MOLLY GREEN has travelled the world, unpacking her suitcase in a score of countries. On returning to England, Molly decided to pursue her life-long passion for writing. She now writes in a cabin in her garden on the outskirts of Tunbridge Wells, Kent, ably assisted by her white rescued cat, Dougie.

Also by Molly Green

The Dr Barnardo's Orphanage series:
An Orphan in the Snow
An Orphan's War
An Orphan's Wish

The Victory Sisters series:
A Sister's Courage

A Sister's Song

MOLLY GREEN

avon.

Published by AVON
A division of HarperCollins*Publishers* Ltd
1 London Bridge Street
London SE1 9GF

www.harpercollins.co.uk

A Paperback Original 2020

A catalogue copy of this book is available from the British Library.

ISBN: 978-0-00-833247-1

This novel is a work of fiction. References to real people, events or localities are intended only to provide a sense of authenticity, and are used fictitiously. All other characters and incidents portrayed in it are the work of the author's imagination.

Typeset in Minion Pro by
Palimpsest Book Production Ltd, Falkirk, Stirlingshire
Printed and bound in UK by CPI Group (UK) Ltd, Croydon CR0 4YY

This book is produced from independently certified FSC™ paper
to ensure responsible forest management.

For more information visit: www.harpercollins.co.uk/green

To the people of Malta who bravely endured
the Siege of Malta
from June 1940 – December 1942,
their Island being harder hit than the London Blitz,
and to the RAF, the Navy and the Merchant Navy who
defended the Island, sacrificing many,
but who won against all odds.

To all the entertainers in ENSA performing
throughout the Second World War
in Great Britain, Europe, the Middle East and the Far East.
The performers were often very close to
the action but carried on regardless,
keeping up the morale of the troops and
bringing them a little bit of Blighty.

Chapter One

Downe, Near Bromley
Easter 1943

Suzanne stood in the wings of the village hall stage, poised to take her place by the other musicians. She couldn't stop shivering. Although it was mild outside, the hall was always cold – but it wasn't that. She had never before performed the solo in the finale of her favourite violin concerto in front of a real audience.

Oh, no – there was her cue.

Just go and do it, she told herself sternly, holding her violin tight to her chest. Despite her trembling legs, she walked up the three steps to the wooden platform. The eight other musicians turned their heads towards her as she nodded to them, then at the modest audience. She sat down, her fingers instinctively tracing the familiar curving outline of her instrument.

Even though Suzanne couldn't see much in the gloom of the badly lit hall, she couldn't mistake Maman. Swathed in her fur coat, which she refused to discard until May, her tiny hat perched on her curls, her mother sat in the front row on one of the hard chairs, no doubt on the cushion she always brought with her. But where was Ronnie? She should be by Maman's side. But this was no time to start asking questions. The conductor looked at her with raised eyebrows. Suzanne settled her violin under her chin, took up her bow, and nodded.

As soon as she played the first notes she relaxed, now sure of herself. Barely aware of her surroundings, she half closed her eyes, the music filling her brain, her heart, and flowing through to the tips of her elegant fingers as the bow caressed the strings of her beloved violin.

Her whole being was immersed in Mendelssohn's wonderful concerto when suddenly the wail of an air-raid siren stopped her in mid-stroke. Her heart jumped with fright. The sound rose and fell over and over again. She'd never heard one so close. Dear God, the Luftwaffe must be heading straight for Biggin Hill. Or Bromley. Or even Downe! Blood pounded through her temples. Her fingers fluttered. Would the hall be struck? Why weren't people rushing out of the door?

Everyone on the platform stopped. Suzanne's heartbeat sounded in her ears as she looked over to the audience. One tall man at the back immediately sprang up, caught her eye for a brief moment and nodded, then shoved his hat on and quickly left. *He* certainly wasn't going to risk it by staying, and she couldn't really blame him. Oh dear, there was Maman on her feet. Should she go to her? No one else moved. They sat quietly on the hard seats, faces upturned, as though expecting to hear the rest of the piece. To her relief she saw her mother look round at the others and quickly sit down again. Suzanne glanced at Mr Rubenstein, the elderly conductor, who tapped on his stand and said:

'Back to the beginning of the solo, please, ladies and gentlemen.'

There was nothing for it but to obey. She nodded, her

hand shaking as she took up her bow, waiting for her introduction.

Just as she was about to begin, the siren started up again. This time the audience stirred. Although the wailing probably lasted no more than a minute, it felt to Suzanne like an hour. Then a silence. The tension in the hall suddenly tightened as a droning noise, followed by a high-pitched whine – different from the siren – sounded overhead. *BOOM!* An explosion rattled her eardrums as the very platform she sat on shook with the vibration. She couldn't move.

Then a deafening bang and the shattering of glass. Suzanne gasped. Dear God, they were all going to be killed! Her heart pounded. Her chest felt so tight that for long seconds she couldn't breathe. What should she do? What were the others going to do? Squashing the feeling of panic she saw heads and hats turn briefly towards the two smashed windows, then back again to the small orchestra. Still no one else got up to leave. Mr Rubenstein gestured for Suzanne to continue.

Somehow the bravery of her audience transferred itself to her and she played the last section, her fear replaced by her love of the joyous music. Although still trembling, she poured her heart and soul out to the audience, letting the music flow and comfort them. She played the final note, completely spent.

There was a hush. Then the sound of applause echoed round the hall.

Her cheeks flushed with embarrassment at such an enthusiastic response, Suzanne faced the audience. She could see Maman clapping louder than anyone else, but it was strange that Ronnie hadn't appeared. Suzanne knew her younger sister didn't much care for classical music, but she'd said only this morning she'd be coming with Maman. Then it struck Suzanne why she wasn't there.

Don't let something have happened to Ronnie in the air raid.

Pushing down her unease she pasted a smile on her face for Maman and was rewarded by the little hat bobbing up and down as her mother waved and blew kisses in her daughter's direction.

Mr Rubenstein gave a bow and gestured to Suzanne. Still shaken from the noise of the bombs she bent forward and briefly lowered her head. Next, the other musicians stood, looking towards her, clapping and smiling.

And then the whine of another siren filled the hall, but this time it built to a high crescendo and wailed for more than a minute. Suzanne breathed out slowly and smiled back at the musicians and then the audience. It was the welcome sound of the All Clear, practically swallowed up by more clapping and some loud whistles from the concertgoers.

'That was close,' Mr Rubenstein said, addressing the audience. 'And we would have completely understood if you'd left for the shelter, so I want to thank you for having such faith that we would all come through this latest attack together.'

'Bit like the *Titanic*,' a man at the back called out. 'The band kept playing even when the ship was sinking, so we thought we'd better stay, too.'

'This in't the first war for most of us,' a large woman with a voice to match put in. 'If London can take it, then so can Downe.'

There was laughter and cheers and more clapping, until the musicians sat down again and began to play the first notes of 'God Save The King'. Immediately, the audience sprang to their feet and sang with even more gusto than usual.

People were still chattering as they trooped out of the village hall into the cool early April night.

'Wasn't that lovely?' Suzanne heard Mrs Holmes, one of their neighbours, say to her friend. 'Something beautiful to listen to . . . and almost spoilt by those dreadful Nazis. But they have us all wrong if they think we're scared of them.'

'Yes, I'm glad we stayed 'til the end,' Mrs Holmes's friend agreed, 'but I wonder where those bombs dropped. Downe's been lucky so far, though Bromley's had its share.' She clicked her teeth. 'Well, we'll soon know what damage they've done, that's for certain.'

'Maman.' Suzanne turned to her mother who was gripping her arm. 'Constable Mason is over by the door. I'm going to have a word with him.'

'I wish to go straight home and find out what has happened to Véronique.'

So Maman was worried as well.

'I want to ask if he's seen her, so just wait a moment . . . please, Maman.'

'Very well. But do not keep me waiting.'

Suzanne broke from her mother's grasp and hurried over.

'Oh, Mr Mason, do you know if anyone was hurt in that raid just now? I'm worried about Ronnie – you know, my young sister.'

'No one 'urt, miss, as far as I know. They all got safely into the shelter – except all of you in the village hall,' he added. 'You want to think yourselves lucky you and your ma didn't come a cropper.'

'But have you seen Ronnie?' Suzanne persisted. 'You know – Véronique.'

'Not that I remember.' PC Mason stroked his chin, making a rasping noise. 'Mind you, they was all packed in tight so I might have overlooked her. She's smaller than you and your other sister, in't she?'

Suzanne nodded. 'I can't help being worried because she was supposed to have come to the concert this evening.'

'I 'aven't 'eard nothing to the contrary,' the constable said. 'Lucky the bombs all dropped in the field, so no real damage, thank Gawd. Even the cows and horses was spared, so I shouldn't worry too much.'

Suzanne thanked him and turned to see Maman hovering behind her, impatiently tapping her foot.

'What did he say?' Simone demanded. 'Has he seen Véronique?'

'No, but he said everyone got into the shelter and no one was hurt.'

As far as I know, PC Mason had added. Suzanne swallowed. She didn't want to alarm her mother, but she wouldn't feel happy until she saw her sister, unharmed, with her own eyes.

'That is a relief.' Maman dabbed her eyes with a pristine handkerchief. 'You made me worry for a moment. Let us go home and put the kettle on.'

'You sound like a real Englishwoman,' Suzanne said, smiling, as she tucked her arm through her mother's for the short walk to the Victorian cottage that was home.

'That is not a compliment for me,' Simone admonished, the cloth bag holding her cushion looking like an elegant accessory as it dangled from her wrist. She stepped along the pavement, her high heels tapping rhythmically.

'Just teasing, Maman. I know you're French through and through and could never pretend otherwise.'

Her mother flashed her a smile of forgiveness. 'I do not understand teasing, as you well know, Suzanne, but if you say it was only a joke, I will believe you.'

The whole way home Simone went over and over the unexpected air raid, each exclamation more dramatic than the one before.

'Mr Rubenstein was taking a bad risk. We could all be dead now.' Her mother increased her walking pace. 'I want to see my little Véronique – to know she is safe.'

'She told me she was coming with you.'

'She told me the same.' Simone's breath came in short bursts. 'And I do wish you would call her by her proper name, Suzanne. How many times do I ask you?'

'She doesn't like being called Véronique,' Suzanne said. 'You know what a tomboy she is, and she doesn't feel it suits her. In a way, she's right, but she'll change when she's a bit older and starts to notice the boys.'

'She should be proud of her name,' Simone said. 'I gave you all beautiful French names and she and Lorraine refuse to use them.' She glanced at Suzanne. 'At least you do not call yourself Suzy like your sisters do. If you did, I would be very upset.'

'Did you see Ronnie before you left?' Suzanne asked, wanting to change the subject about their names that Maman brought up time and time again. She was resolute in trying to work out what could have happened to Ronnie.

'She came in from a walk. I told her to wash her face and change into something presentable, but that I must leave so I am not late.' She shook her head. 'Sometimes I cannot believe my own daughter finds it so hard to wear anything suitable. Perhaps she decided to remain at home.'

'I don't think that would be her reason,' Suzanne said worriedly. 'She doesn't really care about whether she's dressed appropriately or not.'

'Well, she should.' Simone's tone was non-compromising when it came to fashion and appearances.

'I do hope she found somewhere safe in the air raid.' Suzanne bit her lip. 'But if she'd started out for the village hall and heard the siren, she didn't go into the shelter – at least, Constable Mason couldn't remember seeing her there.'

'She knows to go under the dining table,' her mother said firmly. 'That is where we will find her.'

Suzanne gripped her violin case closer to her side, and unable to ignore the knot of anxiety growing in her stomach, prayed silently that her mother was right.

They heard a dog barking as they walked up the path to the front door.

'That noise is coming from inside our house,' Simone said, annoyance coating her words. 'If Véronique has brought in a dog—'

Her mother didn't finish her sentence but unlocked the front door. Suzanne followed her in, only pausing to flick the lock. She heard muffled sounds coming from the kitchen as though an animal was being smothered. Then she heard her sister say, 'They're home, so be a good boy.'

Simone turned to Suzanne. 'There is a dog in there. I will not enter the kitchen until it goes. You can tell your sister. You will have to find your own supper. For me, I am not hungry.'

Suzanne pushed the door open and there was Ronnie sitting on a chair with a dog straddled across her knees. Its tail was wagging feebly. They both looked up at her entrance and Suzanne couldn't help smiling. The dog's head was cocked at the same angle as her sister's, and the two pairs of eyes shone.

'This is Rusty.' Ronnie beamed. 'Isn't it the perfect name for him? It matches the colour of his head.' She caught hold of the dog's paw and gave a pretence of waving at Suzanne. 'See, he knows his name already.' The dog licked Ronnie's hand. 'Sorry I can't get up. He's rather weighing me down.' She sighed happily.

Suzanne knelt by the chair and stroked the dog's head, which could possibly have been described as rust-coloured once upon a time, together with a few rusty patches on an otherwise unkempt white coat. His shaggy fringe flopped into sunken eyes, now looking a little worried, or so Suzanne fancied, and his over-long ears sagged forlornly.

'Hello, boy,' she said. 'Where've you come from?'

'You won't believe it,' Ronnie said. 'I started out for the village hall soon after Maman, but I got caught in the air raid. It was very near.' She looked at Suzanne. 'You must have heard it.'

'Yes, we did,' Suzanne said, looking at her sister anxiously. 'Are you all right?'

'I am now, but Rusty wasn't.' Ronnie stroked the dog's head. 'The warden spotted him – not our usual one but someone younger and so nice. Tall, dark and handsome. At least I imagine he was dark under his hat.' She giggled. 'Anyway, he picked Rusty up but I could see he was trying to stop some children from panicking, so I took the dog out of his arms and said I'd look after him. The poor little thing was trembling with fright. Anyway, we all rushed down the shelter steps. I knew you and Maman would be in the shelter by the village hall so I didn't feel quite so bad that I'd missed the concert.'

'Funnily enough, no one left,' Suzanne said.

Ronnie's mouth fell open. 'Really? You mean they all stayed even after the bombs fell?'

'Yes,' Suzanne said, then remembered the tall man at the back. 'Well, all except one man.' She remembered how he'd given her a kind of apologetic nod. 'Two of the windows shattered,' she went on. 'That gave us all quite a scare. I thought everyone would dash out, but they didn't – even Maman stayed, and you know how frightened she gets.' She stroked the dog's head. 'But I don't know what we're going to do about you, Rusty. Maman won't allow you to stay – that's definite.'

Rusty gave a little whine as though appealing to the two girls.

'I've given him a bit of Maman's leftovers and he scoffed it down as though he was starving.' Ronnie suddenly grinned. 'He wasn't at all critical of Maman's cooking.'

Suzanne smiled back, but when she studied the dog her expression changed. 'He *is* starving,' she said. 'He looks pitiful.'

'But he's such a dear little fellow, and so grateful now he's found me,' Ronnie said, her face serious as she gently stroked the thin body. She looked up and sighed. 'I'm sorry I didn't come to your concert, Suzy, but I couldn't leave him. Did you remember all your notes?'

Suzanne nodded. 'Thankfully, yes. And everyone seemed to enjoy it.'

'Oh, that's good.' Ronnie lowered her voice. 'I knew Maman would be furious about Rusty, so I put him in the shed in a cardboard box with an old cushion, hoping after I'd fed him he'd go to sleep before she came in. Then I was worried about him and brought him back into the kitchen. It's warmer in here for him. And Maman would have to see him sooner or later, but I thought you'd talk her round when you saw what a darling he is, and how he needs us. I know she'll take notice of you to let me keep him because you're her favourite.'

'You and Raine are always going on about that, and it's simply not true.'

'What – being the favourite?'

'Yes. She loves us all the same.'

'Suzy, you're so sweet but she doesn't.' Ronnie looked at

her older sister pityingly. 'Anyone can see that. But it doesn't alter anything about Rusty. So will you have a word with her?'

'Of course I'll have a word,' Suzanne said. 'But you know how Maman is. Once she says no to something it's difficult to persuade her to change her mind. And she does have a real fear of dogs.'

'But not Rusty,' Ronnie said firmly. 'Who could possibly be frightened of him?'

Suzanne leaned across and twiddled Rusty's ear. 'Poor little chap,' she said. 'You must have thought you'd found a lovely new owner when Ronnie took you home, but I'm afraid it's Maman you have to bring round to your way of thinking. And being French, she's very stubborn.'

Rusty gave a short bark as if he understood.

'You are calling me stubborn, Suzanne?'

The two sisters' heads swivelled to the kitchen door where Simone stood quivering with anger.

'Maman, the dog desperately needs some love and attention,' Suzanne said. 'Couldn't you give him a chance if he behaves himself? He'd be company for you as well when we're at school.'

'I do not want the company of a dog,' Simone snapped.

'But, Maman—'

'I have said you may not have a dog and you are going against my wishes.'

'Suzy, please tell Maman—'

'It is nothing of Suzanne's business, Véronique,' Simone rounded on her. 'He is to go out – now!'

'I can't send him out,' Ronnie said, looking up at her mother defiantly, and holding on to the dog even more firmly. 'He's hungry. Look at his ribs sticking out.'

'I am not interested in his ribs,' Simone said, stepping into the room. Rusty flinched and started to whine. Simone's eyes darkened with anger. 'This is the reason you do not attend your sister's concert – because of some smelly dog with fleas. How could you, Véronique? To put a stray dog before your own sister.'

'It wasn't that,' Ronnie protested. 'I was already on my way until the siren went off. Anyway, Suzy understands – she loves animals too.' She glared at her mother. 'And he doesn't smell, nor does he have fleas,' she added indignantly. 'But he does need my help . . . and I'm going to see he gets it.'

Simone pursed her lips. 'As long as you are under my roof you will do as I say . . . and that goes for both of you. I do not like dogs and this one is not healthy.' Her glance fell on the dog who was watching her. She quickly averted her eyes. 'We have no money for medicine and we have no spare food for an animal. He must go to the vet. They will find him a home.' She paused, her eyes sweeping over her two daughters.

'But, Maman, they'll put him down,' Ronnie said, tears springing to her eyes. 'I saw a government leaflet in the library that said it's the kindest thing to do to dogs and cats now we're at war, even if they're already people's *pets*. A vet had to put a dog down the other day that was only two years old. The owner forced him.' She looked pleadingly at Maman, and Suzanne's heart leapt to her throat. 'It's not being kind, it's cruel to put perfectly good animals down.' Ronnie gently patted the dog's head. 'He's a living being – just the same as us. And he'd only need scraps. Please give him a chance. He deserves it.'

'*Non*,' Simone said. 'The dog must go. And they are my final words.'

Suzanne braced herself to speak to Maman on her own after supper, so when Ronnie had sneaked Rusty upstairs, Suzanne tackled her.

'Maman, I must talk to you about Ronnie,' Suzanne said, as she collected the dirty plates to take into the kitchen.

'Do you not mean about the dog?' Simone said shrewdly.

Suzanne's cheeks turned pink. 'Well, yes, I suppose so,' she conceded. She took in a breath to steady her voice. 'Maman, I do think you could bend on this occasion. Ronnie hasn't been herself since Dad died, and she's crazy about animals. She's always the one who comes to the rescue of any animal or bird who needs it. She's an example to all of us. We should all be willing to help the underdog.'

'That is a good description for that stray,' Simone flashed.

'It would give her something of her own,' Suzanne said, ignoring the jibe. 'Being the youngest, she's always felt left out.'

'Nonsense.'

'It's true,' Suzanne returned, 'but she covers it up.'

Maman pursed her lips.

'She's asked you for a dog so many times and you always say no. When Dad was alive I even heard *him* say you should allow her to have a dog.'

'And how does she feed him and walk him when she is at school?'

Was Maman softening?

Suzanne took the plunge. 'She can take him for an early walk and feed him before she goes to school. And I'll help out as well when I come home.'

'And what happens to him during the day?' Simone challenged. 'I am doing my bit for the war effort . . . although no one gives me any credit,' she added. 'I cannot be here all the time. If he is left alone he will destroy my last good pieces of furniture.'

'We can put a cardboard box in the shed, and plenty of water. He'll have to just wait for Ronnie and me to come home from school.' She looked at her mother. 'Please, Maman.'

'I am sorry, Suzanne. It is completely out of the question. But one thing . . .' She gazed at Suzanne. 'I have also not been myself since your father died. But all of you seem to forget that.'

'No, Maman, we never forget,' Suzanne said quickly. 'But Raine has her flying, and I have my music. It's important that Ronnie has something precious of her own as well. Something to care for, to take responsibility. It will do her the world of good. So why can't it be Rusty?'

Suzanne bounded up the stairs and knocked on Ronnie's bedroom door.

'Shhhh, Rusty,' she heard Ronnie say.

Ronnie came to the door, Rusty in her arms. He wagged his tail, his eyes fixed on Suzanne.

Ronnie looked at her face. 'Oh, Suzy, did Maman say I could keep him?'

'Not exactly,' Suzanne said, 'but he's been given a short reprieve. She said he could stay for one week, but only if he doesn't disturb the neighbours with barking. And he cannot come anywhere in the house except your bedroom. If you want to put up with the fleas, it's up to you, Maman said. She also said that one of us has to be with him when he's indoors to keep him under control. In other words, you can't leave him in your bedroom all day. And you must put a notice in the post office and the village shop to ask if anyone has lost him. You've got to do that right away.'

Ronnie's face fell. 'What if no one claims him? Did Maman say I'd have to take him to the vet to be put down?'

'She didn't say,' Suzanne said, 'but it gives him a week to get him used to us and learn his manners.' She gently patted

Rusty's head. 'He'll feel better with some regular food inside him. I'm sure we can spare a small piece of soap to give him a bath tomorrow so he doesn't smell—'

'He *doesn't* smell,' Ronnie cut in.

'He does a little,' Suzanne grinned. 'But he won't by the time we've finished with him. Then maybe he might win round Maman.'

Ronnie broke into a beam. 'Oh, Suzy, you are wonderful. Only *you* could persuade her. But I knew you would.'

'Don't get too carried away, Ronnie,' Suzanne said, allowing Rusty to give her hand a lick. 'Rusty's not safe yet. But we'll do everything we can to see that he stays – unless someone claims him first, of course.' She glanced down at the dog who was looking up at her as though he knew his fate was in her hands. 'Though I can't see a queue of people fighting over him,' she laughed.

Chapter Two

'I have received a letter from your music teacher,' Simone told Suzanne a few days later when she came home from school and they were having tea in the dining room.

What on earth was Miss Reeves writing to Maman about?

'It is serious,' Maman said, 'so I will read it to you.' She unfolded a sheet of paper.

'Dear Mrs Linfoot,

'I am writing to you regarding your daughter, Suzanne. I am sure you are aware that she is a very talented musician, both as a violinist and also a pianist, and I believe she has the potential to develop her talent much further. Yesterday I had a telephone conversation with Mr Rubenstein. He said her solo performance in the village hall recently was truly exceptional for such a young girl (I'm afraid I couldn't attend owing to family sickness) and has suggested she should attend the Royal Academy of Music in London, full-time, starting this September.

'If Mr Rubenstein recommends Suzanne and she is accepted, this is such a wonderful opportunity. I have already spoken to Miss Robson, the headmistress, and she has given her whole-hearted approval if Suzanne takes what could be a life-changing opportunity.

'But before we go any further, we would obviously like to know your thoughts. If you would both like to come in and see me next week, I would be happy to discuss this further.'

Suzanne's heart beat fast. This was so unexpected. She'd had no idea Mr Rubenstein had found her performance exceptional in any way. It had once been her dream to be accepted into a prestigious music school and one day take her place in the London Philharmonic Orchestra. But Miss Reeves had dashed her hopes when she said in a matter-of-fact tone that women were rarely accepted in a professional orchestra.

'Unless you play the harp,' Miss Reeves said, her glasses practically falling off her nose. 'And even then, you wouldn't be seen by the audience – your place would be well and truly in the wings.' The tutor grimaced. 'You wouldn't even be acknowledged on the programme.'

'That's so unfair,' Suzanne blurted.

'I'm afraid you'll find that life's unfair,' Miss Reeves said, a slightly bitter edge to her voice as she pushed her glasses back into position.

At the time, Suzanne had been bitterly disappointed, another dream in ashes. Why on earth should she learn the harp? What a ridiculous rule it was, but she'd had to accept it.

Simone looked up from the letter. 'So, *chérie*, what do you say?'

Suzanne's thoughts flew in different directions. Maman impatiently tapped her foot.

'You were always very firm about me taking my Higher Certificate,' Suzanne said, playing for time.

'Because Lorraine let the family down by leaving school

before her final year,' Simone said. 'She would not listen to me. She does not stop to think how I worry about her constantly, flying those dangerous contraptions that girls should not be allowed to operate. But this letter, Suzanne—' she waved it in the air '—it changes everything. You will have wonderful training for a music career. Something to be proud of.'

'Well, *I'm* proud of Raine,' Suzanne returned. 'She's doing something *very* worthwhile. She's *directly* helping the war effort.'

'Music is worthwhile, also,' Simone said sharply, her cup clattering onto its saucer.

'Yes, I agree. But it's not that simple.' Suzanne regarded her mother. 'Did you know it's almost unheard of for a woman to be accepted in professional orchestras?'

'What nonsense,' Simone retorted. 'You play as well as any man. If not, why did this Mr Rubenstein make this suggestion?'

'Maybe he thinks I'd be a good teacher . . . but that's not what I want.' Suzanne paused. 'So you really are in favour of me leaving school?'

A dreamy smile broke out on her mother's face. 'My daughter at a London *conservatoire*. Nearly so good as the one in Paris.'

'I'd like to think about it,' Suzanne said. 'It's a big decision.'

'*Mais bien sûr,*' Simone said, getting up and kissing her cheek. 'But you will answer me "yes", will you not? And then one day everyone will know your name.'

Suzanne could tell her mother was excited about the prospect of her daughter becoming famous, but fame was not Suzanne's idea of happiness. She would rather be known for bringing joy to people, especially where there was precious little. And because the country was in the middle of a war, she desperately wanted to help make a difference, however small. But what could she do?

'I'll think about it, Maman,' she repeated.

Her mother frowned. 'Do not be long thinking,' she said. 'The opportunity might not always be there for you. And you will only have yourself to blame.'

Maman couldn't have made herself any clearer.

If only Raine was here, Suzanne thought, as she changed the sheets on her bed, top to bottom, then smoothed a fresh one on the top as she did every fortnight. Raine would understand. Her sister had had a terrible time defying Maman but she'd won in the end. Raine was the strong one. She'd sent Suzanne a letter wishing her good luck for the concert and she was sorry to miss it but the ferry pool was going full pelt. She mentioned she'd just completed the third twelve-hour day in a row. Suzanne smiled to herself. This wasn't a grumble from her older sister. She knew Raine adored her work as a ferry pilot as much as *she* loved playing her instruments.

The trouble was, unlike Raine, Suzanne found it hard to stand up to her mother. Dad had lost so much money not long before he died, which put the family in a difficult situation, but her mother had still managed to continue to pay for one of the best music tutors in Bromley, funding the extra violin lessons from her own nest egg.

It was the war. This was what changed everything. It wasn't so bad at the moment while she was still at school, but she'd be taking her final exams this June. Some of her friends had already left school at sixteen and seventeen to work in munitions factories or hospitals, or join one of the forces, determined to do their bit for the war effort, whereas she, at eighteen, hadn't planned anything.

She couldn't help feeling guilty but she knew she didn't have the kind of grit one needed to join the military. All that marching to bellowed orders from her superiors, shrieking at her when she made a mistake or had left a button undone or scuffed a shoe, made her tremble with anxiety. Conscription had recently come in for single women between twenty and thirty, but that could change at any time.

'Come and join the WRNS with me, Suzy,' her friend Rita had said a few weeks ago. 'It'll be fun being together and you could probably play in the band in your spare time.' She regarded Suzanne with a worried frown. 'Thing is, you'll be twenty before you know it and then they might choose for you, and you'll probably be made to join the ATS . . . and their uniform isn't half as smart as the Wrens',' she added slyly.

'But I've never learnt to play any of the brass instruments,' Suzanne protested. She didn't add that playing in a military band had no appeal.

'With your talent you'd soon learn,' Rita came back quick as a flash.

The trouble was, if she had to learn another instrument from the beginning she'd be neglecting her violin practice. Her violin that she loved as an extension of herself. And she definitely wouldn't have any spare leisure time to play the piano. She'd never hear the last of it from Maman. And she wouldn't blame her.

'I'll think about it,' Suzanne had told Rita.

But she knew she wouldn't. There had to be another way of helping the war effort. There just had to be.

And now this. Her mother wanted her – no, she'd more or less *ordered* her – to go to London to study music. No doubt it would be for at least three years. Her old dream come true, but she'd be protected from the outside world, and wouldn't be helping the war effort. But what choice did she have?

Suzanne sighed as she plumped the pillow and folded her nightdress, tucking it inside its cover that she'd embroidered in sewing class. It wasn't a foregone conclusion that she would even be accepted at the music school, but she owed it to her mother to try. Maman loved classical music but had never learned to play an instrument, saying she had no aptitude, so she was putting all her dreams into her talented daughter, as she often freely admitted. Suzanne shrugged. Maybe a miracle would happen and the war would end soon and she could go off to London with a glad heart. Although watching Pathé News at the cinema last week when she and Rita had gone to see Sally Gray in *Dangerous Moonlight*, she wasn't at all convinced it was about to happen.

'Suzanne!' Her mother's call broke into her thoughts.

'Yes, Maman?'

'I have made coffee. Véronique has gone to the library with that dog, so we can talk without being disturbed.'

Suzanne's heart sank. Maman would expect an answer, but only the answer she insisted upon. With a sigh she turned and slowly walked out of the bedroom and down the staircase where her mother was waiting for her.

'Well, Suzanne?'

'I will go to London, Maman, if you think it is the right thing for me to do, even with a war on.'

'I, and many others, it seems.' Simone's face lit up. 'It is a very sensible decision. You must not waste your gift – even with the war. I will telephone Miss Reeves tomorrow morning to discuss the next step.'

'Everyone's talking as though I've already been offered a place,' Suzanne said. 'I'd have to do an audition first before they accept me.'

'You will do it standing on top of your head,' Simone said.

'I hope it doesn't come to that.' Suzanne gave a wry smile.

She was glad she'd made her mother happy, but there was still that niggling doubt in her mind.

'I see,' Suzanne heard her mother say into the receiver. 'Well, it is most inconvenient, but I suppose it cannot be helped.' Her mother tilted her head. 'No, thank you, Miss Reeves is the lady I must talk to.' Simone put her hand over the mouthpiece. 'Miss Reeves is away,' she muttered to Suzanne who was putting her coat on to go to her rehearsal. Her mother removed her hand and spoke to whoever it was on the other end. 'When she is returned, would you please ask her to telephone me?'

There was a minute's pause while her mother listened, then rolled her eyes to the ceiling.

'Yes, yes, I understand. The Easter holidays. Maybe a delay. Thank you.' Simone slammed the receiver down and swept into the dining room.

'That was Miss Robson, your headmistress,' she said. 'Miss Reeves is still attending to the sick family member. They do not know when she is coming back.'

Her mother would be even more annoyed if she suspected the flicker of relief in her middle daughter's heart, Suzanne thought, as she shut the front door behind her and briskly walked to St Mary's Church for the rehearsal.

As usual, the sight of the pretty flint-built parish church with its stained-glass windows lifted her spirits. She thought of Charles Darwin's family attending the Sunday service so many years ago. People had gone before her and people would go after her, but this was today and it was her turn to appreciate its special ambience.

She heard the others tuning their instruments before she'd

heaved open the heavy oak door. She smiled. Although she was happy playing set pieces in her bedroom when no one was around, it was wonderful to be with other musicians. They could tackle different pieces when they were together. That was when she felt part of a real orchestra even though it was only a fraction of the size.

She stepped inside and looked round to see who was there and spotted Mr Rubenstein neatly folding his coat like a parcel and leaving it on one of the chairs. Four men and four women had already assembled.

It's lovely to know our little group isn't bound by the stiff regulations of professional orchestras, Suzanne thought, as she smiled and nodded to everyone.

All the men were older, most of them having already played their part as soldiers in the Great War and now finding comfort in music. Mr Barton had a missing leg but it didn't stop him from being a superb cellist. Three women were in their fifties or even sixties, and only Wendy was younger – maybe in her mid-twenties – much too young to be a widow.

The smell of the interior was comforting – a mix of candles and old books and furniture polish. Very little warmth escaped from the two paraffin stoves; any heat they managed to produce rose straight up to the high oak-beamed ceiling. Yet however cold she was before she began, once she started playing, all discomforts evaporated and she was totally absorbed.

The conductor was now turning over his sheets of music, frowning. She wondered if she should say anything in front of the others to thank him for recommending her to attend the Royal Academy of Music. Maybe best not to. It might look like favouritism, or that she was bragging. She'd have a word after the rehearsal if she could get him on his own.

The rehearsal was not one of their best. Suzanne found it

difficult to concentrate, and more than once she didn't come in on perfect time. Mr Rubenstein said nothing but raised his eyebrows in question. Some of the others stumbled with their pieces, which was unusual as they'd played Dvorak's 'Slavonic Dances' several times before.

'We'll have a tea break,' Mr Rubenstein said a half an hour later, putting down his baton. 'Maybe that will buck you all up.'

'Tea's all ready, sir.' Mrs Jackson, one of the volunteers, bustled through from the kitchen. 'And there's some nice ginger cake Mrs Henry made this morning especially for you all.'

While the group were chatting together and enjoying Mrs Henry's cake, Wendy lightly touched her arm.

'I need to talk to you about something, Suzanne,' she said, her green eyes gleaming. 'Bring your tea over to one of the tables.'

When they'd settled on the hard chairs, Wendy leaned forward.

'I didn't want to mention it until it was definite, but I've heard now that I'm in,' she said in a conspiratorial whisper.

'In what?' Suzanne found herself whispering back.

'I've joined ENSA.' Wendy waited to let her words sink in. 'I'm just waiting to hear when I actually start.'

Suzanne shook her head. 'I don't know what you're talking about,' she said. 'What's Ensa?'

'E-N-S-A,' Wendy spelt it out. 'Capital letters. It's an organisation they set up at the beginning of the war to entertain the troops. They go all over the place, sometimes even abroad – wherever the fighting boys are – like Vera Lynn does. You must have heard of it. They call it "Every Night Something Awful".' She giggled. Suzanne realised it was the first time she'd ever seen Wendy so animated.

'Why would you want to play with them if they're awful?'

'It's not the official name,' Wendy said, still chuckling. 'It's Entertainments National Service Association.'

'How did you find out about it?'

'Through *The Stage* magazine. They were advertising and I thought, why not?'

'Well, I've heard that Vera Lynn sings to the troops,' Suzanne said, 'but what's that got to do with the kind of music *you* play? Unless you sing as well.'

Wendy's face flushed with eagerness. 'Funnily enough, they gave me an audition to sing a few songs as they'd been let down by one of the singers.' She laughed a little self-consciously. 'How did they guess it's something I've always fantasised about doing? Anyway, I put my heart and soul in it—' She stopped and giggled again. 'Actually, that's what I sang at the audition – "Heart And Soul" – and they said yes!' She looked round the room but everyone was chatting and intent on enjoying Mrs Henry's ginger cake. 'Oh, Suzanne, I'm so excited – I can't wait to go.'

Suzanne felt she was being swept away with Wendy's enthusiasm. Her heart beat a little more quickly.

'Tell me more about this ENSA.'

'Well, it's quite varied. They've always had comedians and singers and drama groups – often with famous actors like Jack Hawkins – but they're big on swing bands.'

Suzanne's mouth fell open. 'And you can really sing to that kind of music?'

'I sing along with the wireless all the time.' Wendy grinned. 'Look, why don't you join up, too? It'd be fun – if you like swing and jazz, that is.' She took a gulp of tea and sat back, keeping her eyes fixed on Suzanne.

'Who doesn't?' Suzanne said, her heart leaping. Was this the sign she'd been waiting for? She wouldn't have dreamt of being a jazz violinist in normal times – she could just picture Maman's face – but these weren't normal times. She gazed back at Wendy, stupefied.

'Do they allow women musicians?'

'Course they do. Bands aren't stuffy like orchestras. You must've heard of Ivy Benson?'

'Yes, I love her band. I saw them play when my sister and I went to the Palais in Bromley once, but she's different. It's all female. And because it's her own band she can make her own rules, and for once turn the tables and not let the men in.' Suzanne relaxed into a smile for the first time in the conversation.

'That's true. But with men being called up to fight, they're leaving plenty of gaps in big bands for women.' She grabbed Suzanne's hand. 'I'll introduce you to George Johnson. He's ever so nice. I'm sure you'd like him.'

'*George Johnson?*' Suzanne's mouth fell open. 'You're in George Johnson's band?'

'Yes, but a smaller version as it's too big a band for them all to go.' Wendy rose to her feet as Mr Rubenstein called the group to return to their places. She looked down at Suzanne who remained glued to her chair. 'You'd have to be "Suzy" from now on because "Suzanne" doesn't sound right at all for this sort of music. It needs something more modern.' She gave her a sly smile. 'It'll be such fun. You need to live a little. Come on, I dare you.'

'I don't know anything about this ENSA,' Suzanne said. 'I'm not sure I'd be suitable.' She hesitated. 'Although it does sound exciting.'

Wendy reached into her handbag and pulled out a small notebook. She scribbled something down and tore out the page.

'Here,' she said, slipping it into Suzanne's coat pocket. 'I want you to think about it seriously. It would do you good to break free.' Suzanne startled and Wendy laughed. 'It's obvious,' she said. 'Didn't you tell me your sister is a pilot against your mother's wishes? She's managed to break the chains, but that probably means you're bound even tighter now.'

Suzanne hesitated – caught between irritation that it should be so obvious, and loyalty to her mother.

'Sorry,' Wendy said, and laughed. 'I might be completely barking up the wrong tree.'

'No, you're not, if I'm truthful.' Suzanne surprised herself by her response. 'Wendy, when's your last rehearsal with us?'

'One more after tonight,' Wendy said. 'I'm telling Mr Rubenstein it's no good rehearsing for something I shan't be playing.'

'Oh, Wendy, I'm going to miss you.'

'Ladies,' Mr Rubenstein called to them. 'Would you please stop talking and take your seats, so we can all get home at a reasonable hour.'

Somehow Suzanne couldn't put her heart into the pieces Mr Rubenstein had chosen. She kept thinking about Wendy and the different turn her friend's life was about to take.

'See you next week, Suzy,' Wendy winked, after the rehearsal. Then she was gone.

Chapter Three

Oh, Wendy, if only you knew how I couldn't possibly join these ENSA people.

Suzanne picked her way home after the rehearsal in the nightly blackout. Holding her torch pointing downwards, with its regulation cover of a double piece of tissue paper secured by an elastic band, it didn't give more than the merest glow under the smothering blanket of pitch darkness. It was unnerving not seeing where she was going. Someone could jump out at her. Rob her of her violin. Fear crawled over her scalp. She was being childish, she knew, but she'd always hated the dark and dreaded this twice-weekly walk. Wendy lived in completely the opposite direction. Sometimes one of the other members who lived further down her street, a kind elderly gentleman, accompanied her. But he hadn't shown up this evening.

I hope he's not poorly or had an accident, she thought, as she stumbled along.

Something brushed against her leg. She bit back a scream. Dear God, what was it? 'Who's there?' Her voice shook as her fingers gripped the violin case tighter. There was a plaintive mew. Then she saw a pure white cat slink into a side alley between some houses. Berating herself for being so nervous, she couldn't help smiling. People nowadays often tied a white band over their coat at night so they didn't get run over in the blackout. This cat carried its own permanent safety covering as protection.

Suzanne kept close to the shop entrances where it was safer in an unexpected air raid. But a few steps further she heard her violin case bang against something. Damn! She shone the weak light onto the shape of a pillar box. If she wasn't more careful she'd have a nasty accident. In the dark she glared at the offending torch, and in a moment of uncharacteristic rebellion she tore off the cover. Ah, that was so much better. A proper light. She could actually make out where she was going.

Calmer now, Suzanne turned her thoughts again to Wendy, and the piece of paper with ENSA's address mocking her loyalty to her mother's wishes.

She had to admit Wendy had come alive this evening. The young widow had seemed a romantically tragic figure to Suzanne, as she'd told her that her husband had been killed in the first month of fighting. But Suzanne had noticed Wendy's fingers were ringless. Maybe they hadn't been as happy as she'd imagined. Or maybe this was Wendy's way of trying to shut out the dreadful tragedy of her past and look to the future. Well, whatever the reason it wasn't her business.

She and Wendy had been drawn to one another as the two youngest members. Apart from rehearsals they'd been to the pictures occasionally, and last summer Wendy had invited Suzanne and a couple of friends for an afternoon tea in her garden. But tonight had been different. Wendy was suggesting something Maman would consider outrageous and the ruin of everything she had planned for her daughter. Her mother would never let her forget she'd paid out all that money for music lessons when they could ill afford it.

Oh, but how tempted she was. She'd never played jazz although she could listen to it all night. That evening – was it really two years ago? – she'd gone to the Palais with Raine, and Ivy Benson and her girls had shared the bill with another swing band. She hadn't made up her mind which band she'd enjoyed most that evening, but she'd been particularly intrigued with Ivy Benson's. That lady hadn't been at all perturbed that she'd been barred from playing in a professional orchestra. She'd simply formed her own. And she and her girls had all looked as though they were thoroughly enjoying themselves that evening. Suzanne remembered how she'd almost wished she was up there playing with them. She wondered if they were also in this ENSA.

It was the same night she and her sister had met Alec Marshall, who'd made it clear he had his eye on Raine, and Raine had been so horrible to him. He'd said they didn't even look like sisters and not just because Raine was dark-haired and Suzanne was blonde. It was because Raine had been so bad-tempered that evening. Suzanne smiled at the memory.

Her thoughts switched to Wendy again. Wendy, the violinist, becoming a singer in a band. How brave she was to try something so new. Jazz was so different with its strange, inconsistent beats . . . so fast and loud, but there was something about it that was infectious. Well, heady, if she was honest.

It started to rain. At first it was a drizzle but it intensified within minutes. Suzanne struggled to pull up the collar of her coat but failed as she couldn't let go of the violin case or the torch. Water splashed down the back of her neck in cold rivulets. The damp seeped into her bones. Oh, why had she put her felt hat on this evening? It would be soaked and Maman would be annoyed with her. Hats, to Maman, were the key to being a lady. Suzanne's shoulder bag slipped down her arm, the one carrying her violin case, and she tried to shrug it back up, all the time gripping her torch and shining it ahead so she didn't smash into anything else.

'What the devil are you doing waving that torch around?'

Suzanne startled, every muscle in her body rigid with the shock of a man's voice from behind. Her heart thumped against her ribs as she set the violin case down to see who was being so rude. She knew she'd broken the law and that she might have to pay a penalty, but it had seemed worth the risk to get home safely. But it hadn't paid off. Maman would be furious that she'd disobeyed the rules.

The next thing she knew was a light shining on her face. She blinked.

'Don't you know you're supposed to keep your torch pointing downwards so you don't give any signal to the enemy, young lady?' When she didn't answer he said, 'I'm going to have to take your name and address.'

She was cold and tired and scared. Now this.

Something snapped inside her.

'Who are you?'

'The ARP warden.'

Without thinking she shone her own torch several inches up into his face and almost gasped aloud. He certainly didn't look like Mr Draper, the village ARP warden. Quite the opposite, in fact. Much younger and much more attractive. She wondered if he was the one Ronnie was on about who'd first found Rusty. She lowered the beam.

'Oh, I see why your torch was so bright,' he said, glowering down at her. 'You didn't cover the glass.'

'That's right,' Suzanne said firmly, sure of herself now. 'It was covered when I left the village hall, but when I started walking home it was so pitch-black I couldn't see where I was going and—'

'But you know the law – don't you?' he interrupted, his tone remaining stern.

'Yes,' Suzanne admitted. 'I also know the law says ARP wardens are supposed to be in uniform so the public know they're dealing with an official. As you're not wearing one, I have no idea who you are, so I will certainly *not* be giving you my name and address.'

She turned on her heel, but her foot caught the edge of the kerb. With a cry she tumbled to the pavement, still grasping the handle of her violin case, which banged on the concrete. Her torch flew from her fingers and she heard the tinkle of thin glass shattering.

'I'm sorry, but I tried to catch you. Are you hurt?'

The man had crouched down beside her. His tone had changed to one of concern. She shook her head and tried to sit up. 'My knee.' She'd torn her stocking and she could see blood seeping through. But never mind the blood. They were her last good pair. Damn and blast! If he hadn't stopped her she'd be home by now.

'You need to get that knee seen to.' Gently, he pulled her gloved fingers from the violin case.

'My violin! Oh, I hope I haven't damaged it.' Tears of anger welled in her eyes. 'It's the second time I've banged it tonight.'

'I don't think it will have come to any harm. That's what the case is for.' She heard him set it down. 'Here, let me help you up.'

Reluctantly, she took his hand and he hoisted her to her feet, then pulled her close to steady her. For a long moment she was aware of the strength of his arms. She felt her cheeks flush and was glad it was too dark for him to see.

There was a silence. Then he said, 'Look, why don't you come with me to my mother's house. She only lives round the corner. Let me take you back and we'll look at that knee.

And you can check your violin is none the worse in a safer place than on the street,' he added, invitingly.

Suzanne opened her mouth to say she would do all that when she got home. But her knee was throbbing alarmingly.

'You're right in one respect. I'm not a certified warden although I am one this evening.' He pointed to a white armband with 'ARP' printed on it, which she could just make out. 'Brian Draper asked if I could stand in for him a few days. He's come down with the flu.'

Feeling more confident, Suzanne said, 'So who are you really?'

'James Mortimer, at your service. I'd give you a bow if you could see it.'

His voice carried a hint of amusement. It was so different from how he'd spoken to her at first, telling her off about her torchlight, that it threw her into confusion.

She knew the name. Maman had mentioned a Mrs Mortimer in her knitting group.

'I'm in the Royal Navy, on leave at the moment and staying with my mother, so you'll be perfectly safe.'

'Thank you. It's very kind of you, but I'm quite able to walk home now,' she said, coolly, picking up her case. 'Thank you for helping me but all I need now is my torch.'

'I've got it, but I'm afraid it's had it.' He handed it to her. She glanced at the smashed glass and, furious with him and herself, shoved it in her pocket. 'I don't think you have any choice,' he said. 'It'll be too dangerous to try to find your way home with a bad knee and no light at all. And unless you live nearer than two minutes away, my mother's is the best option.'

She hesitated. He was right. She didn't have any choice.

Biting back her annoyance, she said, 'All right. Thank you.' She hadn't meant it to sound quite so churlish but he didn't seem to notice.

'And you'd better hang on to me. You don't want to risk another fall.'

She felt for the crook of his arm and slipped her hand through it. She wished she could see his face again, but it was impossible. All she could do was limp alongside him, her hand gripping his arm like a lifeline, and him asking her once or twice if she was okay.

She was thankful when they rounded the corner and James Mortimer pointed to a house standing on its own and set back from the street, the windows carefully blacked out with blinds.

'Here we are,' he said. He took a key from his pocket and shone his torch for a split second on the front door. 'Come on in.' He helped Suzanne through and into the hallway. He hung his hat on a hat stand in the wide entrance hall where a light from a lamp on a table sent out a feeble glow.

Trying hard not to stare she couldn't help noticing she hadn't been wrong about his face, now enhanced by nut-brown hair, the front flopping over a smooth forehead, a strong nose and jaw, and intelligent grey-blue eyes, under dark brows.

Those eyes caught hers and he grinned.

'Is that you, James?' a voice called.

'Yes, Mother. And I've brought someone to meet you.'

He took Suzanne's arm and led her through one of the doors. She found herself in a large sitting room, where a woman who looked to be in her fifties, the same nut-brown hair in a carelessly pinned chignon, was sitting by a dying fire, embroidering. She immediately rose to her feet.

'Hello, my dear. Won't you come in?' She turned to her son. 'James, help the young lady off with that wet coat.'

'I'm sorry it's so late to barge in like this,' Suzanne started, as James took her violin case and released her from the coat, 'but—'

'But she fell over and I was the knight in shining armour. Well, not at first, I'm afraid. I told her off for having her torch on full beam. She gave me a piece of her mind.'

Mrs Mortimer smiled at Suzanne. 'He can be a bit too quick to judge sometimes,' she said. 'I do apologise if he was rude in any way.'

'I think he was taking his new duty a bit too much to heart,' Suzanne said, managing a smile.

'Just like his father. Whatever he did, he had to do it perfectly. And James is exactly the same.'

Suzanne threw a glance at him and he grinned like a naughty schoolboy. 'Don't listen to Mother. She loves me really.' He paused. 'Here, let me take your hat. It looks rather a sorry sight from that downpour.'

'Sit down by the fire – for what little warmth it gives with coal now rationed. You look frozen.' Mrs Mortimer's face was one of concern. 'James, be a dear and pull that chair nearer.'

'Oh, please don't go to any trouble,' Suzanne said, taking her hat off but keeping hold of it. 'It's getting late and my family will worry where I am.'

'I think you must at least let us look at your knee before you go,' James said. 'Come and sit here and I'll take a dekko.' When she didn't say anything, he said, 'No need to worry about my credentials – I'm certified in First Aid.'

She'd have to roll down her stocking. No, she couldn't do it in front of a man. As though Mrs Mortimer understood her hesitation, she said, 'James, go and put the kettle on. She's—' She broke off. 'I'm so sorry, my dear, I don't know your name.'

'Suzanne Linfoot.'

'Oh, I know your mother,' Mrs Mortimer said. 'She comes and knits with us – shows us where we're going wrong, even though we've all been knitting donkeys' years longer.' She laughed, but it was a nice laugh. 'Are you on the telephone at home?'

Suzanne nodded.

'Well, give me your number and I'll ring her and tell her what's happened. Then she won't worry, and you can sit here and have a cup of tea. You've had a shock and I'm not sending you out again until I feel quite satisfied that you'll be all right.'

'It's too much trouble,' Suzanne began, but Mrs Mortimer wouldn't hear of it, and a minute later she could hear Mrs Mortimer speaking to Maman.

'There, that's settled,' Mrs Mortimer said, coming back into the room and reclaiming her chair. 'I told her James will see you home safely.'

'Did I hear my name?' James put his head round the door.

'Yes, dear. I told Suzanne's mother you'd go with her when she's had her cup of tea and is fit enough to walk home.'

'There's no need, honestly,' Suzanne said. 'I'll be perfectly all right.'

'That's as may be,' James said, grinning, 'but funnily enough, I was going that way myself later on this evening. I'll just be a few minutes earlier, that's all.'

Suzanne laughed at the absurdity. Why fight against them? They were being kind and fussing over her. She had to admit it was rather nice.

'Anyway, kettle's boiling. I shan't be a minute.' He disappeared again.

'While he's gone you can ease down your stocking,' Mrs Mortimer said. 'I should let him have a look. He really *is* good at first aid.'

Suzanne rolled down her stocking. Blood had seeped through the broken skin that was already swollen with an angry purple bruise emerging.

When James came back carrying the tea tray he glanced over to her, and his eyes dropped to her legs.

'Good. I'll have a look at that knee before I pour.'

He set the tray down and pulled up a low stool. Embarrassment flooding through her body, she thrust out her leg.

'Hmm, that's a nasty graze,' he said. 'A dab of TCP wouldn't come amiss.' He was back in an instant waving the familiar bottle and a white flannel.

'You can't beat it,' he said, 'but the sting is awful.'

'The smell is bad enough,' she said, smiling, but as the flannel soaked with TCP came into contact with the still-bleeding graze, she couldn't stop her sharp hiss of breath.

'Agggh, that really hurt.'

'I have to be cruel to be kind,' he said, looking up and meeting her eyes. 'You know, Suzanne, now I can see you more clearly, I realise it was *you* I heard playing the violin solo the other evening in the village hall. Mendelssohn, wasn't it?'

'Yes,' Suzanne said, irrationally pleased he'd heard the concert. 'But I don't remember seeing you.' She wished she could have bitten the words back. He'd think her awfully forward.

But he didn't seem to think anything of the kind. 'I had to leave when the air-raid siren went off, so I only heard the first bit,' he said. 'That was my first day standing in for Brian Draper.'

'Oh, I noticed someone leaving,' Suzanne said, breaking into a mischievous grin.

'Did you think I was rushing off to the shelter?' James's eyes were teasing. He was still looking up at her. 'Well, I was, but not in the way you might have thought.'

'N-no, of course not,' she said, feeling her cheeks warm. 'But even if you had been, I couldn't blame you.'

'Hmm. Your face tells me something different.' He laughed again and gave another dab of the flannel.

'Don't take any notice of him,' Mrs Mortimer said. 'He's a terrible tease.' She looked over at the violin case. 'You must be the musician in the family. Your mother's always mentioning how talented you are. She's very proud of you – I can tell. I was sorry to have missed the concert. I'd bought a ticket but had to do an extra shift at the Red Cross.'

'That reminds me,' James said, getting to his feet. 'You wanted to check the violin hadn't come to any harm. Do you trust me to open it and have a look? I've got quite a sharp eye.'

Suzanne nodded.

Carefully taking the violin from its case, he turned it this way and that, then held it up to the ceiling where the light fell in a weak pool on the instrument.

'No sign of any dent,' he said triumphantly, handing it back to her.

Taking him at his word, Suzanne laid the violin back in its case and snapped the clasps.

She found herself relaxing in the Mortimers' company. There was no awkwardness in the conversation, considering she'd never set eyes on either of them before.

She finished the welcome cup of tea, then stood.

'I really must go,' she said, 'but I can't thank you both enough for your kindness.'

'Pop in any time you'd like a chat, my dear,' Mrs Mortimer said, rising to her feet. 'If I'm home I'd love to see you.' She picked up a pencil and jotted something down on the back of an envelope, then handed it to Suzanne. 'Our telephone number,' she said, the same grey-blue smiling eyes as her son lighting her handsome features. 'So there's no excuse. Come for a cup of tea . . . any time.'

'I'd love to do that,' Suzanne answered, picking up her coat and thinking she just might take Mrs Mortimer up on the invitation.

James immediately took the coat from her and helped her on with it. Her knee was sore and throbbing now but she mustn't let them know. She felt as if she'd already overstayed her welcome.

'Right, shall we go?'

She nodded. He opened the front door and they stepped out into the damp night.

James broke the silence. 'At least the rain's eased off.'

He insisted she hold his arm again, and this time he carried the violin case, his torch in the other hand. Grateful he'd set a gentle pace, she couldn't resist glancing up at him.

'I thought I was getting to know a lot of people by now,' she said, 'but I've never seen you in the village before.'

'Probably because I'm rarely here. I'm based in Scotland.'

'Oh.'

He didn't elaborate so she didn't pursue it. He obviously wasn't allowed to say where. He asked her about her family and she briefly told him about Raine and Ronnie.

'Sounds like Raine is doing a magnificent job in the war effort,' he said.

'She is. I wish I was doing something important to help as well.'

'I'm sure it will happen. You're still young.'

'Not so young,' she said defensively.

He grinned. 'You are to me. I'm twenty-four in a few days. It feels ancient sometimes, especially in this damnable war.' He looked at her. 'Sorry, I shouldn't swear in front of a lady, but it *is* bloody damnable.'

Suzanne laughed. 'At sixpence a go, that's one-and-six you owe the swear box – even though I agree with you.'

He joined in her laughter. It was strange how perfectly comfortable she felt with him by the time they turned into her street. She almost wished their conversation could have carried on longer.

At the gate outside her small front garden he carefully set down the case.

'Thank you for rescuing me, Mr Mortimer,' she said, holding out her hand. 'It was very kind of you. And for administering the dreaded TCP.'

He chuckled. 'It works, though. But I'll only accept your thanks if you call me James.'

He gazed at her, then took her hand in his, and although the night air was cool, his fingers encircling hers were warm. For a mad moment she wondered what it would be like to feel his mouth on hers. She drew her hand quickly away.

'I couldn't very well mention this in front of my mother,' he said, studying her face intently, 'but even though it's dark and a bit foggy, you do have the most incredible eyes, Suzanne. They're like purple pansies.'

She smiled a little self-consciously. 'My mother and sisters all have the same colour. Raine calls it the Linfoot trademark.'

He nodded and smiled. 'Talking of mothers – do go and see mine. She meant it, you know.'

'I know she did.' Suzanne picked up the case. He stepped forward and opened the low front gate. She passed through and clicked it shut behind her, then turned to face him. 'Goodnight – and thank you again . . . James.'

'Goodnight, Suzanne.' He looked directly at her. 'I'm sorry I was a bit rough on you, but you do understand we have to keep strictly to the regulations.'

'You were doing your job . . . even if you *were* in civvies,' she added with a smile.

'*Touché*.' He smiled back and something stirred in her blood. 'I hope we might bump into each other again.'

'Perhaps we will.'

'Then let it be soon because they don't give me much time off.' He touched his hat and strode away.

Her heart beating a little too fast, she rang the bell of her front door.

'You had me worried to death,' her mother said, as she let her in. 'Come and take off those wet clothes. I want to hear all about Mrs Mortimer's house.'

Chapter Four

'Beatrice Mortimer is a widow with only one son,' Simone remarked when Suzanne brought her in a cup of cocoa. She fixed her eyes on her daughter. 'You know he is in the Royal Navy?'

'That's what he told me.'

'An officer, I believe.' When Suzanne didn't reply, Simone persisted. 'Suzanne, I warn you – you must not fall in love with him. He will be away at sea for long periods, and that is not good for the wife at home.'

'What on earth are you talking about?' Suzanne rounded on her mother. Really, Maman was too dramatic for words. 'I fell over. He took me to his mother's to put some TCP on my knee. Then I had a cup of tea with them, and as I'd broken my torch in the fall, he kindly brought me home. He's a total stranger. But you've already pegged me as his wife.'

'These things can happen very quickly,' Maman said, her eyebrows raised as she studied her. 'Especially in times of war. And Mrs Mortimer is a powerful lady. She dominates the knitting class.'

'She also works for the Red Cross.'

Maman raised her eyebrows. 'You seem to know much about her,' she said.

'Well, there's no need for you to read anything into the evening,' Suzanne said firmly. She stood up. 'I'm going to see Ronnie and Rusty, and then have an early night.'

Maman had made it clear that she was wary of the Mortimers. And although she loved her mother, it made Suzanne determined to take no notice of her opinion.

The rest of the week flew by and by the end of his probation period Rusty looked like a different dog. He was still thin but his ribs weren't so prominent, and his head and the patches on his coat now lived up to his new name since Suzanne had helped Ronnie give him a bath in an old tin tub. No one had answered Ronnie's 'lost dog' messages she'd pinned up on the board in the post office and village shop, but every time the telephone rang Suzanne noticed her sister jump up to take the call. And every time it was someone for Maman, Ronnie would hand over the receiver, a relieved grin on her face.

'You've been a very good boy, Rusty,' Ronnie said on his last day. 'I'm going to beg Maman to let you stay. I don't see how she can refuse you now.'

Ronnie had rushed to the shed after school and brought him out. After a few joyful barks he was now sitting quietly by her feet in the kitchen, looking up at her adoringly as Suzanne made the tea.

Their mother hadn't set eyes on Rusty since that first day.

'He's part of the family now,' Ronnie said, patting him. 'Maman can't make me take him to the vet now, surely.' She puckered her forehead and looked at Suzanne. 'Do you think I should take him in to see her and show her how much better he looks and how well he's behaving, Suzy?'

'I shouldn't. I know you're hoping to soften Maman's heart but I wouldn't remind her it's a week today,' Suzanne said.

'We'll just have to cross our fingers that Maman hasn't realised.'

Ronnie shut Rusty in the kitchen while they took the tea tray and some broken biscuits, all the grocer had been able to offer Maman, much to her disgust, into the front room where she was writing a letter.

'*Merci, chérie.*' Their mother blotted her letter and smiled as she graciously extended her hand to take the cup. 'You will both join me?'

'Yes, of course, Maman,' Suzanne said, jumping up to fetch two extra cups. They'd been going to have theirs in the kitchen with Rusty to leave Maman in peace, but it appeared she wanted their company. Suzanne's heart fell. Perhaps her mother was going to say it was time for Rusty to go. Ronnie would be heartbroken.

When the three of them were sipping their tea, Maman broke the silence. She looked across at Ronnie.

'Well, Véronique, did you have an answer to your notices in the post office and the shop about the dog?'

Suzanne could barely look at her sister's face.

'No, nothing,' Ronnie said, her voice anxious. 'Maman, would you have a look at him? He's turned into such a lovely dog.'

The clock on the chiffonier ticked loudly in the silence. Suzanne felt her own heart almost stop beating, so goodness knew how Ronnie must be feeling.

'I do not wish to see him.'

'Maman, please don't make me take him—'

'But I will allow you to keep him as long as he remains under full control and stays in the shed while you are at school.'

Ronnie sprang to her feet, her face wreathed in smiles. 'Oh, Maman, you won't regret it, I promise. I won't let him disturb you. He's been such a good dog, just as though he knows.' She tried to hug her mother, but Simone brushed it off almost as though she was embarrassed.

'So long as you do,' Simone said. 'Now, I will prepare supper.'

The two girls exchanged horrified looks but before they could stop her, Maman was on her feet and out of the door. She opened the kitchen door and they heard Rusty barking his head off.

Ronnie flew after her.

'No, no, go down. Sit! Sit!' Maman's voice was almost hysterical.

'Rusty, here boy.' Ronnie grabbed him by his new collar. 'This is Maman. You mustn't jump up. You have to be a good boy and behave because if you do, Maman says you can stay.'

'I am beginning to regret my decision already,' Simone said, 'so please keep him out of my way.'

'You've been awfully quiet lately, Suzy,' Ronnie remarked when Rusty was safely shut in her bedroom.

'Have I?' Suzanne said.

'You look as though you're dreaming,' Ronnie said sharply. 'Wake up.'

'Don't be silly. I *am* awake. I'm just thinking, that's all.'

'What about?'

Suzanne couldn't answer. Since she'd met James her emotions had been in a turmoil. He was so unlike the kind of men she usually met in her small circle. For one thing, he was much younger than any of the ones in the village orchestra. And he seemed so natural, not putting on any airs and graces, and yet he obviously came from a good family.

She'd taken to Mrs Mortimer right away, and James had

turned out to be quite different when he'd dropped the ARP warden patter after the first few minutes of their encounter. Suzanne smiled to herself, and Ronnie immediately pounced and demanded to know the joke.

Two days later Suzanne was up early when the postman knocked on the door.

'Oh, you're just the person, Miss Linfoot,' he said, handing her a buff-coloured envelope. 'It's for you. Looks most official.'

She glanced down in surprise. Who was writing to her? It was neatly typed.

'It's from London,' the postman added helpfully.

She smiled and thanked him. She realised now where it was from. Instinct told her to read it in private in her bedroom, the one she used to share with Raine. Oh, how she missed her sister, even though it was lovely to have the room to herself.

Sitting on the edge of the bed, she opened the letter carefully with the paperknife her father had given her the Christmas before he died.

29th April, 1943

Dear Miss Linfoot,

As you are probably aware, Mr Rubenstein has highly recommended you for a place at the Royal Academy of Music to study full-time.

We are pleased to invite you to attend for an audition at 11 a.m. on Tuesday, 11th May.

The piano is, we understand, your second instrument, so we would ask you to play three violin pieces of your choice, providing they are different composers, or two violin pieces and one piece of piano music.

If you wish to proceed, please confirm the date, and indicate the pieces of music you wish to play.

I look forward to hearing from you.

Yours sincerely,
Richard Glover (Principal)

Suzanne read the letter once more before folding and tucking it back in the envelope. She sat for a minute completely still.

If we weren't at war I'd be so excited.

But the niggling feeling that she should be involved in the war effort was growing stronger by the day. Not just 'should be' but she *wanted* to be involved. Wendy had taken the step. The idea of joining ENSA as a violinist in a swing or a jazz band was becoming more and more alluring. She chewed her bottom lip, considering whether she should keep the letter from her mother. She could never make Maman understand. Normally, she would have turned to Raine, but her older sister wasn't here to ask for advice and Ronnie was too young to give it.

'Come in, my dear, won't you?' Mrs Mortimer said, her face wreathed in smiles as she held the door wide for Suzanne. 'How lovely to see you again.'

Suzanne followed the matronly figure to the same sitting room as the other night. This time the fire was a little brighter but there was still a chill in the room, although Mrs Mortimer's warm welcome more than made up for it.

'The tray's all laid up so I'll get the kettle on. Just make yourself at home.'

'Thank you.'

Suzanne took the same chair as a few nights ago. She

glanced to the chair on her left, which James had occupied. She remembered his strong profile, the way his mouth turned up at the corners . . . She was glad she'd decided to take up Mrs Mortimer's invitation to come for tea at any time and had telephoned her this morning. It made a nice change, sitting in a comfortable home and being waited on. She refused to admit to herself that by not leaving it any longer there was a chance she might see James as well.

Then she realised Mrs Mortimer was speaking to her from the doorway.

'I'm sorry, I didn't quite catch that.' Suzanne turned to her hostess, her cheeks growing warm.

'One sugar or two?'

'Just the tip end,' Suzanne said. 'I've cut down from two since it was rationed, but it's that last little bit that's somehow the worst.'

'I know exactly what you mean,' Mrs Mortimer smiled as she disappeared.

Suzanne got up and wandered around the room. Her eye caught sight of several photographs displayed on top of a walnut chiffonier. She couldn't help herself. She picked up the one in the centre, which had obviously been given pride of place. It was James in his naval uniform. No doubt Maman was right – he was an officer by the look of the two gold-braid stripes on his sleeve, the top one in a loop, though she wasn't sure of the naval ranks. A strong face. One who was used to giving orders. But there was no hint of steel in the warm twinkling eyes that smiled back at her from beneath his cap, and there was a lift to the corners of his mouth as though he might break into laughter at any time . . . She thought she heard noises and hurriedly returned the frame to its position.

There was no further sound so she walked over to the

bookshelves, glancing at the titles and authors. Someone obviously loved the classics, especially Shakespeare. It looked as though every play was represented. Charles Dickens also had a prominent place although *Great Expectations* was the only one she'd read at school. She eased one of Dickens' other novels off the tightly packed shelf. Standing with the book in her hands she was soon absorbed.

'Ah, you've succumbed to the attractions of our little library.' Mrs Mortimer came into the room holding a tea tray. 'Which one's caught your fancy?'

'*The Pickwick Papers*,' Suzanne said, about to put it back on the shelf. 'I've never read it.'

'You're very welcome to borrow it. James won it as a prize at school for being top in English.' Suzanne loved the note of pride in Mrs Mortimer's voice. 'It's one of Dickens' most comical novels. I think you'll enjoy it.'

'If you're sure your son won't mind,' Suzanne said.

'He won't mind a bit,' Mrs Mortimer said. 'He'll be sorry to have missed you. He's gone to see one of his friends before he goes off again – James, that is.' Suzanne noticed a shadow pass over Mrs Mortimer's face until she smiled warmly. 'Now come and sit down while the tea's hot. I have a feeling you want to chat something over with me.'

'How did you guess?' Suzanne said as she took the cup and saucer from Mrs Mortimer.

'Put it down to experience,' Mrs Mortimer chuckled. 'Now, what's on your mind?'

It was difficult to know where to start. But once Suzanne plunged in, the words poured out. She told Mrs Mortimer about Raine in the Air Transport Auxiliary delivering aeroplanes all over the country to the boys in combat, although she didn't go into any details of places or times. Raine had drummed the security risk into her and Ronnie too often.

'It's always been my dream to attend a music school in London,' Suzanne finished, 'and now I have an opportunity – if I pass the audition, that is – but I'm not sure it's what I want, after all.'

'Do you know what might have changed your mind?'

'Yes,' Suzanne said without hesitation. 'It's the war. I want to do something where I can make a difference. But Maman has paid for my music lessons all this time when she couldn't really afford it. This is what she's always wanted for me – war or no war.'

'The war has changed our outlook as to what's important,' Mrs Mortimer said. 'You're obviously very talented so your music has taken priority up to now, but maybe that could go on hold for a while – at least until the war's over.' She caught Suzanne's eye. 'Do you have any idea – some plan – of what you might do instead?'

This was the part Suzanne was most worried about. She just hoped Mrs Mortimer wouldn't look askance at such an admission. She took a deep breath.

'I'm seriously thinking of joining an entertainments group,' she said. To her surprise Mrs Mortimer didn't look at all shocked.

'Ah, that's probably ENSA,' Mrs Mortimer said immediately. Her eyes were warm with encouragement. 'But I didn't realise they sent classical musicians to entertain the troops.'

'I'd be playing in a jazz band – swing band – that sort of thing,' Suzanne said feebly. It sounded crazy now she'd actually put it into words. 'My friend in the village orchestra has already been accepted and has asked me to go with her. She says the boys really cheer up when they hear the music, or any of the variety acts they put on.'

'And you're worried what your mother will say – is that it?'

'Yes,' Suzanne admitted. 'I told Maman I would attend the school if I get through the audition, and she was so happy that for the moment I was happy, too. But if I tell her I've changed my mind and want to play in a band and travel round the country, she'll . . . well, I don't know what she'll do.'

'Suzanne, listen to me.' Mrs Mortimer put her cup down on the saucer. 'This is *your* life, not your mother's. It's your mother's dream for you to go to the music school, but it's not yours *at the moment.*' She emphasised the last three words. 'You can pick it up later. And if you and the band can bring some reprieve to our fighting lads who are going through hell – make them forget for a while and enjoy it at the same time, as I think you would – then I believe it's a very worthwhile choice to make.'

'Do you really?' Suzanne said, feeling her face glow at the thought.

'Yes, I do, my dear. I think you've already made up your mind to do something more personal to help the war effort and if I'm right, the sooner you tell that charming French mother of yours that you've changed your mind about the music school, the better.' She looked serious for a moment. 'Just one thing – if you *do* take this path, make sure you tell her it's only for the time being so she knows you're not ignoring her wishes for you to have a musical career – which I think is completely understandable when you're obviously very talented.' She paused. 'I'd want the same for my daughter – if I had one,' she added wistfully.

'Thank you, Mrs Mortimer,' Suzanne said, finishing the last drops of her tea. 'I'll certainly consider everything you've said.'

The next half an hour passed in pleasant conversation until Suzanne rose.

'It's been lovely, Mrs Mortimer,' she said. 'Thank you so much for listening. It's helped me to think more clearly.'

'I'm glad.' Mrs Mortimer saw Suzanne to the door and kissed her cheek. 'Come any time you feel like it.'

Chapter Five

Easier said than done, Suzanne thought, as she walked home, the copy of *The Pickwick Papers* that Mrs Mortimer had put in a brown paper bag safely tucked under her arm. All the while Mrs Mortimer had been speaking so persuasively Suzanne had felt confident she wasn't throwing away an opportunity that might never come again. But as soon as they'd said goodbye Suzanne's optimism evaporated. Maman would be terribly upset if she said she wouldn't be going for any audition after all because she was going to join a light entertainment group to play for an audience of soldiers.

There was no sign of life in the house even though the back door had been left unlocked. She stepped into the kitchen where there was a note on the table in Maman's flamboyant writing.

> *Chérie, I have gone to visit Mrs Bond. Please peel the potatoes for supper. Véronique has taken that dog for a walk.*
>
> *Maman*

Suzanne grimaced. Maman refused to use Rusty's name or even acknowledge him properly, but at least she'd allowed him to stay so long as he remained out of her sight. It was a great pity as he was such a loving animal.

Suzanne hummed to herself as she peeled the potatoes. There was a tune running in her head that she'd heard The Andrews Sisters sing on the wireless last night. Their happy voices and the beat were so infectious that she couldn't let go the tune. Knowing there was no one around she burst into song, her shoulders keeping time as she dropped the chunks of potato into a saucepan of cold water.

'Pardon me, boys, is that the Chattanooga choo choo?
Right on track twenty-nine . . .'

She grinned. No, that last line wasn't quite right. But it went something like that. She laid out the cutlery on a tray, the salt and pepper, and a butter dish of part butter but mostly margarine she'd mixed together, not that the result would fool anyone. She took the tray to the dining room and set it on the table, all the while singing. Grabbing hold of a bottle of salad cream she held it up to her mouth like a microphone, her body swaying to the rhythm.

'. . . dinner in the diner, nothing could be finer
Dum de dum de dum Carolina . . .'

'Suzy!'

Abruptly, Suzanne stopped, the salad cream bottle still held in microphone position, as Ronnie's head appeared round the door, her eyes wide.

'What's going on?' Ronnie demanded.

'I got carried away,' Suzanne said, a little pink. 'I can't get that song out of my head.' She laughed. 'Did I frighten you?'

Ronnie came in. 'No, not in the least. Actually, you sounded really professional – just like those singers on the wireless.'

'Thank you, little sister, for such a compliment,' Suzanne

said, as she smoothed a tablecloth on the dining table and set out the knives and forks.

'Has Maman heard you?' Ronnie asked curiously.

'What has Maman heard – or not heard?'

Two pairs of eyes flew to the doorway where Maman stood, immaculate as always, even though she'd only popped over to see one of the neighbours. Instantly, Suzanne's flushed cheeks deepened a further shade.

'You look as though you're ashamed of something, Suzanne,' Maman said, stepping into the room. 'Or hiding something. Which is it to be?'

'Ronnie's just being an annoying baby sister,' Suzanne said in a tight voice. This was not the right moment to tell her mother about not going to London after all.

'She could easily go on the stage like Sally Rivers,' Ronnie persisted. 'Only Suzy has a better voice.'

'What are you talking about, Véronique?' Maman said, sitting on one of the upright chairs and not taking her eyes off her youngest daughter.

'Suzy. I caught her singing away, pretending she had a microphone, only it was a bottle of Heinz Salad Cream,' Ronnie said, giggling and nodding towards the bottle, now standing innocently in the middle of the dining table.

'What is this nonsense, Suzanne?' Maman demanded.

'She's just trying to irritate me,' Suzanne said, determined not to be drawn in. Why did Maman never leave anything alone, once she'd got her teeth in it? She tried to change the subject. 'Ronnie, why don't you give Rusty his dinner?'

Ronnie looked as though she wanted to stay and hear what they were going to discuss, but Suzanne threw her such a warning look, her sister scurried off, giving her a backward grin as she pulled the door shut behind her.

'Have you done your practice today, Suzanne?' Maman said.

'Er – no, not exactly.'

'What do you mean? It is either exact or it is not. What have you then been doing this morning besides the ironing I left you?'

Suzanne gave a start. In her hurry to talk to Mrs Mortimer she'd forgotten completely about the ironing.

'Or have you not found the time to do it?'

'I'm sorry, Maman. I'll do it this afternoon.'

'That is when you must practise your pieces for the music school,' Maman said, her lips tightening. Then her face relaxed into a smile. 'Ah, *oui. Je comprends.* You wish to discuss the pieces you have chosen for the audition. And you are still not sure if you have made the right choices. But do not worry, *chérie*. We will make the final decisions together.'

Suzanne briefly closed her eyes in resignation. Once again Maman had got hold of the wrong end of the stick. Or was it on purpose? Well, it wouldn't hurt to wait until after supper so they could all eat in peace without a row hanging over them. She immediately reprimanded herself for being such a coward. But the moment had gone.

'Let's have supper first,' she said mildly. 'I've done the potatoes but what are we having with them?'

'You can heat a tin of peas,' Maman said. 'The butcher kept me some sausages I will fry.' She pursed her lips and shook her head. 'Although they are not the same as the delicious French *saucisson* . . .' She touched her fingers to her lips and blew out a kiss.

At that moment Rusty leapt into the room with Ronnie flying after him.

'Get that dog out of here.' Maman lifted her heels a few inches off the floor.

'Rusty, be a good boy. Come here.'

Rusty halted and turned his head towards his new mistress. He stood still and let Ronnie put his lead back on.

'There,' Ronnie said triumphantly. 'See how obedient he is.'

'Hmm,' their mother said, obviously not daring to put her feet back on the floor, in spite of Rusty wagging his tail and looking up at her with a beseeching expression.

'Let him stay a few minutes, Maman,' Ronnie said. 'You'll never get used to him if you never allow him in.'

'I do not want to get used to him,' Simone said firmly, but at least she lowered her feet to the floor. She caught Suzanne's eye. 'And after supper, Suzanne, we will have the happy discussion for your beautiful classical pieces. If you want my opinion—'

'Maman, later.'

'*D'accord, chérie.* We eat first. And after we talk you will go upstairs to practise for the audition. That is very important. You must give a perfect rendition.'

Maman had fried the sausages in too much lard. After only one mouthful Suzanne thought she would choke on it. Feeling like a naughty schoolgirl she surreptitiously took her handkerchief out of her pocket and wrapped it up. Rusty would love it for a treat later.

'The sausage was even worse than I suspected,' Maman said after she'd chased a few peas around her plate and tried a little mashed potato.

'It was nice,' Ronnie said smiling at her mother and putting her knife and fork together on her empty plate.

Dear Ronnie. She'd eat anything that was put in front of her.

'If we were in France,' Maman began, 'we would finish our meal with a beautiful coffee.'

Suzanne managed to stop her eyes from rolling up to the ceiling. *Have you noticed, Maman,* she wanted to scream, *we're not in France? And thank goodness. You've said it yourself many times that since the occupation, France is no longer France. France is now Germany. French people are desperately trying to escape from their own country.*

'Véronique, please clear the table. You may start to wash up. As soon as your sister goes to her practice I will come and help you – so long as the dog is not there.' She looked at Suzanne. 'Come, *chérie*, we will go in the front room and be peaceful.'

Suzanne followed her mother into the front room. If only Dad was here. He would have stuck up for her, she was sure. But it was no good dwelling on it. She'd have to face Maman and get it over with.

'Sit with me, *chérie*.' Simone patted the space next to her on the sofa. 'Now tell me the pieces and I will give my opinion.'

Suzanne drew in a deep breath.

'Maman, I'm not absolutely sure—'

'No, of course you're not,' Simone interrupted. 'It is too important to make any hasty decisions. The pieces must be complicated so they know you are capable, but not so much that you do not perform them correctly.'

'You don't understand,' Suzanne tried again. 'I'm having serious doubts about going there in the first place.'

There. She'd said it. She sneaked a look at her mother's face. Maman's expression was frozen. There was not a flicker of life. Until Suzanne saw the glint of anger burning in her mother's eyes.

'What are you saying, child? Of course you are going. We are talking about the audition pieces, are we not?'

'No, Maman. I want to have a serious talk about *now* . . . with the war on.'

Simone frowned. 'You cannot change the war.'

'I know I can't. But I've been talking to Wendy . . . you remember . . . she's another violinist in our orchestra. She said she's going to join an entertainments group, and I'd like to find out more about it. Which means that I don't want to do any audition at the moment as it could be wasting their time.' She paused, remembering Mrs Mortimer's warning. 'It's only for the time being. I'll apply to the music school when the war's over and I've done my bit.'

Simone's delicate features hardened. 'The war does not show a sign it is coming to the end. Maybe another year, maybe two, maybe longer. By that time you will have lost your chance. I will not let that happen. Your father would be very angry with me if I did. It is your future I am talking about. And your future is your beautiful music. You have a wonderful talent and I will not allow you to throw away your career because you want to do the same as your foolish friend.'

'Wendy's not foolish,' Suzanne protested. 'She's—'

'I will hear nothing more. You must now go and do your practice. I have the 'eadache and will go to bed for an hour. Then you may bring me some tea.'

Suzanne looked after her mother's retreating back. Why wouldn't Maman just listen for once to what she had to say? She blew her cheeks out. She was sure now that her mother suspected she'd already made up her mind not to attend the audition, but that if she refused to stop and hear those words from her daughter, Suzanne would eventually comply.

Chapter Six

May 1943

'Raine! What a wonderful surprise. Why didn't you tell us you were coming?' Suzanne said, her face lighting up as soon as she set eyes on her older sister the following Monday morning. Raine's timing couldn't have been better.

'It was all last minute,' Raine said, hugging her back and planting a kiss on her cheek, 'and I'd rather hear all the news in person.'

Somehow Raine always made everything seem right. Suzanne watched as her sister shrugged off her coat and hung it in the hall, then popped her forage cap on the hook above.

'Just look at you,' Suzanne said, admiringly. 'You look so smart in your uniform . . . and the gold wings you've worked so hard for.'

'Yes, although I'm much more comfortable in trousers, but we're not allowed to wear them off duty. Thank goodness we can in the cockpit. You didn't used to be able to. I think the men wanted to admire our legs.' Raine gave a short laugh. 'I must say, wearing a skirt feels quite dressy these days.'

Suzanne thought it must be wonderful to have such a

sense of belonging in such a worthwhile organisation. Raine oozed confidence and positively glowed. She pulled the elastic from her dark wavy hair and let it fall to her shoulders.

'I'm sorry I couldn't get home for Easter, or your concert.' She flung the words over her shoulder. 'But we've been rushing all over the place.'

'Don't worry. I know you would if you could.'

'Did it go well? Did Ronnie enjoy it? I know she's not that keen on your kind of music.'

'She wasn't there,' Suzanne said, ushering her sister into the front room. 'I'll put the kettle on and tell you all about it.'

'What's that noise?' Raine tilted her head to the ceiling. 'It sounds like a dog. Is it next door's?'

'Yes, it's a dog, and no, it's not next door's,' Suzanne grinned.

Raine's jaw dropped. 'Don't tell me Maman's relented at last and let Ronnie have one.'

'Not quite relented,' Suzanne said. 'Rusty's permanently on borrowed time. He has to live in Ronnie's bedroom when she's home or the shed when she's at school.'

'Ah, I thought Maman's change of heart was too good to be true,' Raine said, chuckling. 'Maybe she'll get used to him and give him a reprieve.' She made towards the door. 'I'd better go and say hello to her and then I'll go and see Ronnie and meet Rusty while you're making the tea.'

Ten minutes later the three sisters and Rusty were in the dining room, Rusty mad with excitement that another sister seemed to want to be his friend.

'You've only one more person to conquer, Rusty,' Raine said, fondling his ears. 'But it may be your most difficult challenge yet.' Rusty stuck his wet nose in her hand and wagged his tail. 'He's very thin,' Raine commented, giving him a gentle pat on his head.

Rusty gave a little whine of pleasure.

'You should have seen him when I found him,' Ronnie said. 'He was starving. You could see his ribs through his coat.'

'I'm really pleased you have him,' Raine said. 'And Maman will come round eventually.'

'What must I come round to?' Maman stood at the doorway, then saw Rusty and backed off. 'Véronique, I told you that dog is not to be in the house except for your room.'

'Raine wanted to meet him,' Ronnie protested. 'And he wanted a change. It's awful how his life is nearly all in my room or the shed.'

'They are the conditions,' Maman said. 'If you do not like them then you must get rid of him.' Her eyes caught sight of Raine. 'So Lorraine, you have come to see your mother at last.'

'Hello, Maman,' Raine said, getting up and kissing her mother's cheek. 'Sorry I couldn't let you know, but I'm only here for one night. I have to leave first thing in the morning.'

'Then we must make the most of it,' Maman said. 'And it must start with that dog—'

'Maman, please don't keep calling Rusty "that dog",' Ronnie said. 'He hates it. You know his name.'

'I do not know anything of the kind,' Maman said. 'But I know I will not rest until he is out of this room and I can enjoy my cup of tea. I do not think it is too much to ask.'

'I'll take him for a walk,' Ronnie said. 'If anyone wants to go with me, they can.'

'I'll stay with Maman as I've only just arrived,' Raine said. 'You go with her, Suzy.'

'You may all go and leave me in peace,' Maman said firmly.

'Doris Strong left me *The Lady* last week and I have been too busy to read it. I will be happy on my own with a cup of tea and the magazine.'

'Can't you join a proper orchestra with this ENSA?' Raine said. 'Then at least Maman won't be able to moan about the waste of lessons.'

The two of them were sitting in Suzanne's bedroom chatting, just like they did before Raine left home to join the ATA.

'It doesn't appeal to me as much as being part of a jazz band,' Suzanne said, surprised that it was true. 'And on Pathé News when you see the soldiers having a dance with the girls, the music's always jazz and swing. Besides, I'm ready for a change.' She looked at her older sister. 'I told Maman I'd go back to classical but she won't have it. She says I'll have thrown away my chance of a musical career. But this war has changed everything. Things that were so important to me aren't so much any more. I want the challenge of learning something completely new and I think the soldiers will respond to jazz more.' She looked at her sister and laughed. 'Listen to me, rambling on.'

Raine smiled. 'You know, Suzy, I think it might be absolutely right for you. You do tend to be a bit serious with all this classical stuff, beautiful though it is, and I do genuinely enjoy it. But I can see what you mean from the soldiers' point of view.' She paused, frowning slightly. 'There's only one thing I can see against it and that's Ronnie. If you'd gone to the music school you'd have come home every day and been a support for her, but who knows where you might end up with ENSA. As far as I know, you can be sent all over the place – all over the world, in fact.'

'I've thought of that,' Suzanne said. 'Ronnie's one of the

reasons why I stupidly told Maman I would go and do the audition.'

'And Maman was the other,' Raine said immediately. 'Have you talked to Ronnie about it?'

Suzanne shook her head. 'No, but I will before I make a definite decision.'

'I think you've made up your mind,' Raine said, 'and Ronnie will tell you to go ahead with your plan. She's such an independent creature. She'd be furious if she thought you were staying behind for her.'

'I know,' Suzanne said. 'But I do feel guilty. She's only sixteen. A child still. And Maman can be very difficult sometimes.'

'Don't I know it,' Raine said grimly. 'Do you want me to speak to Ronnie?'

'No,' Suzanne said. 'This has to be between her and me.'

'Don't forget that Maman could easily use Ronnie as a weapon against you joining ENSA to make you feel guilty, when really it's *her* who wants to keep you by her side. Like she did with me.'

'I know,' Suzanne said. 'I've thought about the way she treated you. But you were completely focused. I wish I had your strength of mind.'

Raine gazed at her. 'You've got more strength of mind than Ronnie and me put together,' she said. 'You just haven't had the opportunity yet to prove it.' She paused. 'You know, Suzy, there's something different about you and I'm not sure it's just this change of heart about the music school. Do I detect an extra sparkle in your eye?'

'I don't know what you're talking about.' Suzanne gave a short laugh. 'It's still the same old routine here – well, except for Rusty making his appearance.'

'No, it's not Rusty.' Raine gave her sister a mischievous wink. 'I think you've met someone.'

Immediately Suzanne tensed. She'd made up her mind not to discuss James. It was only an accidental meeting. He'd made no suggestion of—

'I'm right, aren't I?' Raine demanded. 'There's no point in denying it, Suzy, because you're blushing.'

'I wouldn't exactly call it *meeting* someone,' Suzanne said, smiling now. Raine could read her like a book. Maybe it wasn't a bad thing to tell her sister about the fall and James coming to the rescue. At least it was something new to say. And she could always put the attention onto his mother.

'James and his mother sound lovely,' Raine said when Suzanne had related her story. 'So when do you think you'll see him again?'

'I probably never will,' Suzanne said. 'Unless I bump into him. He's in the Navy so I imagine he's away a lot.'

'That shouldn't present a huge problem,' Raine said. 'They do get time off. And he was on leave when you met him.'

'I actually went to see his mother yesterday,' Suzanne said. 'She invited me to go round for a cup of tea any time I liked so I thought I'd take her up on it.' She hesitated, not wanting to hurt Raine's feelings. 'We did chat about ENSA – she'd heard of it – and she understood my problem about the music school and Maman. She didn't try to persuade me, or anything, but she helped me to see that if I decided to go ahead, she thought I'd be doing something worthwhile and that I could go back to my music later.' When Raine didn't answer, she said, 'I would have discussed it with you if you'd been here, Raine. But as you weren't, Mrs Mortimer was the only other person I trusted to have a sensible opinion.'

Raine's eyes narrowed. 'Or was it that you thought you might have another stroke of luck and run into the rather good-looking son – I believe that's how you described him?'

'Did I say that?' Suzanne felt the warmth rush to her cheeks.

'Yes, you did,' Raine said firmly. 'And you also implied I was sensible – not something I hear that often.' She grinned. 'But you were saying . . .?'

'I think that's about all. Oh, and she knows Maman. They're in the same knitting group.'

'Perfect,' Raine chuckled. 'Our dear mother will be delighted. A nice steady man in the Navy from what sounds like the sort of family she'd approve of.'

'Raine, please stop rushing ahead. You're sounding as bad as Maman. She's already warned me not to fall in love with him. Do you know, she had us married and me sitting all alone waiting for his ship to come in.'

Raine laughed. 'That's Maman.'

'And talking of approval – she doesn't approve of Mrs Mortimer all that much. She says she dominates the knitting group. I had to smile. If anyone dominates the conversation, it's Maman.'

Raine laughed. 'Don't try to change the subject.'

'Raine, I'm telling you – James and I only met once and started off on the wrong foot. I think he likes me well enough, as I do him, but there's no hint it could develop into anything remotely along the lines you're talking about.'

'Hmm. We'll see what fate has to say about it,' was all her sister said.

Chapter Seven

Suzanne lay in bed that night thinking that talking about James Mortimer to Raine had stirred up that same strange flutter. She remembered the pressure of his hand when he'd said goodnight. She shrugged. Raine had simply been teasing her when she'd insinuated that fate would decide.

She opened the book – James's book – by her bed, thinking she would begin reading it tonight. When she'd flicked through it at Mrs Mortimer's yesterday she hadn't noticed the inscription on the frontispiece in bold handwriting:

James Mortimer, aged 12, Class 2A.
Prize for top in English Literature.
Randolph Sweet (Headmaster)

Suzanne smiled, picturing James at that age. He'd be a dark-haired lad, tall for his age, with laughing eyes, wearing a cap and a cheeky grin. She wondered if he'd read the book. She gently ruffled the pages and scrutinised several of them minutely, but she couldn't tell. He either hadn't read it or he'd been very careful to keep it in such pristine condition. She opened the cover at the very end. There, on one of the blank endpapers, written in pencil, she read: *This one is my favourite by CD. I particularly like the characters. Their names fit their personalities and both things made me laugh. James Mortimer, 10th November 1931.*

She smiled and turned again to Chapter One, and even though she could hear Maman and Raine's murmurs downstairs, this time she was able to read and become absorbed until her eyelids drooped.

Raine had already left to catch an early train by the time the postman arrived. Suzanne was making herself a cup of tea but rushed to the door when she heard the letterbox rattle. She bent to pick up the letters. Two for Maman, looking like bills, and one for Raine, which she would forward on, and one for herself in beautiful italic writing. It was postmarked Bromley.

Curiously she slit open the cream envelope and pulled out a cream-coloured sheet of Basildon Bond notepaper. Her eyes scanned down to the signature: Beatrice Mortimer. How strange.

Dear Suzanne,

I did enjoy our chat and I was wondering if you would like to come to an afternoon tea this coming Saturday at 4 p.m. It's James's birthday (the 8th). He's made it quite clear, though, that he doesn't want any present from me this year while the war's going on so please don't bring anything. But I know he'd be delighted to see you, although this little 'do' is meant to be a surprise.

Don't worry about letting me know – just come at any time if you can. James has to go back to his ship on Monday morning early.

I look forward to seeing you again.

Sincerely,

Beatrice Mortimer

P.S. I also look forward to hearing about your decision!

Suzanne skimmed the letter again, biting her lip. She wished now she'd mentioned she'd been to see Mrs Mortimer again. As it was, she'd have to confess to Maman if she decided to go – unless she went without telling her. But she couldn't do that. She wasn't in the habit of doing things behind her mother's back, but the worry was that Maman would insist upon going with her so she could control what Mrs Mortimer might have to say. After all, her mother knew Mrs Mortimer from the knitting class. Oh, why did life have to be so complicated?

She'd go right now and tell Maman she was going to a birthday afternoon tea on Saturday for Mrs Mortimer's son, James. And that she'd definitely made up her mind to join ENSA. Get it all over in one go.

'Was that the postman, *chérie*?' Simone called out from the dining room.

'Yes, Maman,' Suzanne answered, resolutely raising her chin. 'I'm just coming.' She took her cup of tea into the room where her mother sat eating a piece of toast and sliver of cheese at the table.

'Is there something for me?' her mother asked.

'Yes, but nothing terribly exciting, I don't think.' Suzanne handed her the envelopes and sat down opposite.

Her mother looked at one, then the other, and tossed them unopened onto the table. She gazed at her daughter. 'You are looking a little pink, Suzanne. What has happened?'

'I've had a letter from Mrs Mortimer.'

Simone's mouth fell open. 'Beatrice Mortimer? Why is she writing to *you*?'

'It's an invitation to have afternoon tea with her – she's doing a birthday tea for her son.'

Simone's eyes narrowed. 'Why would she do that? You've only met her once. Who else is invited?'

'I think she's inviting a couple of his friends as well,' Suzanne said, ignoring Maman's first question.

'I see.' Maman pressed her lips together as if she didn't see at all. 'You are hiding something from me,' she said eventually. Suzanne's heart sank. 'I would like to see this letter, *chérie*. You will show it to me.'

'I have it in my pocket.' Suzanne pulled out the folded paper. 'I'll read it to you.'

'*Non*, I wish to read it myself.' She held out her hand.

Suzanne passed it over. If it confirmed to Maman that it was all above board, then that was just as well. Too late she remembered Mrs Mortimer's postscript. She held her breath as Maman read the letter, her expression hardening. Suzanne swallowed.

'What does this mean at the bottom?' Her mother tapped the offending letter with her manicured nails.

'Maman, this time you must listen to me. I want to join that entertainments group I told you about. They go round the various stations where the troops are – our soldiers fighting for King and country – who desperately need cheering up,' she gabbled.

Simone threw her hands in the air.

'I cannot believe you are saying these things. I am sorry, Suzanne, but I will not allow you to waste your life. And if your father was alive he would agree with me. No, you will not go. You will accept the audition date. If you do not, I will write to the person myself to say you will be attending.'

'Maman,' Suzanne said as gently as she could, 'you want this for me, and I love you for it. I wanted it, too—'

'Then what is changed?' Maman demanded.

'The *war*! It's changed everything. Oh, Maman.' Suzanne tried to take her mother's hand in hers. 'Don't you see? I'm not a child any longer, even though you still call me one, and I want to help in the war effort.'

'And you *will* be helping,' her mother said, gripping Suzanne's arm and fixing her eyes on her. 'You will be playing beautiful music for people to hear. It is as important to keep up the spirit of people here at home in these terrible times. We all need food. But the soul also must be fed. And you will do that with your music.'

'But if I was accepted I'd have to stay for several years,' Suzanne protested.

'*Absolument.*'

'The war will be over by then. I want to do my bit *now*. Play to ordinary soldiers who are on the battlefields fighting for us – risking their lives every day. I want them to have some fun.'

'Classical music is not for fun,' Maman said huffily. 'It is music for the soul. For here. Deep inside.' She pressed somewhere near her heart.

'Exactly my point. Maman, I'd be in a swing band where I can still play my violin, but to a different beat. I want to entertain people who know the kind of music they like. I want to help them forget for a few hours the hell they're going through.' She looked at her mother, desperate for her to understand. 'Is that really so bad?'

'You are wasting your talent, Suzanne, after all the music lessons I have provided—'

'Maman.' Suzanne had to force herself to keep calm. 'You know how grateful I am. But you're insinuating that the musicians in bands aren't talented.' When her mother opened her mouth to argue, Suzanne quickly added, 'But of course they are. The jazz and swing bands here and in America are wonderful. They bring the people together to show Hitler we haven't lost our spirit and will go on fighting until we win. The music gets them on the floor dancing and laughing. And I wouldn't be accepted in any band if they didn't think I had any talent.'

She looked anxiously at her mother who sat in silence. After a minute her mother spoke in an even tone.

'I always thought you were very different from Lorraine. More loving. More understanding and would listen to your *maman*. Not headstrong, like she so often is. But I am wrong.' She gave a long sigh. 'It is a great pity you have inherited such an unattractive trait.'

Suzanne looked her mother directly in the eye. 'What are you saying, Maman? You can't inherit a trait, good or bad, from a sister . . . even if she is older,' she added with a smile, trying to ease the tension.

Her mother clamped her mouth shut. She gazed at Suzanne and shook her head. 'I am disappointed, that is all.' She rose to her feet. 'I will leave you to think what you are doing to me, your *maman*. And I will tell you one thing – I do *not* approve of this . . . what they call *swing* music, and this – this *jitterbug* from *America* . . .' She practically spat the words out. 'And I will *not* have my daughter in any part of it.' She peered at the letter again, then at Suzanne. 'What I do not understand is why Mrs Mortimer is involved in this change of mind.' Her voice was ice.

'Maman, please give me a little credit. I'll make up my own mind. Mrs Mortimer has nothing—'

'Stop!' Simone raised her hand. 'You have spoken to Beatrice Mortimer behind my back. You have asked her opinion and she has told you to go with this entertaining group. *Nom de Dieu!* How *dare* you do this to your mother. And listen to a *stranger*. She will hear from *me*.'

She swept out of the room.

Suzanne sat in stunned silence. She'd known her mother

wouldn't at first approve, but she'd hoped that after Maman had had time to let it sink in, she would see that it was important for her to do something towards the war effort. But she realised with thumping heart she'd completely misjudged her mother. And Raine would have been the first to point out the power of Maman over them all.

She blinked back the tears as she cleared her mother's dishes, then poured the untouched cup of tea down the sink. Whatever Maman threatened, Suzanne vowed she would not allow her to take control of her life. She would not.

Chapter Eight

'You could be conscripted any time,' Ronnie said, when Suzanne related the scene with Maman that afternoon when they were taking Rusty for a walk. They'd got into the habit during the Easter holiday and Suzanne enjoyed chatting with her young sister who sometimes surprised her with her wisdom. 'And they could send you anywhere. You won't have any choice. Maman will be on her own one day, so you'll have to be cruel to be kind. At least when it's *my* turn she'll be used to two daughters leaving home, which will pave the way for *me*,' Ronnie giggled, handing the lead over to Suzanne.

'I'm not sure she'd be very happy with that reasoning,' Suzanne said. 'Stop pulling, Rusty. We'll let you off in a minute when we get to the park.' The dog was barking joyfully at all the smells, tugging on his lead, then making them wait while he sniffed and snuffled. 'The worst of it is that she's threatened to see Mrs Mortimer.'

'Mrs Mortimer sounds like a lady who can stand up for herself so I shouldn't worry about it,' Ronnie said. 'No, Rusty, put that filthy rag down immediately.'

'It's just that she was so kind to me – and I don't want Maman to upset her.' She bit her lip. No need to mention to her young sister that she equally didn't want Mrs Mortimer's very nice son, James, to be upset either. Ronnie would learn about such grown-up matters when the time came.

'I am afraid you will not be welcome at Beatrice Mortimer's house on Saturday, *chérie*.'

Suzanne startled. 'What do you mean, Maman?'

'I have spoken to her on the telephone and told her to please mind her own business and not to interfere in the future of my daughter.'

'Oh, Maman,' Suzanne said, dismayed, 'you didn't have to do that. I feel so embarrassed. She didn't try to persuade me in the least.'

'I have nothing more to say.'

No, I don't suppose you have. You've done your worst by what you said to Mrs Mortimer.

The more Suzanne thought about what her mother had said to Mrs Mortimer, the more upset she became. Well, there was nothing she could do. Her mother had purposefully made trouble so that Suzanne could never again confide in the lady.

A ripple of anger coursed through her. Deciding to go for a walk to calm down, she removed her jacket from the hook and didn't bother to put it on until she was outside. At least the orchestra would be rehearsing again tomorrow and she'd have a chance to speak to Wendy again.

Suzanne mooched along, head down in thought, when she heard a motorcar pull up beside the pavement. The driver leaned over and wound down the window.

'It *is* Suzanne, isn't it?'

She recognised that voice. Melodious. She peered in to see James grinning at her.

'Yes, it's me,' she said flatly. When James found out what Maman had told his mother he wouldn't be so friendly.

'Oh, dear. You look very serious. Has something happened to upset you?'

She shook her head.

'Sorry, I don't believe you. Why don't you jump in and we'll have a tea or something at the café? I'm a good listener.'

What would be the harm? Then the image of her mother's face, livid with fury, made her hesitate.

'I'm afraid I can't. I—'

'Please.' James looked at her imploringly. 'I'm a bit low myself. I hate leaving my mother worrying herself to death when I go back to my ship on Monday.'

'All right,' she said, without thinking. 'Just a cup of tea, then. I was only walking into the village to get some exercise. Trying to clear my head . . .'

'Ah, so there *is* something you need to get off your chest.' He came round to her side and opened the door, and a little self-consciously she folded herself into the small space.

'I didn't think anyone could get petrol these days,' she commented for something to say when James pulled into the road.

'I'd topped up the tank before the rationing, and because I'm mostly at sea I've barely touched it.' He turned to her. 'Actually, we could go into Bromley. I know an exceptionally good cake shop . . . and we wouldn't run into any gossiping villagers,' he added, with the same wide smile.

If she said no, she knew she'd regret it. Today was Wednesday. He was going back to his ship in less than a week. Although the Allies had dramatically turned the tide in the war against the U-boats, it was still possible for a ship to be torpedoed. A shiver ran up her spine. Not just for James, she told herself, but all the crew he'd be sailing with. She wouldn't allow herself to think further.

'All right, you've tempted me,' Suzanne said, returning his smile with a shaky one of her own.

'Good-o,' James said, pressing his foot on the accelerator.

In the café, James helped her off with her coat and ordered tea and scones with jam.

'Please make sure it's real butter,' he said, smiling up at the bleached blonde waitress. She nodded and disappeared. He grinned at Suzanne. 'They palm you off with marg if you don't specify.' He paused. 'Do you mind if I smoke?'

Suzanne shook her head. She noticed the shape of his hands as he lit a cigarette. He had long fingers, not as slender as a musician's, but more like someone who would roll their sleeves up and work, if need be. She imagined him on a ship, issuing orders.

'Now tell me what's on your mind,' he said, and for a moment she thought he meant what she was thinking and visualising at this minute. Feeling her cheeks flush, and hoping he'd think it was the warmth of the café, she came back to the present, swiftly telling him about Maman insisting she attend the Royal Academy of Music, and her own desire to join ENSA.

'I went to see your mother again,' she said.

'I know,' James smiled. 'She told me you'd had a chat. She was delighted you went to her.' He touched her hand briefly and she felt a tingling up her arm. 'Was it about your dilemma?'

'Yes. She really listens when you say something,' Suzanne said, fidgeting with the condiments on the table. 'Something Maman finds very hard to do. Your mother reminded me that if I did decide to join ENSA I could take up classical music again when this war is over – if it ever is.' She looked up to see James watching her with those twinkling grey-blue eyes. They were the same colour as the sea on a summer's day when Dad used to take them on a caravan holiday in Hastings. Like his mother, James was also listening intently. 'And I would still try to keep up my practising,' she hurried on, not wanting him to realise how his eyes affected her.

'Well, I can't see any problem, so far,' James said, tapping his cigarette over the ashtray.

Suzanne watched the piece of ash drop into the glass dish as if it were the most fascinating of movements.

'Did your mother also tell you that Maman telephoned her and told her it was none of her business to advise me on my future?' she said finally.

'No, I can't say she did,' James said, inhaling and then blowing out the smoke away from her face. 'But my mother wouldn't take much notice, so don't worry that her feelings are hurt.'

'Well, I do,' Suzanne admitted. 'I was so embarrassed.'

'I expect the truth of the matter is that your mother worries about you going off on your own. I don't know how old you are—' he leaned towards her '—but I imagine you haven't got the key of the door yet. That's why she worries. As far as she's concerned, you're still her child and need to be under her authority – she doesn't see it as control. She sees it as doing her best for you.' He gave her a rueful smile. 'Maybe in her own life, when she was young, there were things she wished she could have done but was stopped by the effects of the last war. Who knows? I suppose you have to try hard to be patient, but that's not to say you have to give in to all her suggestions if you feel deep inside that they're wrong for you.'

Suzanne didn't know quite what to say. If she admitted the truth that Maman was aggrieved she'd gone to *his* mother and discussed her problem, she'd feel disloyal. And maybe James had a point about Maman not fulfilling her own dreams. Before she could answer, the waitress hurried over carrying a full tray and briskly set out the crockery, teapot, milk jug, and a small bowl with four sugar lumps on the table. 'I'll bring the scones straightaway,' she said.

'Shall I pour?' James asked.

'Please.'

He picked up the teapot and poured out the two cups, then added some milk. He pushed the sugar bowl towards her, but she shook her head.

'Does this mean you won't be coming to the birthday tea Mother is preparing?'

'Oh, you're not supposed to know anything about it,' Suzanne blurted.

James grinned. 'I know I'm not – but I do. Lance Boswell stopped me when I was in Bromley library yesterday, and said he'd be there, but none of my other friends have any leave. Poor old Lance has only just recovered from a nasty wound on his leg.' He sucked in his breath. 'What a bloody awful war – excuse my French.'

The blonde waitress who had just set down the plate of scones gave James an admiring look and giggled before she turned to look after another customer.

'Oh, dear, that's two ladies who've heard me swear in the space of ten seconds.' But he was grinning widely.

Suzanne smiled. 'I doubt you've offended either of us. It *is* bloody – literally.' She hesitated. 'You might be right about Maman, but she's being unreasonable. After all, you're only up the road. I wouldn't be doing anything *that* wild.'

'More's the pity . . .' James chuckled, a wicked gleam in his eyes. 'Sorry, Suzy, I couldn't resist that.'

She couldn't help laughing. They talked a little more, and Suzanne enjoyed the novelty of being with a man who seemed to find what she had to say of interest. She liked listening to the sound of his voice without always taking in everything he was saying. She liked hearing him call her Suzy.

'Well, what are you going to do about this ENSA company?' he said, finally, pulling her out of her reverie.

'I definitely want to find out more about it,' she said, taking a bite of the delicious still-warm scone, 'so I'll speak to Wendy tomorrow.'

James dropped her off outside her house, then wound the passenger window down and stuck his head out.

'Shall we see you Saturday afternoon then?' he asked.

'I'm not sure,' she said. 'Your mother said I didn't need to reply. Just call in if I was able to.' She looked directly at him. 'Can we leave it like that?'

'Of course.' He switched the engine on again. 'Suzy, I'm the last person who would want you to get into trouble with your mother, but I'd be so pleased if you came on my birthday – and if you do, please don't bring me anything. I don't want or need anything at all. Just bring yourself.'

She watched as his car disappeared in a cloud of smoke with a roar of the engine.

Chapter Nine

That evening as Suzanne walked to the village hall to her rehearsal, her mother's words would not stop rolling around her head. She tried hard not to think badly of her but really, Maman had behaved disgracefully to Mrs Mortimer. Then she softened. Maman had lost Dad and must be constantly worried about Raine having an accident in 'one of those flimsy contraptions', as she called the aeroplanes. Suzanne realised this was all part of the problem. If she left home to join ENSA, it would just be Ronnie and Maman. And another daughter being sent goodness knew where for her to worry about. With a stab of guilt, she remembered how non-judgemental James had been, suggesting Maman might have had her own dreams curtailed.

Suzanne opened the village hall door to the sounds of chattering and a couple of musicians tuning their instruments. They looked up and smiled, calling hello. She might not know much about them personally, but she liked them because they were enthusiastic and serious about the music they were playing, and even with the war on, rarely missed a rehearsal.

'Ah, there you are, Suzanne,' Mr Rubenstein said when she stepped in and shrugged off her coat. 'Can you believe it's this cold in May?' He rubbed his hands briskly together. 'I think we're just waiting for Wendy.'

He was right about the cold, Suzanne thought. It certainly

wasn't spring weather. She hung up her coat and glanced at the clock in the kitchen as she came back into the main hall. Almost half past. The conductor liked to start dead on half-past five. She'd been worried that she'd be late this evening as she'd helped her mother prepare the supper in advance, Maman barely saying a word.

The door opened and Wendy appeared, holding the hand of a child of four or five with a halo of golden curls. 'Oh, good, you haven't started yet,' she said. 'I'm afraid I've had to bring Rosie to the rehearsal.' She lowered her voice. 'She's my goddaughter and her mother asked if I could babysit while she and Tony went to the pictures tonight. It's the first time her Tony's been home for almost a year, so I said yes. I hoped you wouldn't mind, and I thought Rosie might even enjoy listening to us.'

'We can't normally accommodate children,' Mr Rubenstein started, 'but seeing as you haven't any option, then she can sit over here.' He smiled at the child. 'Do you like music?'

Rosie nodded. 'I like singing too.'

'That's excellent. But we won't be singing this evening.'

'I can hum quietly.'

Suzanne smiled. Rosie seemed a confident child who knew exactly what she did and didn't like.

'She'll be a good girl, won't you?' Wendy gave the child a little tug on her hand.

Rosie nodded. 'I bought Teddy to listen, too.'

'I *brought* Teddy,' Wendy corrected.

'Right.' Mr Rubenstein looked at his watch chain. 'We need to start. Everyone, please take your seats.'

After the rehearsal – which had gone better than the last one, and was livened up by an audience in Rosie, who clapped after every piece – Suzanne stopped Wendy as she was putting her coat on.

'Do you have a moment, Wendy?'

Wendy glanced at Rosie who was staring up at both of them. 'Look, why don't you come to the cottage? Rosie's going to stay with me the night and I've got enough supper for all of us. Then we'll put Rosie to bed and be free to have a natter. How about that?'

Suzanne hesitated. Normally, her mother might have encouraged her to spend an hour or two with a friend, but she doubted Maman would allow it this evening, the mood she was in, especially knowing she was with Wendy.

'I'm on the telephone so you can ring your mother.'

It hadn't worked so well the last time when Mrs Mortimer had rung her mother to say her daughter would be late, owing to an accident. She bit her lip. If she allowed Maman to direct every aspect of her life from now on, without any say in the matter, she'd never escape her clutches.

'Thank you, Wendy, I'd love to.'

Wendy lived down a winding lane, pitch-dark tonight with the blackout, but it was only ten minutes' walk from the village hall in the opposite direction from Suzanne's home. Rosie began to whine that she was tired.

'You won't want your supper then,' Wendy said, as they approached the pretty little thatched-roof cottage that she rented.

'I will, yes I will.' Rosie hopped up and down.

'Come on, then. Let's get in out of this cold.' Wendy unlocked the front door. 'Let me go ahead and do the windows so we can put the light on.'

Suzanne followed her into the square hall with rafters that rose to the roof. She watched as Wendy pulled the blackout curtains firmly together and switched on a side lamp. It threw a weak light onto a long refectory bench piled with books, and a row of pegs acting as coat hooks, and cast eerie shadows, making the hall look and feel completely different from when she'd seen it the one time before on a beautiful sunny afternoon.

'Go through,' Wendy called. 'And mind your head.'

Suzanne's shoes clattered on the stone floor as she ducked into the opening to the sitting room, reminding her, as it had the last time, of walking into a forest of tree trunks. The ceiling, only inches above Suzanne's head, was heavily beamed, with more timbers holding up the walls. At one end of the modest-sized sitting room was an enormous inglenook, stretching almost end to end.

It would look so warm and cosy if it was lit, was Suzanne's first thought, but of course Wendy could hardly have left a fire burning all evening while she was at rehearsal.

'Ooooh, it's cold in here,' Wendy said, folding her arms across her chest and rubbing them. 'It's too late to light a fire. I'll put the electric one on. Rosie, you show Miss Linfoot where to hang her coat.'

Suzanne obediently hung her coat on the peg Rosie pointed to and went back to the sitting room.

'The telephone's by that green armchair,' Wendy said, as she stood on a small stepladder to reach the ceiling light. 'Help yourself.' She plugged in the fire, letting the long wire dangle from the ceiling into a coil on the floor. 'It's not ideal,' she said, stepping from the ladder, 'so don't trip over it, whatever you do.' She looked at Rosie. 'Rosie, are you listening?'

'Yes, Auntie Wendy.'

'Let me finish preparing the supper and while I'm doing that, you can telephone your mother.'

Suzanne's stomach tightened as she braced herself for Maman's instructions. To her relief it was Ronnie who answered.

'Don't worry, Suzy. I'll tell Maman. Have a nice time with Wendy. Don't come home too late or else we'll worry – well, Maman will worry, but I shan't, of course.' She heard Ronnie's giggle.

'You monkey,' Suzanne chuckled. 'Anyway, I won't be late.'

She put the receiver down, feeling at once relieved and apprehensive. Relieved that she couldn't do anything about it now – the deed was done – but apprehensive knowing she had it all to face later.

After the three of them had finished a delicious stew, and Suzanne had gone with Wendy to tuck Rosie up in bed in the small windowless boxroom, Wendy made a pot of tea.

'Here, Suzy, put your feet up.' Wendy pushed a covered stool towards Suzanne with her foot. 'Make yourself at home.'

'I'd never be allowed to do this at home,' Suzanne said, as she stretched her long slim legs onto the stool.

'Hmm.' Wendy caught her eye in a direct gaze. She pulled out a packet of cigarettes and offered one to Suzanne.

Suzanne shook her head. 'I've tried them but they just make me feel sick. And if Maman knew I was smoking she'd practically disown me.' She glanced at Wendy. 'You must get lonely here sometimes.'

'Not at the moment with Rosie around, though I don't see that much of her. But she's a smashing little kid. I love her to bits.' Her smile faded. She struck a match to light her cigarette. 'I'd love to have had my own. When I met Bill it was love at first sight. I haven't told you much about him, have I?'

Suzanne shook her head.

'He was in the Merchant Navy and away for long spells so we decided on his next leave to get married.' She paused and gave Suzanne a rueful smile. 'You've probably guessed – I was pregnant. But we were both thrilled. It didn't matter that we did things the wrong way round. But before we had time to get married his ship was torpedoed. And that was the end of him.' Her voice cracked. 'With all the worry I lost the baby. I lost everything – the baby, Bill, my dream of marriage and my happiness.'

A shiver ran the length of Suzanne's spine. She thought of James in his ship. The same thing could happen to him. She swallowed and looked across at Wendy whose head was lowered, consumed by her memories. Poor Wendy. She realised now why Wendy didn't wear a ring. She and Bill had never had time to get married. Impulsively, she sprang up and put her arms around the slumped figure.

'Wendy, that's the saddest story I've ever heard. I'm so sorry. But you'll meet someone again. Maybe have another child. It's not too late.'

'I'll never love anyone like my Bill,' Wendy sniffed, reaching for her handkerchief again. 'But thank you for listening.' She blew her nose. She looked up, her eyes still glistening with tears. 'What I'm trying to tell you is that life is precious, and you must do whatever's in your heart. And I believe you'd get a hell of a lot of satisfaction from entertaining our boys who are risking their lives every moment of every day for *us*.'

'I'm seriously thinking about it,' Suzanne told her, smiling, 'so I wondered if I could go with you when you have your first rehearsal – just to get a feel and talk to someone who would tell me more about it, and the kind of places they go to.' She hesitated. 'Anyway, even if I say I'd like to join, they might not want me.'

Wendy broke into a grin, transforming her plain features. 'They'll want you,' she said. 'No doubt about it.' She jumped up. 'I think you're coming round to the idea so this calls for a celebration. I've got some sherry somewhere.' She disappeared into the kitchen and came back with a bottle in one hand and two glasses in the other.

'Let's have a toast,' she said as she poured the glasses. She handed one to Suzanne. 'To us. May you say "yes" and may we cheer up those boys and have a bit of fun ourselves at the same time.'

Suzanne chuckled, glad to see her friend looking happier.

'It's perfect timing.' Wendy tapped her ash into the saucer. 'I have my first rehearsal with them in London tomorrow afternoon. You can come with me.'

Suzanne was silent.

'Will that be a problem?' Wendy asked.

Suzanne shook her head. 'I won't let it be. What time will you leave?'

'I want to allow plenty of time for any hold-ups on the train. I thought around ten.'

'My mother's rarely downstairs before nine,' Suzanne said. 'But I'd rather be out of the house earlier.'

'Come for breakfast,' Wendy said, smiling. 'Rosie would love it. We could catch an earlier train and maybe go to Oxford Street. Have a look in the shop windows. Selfridges is always eye-catching – it's so different from all the other department stores.'

Suzanne had never been to Oxford Street. A frisson shot through her at the thought of a day out in London instead of attending school. She'd never played truant in her life. But this was different. There was a war on. Nothing was how it used to be. And it would never go back to being the same – of that, she was certain.

'What do you think, Suzy?' Wendy said, then hesitated. 'Do you mind being called Suzy?'

'I'm used to Raine and Ronnie calling me that,' Suzanne smiled. 'Even though Maman frowns when they say it.' She caught Wendy's eye and grinned. 'Do you think it suits me then?'

'It *will* do when you're up on that stage playing jazz on your violin in completely different surroundings to the village hall or the church.' Wendy chuckled as she put down her empty glass. 'Let's run through the plan. You be here by seven for breakfast. Then we all leave together just before eight. We'll catch the bus from the village into Bromley, drop Rosie off at her mum's, then catch a train into Charing Cross. We'll be early so we can get the tube to Oxford Street. Have a coffee. From there we'll get the tube to Covent Garden and it'll be time to stop for a sandwich or something. Then it's just a short walk to Drury Lane.'

'What time is the rehearsal?'

'Not until half-past two,' Wendy said. 'But we'll aim for two so I can introduce you to Elizabeth Foster – she's in charge of new recruits in ENSA and knows it inside out.'

'Is she nice?'

'She seems to be. I've only met her that one time.'

Suzanne glanced at her watch and rose to her feet.

'Are you off already?'

'I must. I'm sorry to have to leave your beautiful little cottage . . . it's lovely and warm now, but I don't want to be late home. And thank you for everything, Wendy. I'm so glad we've had our chat. I feel we're really proper friends.'

'Most definitely,' Wendy said, springing up and giving her a kiss on the cheek. 'Until tomorrow – seven o'clock sharp. I'll have the kettle on.'

Chapter Ten

Suzanne shot up in bed, her heart hammering in her ears. She rushed over to the window in time to see the back of a fire engine, its bells clanging. She shoved up the sash, bracing herself for another explosion, as that must have been what had woken her up, and stuck her head out. No aeroplanes roaring in the sky. No nothing. Puzzled, she climbed back in bed, glancing at the clock on her bedside table. Twenty minutes to five. She'd planned to get up at six so she still had more than an hour left, but her sleep had been well and truly broken. She stared up at the ceiling in the dark, letting her heartbeat quieten down.

Poor Wendy. What a sad story. It was bad enough losing your fiancé in this terrible war, but to think she'd been going to have a baby and even that life had been cruelly snatched from her. No wonder she felt so close to little Rosie.

At least Wendy had been brave enough to change her life and even her music to join ENSA. After all her unhappiness Wendy wanted to have some purpose in her life. Surely her friend would find someone else one day who would truly love her and they would have a family. Suzanne smiled in the darkness. Wendy would make a lovely mother.

The thought calmed Suzanne and she was just about to doze off when another emergency vehicle screeched past. By the time she'd scrambled out of bed and peered through the window again to see whatever it was, police or maybe an ambulance, it had disappeared. She grimaced. It was hardly worth going back to sleep now.

Ronnie came down the stairs yawning, Rusty at her heels, just as Suzanne picked up her coat, ready to leave.

'I thought I heard you,' Ronnie said, going to the larder to find Rusty some breakfast. 'Why are you up so early?' She looked at Suzanne, her eyes wide. 'And why are you in your best Sunday costume?'

'Because Wendy – you know, the other girl who plays the violin – wants me to go with her to London to meet the ENSA woman who recruits new members.'

'You've been going on about it,' Ronnie said, chopping up a slice of Spam for Rusty who was whining with delight at the meaty smell, 'so now you're finally going to do something.'

'I haven't made any decision yet. And if I did, I'd worry about leaving you to cope with Maman.'

'Oh, don't worry about me,' Ronnie said airily. 'I'm practically out all the time with school starting today and doing the garden. Besides, I've got Rusty now. Just look at him. He's my little friend. I couldn't wish for anyone better.'

Rusty was looking up adoringly at his mistress, giving little excited whines.

'He's a darling,' Suzanne said, patting his head. 'I'll tell you all the news this evening. I should be home in time for supper.'

'What have you told Maman?'

'That I'm rehearsing. It's near enough the truth if they decide to audition me.'

Ronnie giggled and waggled her finger. 'Mind you're back or you'll have Maman to face. But I'll cover for you. And when I need the same in return I'll know who to come to.' She set Rusty's plate down. 'Good boy . . . there you are. Lovely Spam.' She turned to Suzanne and pulled a face. 'Ugh. One of the only things I can't stomach. It's revolting but he loves it.'

Suzanne laughed and kissed her sister.

'Good luck at school today, Ronnie.'

'Good luck at ENSA,' Ronnie answered. 'Knock 'em dead.'

Suzanne smiled to herself as she walked towards Wendy's cottage. Ronnie certainly had her own mind. Suzanne couldn't see her younger sister humming and hawing over any decision or feeling guilty once she'd made it. She wished she could be more like her, but today was a fresh day in every sense. The sky was bright – a hopeful sign that the sun might come out.

She loved being out this early, having the road to herself except for the milkman and his horse doing their last round.

'Morning, miss.' The milkman raised his cap. 'Look at you all done up. And very nice, too, if I may say so.'

Suzanne smiled. If she said anything it would be bound to reach Maman's ears.

'Going somewhere special?' he persisted.

'Just having a walk.'

'You enjoy it, love,' he said, and flicked his whip for the horse to continue the round.

She couldn't help it. Quietly singing 'Don't Sit Under The Apple Tree' to herself, and chuckling at her unconventional rendition, she hurried along.

'*. . . with anyone else but me, anyone else—*' She suddenly broke off. The air smelt odd. By now she was nearing the lane where Wendy lived. She screwed up her nose. What on earth—? It smelt like something burning. Somebody must have a bonfire. But she couldn't see any smoke.

And then her throat tightened with a terrible foreboding. She began to run. She ran until her chest ached. Until pains spread across the top half of her body. But she didn't stop.

She turned the corner of the lane. The smell was worse. Not just of burning but something so foul she began to retch, but she couldn't stop running. She had to get there. Holding her hand to her nose she ran towards the row of cottages where a dozen or so villagers had already gathered, pointing and shouting. Then every muscle froze. She stared in horror. Wendy's beautiful thatched cottage was unrecognisable. The thatched roof had completely gone, and half the side of the house had disappeared.

She fought down a scream. *Dear God. Wendy and little Rosie. Please let them be safe.*

Who to ask? Where was someone official? Frantic, she turned to a man standing next to her in the crowd who was shaking his head.

'I saw the fire engine go past early this morning,' she said in a shaky voice that didn't sound like hers. 'I never dreamed it was my friend's house. I was only here yesterday evening having supper with her and a little girl. I need to know they're safe.' She looked at him in desperation. His expression told her everything.

'The ambulance already took them away.' He averted his eyes but not before she saw they were wet with tears. 'I'm sorry, love.'

'B-but they're alive?' Suzanne gulped. She grabbed his arm. 'Aren't they?' Her voice rose.

'I doubt it,' the man said. 'They said the fire was well under way when the fire engines turned up. And because it was a thatched roof, the blaze was fast and furious. It must've caught the two of them unawares at that time of night. They wouldn't have stood a chance.'

Oh, dear God.

'Where've they been taken to?' She tried to shout above the noise but her voice came out in a squeak.

The man shook his head. 'I wouldn't know, love, but probably Bromley General.'

She didn't even wait to thank him. The buses probably wouldn't be running yet but she had to get there right away. *Before it's too late,* a little voice inside her said. She shuddered. There was only one person she could turn to.

Outside the gate she almost fell with exhaustion. Steadying herself she ran up the drive and banged on the front door.

There was no sound. *They must both be asleep.* She couldn't think what to do next. Then a sash window above her opened and a man stuck his head out.

'Suzanne! What's the matter? No, don't tell me. I'm coming right down.'

Seconds later the door opened. He stood there in his dressing gown, his chestnut hair in spikes.

'James, I'm sorry to—' She couldn't get her breath.

Without speaking he drew her inside. 'What's wrong?'

She squeezed her eyes shut for a second, biting her lip hard. 'James, have you still got some petrol in your car?'

'Yes,' he said. 'Where do you need to go?'

She breathed out. 'Can you take me to Bromley right away? To the General Hospital. I think that's where they've been taken.'

'Who's "they"?'

'My friend and a little girl who was staying with her.' She tried to dislodge the lump trapped in her throat. 'Oh, James, their house caught fire in the night and they've been taken off in an ambulance. A man I spoke to said they d-d-didn't stand a chance.' She broke down in sobs.

The next thing she knew, she was in James's arms. 'Don't cry, Suzy,' he whispered against her hair. 'I've got you.'

She stayed leaning against him for a few grateful seconds, then pulled away.

'Let me get you a glass of water,' James said, leading her into the sitting room, 'and then I'll go and get dressed. Just sit down and wait. I'll only be five minutes.'

She heard the tap running and he was back with the glass. She sank into a chair and gratefully took it. The water eased her throat a little, but horrific images rushed to her mind of the two of them: Rosie in the boxroom next to Wendy's, both sound asleep. Not hearing anything amiss. She wondered who'd woken up first. She shuddered.

Please, dear God, don't let them die.

James didn't question her further as he drove into town. She saw him glance at her every so often as though to confirm to himself that she was all right, but she couldn't say a word. All she saw were the terrible images of Wendy and Rosie screaming for help. Until it was too late.

'We're here,' James said, breaking the silence. He parked and she was out of the door before he came to open it.

She rushed up to the reception desk where a woman was speaking on the telephone.

'Please . . .' Suzanne began.

The woman acknowledged her with a nod and went back to her phone call. She scribbled something on a pad and put the receiver down, then smiled at Suzanne.

'May I help you?'

'My friend, Wendy—' Suzanne's brain froze. She couldn't remember Wendy's surname. 'I'm sorry, I don't know . . .'

How stupid that sounded, when she'd told the woman she was a friend. 'She was w-with a little girl,' she stuttered. 'The ambulance brought them in. Their house caught fire in the night in Downe. Please tell me they're safe.'

'And the child's name?'

'Rosie. Wendy's goddaughter . . . and I don't know her parents' names either. I'm sorry.'

If the woman asks one more question, I'll choke.

'Let me find out for you where they are. What is your name?'

'Suzanne Linfoot.'

'Are you on the telephone?'

Suzanne nodded and the woman wrote down her details, then left her desk and spoke to a passing nurse.

'She's going to make some enquiries,' she said. 'It might take a little while. Take a seat.' She pointed to a few chairs grouped together.

Suzanne hesitated. She didn't want to sit. Fear gripped her.

'Suzy,' James said, gently taking her arm. 'Let's do what the lady said. We can't do anything until we know more.'

He led her over to the visitors' chairs and sat down beside her. She felt him take her hand in his and she clung to it, the only shred of comfort in the anonymous space of the hospital reception area.

'Oh, James.' She couldn't say anything more.

He squeezed her hand. 'Try not to worry until we know exactly what's happened.'

She looked at her watch. Five to eight. She and Wendy and little Rosie should be at the bus stop by now. Tears filled her eyes again but she mustn't cry. She needed to be strong for Wendy.

It was getting on for nine when a doctor came up to the

reception desk and the woman behind it gestured to Suzanne. He nodded and went over to them. He had a kind face but he didn't smile. Suzanne's stomach turned over.

'I'm Dr Raynor. Are you Suzanne Linfoot – Wendy Rushton's friend?'

'Yes.' Suzanne turned to James. 'And this is—'

'James Mortimer,' James said firmly. 'Miss Linfoot's friend.'

He nodded. 'Then would you both like to follow me.'

The smell of the disinfectant was strong in her nostrils, making her feel nauseous again, as the doctor led them along a corridor and into a small private room. Four chairs were set around a table. He gestured for them to sit.

'They were brought in at five o'clock this morning,' he said. 'I'm afraid it's bad news for your friend. She was overcome with smoke and already dead when the ambulance men put her on the stretcher.'

Dear God.

Bile rose to her throat. Poor Wendy. Suzanne looked at the doctor, hope flickering – he hadn't mentioned Rosie. She took in a deep breath.

'And Rosie?'

'She's lucky. Your friend saved her life. She has a small area of second-degree burns on her legs but mostly they're only minor.'

'What does that mean?' Suzanne asked, hanging on to the word 'only'.

'It means she's going to be fine,' Dr Raynor said, giving her hand a gentle pat. 'There's hardly any blistering so there'll be minimal scarring – maybe none. She'll be home in a week or two with her mum and dad. That's the best place for her to recover.'

'Thank heavens she's all right, and thank you, Doctor, for all you've done.' James stood and held out his hand to steady

Suzanne. 'Come on, Suzy. We can't do any more so let's get you home.'

Suzanne swallowed her tears. Poor, dear, brave Wendy. Then she remembered something.

'Doctor, I only saw them a few hours before . . . They were perfectly all right then. So how could something so terrible have happened in such a short time when there wasn't any explosion?'

'It's early yet, but we understand it was an electric fire that started it.'

'You're coming home with me,' James said as Suzanne wordlessly sat by his side in his motorcar. 'Mother will look after you.'

'I can't let her do that,' Suzanne said. 'I'll be all right.'

She would be if she could only stop shaking.

'You're in shock.' James glanced at her. 'It's terrible for you.'

'I couldn't give that receptionist any proper information. I felt more trouble than I was worth.'

'It wasn't your fault,' James said. 'They'll find out who to contact. It won't be the first time they've had to deal with this sort of thing.'

'Wendy's poor parents,' Suzanne said, her voice shaking. 'What a shock for them.' The tears welled. 'Wendy risked her own life to save Rosie. She loved that child because she'd had a miscarriage.' She wouldn't tell James it was the shock of Bill's ship being torpedoed.

'From the sounds of it, Wendy would want it that way . . . that she'd saved Rosie,' James said quietly. 'That's what you must hold on to.'

Her knees kept buckling under, even with James's supporting arm around her shoulders as she stumbled with his help up the Mortimers' drive. He wouldn't hear of her protests. But when he called out to his mother that he'd brought Suzanne there was no answer.

'Go and sit on the sofa,' he said. 'I'm going to make a pot of tea. I think we could both do with one.'

Immediately Suzanne began to feel uncomfortable. She'd clung on to the fact that the motherly Mrs Mortimer would be at home. Now she was alone in the house with her son. Maman would be furious that she was 'giving herself a bad name'. *What will the neighbours say?* she could hear her mother's voice in her ear. She bit her lip hard to stop the tears. What did it matter what the neighbours thought?

'Mother's left a note,' James called from the kitchen. He came through and read it out:

'James, dear, I've had to pop out to get something. Not sure when I'll be back, but not late. Mother.'

He looked up. 'I expect she's forgotten something for Saturday.' He disappeared again.

Suzanne's brain tried to work. Of course. James's birthday. And then he'd be gone to his ship on the Monday. And that would be that.

'By the way, have you had any breakfast?' James asked as he set the tray down.

She shook her head, then wished she hadn't when her head began to spin. She took in a deep breath. 'No, I was supposed to have breakfast with W-Wendy and Rosie.' She put her head in her hands. She'd tried so hard not to cry in front of James again, but now the tears spilled between her fingers.

She felt his presence as he sat next to her, a strong arm pulling her close to his side. She was so tired. She rested her head on his shoulder and they sat for a minute or two in silence.

Reluctantly, she drew away and looked at him with a tear-stained face and sniffed. 'I'm sorry, James. I'm being stupid.'

'You're not,' he said, handing her a handkerchief. 'Here, blow your nose.' He waited a few seconds, then said, 'It's understandable and better to let it out than have it choking you inside.' He kissed her forehead. 'Why don't you pour the tea and I'll make us some toast. I can't remember having any breakfast either.'

She gave him a watery smile. 'I couldn't touch anything, but *you* must have something.'

'*We* must have something,' he corrected her. 'I'll be back in a jiffy.'

The smell of hot toast was comforting as she sipped her tea, thankful her hands had stopped shaking. Moments later James appeared with a plate piled high.

'I found some butter at the back of the larder,' he said grinning. 'No matter how hard I try I can't get used to marg, even disguised with marmalade, which by the way, I've taken the liberty of putting on for you. You need the sugar.'

Feeling a little calmer she munched the toast gratefully, content to be sharing the simple breakfast with him.

'Why were you going to Wendy's for breakfast?'

'She was attending her first rehearsal with ENSA,' she said, 'and she was going to introduce me to the recruitment lady to tell me more about it.'

'I'm taking it that'll be London.'

'Yes, Drury Lane. Wendy told me how we'd get there. But I can't even think about it now. Not after . . .' She trailed off and turned her face away.

'Suzy, look at me.' He gently tilted her face towards him. 'There's a war on. I know this fire wasn't part of it, but terrible things are happening all the time. But I understand you're under a great deal of strain today. Did you have an actual appointment?'

She shook her head.

'Well, don't put yourself under any further pressure for a few days. Maybe write to them asking if you can go and meet them in a few days' time. Does that make sense?'

She nodded. 'I'm not even sure I'm interested any more.'

'Really?' James's eyes were warm with concern. 'I wonder what Wendy would say about that.'

Suzanne swallowed. 'She'd probably tell me not to be so daft if it's because of her.'

'That's exactly what *I* would say.' His finger lightly brushed a crumb from the corner of her mouth. 'There, that's better,' he smiled.

She heaved a sigh. Was James right? She felt completely drained – unable to think straight. Was she letting Wendy down if she didn't at least go and talk to this Miss Foster? Suzanne licked her lips that had suddenly gone dry. She remembered Wendy's enthusiasm for bringing some cheer to the soldiers who were going through so much misery and fear – even at this very minute. She drew in a jagged breath, then looked directly at James.

'I keep seeing Wendy's face. She'd be so cross if I didn't go at least to talk to them after all her plans.' Suzanne gave him a small smile. 'But I think she'd understand if I left it for a day or two.'

James gave her hand a light squeeze. 'Then that's settled. For now, you need to go home and rest. Doctor's orders. I'll drive you back.'

Suzanne leaned her head on the back of the car seat and closed her eyes. An actual pain seemed to have settled in her chest and she dreaded the moment when James would leave and she was left to cope with the terrible events of the morning. If only the short journey home would take ten times longer. But all too quickly James pulled up outside the cottage and switched off the engine. He came round to her side and opened the car door, offering his hand.

Gratefully, she took it.

'Will your mother be home?' he asked.

'No,' she said, hoping it was true. She wasn't ready to face Maman.

'I'll see you inside,' he said.

It would only delay the inevitable moment.

'No, James, I'll be all right – honestly. I need to be quiet for a while.'

'If you're absolutely certain.'

'Absolutely.'

'Then may I telephone you this evening to see how you are?'

'May I call *you* instead?' she said, not wanting Maman to answer the telephone.

'Yes, of course – if you promise to,' James said, smiling. 'You've got our number.'

She was aware he was still holding her hand and somehow his strength transferred itself to her. Wendy's death mustn't be allowed to go in vain.

Chapter Eleven

The house felt empty when Suzanne walked through the unlocked kitchen door. She knew Ronnie was already at school but her mother didn't answer her call. Then she heard Rusty bark and she ran upstairs to let him out of Ronnie's bedroom. With a woof of delight he flew down the stairs in front of her and into the kitchen where Simone had left a note on the table to say she would be back before her girls.

Suzanne couldn't help the flood of relief that she had the house to herself. If she couldn't have the understanding company of James, she'd rather be on her own at this minute. She ran a glass of water and took it into the front room with Rusty at her heels, then sank into her father's chair.

If she could only stop the terrible image of Wendy desperately trying to save Rosie. But it flashed before her again and again until she thought she would faint. She took some deep breaths, then sipped the water. Rusty sat quietly at her feet, and as though he knew how upset she was, he kept licking her hand.

'I'm glad you're here, Rusty,' she told him. 'I'll take you for a walk in a few minutes, but I need to sit here for a little while, so you'll have to be patient.'

And then without warning she dropped her head in her hands and sobbed.

It was only Rusty's whining that brought her out of her misery, as he nuzzled her legs.

'All right, boy. A walk will probably do us both good,' she said, as she rose to her feet.

The walk to the church and back had done her good. It had turned out to be a fine day, for a change, though she'd barely noticed this morning, but at lunchtime she *had* noticed it felt milder in the sun. She was cheered up by several displays of daffodils – very late this year because of the unseasonal cold weather – dotted around the gravestones. Back at home she felt calmer as she put Rusty's lead on its hook. She even felt a pang of hunger and set about making herself a round of cheese on toast, carefully eking out two teaspoons of grated cheese. That made her think of James again, and how kind he'd been. Brushing the ready tears away she set her jaw. She'd make a cup of tea and settle with James's book for an hour or two before Ronnie came home from school.

'I didn't think you'd be back already,' Ronnie said as she burst through the back door. 'How'd you get on?'

Suzanne set down the book and began to tell her sister about the tragedy. She left out the worst of the details but she couldn't stop the tears running again.

'Oh, Suzy, how awful,' Ronnie said. 'What a dreadful thing to happen. Poor Wendy. But thank goodness Rosie wasn't badly harmed, and James came to the rescue. He sounds lovely – a knight in shining armour.'

'I don't know what I'd have done without him,' Suzanne said with feeling. 'But please keep all this to yourself, Ronnie. I don't want Maman to know anything yet until I've been to see the ENSA lady.'

'When will you go?'

'I'm not sure.'

'You shouldn't leave it too long,' Ronnie said. 'They'll be wondering why Wendy didn't turn up for her first rehearsal. And *you're* the only one who can tell them.'

Thankfully, at supper her mother was full of news of her friend, Mrs Garland, who had the dress shop in Bromley.

'I wish Lorraine had taken up her offer to be trained as a buyer,' she said. 'A more fitting position for a well brought up young woman.'

'Raine wouldn't have been happy,' Ronnie said. 'She loves what she's doing now.'

Simone grumbled for a few more minutes about women taking men's jobs when they had no business to – it should be left to the men, how dangerous it was flying one of those contraptions, Lorraine never listened, she was so stubborn. On and on Maman went until Suzanne was on the verge of screaming. Just when Suzanne was about to cover her ears her mother said she was tired and would retire to bed early with her magazine.

But it was nearly half-past nine by the time Simone disappeared upstairs. Ronnie was already catching up with her homework in her bedroom, and downstairs had gone miraculously quiet. Suzanne tiptoed into the hall, lifted the telephone receiver and dialled.

'Suzy?'

She loved the warmth of his voice. 'Yes, it's me. I'm sorry it's so late.'

'It's not late at all. I've been worrying about you. Are you all right?'

'I think so – better now, anyway.' Suzanne hesitated. 'James, I've been thinking . . . Ronnie mentioned I shouldn't leave it too long to speak to someone at ENSA because they'll be wondering why Wendy didn't turn up for her appointment. Even if they ring her house, there won't be any answer and—' She gulped.

'And you're the only person who can explain,' James finished.

'Yes.' She paused while the line crackled. 'James? Are you still there?'

'I'm here,' he said. 'When are you planning to go?'

'I thought I'd go tomorrow. I think I'll feel much more like it in the morning.'

'Good.' James's tone was reassuring. 'What time do you want to leave so I can pick you up?'

'Honestly, you don't have to.'

'I know I don't have to – but I *want* to.'

'That'd be lovely. Would eight o'clock be too early?'

Maman wouldn't be up.

'Not at all. I'll be there. Now go and get a good night's sleep. Try to think of pleasant things. Me, for instance.' He chuckled. It was a nice sound.

She smiled into the receiver. 'I'll try.'

She was waiting outside at ten minutes to eight, and five minutes later she saw his car.

He leapt out and opened the passenger door.

'I wish I was going with you,' he said, glancing at her. 'I could, you know. Mother doesn't want me hanging around all day when she's trying to hide the preparations for the birthday tea.'

'I'm better doing this on my own,' Suzanne said. 'I know I was in a bit of a state yesterday—'

'It was understandable,' James said, giving a cyclist a wide berth. 'But I'm glad to see you look more like yourself this morning.'

Despite her protests he insisted upon paying her train fare and bought himself a platform ticket at the same time.

'I have to see you off,' he said, putting the change in his pocket and taking the tickets. 'You know, Suzy, when they set eyes on you, I bet they'll audition you right away.'

'I'm not sure I'm ready for that,' Suzanne said, 'but I owe it to Wendy to tell them what happened and to find out more as I told her I would.'

'So when you come to the birthday tea tomorrow you'll be able to tell me all about it,' James said, smiling. 'I can't wait to hear.' He looked at her. 'You will come, won't you?'

'I'm planning to.'

They strolled along the platform, James holding her hand firmly in his. It felt right. Comforting. Wonderful.

'Here's your train.' James's words were practically drowned by the great beast as it drew to a shuddering halt, belching steam and soot. He bent his head and for a moment she thought he was going to kiss her. Her heart hammered. He must be able to hear it. She waited. He seemed to hesitate, then swiftly kissed her cheek.

'Good luck, Suzy,' he said, smiling down at her. 'Or "break a leg", as they say.'

She laughed. 'That's the last thing I want to do,' she said. 'I've already turned up at your house with a bad knee. I don't want to arrive there on crutches tomorrow.'

Chapter Twelve

Suzanne leaned out of the window to wave to James as the train lumbered out of the station. She watched until he was a dot, then drew back into the crowded, smoky corridor, her confidence waning. It was the first time she'd done anything like this on her own and she was suddenly terrified she wouldn't be able to cope. She'd get lost. No one would be able to direct her to Drury Lane. They wouldn't know what she was talking about. ENSA? Never heard of it.

She told herself not to be so ridiculous. She wasn't a baby. People were very kind and everyone pulled together in the war. And anyway there was bound to be a bobby she could ask. Nevertheless, she wished she had a street map so she'd at least know she was walking in the right direction. Telling herself she'd be fine, she edged past the people packed along the corridor – nearly all men and women in uniform, the men sending her admiring glances and one or two appreciative whistles – to see if there was a spare seat in one of the carriages. No luck. Every compartment had soldiers standing between the two rows of seats. She turned back to the corridor where a notice was pinned up saying if enemy action developed overhead you were to lie down on the floor. If it were to happen right now, Suzanne thought grimly, the bodies would be layered like piles of sandwiches at the latest village hall 'do'.

Luckily, there was only one short delay of a few minutes and they were off again, very slowly at first, and finally gaining speed. When they pulled into Charing Cross Station she glanced at her watch – it had taken just over an hour. She was pleased. If she did decide to join ENSA, providing she was suitable, she wouldn't be too far from home if and when they were given a day off.

Servicemen streamed in and out of Charing Cross Station as Suzanne made her way to the entrance, half choking on the smoke from two trains belching around her, the one she'd just arrived on, and another departing. Her stomach clenched. It was the first time she'd set foot in London since Dad had taken her and her sisters to the zoo when they were children, but she remembered little of that time except the joy of seeing the animals.

Pull yourself together, Suzanne. You're no longer that child – you're an adult with a mission.

She glanced at her watch. Even after a much later start than she and Wendy had planned, she was still too early for Drury Lane. She turned into Charing Cross Road, shocked at so many smashed windows waiting to be boarded up – shops that were once the livelihood of enterprising owners razed to the ground or not looking safe enough to reopen until major repairs were carried out. She noticed one bookshop had its contents scattered everywhere except the shelves they'd been displayed on. Filth and rubble coated them. They'd be ruined.

Dear God, how did these Londoners cope with such devastation and misery, day after day? People who were passing her right now, some of whose lives must have been wrecked with telegrams stating their son or brother or husband was injured or missing – or worse – yet still they managed to put on a brave face. A middle-aged woman, her hair tucked under a turban, wearing a faded dress and overall, with a basket over her arm, caught Suzanne's eye and nodded as she jostled by. It was just as Suzanne had been told – Londoners refused to cower from the relentless beatings they'd received from Hitler's terrifying Luftwaffe. Apparently, it had had the opposite effect – only making them even more determined to carry on.

Wendy had mentioned looking round the department stores in Oxford Street, but Suzanne didn't feel in the mood now Wendy wasn't with her. She squeezed her eyes shut to stop herself from bursting into tears. She had to carry on, just like everyone else. She could almost hear Wendy ordering her to do so. But shopping? She had no spare money for such luxuries as shopping in places like Selfridges, and window shopping didn't excite her in the least if she couldn't buy even a little something. She'd only agreed to look at the shops because Wendy had seemed so keen. No, she'd go straight to Covent Garden and have a look round, and maybe have a sandwich.

Oh, Wendy, why did you have to die?

As she opened her eyes the tears rolled down her cheeks. Embarrassed, though no one was taking any notice of her, she quickly brushed them away. This wasn't doing anyone any good. If Wendy was right, she told herself firmly, Covent Garden should be within walking distance of Drury Lane theatre. It didn't matter that she'd be early. She could stroll around the area and get her bearings.

As it was, Suzanne was able to catch a bus that dropped her at the heart of Covent Garden. The area around the station had brought it home to her that London had taken a terrible beating. Looking through the bus's smeary windows, she bit her lip at the recent evidence of collapsed buildings. People and even children were searching among the rubble, perhaps for a precious toy, or a pet. She was thankful to finally alight and wander round the pretty little shops that hadn't been caught in the worst of the bombing.

She followed a group of people who looked as though they knew where they were heading, and came face to face with a beautiful building, reminding her of a Greek temple she'd once seen in a library book on Ancient Greece.

'Gorgeous, isn't it,' remarked a tall, striking-looking woman of maybe forty, fashionably dressed in a cream coat, her smooth dark hair in pageboy style topped by a perky little hat. She paused for a moment in her high heels to stare up at the neo-classical façade.

'Is it a theatre?' Suzanne asked.

'It's the Royal Opera House,' the woman said, stopping and smiling at Suzanne. 'They have concerts and ballet there as well. I've often been. But nowadays they've changed it into a huge dance hall. I just hope they put it back to how it was when this war is over.' She gave a short laugh. 'But the young ones love it. They're not so interested in classical music. They prefer the latest dance crazes from America, like the jitterbug . . . whatever *that* is.' She looked at Suzanne with a raised eyebrow. 'Though I expect you know them all, being young.'

'Not really,' Suzanne smiled. 'I can manage a waltz and a quickstep but I wouldn't have a clue how to do the jitterbug.' She paused. Wendy's face flashed in front of her. 'But I do play the piano and violin, and I can't be the only one.' She swallowed, hoping she hadn't sounded rude but for some reason she wanted to tell this woman that some young people *did* love classical music. She gave the woman another glance. There was something vaguely familiar about her. Was it the dreamy, slightly hooded eyes? The sensuous mouth?

The woman was regarding her with more interest. 'Is that

right? But you're far too young to play professionally. You must still be at school.'

'I've more or less finished,' Suzanne said, 'and thinking about joining ENSA. That's where I'm going this afternoon – to the Theatre Royal in Drury Lane to see about it.'

The woman raised her dark eyebrows. 'Oh. Have you an appointment?'

Suzanne shook her head. 'Not really, but I was supposed to be going with a friend who recently joined to sing in a jazz band, but she . . . she—' Another tear ran down her cheek. 'Excuse me,' she said, fishing in her handbag for a handkerchief. She turned her head and blew her nose soundly. Breaking down in front of this stranger would be the final straw.

'Something's upset you,' the woman said, her eyes searching Suzanne's. 'Look, why don't we have a cup of tea over there.' She gestured towards a Lyons teashop on the other side of the square. 'You can tell me about it, if you want to. And I can tell you all about ENSA.'

'Oh . . . well . . . thank you,' Suzanne stammered as the woman took her arm and led her across the square, despising herself for being so weak in front of a woman she'd never before set eyes on. Yet instinctively, she felt she could trust her.

Inside, it was full of chattering diners, smoke curling from several tables as people took a break from work. A waitress showed them a table, but the woman waved her arm as though warding off a fly.

'No, thanks, we'll take that one.' She pointed to a table tucked in a corner.

'I'm afraid it's already reserved, madam,' the waitress said apologetically, gave the woman a glance, then took a step back, her eyes wide. 'I hope you don't think me forward, madam, but are you Miss Miller – Miss Fern Miller?'

'Yes, I am.' Fern Miller grinned at Suzanne who stood staring in amazement. 'You didn't recognise me, did you, darling?'

Suzanne felt her face flush. 'I never dreamed I'd ever come face to face with one of my mother's favourite actresses – and mine,' she added hastily.

'Now you're flattering me.'

Fern Miller's voice was husky . . . distinctive. That was what Suzanne now realised had seemed familiar.

'Do come this way, Miss Miller,' the waitress said, excitement and awe coating her words, practically ignoring Suzanne, much to her amusement. 'I can find you a nice table over on the other side by the window . . . that is, if you don't mind being stared at.'

'It's what I live for.' Fern Miller was still chuckling as she and Suzanne followed the waitress.

When they'd ordered tea and at Fern's insistence two rock cakes, the actress took out a cigarette holder and a silver cigarette case. She offered it to Suzanne who shook her head.

'I don't blame you,' Fern Miller said ruefully. 'A bad habit, but I love it.' She laughed as she lit the cigarette with a gold lighter, inhaled, then leaned back in her chair as she waited for her tea. 'Don't ever start – that's the key.' She blew out a stream of smoke through painted red lips, all the while regarding Suzanne under hooded eyes. 'Now, tell me what's upset you . . . and by the way, call me Fern.'

Suzanne briefly told her what had happened in the early hours of yesterday morning to her friend and little Rosie while the waitress brought their tea and rock cakes. Fern put out her hand and clasped Suzanne's.

'How awful for you,' she said. 'Somehow, it's almost worse than if a bomb had dropped on the house. We have to expect death in wartime, but that was a tragic accident that needn't have happened.'

'That's what I keep thinking,' Suzanne said. 'If I hadn't gone back with her to her house the day before she might not have felt obliged to plug in the electric fire. I didn't like the look of the wire dangling from the ceiling, and they think that was the culprit. The wire caught fire and it was a thatched roof. The house was ablaze before the fire brigade arrived.'

'Well, you mustn't blame yourself.' Fern's eyes were warm with compassion. 'Your friend would have done exactly the same if you hadn't been there. Even if she put up with a cold room herself, she wouldn't have allowed the little girl to catch a chill.'

'I hope you're right,' Suzanne said, feeling a little consoled.

'And she'd want you to carry on,' Fern said. 'You mentioned she'd already joined ENSA and was going for her first rehearsal in a jazz band. So presumably she was going to introduce you to Elizabeth Foster who's in charge of the recruits.'

'Yes, she planned to.' Suzanne took a sip of hot tea, feeling comforted by it, hardly believing she was with a famous actress who was being so kind. What on earth would Maman say? For once, she'd probably approve, Suzanne thought, wryly.

'I can tell you're feeling a bit better,' Fern said. 'It's often good to talk over something painful with a stranger. Although I hope we won't be strangers for long.'

'You mentioned you'd tell me about ENSA,' Suzanne said, then boldly asked, 'Are you a member?'

'Yes, I am. I'm in a play and we tour together with other acts such as comedians, dancers, swing bands . . . that sort of thing,' she added, smiling broadly. 'We visit the stations and entertain the troops who always greet us with open arms – especially when they can feast their eyes on some women at long last. Some of them have been away for months, even years, in remote areas, and are desperately homesick for their wives and sweethearts. And from what you've told me about Wendy, she was determined to help the war effort, so I think it's a perfect way for you to keep her memory alive . . . if you've made a decision to join us, that is.'

With rapidly beating heart Suzanne entered the Theatre Royal with Fern Miller. Immediately, the doorman bowed to Fern.

'Afternoon, Miss Miller,' he said, touching his hat. 'Good to see you back. Your group are going to be in the auditorium, and George Johnson's band will be using the rehearsal room. All the other acts rehearsed this morning.'

'Thank you, Jeffries.' Fern nodded, glanced at her wristwatch and took Suzanne's arm. 'I don't need to go on for another twenty minutes, so I'll take you now to see Elizabeth Foster.'

'Oh, thank you,' Suzanne said eagerly, hardly believing she was at the famous theatre, about to talk to someone who might change her life.

They went down a passage and Fern stopped outside one of the doors labelled ELIZABETH FOSTER. The actress knocked and a voice from within instructed them to enter.

Suzanne paused a second or two in the doorway, allowing Fern to go on ahead. There was a tangible smell of excitement from the people rushing past, some of them not fully clothed, calling 'darling' to one another or muttering lines under their breath. Swing music squeezed through the gap of one of the closed doors near where she was standing. She breathed it all in. This was it. No more dithering. Threats from her mother had no power over her decision now. If they'd have her, she wouldn't hesitate.

Suzanne couldn't help staring. She'd never seen a woman in trousers except Raine once in her boiler suit when her sister had cadged a lift into Biggin Hill aerodrome and come straight home to Downe. But *that* was a practical working outfit. *This* appeared to be deliberate. Miss Foster, almost as tall as Fern but much bigger-boned, wore a crisp white shirt with a cameo brooch at the neck, and pinstriped charcoal-grey trousers. A matching jacket was tossed over the back of her office chair. As soon as Fern appeared, she jumped up and came from behind her desk.

'Darling,' Fern cooed, kissing her on both cheeks, 'how marvellous to see you again. You're looking wonderfully well, as usual.'

'I bet *you'd* hate to be described as "wonderfully well",' Elizabeth Foster said with a hearty chuckle. 'And to be truthful, it wouldn't be at all adequate. You look sensational – as you always do.'

'And *you* always say the right thing.' Fern beamed, pressing Suzanne forward. 'Liz, darling, I've brought someone to meet you. Miss Suzanne Linfoot – a friend of Wendy—' She broke off and raised an eyebrow to Suzanne. 'I'm sorry, I don't know her last name.'

'Wendy Rushton,' Suzanne said in a small voice.

'Ah, yes, Wendy,' Miss Foster said. 'She didn't turn up yesterday for her first rehearsal.' She looked sternly at Suzanne. 'Don't tell me she's changed her mind. That would really be too inconvenient.'

'It's rather a sad story . . . This young lady will enlighten you,' Fern said, turning to Suzanne. 'I'm going to leave you in the capable hands of Elizabeth, Suzanne.' She gave her an encouraging smile. 'I hope to see you again, and at any rate we're bound to run into one another sooner or later. But just in case, here's my card.'

She delved into her shoulder bag and fished out a small white card. 'My address and telephone number, should you ever need to contact me. I don't give it out to many people, so please guard it with your life.'

'Thank you very much, Fern,' Suzanne said. 'I promise I won't let it out of my sight.'

'Good girl.' She turned to Miss Foster. 'Look after this young lady, Liz. I think she's pretty special. I'll catch up with you later but for now I'm going to have to love you both and leave you.' With that, she swept from the room, leaving a trail of expensive perfume behind her.

'So you know Fern Miller?' Miss Foster said brusquely, as if Suzanne oughtn't to know such a famous person.

'I've only just met her. We were admiring the Royal Opera House building and started chatting. She's been very kind to me.'

'Hmm. Fern has a habit of collecting people.' Miss Foster nodded towards one of the chairs. 'You'd better sit down and tell me about Wendy. I hope she's not ill.'

Dreading having to relate the story all over again, Suzanne shakily explained, with Miss Foster listening attentively.

'I'm very sorry indeed to hear that,' Miss Foster said when Suzanne had finished. 'We really took to her. She was so keen to join ENSA and start rehearsals.' She peered at Suzanne over the top of her spectacles. 'You look a lot younger than Wendy.'

'I'm eighteen.'

'You've not thought of joining one of the forces?'

'No, I finish school next month. My mother wanted me to go to the Royal Academy of Music, but when Wendy told me she'd joined ENSA, and told me about the work they did, I wanted to find out more. So she suggested I meet you.'

Miss Foster lit a cigarette, and deeply inhaled. 'Now Wendy can't be with us, there's obviously a vacancy,' she said, blowing out the smoke through her nostrils. 'Did Wendy tell you what we had in mind for her?'

'I understood she was going to be one of the singers, although she's . . . was—' Suzanne gulped '—really a violinist – the same as me.'

'I knew that,' Miss Foster said, 'but we'd just been let down by one of the singers – a crooner. That's what we desperately need. And luckily for us she turned out to have an exceptionally engaging voice.' She paused and tilted her head. 'Do *you* sing, Miss Linfoot?'

The question took Suzanne by surprise.

'Only at home if there's no one about.' She gave Miss Foster a rueful smile. 'Or occasionally with my older sister when she's home and I'm on the piano.'

'And is she also a musician?'

'No, she's a pilot, delivering aeroplanes to the fighter pilots,' Suzanne said with a note of pride.

'Ah, a very worthwhile part to play,' Miss Foster said, nodding her approval. 'But we consider that entertaining the troops, lifting their morale, is extremely important as well.'

'Oh, I do, too,' Suzanne said, leaning forward. 'That's why I'm prepared to give up the music college – against my mother's wishes.'

'So your mother doesn't approve of your joining ENSA?' Miss Foster said quickly.

Suzanne could have bitten her tongue out, but it was too late now. 'She thinks I should stick to classical music. I can't really blame her. She's always paid for my music lessons, even when it was difficult . . .' She didn't want to go into any details as it felt disloyal to her father, but Miss Foster appeared to understand.

'And what do *you* want to do?'

'ENSA really appeals to me,' Suzanne said. 'I'd feel I was directly helping our servicemen to forget for an hour or two what they've been through and still have to face.'

Miss Foster cupped her chin with her hand. 'And if I ask you to audition as a singer in a swing band, instead of a violinist, what would you say?'

'I don't know,' Suzanne answered, her hopes of joining George Johnson's band sinking. 'I don't think I'd be any good.'

'Perhaps that's for *me* to decide.' Miss Foster took a last drag of her cigarette before stubbing it out in the already overflowing ashtray. 'In fact, why don't you come with me. I'll find Bram, our pianist. He can give you the sheet music for one of the songs and play the accompaniment. See how you do.' She studied her a few seconds. 'You certainly look the part with your figure and that blonde hair . . .' She peered closer. 'And eyes a colour I've never seen on anyone before. They're violet.'

Suzanne sat in stunned silence. A singer. But you'd have to be professional. And she wasn't. This interview was not going at all as she'd imagined. But if she refused to do what Miss Foster was offering, it didn't look as though she'd get into ENSA.

Chapter Thirteen

Bram was a man with early thinning hair and twinkling blue eyes. Suzanne's eyes travelled to his hands, noticing his fingers were as short and stocky as the man himself. Not really pianist's hands at all.

'Bramwell Taylor.' One of those hands enclosed hers briefly. 'Everyone calls me Bram. And you're—?'

'Suzanne Linfoot.'

'Hmm. Suzanne. I think you'll have to be Suzy if you sing with us.'

Exactly what Wendy had said.

'Come closer to the piano,' Bram said, as he thumbed through some sheets of music that were half falling from the music stand. One page fell to the floor and Suzanne dived for it.

'Thanks, love.' He took it and arranged it back on the stand, giving her a rueful smile. 'What a terrible thing to happen to poor Wendy. Elizabeth told me about it. And nothing to do with the war.' He tutted and shook his head. 'She was a lovely girl and was so excited to be joining us.' He rifled through some music, apparently spotted a sheet he was looking for, and smoothed it in front of him, then looked up. 'She lived near you, didn't she?'

'Yes,' Suzanne said, hoping he wouldn't ask for any details.

She just couldn't go through it all again. 'We knew each other because she and I both played the violin in a small orchestra in the village where I live. But Miss Foster says the vacancy is for a singer . . . a crooner. But I've never sung professionally.'

'But you *do* sing?' Bram said.

'Only around the house.' Suddenly she remembered the other day when she grabbed hold of the salad cream bottle pretending it was a microphone and belting out 'Chattanooga choo choo'. A smile curved her lips at the embarrassing memory when Ronnie had surprised her, although her young sister had mentioned she had a terrific voice.

'You're smiling.' Bram pounced on her expression. 'That to me means you enjoy singing. So let's see what you can do. I've got here "I'll Never Smile Again". Do you know it?'

Her voice wouldn't be good enough to sing such a slow, romantic song. 'I know the tune and some of the words,' she said reluctantly.

'Here then.' He handed her the sheet. 'You have the words.' He hovered his stubby hands over the piano. 'Just a short intro, then off we go.'

'Should I have a microphone?'

Bram shook his head. 'No. I want to see how you sound absolutely raw. No aids. No nothing.'

'All right.' She took in a breath.

'No, don't suck in your stomach when you need a breath. It should be the opposite. Your stomach should expand . . . slowly . . . nice and full – like this.' He stood and demonstrated, his already protruding stomach now stretching his trousers to their limit. 'Have you ever had singing lessons?'

'No,' Suzanne said, immediately feeling inadequate and slightly piqued. She'd already told Miss Foster and now this Bram that she was a violinist. What did they think she'd been studying all these years? She certainly had no idea that you had to breathe in a certain way when singing.

'No matter,' he said. 'We can give you some training.'

'Could I start with something a bit faster?' she asked boldly.

He raised a bushy eyebrow. 'What do you have in mind?'

'"Chattanooga choo choo".'

He smiled. 'That's really for more than one singer.'

'I know, but it's jazzy, and I think I'd be better singing something with more of a beat.'

'I don't see any reason why not.' He flipped over some pages, nodded, and began to play the introduction.

In her nervousness she missed her cue.

'I'm sorry, Bram.'

'I'll nod the beat before you come in.' He repeated the last two phrases again, then nodded.

'Pardon me, boy, is that the Chattanooga choo choo?

Track twenty-nine . . .'

She sang a few more bars then stopped. It was terrible. So different from when she'd spontaneously sung at home when everyone was out. She wasn't putting any life into it. It didn't sparkle. What a cheek to think she could even stand a chance among the professionals. She wished she'd said firmly that no, she didn't sing, and didn't want to sing.

'That was awful. I don't know what's the matter with me, but I wasn't prepared to sing.'

'Okay. Let's try it in a different key.'

Bram played a few bars up an octave and began to sing in a squeaky voice. She couldn't help a giggle escaping. He looked at her and chuckled. 'That's it . . . relax. Pretend you're in a room full of soldiers. They've been out fighting and now they're desperate for something lighter to take them away from all that. You come on looking absolutely stunning in your evening frock. They'll love you before you even open your mouth. Don't stand so stiffly with your arms by your sides. And don't forget to *smile*.' He looked up. 'Let's see that smile.'

She gave him the widest smile she could manage.

'Now make it sincere.'

She swallowed and thought of James.

He grinned. 'Much better. Off we go.'

Suzanne took in another breath, making sure her stomach went out and not in. She pictured the scene that Bram had painted for her. Those dear, wonderful, brave young men who risked their lives every day for their country – for its people – for her. She clicked her fingers and began to sway. He nodded. She came in perfectly on time.

She began to enjoy herself. She could feel her voice becoming more confident and she sang a couple more verses. Just as she was about to start a new verse, to her dismay, Bram held up the palm of his hand. Her heart plummeted. She obviously wasn't good enough and never would be. In that instant she desperately wished she could sing. That she had the kind of voice the soldiers would love. She gave him a sideways glance but his expression told her nothing. She was finished before she'd even started. Well, Maman would get her wish.

'So that's your fast one, now let's try the slow one.' For the second time he handed her 'I'll Never Smile Again'.

'But what's the point?' Suzanne protested, automatically taking it. 'I'm never going to make it as a singer. I'm a violinist and I should stick to that.'

'Humour me,' Bram said. 'Come on, Suzy, take it nice and slow.'

If anything, her voice was worse than the first effort of 'Chattanooga choo choo'.

'You're rushing ahead of me, Suzy. This is a love song. You want to get right into the soldiers' hearts.'

She tried again but she had no feeling for it. Every word felt false. She stopped abruptly.

'What's the matter?'

'I don't want to sing any more. I can't sing to an audience. I'm sorry but . . .' Tears gathered in her throat as she bent to collect her bag by her side.

'What are you talking about, young lady? You have a delightful voice, as a matter of fact. A little unusual but I like it. You just don't know how to use it. But we can sort that out. I want you to sing it again – this time all the way through.'

She shook her head. 'I can't.'

He sent her a piercing stare. 'Have you ever been in love?'

She blushed at such a question. 'No,' she said. 'Well, maybe a crush, but it didn't mean anything.'

'I ask because you need to put some feeling into the words. You could have the most beautiful voice in the world, but if there's no feeling it will fall flat. But if you put feeling in, then even if your voice isn't perfect it won't matter a jot.' He sent her a searching look. 'Have you never lost someone you love?'

She gulped. 'I lost my father not long ago.'

'Oh, I'm sorry. How did you feel?'

'An ache that wouldn't go away. That I'd never see him again. Never hear his voice. Never feel his arms round me giving me a hug. Even talking about it now is just as painful.'

She'd never told a stranger or even a friend how she'd felt about Dad.

'That's it,' Bram said, playing a few bars. 'He'll never see your smile. So remember your father and how you would give anything to smile at him again.' He sent her his own smile that lit up his plain features. 'The words and notes will follow . . . I promise.'

She did as he asked. After a few seconds she forgot about Bram and auditions and even the soldiers. She only thought about her father. How much she missed him. What a good father he'd always been, wanting the best for his girls, as he always called her and her sisters. Never picking one daughter out as a favourite – unlike Maman. She pushed away a flicker of guilt. Raine and Ronnie often reminded her that she was the favourite in Maman's eyes and she'd always denied it, but deep down she knew it was true. At least it used to be before she'd told her mother she wasn't going to the London music school. Tears ran down her face and she could hardly form the last words of the song.

'*. . . until I smile at you.*'

Bram's fingers drifted on the last few keys until the notes faded away. He turned his body round on the stool and fixed his eyes on her.

'Are you all right?'

She nodded and took a handkerchief from her bag and dabbed her nose. How could she possibly take Wendy's place – stand in Wendy's shoes? She wasn't cut out to be a singer.

'Suzy?'

'I spoilt the song by starting to cry.'

'There's a lovely catch in your voice, Suzy. It reminds me of Judy Garland and will tear the hearts out of the soldiers. It's exactly what we need. You may need a little help with some songs on how you put them across – the jazzy ones, particularly – but you're a natural and I urge you to stay that way. And make sure any accompanist gets you in the right key. You have a very high range.'

'Does that mean—?' Suzanne broke off, the words that she reminded Bram of Judy Garland whose voice she adored ringing in her ears. She didn't dare finish the question.

'Yes, I shall recommend to Miss Foster that you'd be perfect for her second songstress.'

'No need to,' a voice came from the doorway. 'I heard her sing. I'm quite satisfied.' Miss Foster stepped into the room. 'If you would like to take up our offer, we'd be pleased to have you.'

For the first time since hearing the devastating news about Wendy, Suzanne felt something warm and positive stir deep within her.

'I'd like that,' she said firmly.

'Good.' Miss Foster gave her a quick smile of approval. 'I'll give you a couple of forms to take home and fill out. Our next posting will be abroad and we'll be gone at least three months so we'll need one of your parents' signatures allowing you to go.' She fixed her eyes on Suzanne. 'That won't present any problem, will it?'

Miss Foster's words went over and over in her mind as Suzanne slumped in her seat back to Bromley. She hadn't let the woman know that her desire to join ENSA was now impossible, even though Miss Foster must have seen her face fall. She'd tried to cover it up by shaking her head and saying that her mother wouldn't make it difficult. Miss Foster had asked a few more questions and taken note of her address but Suzanne hadn't dared give Miss Foster the home telephone number until she'd spoken to her mother. But she knew the answer before she even asked.

To go abroad for three months? No. Maman would never sign.

Chapter Fourteen

'I've been dying to hear how it all went,' Ronnie said, coming into the kitchen with Rusty. He gave a joyful bark and rushed up to lick Suzanne's hand.

'Has he been for his walk?' Suzanne twiddled his ears and let them flop back.

'Just going. Come with us and you can tell me all about it.'

'Give me a moment. I was making myself a cup of tea. I haven't had anything to drink for hours. Where's Maman by the way?'

'She's setting up a fund-raising group in the village.' Ronnie glanced at the kitchen clock. 'She'll be back soon. We can't be long as I told her this morning I'd get the vegetables ready for supper. She left one of her notes.'

'Yes, I saw it.'

Five minutes later the two of them, Rusty trotting in front, walked down the lane towards a lightly wooded area the opposite end of the village where they could let Rusty off the lead.

'Come on,' Ronnie said. 'I'm dying of curiosity. Did they like your playing? Was it jazzy enough?'

'I didn't play,' Suzanne said. 'They don't want a violinist, jazzy or not. They want a second singer.'

'Oh, I love it!' Ronnie exclaimed. 'You've got a terrific voice. I told you that the other day when I caught you with the salad cream bottle.' She giggled. 'Honestly, Suzy, you'd be perfect for them.' She stopped and looked at her sister. 'Did you get in?'

'Yes,' Suzanne said, forcing down a surge of pride. 'But I don't think I can take up their offer.'

Ronnie's brows shot up. 'Course you can,' she said. 'And if you're worried about Maman—'

'Can you imagine what Maman will say when I tell her not only would I not be playing the violin, but would be a singer, and after she digests that shock, that I'd be going abroad in a fortnight.'

'Really?' Ronnie's eyes were wide with envy. 'Oh, you lucky thing. Where?'

'Bram – that's the pianist – didn't say where. And Miss Foster – the woman in charge of the group – wasn't specific either. I expect it's a security thing.' She sighed. 'It didn't really occur to me that I might be going abroad.'

'But surely joining this ENSA thing means you can be sent anywhere at any time, wherever you're needed. That should be how you base your decision – not worrying about us.'

'Miss Foster said it would be at least three months.'

Ronnie threw a stick for Rusty who galloped off after it. 'We'll miss you, Suzy, but we'll be all right. Maman won't like it but she'll have to accept it. There's a war on, for goodness' sake. She seems to forget whenever it suits her.'

Suzanne sighed. Ronnie, as usual, was wise for her age.

'Even if I do decide to go, Maman has to sign the paperwork to give her permission. And I can't see her doing it.'

'I'm on your side, Suzy,' Ronnie said firmly. 'We'll get her to sign. We can't deprive those poor soldiers of ogling somebody as glamorous as you – when you don't smell of doggie, that is,' she added, chuckling.

Suzanne gave her young sister a dig in the ribs. 'Enough of your cheek,' she said, laughing. 'It's your fault for not having him under control – letting him jump up all the time.'

'He's just excited to see you – to see anyone, when he's shut up for so much of the day.'

'If you could train him better you might have a chance of him being allowed out of your bedroom once in a while.'

Ronnie looked doubtful.

'Come on, Ronnie,' Suzanne said, turning towards the way they'd come. 'We'd better not be out too long. I'd rather be home before Maman comes through the door and tells us off for not being there.'

'Rusty!' Ronnie called. 'RUSTY! Here, boy! We're ready to go.'

But it was another ten minutes before Rusty could be dragged away from all the enticing smells around him. And by the time they got back, Maman was home.

For once Maman's attention was diverted from Rusty and firmly on her daughters.

'Mrs Whitehead dropped the bombshell on us this afternoon,' she said, wrinkling her brow. 'I need a cup of tea. We did not have one as normal. Everyone was shocked.'

'I'll put the kettle on,' Ronnie said, 'and you can tell us all about it.' She rolled her eyes at Suzanne who couldn't help grinning.

'What did I say that was so amusing?' Simone demanded.

'Nothing, Maman. Just something I thought of.'

'And what is that, may I ask?'

'Nothing important. We want to hear about Mrs

Whitehead. What's she done that's put everyone in such a spin?'

Simone narrowed her eyes as though wondering if Suzanne was being sarcastic.

'Véronique is too young to listen,' she said.

'Maman, I heard that.' Ronnie's head came round the door. 'I just wish everyone would stop treating me like a baby.'

'She really is growing up, Maman,' Suzanne said. 'I think we should include her in any discussions that are important.'

Simone shrugged. 'All right. We will wait for her to make tea.'

Suzanne went into the kitchen to lay the tray.

'Are you going to drop *your* bombshell?' Ronnie said in an undertone, taking the cups and saucers from the dresser. 'Might as well let her have two for the price of one.'

'She's going to say no,' Suzanne said.

'Don't take no for an answer.' Ronnie's face was serious. 'Just like Raine said – this is your future. Dad always told us that you have to follow your heart. And I think your heart says you must go.'

'Maybe you're right,' Suzanne said, her eyes stinging at the mention of Dad. 'But let's see what Mrs Whitehead has been up to first.'

Simone made her usual drama of taking her time with her tea, but Suzanne was too lost in her own thoughts to urge her mother to tell them what terrible thing Mrs Whitehead had been up to.

'*Alors, mes enfants.*' Simone put her cup and saucer on one side. 'That is better.' She fixed her eyes on her daughters. 'Mrs Whitehead—'

'Which one is Mrs Whitehead?' Ronnie interrupted.

'She is our new member to join,' Simone said, 'and she has a very big house.' She spread her hands wide as though to show her daughters how very large the house was. 'The last time we meet . . . met in the village hall they said we could no longer be there. They need it for something else.' She sighed out her irritation. 'That is why Mrs Whitehead offered us her house for our meetings. Today was the first time and we all like it. But she said it will be our last time. She is going to join the Women's Voluntary Service.' Simone looked up and caught Suzanne's eye. 'Can you believe it? She'll be serving soups and cups of tea.' She shuddered. 'Coming from that lovely house to work on a *tea van*.'

Suzanne was silent. She'd heard that the women in the WVS set up their vehicles right where the action was, so they were the first 'normal' sight the soldiers saw when they came from the fighting, longing for a cup of tea and a biscuit served by a woman who reminded them of their mum. She couldn't think of a more practical and worthwhile job to do for the boys.

Simone went on, 'She says she wants to do something more useful than fund-raising for those poor soldiers. I said we can start a fund to help make a new aeroplane for the RAF. I have called it the Downe Fighter Fund.'

'That's a really good idea, Maman,' Ronnie said.

Simone nodded. 'Even, I think, Lorraine would approve. But Mrs Whitehead is not interested.' She raised her eyes to the ceiling.

'How old is Mrs Whitehead?' Suzanne asked, imagining a plump elderly lady, her grey hair in a net.

'She is the same age as Lorraine. She married young and is already a widow. I thought she would be occupied by the knitting group and the fund-raising, but it seems it is not enough.' She drained her cup. 'I do not know what her mother is thinking of, allowing such a thing.'

'I think it's marvellous that she's doing something so practical for the war effort,' Suzanne said, risking her mother's annoyance that she wasn't agreeing with her. 'I imagine the soldiers will greet her with open arms when she hands them a cup of tea.'

'Yes, it is what I expected you to say.' Simone closed her eyes, then opened them to fix on Rusty who was lying at Ronnie's feet. 'Véronique, you can take that flea-ridden dog upstairs.'

Rusty barked as though in protest and Suzanne hid a smile.

'He doesn't have fleas—' Ronnie began.

Suzanne threw her sister a warning glance.

'Come with me, Rusty,' Ronnie ordered. 'We'll play a game in the garden.' She stalked out with Rusty at her heels.

'You are very quiet, Suzanne,' Simone said suddenly. 'What are you thinking, child?'

Suzanne sighed. 'I'm not a child. I've been offered a job today to join that entertainments group I keep telling you about. They want me to sing.'

'*Sing*? Are you mad? When did you talk to these people?' Simone's voice cracked with anger.

'I went for an audition today and—'

'And you did not tell me where you were going? My own daughter lying to me.'

'I didn't lie to you,' Suzanne said, her cheeks burning with frustration. 'I just didn't say anything because I knew you would try to stop me.'

'*Certes*, you are correct.' She glared at Suzanne. 'It is most regrettable that you are becoming as deceitful as your sister Lorraine.'

'Maman, that's not fair to Raine. She—'

Simone put the palm of her hand up. 'So you intend to waste your classical training and sing when you have no professional experience.'

'They seem to think I can do it. But I need you to give permission for me to go abroad.'

Simone's eyes gleamed. 'That, *chérie*, I will never do.'

'That's what I thought you'd say,' Suzanne said, standing up. 'I'd better telephone Fern Miller and Miss Foster to say you will not give permission for me to go.'

'What are you talking about?' Simone demanded, her eyes flashing. 'What has Fern Miller to do with any of this? She is a famous actress.'

'I know. I met her in London. She took me to a Lyons teashop and told me she's a member of ENSA. She said how important it was to entertain the troops. Her group are putting on a play and she hopes I'll be joining the same tour and that we can be friends. I told her she was one of your favourite actresses,' Suzanne added, playing the only trump card she could think of.

'You said that to Fern Miller? I do not believe this.'

'I have her telephone number. I could ring her and let you speak to her yourself.'

'*D'accord.* And then we will disclose the imposter.'

'She's not an imposter, Maman. Miss Foster who's in charge called her Fern as soon as we walked into her office. And the waitress in the teashop recognised her immediately. All the heads were turning in the café.'

'*Impossible.*' Simone pronounced it the French way and rolled her eyes. 'But I will talk to her. If she is who you say she is . . .' She didn't finish the sentence.

Suzanne held her breath. Perhaps Maman might, just might, think about giving permission after all if Fern Miller said it was the right thing to do.

But when her mother dialled the number Fern Miller had given her, it simply rang and rang.

'As I said . . .' Maman's lip curled. 'This woman, whoever she is, is an imposter.'

Chapter Fifteen

Suzanne opened her blackout curtains to a clear day, the sun already throwing dappled light on the tree opposite. James Mortimer's birthday. She peered into the wardrobe where a few of Raine's clothes still hung. She was looking for something lighter to finally welcome the milder weather, but there was little to choose from. Maman was always very careful with money and dress material was now rationed. The dark green pleated skirt would have to do. Reluctantly, she took it out and then her eye caught sight of one of Raine's blouses – cream silk with a bow at the neck. Suzanne had made it for herself in her sewing class just before the war, but Raine had begged her for it. Surely her sister wouldn't mind lending it to her for the afternoon.

She tried it on with the skirt and twirled, catching sight of herself in the mirror inside the wardrobe door. She smiled at her reflection, feeling she'd finally become a grown woman. Quickly peeling off the two items she hung them on the cornice of the wardrobe so as not to crease them, all the while wondering what her mother would say when she told her she was going to James's birthday party.

Throwing on her dressing gown and hugging the thought that she'd soon be seeing him, she ran downstairs to put the kettle on. She turned on the wireless but after a few minutes she turned it off. The news was often so depressing.

There were so many tragedies happening nowadays. She thought of Raine, her beloved sister, battling all weathers to deliver aeroplanes to the waiting soldiers. Then those brave young men would take to the skies in those very aeroplanes to fight to protect their country – and sometimes lose their lives in doing so. She swallowed the tears. It was no good dwelling on such things.

Think of something nice, she told herself. James had said he wanted nothing on his birthday but she had to take something – however small. She didn't know that much about him but by his school prize in literature, he obviously loved reading. Her mouth curved into a smile. She'd give him that bookmark she'd made a few weeks ago. It wasn't very manly and she'd embroidered her initials SL on it, but it was the only thing she could think of as at least a token.

She was just about to pour the tea when she heard the front doorbell. Putting her head round the kitchen door she saw the post boy's bicycle leaning against the low front wall.

'Hello, Micky.' She greeted him with a smile.

'Hello, miss.' A youth with ginger hair and face covered with freckles to match gave her a mischievous grin of approval as he looked her up and down. 'Did I wake you up?'

'No, cheeky, I've been up for ages.' She pulled the cord of her dressing gown a little tighter. 'What've you got for us?'

'Something addressed to "Miss Suzanne Linfoot". Looks like you're the one getting all the interesting post these days.'

Suzanne gave him a smile. Micky commented on everyone's post, just as his father, Mr Short, used to. Poor man. He'd got killed in the blackout when he'd gone to London to see his mother only a few weeks ago. He'd always had a remark to make on his deliveries. She'd got used to it, and even found it mildly amusing, but Maman's temper would rise every time.

'Poking his nose in,' she would say. 'I cannot understand the English. It would never 'appen in my country.'

'If you could sign here, miss,' Micky said importantly, handing her a small receipt book. 'It's registered.' He stared at her. 'Is it your birthday?'

Suzanne shook her head. 'No.' She wasn't going to enlighten him further, although she was as curious as Micky Short as to why someone had sent her a registered letter.

But it wasn't a letter. When she'd signed for it he handed her a cube of a parcel, six or seven inches across, and wrapped in brown paper with plenty of string and red sealing wax. She looked at the postmark. London. That didn't mean much. But the writing looked strange. Not like any writing she recognised. It almost looked Gothic, like the lettering they'd once copied at school in art class.

'Thank you, Micky,' she said, and he nodded and grinned again as he hopped onto his bicycle.

Suzanne went up to her room and opened one of her dressing table drawers and took out a pair of nail scissors. She cut the string and put her thumb under the sealing wax to carefully break it, then opened up the flaps of brown paper. Inside was a plain cardboard box. She opened it to find another much smaller package tied with string amongst some balls of crumpled newspaper. She removed it and put it on top of her dressing table, then pulled out all the newspaper stuffing. She shook out the balls of newspaper to make sure nothing more was hidden, but there didn't seem to be.

Suzanne tossed the newspaper stuffing into her wastepaper basket, then on impulse retrieved them and smoothed one of them out. She frowned. It was in French. She did the same with the rest of the stuffing balls and they, too, were torn pages of a French newspaper.

She removed the piece of newspaper that lined the outer box and found it was flatter and easier to read. It was the front page of *Le Figaro*, which she'd once heard her mother say her parents used to read. It was dated *Lundi 9 Novembre 1942*. The headlines screamed out at her.

LES AMERICAINS
ET LES ANGLAIS ATTAQUENT
NOTRE AFRIQUE DU NORD

Suzanne scanned the report from Vichy France by the Marshal – who was Pétain, she thought, grimly – to President Roosevelt, condemning the aggression. But the newspaper had refused to criticise the Anglo-American forces who had landed in French North Africa the day before. Interesting. She translated it into English to be sure she understood, grateful for her stickler of a Mademoiselle, their French mistress at school, and the occasional French conversation with Maman when she was in the mood. What would the Germans make of this outright gesture of defiance? She hoped none of the journalists had got into any serious trouble. But who in England had managed to get hold of a French newspaper?

She looked in the box again and pulled out two small sheets of paper that must have been tucked under the newspaper lining. Hoping it was some kind of letter of explanation, she unfolded them to see it was the same strange handwriting as the Linfoots' address on the outside of the parcel.

Where did the letter come from? But there was no address, not even a date. She lifted off the top sheet and looked at the signature at the bottom of the second page.

Marguerite.

She frowned. A French name. No surname. How odd. It must be someone her mother knew. The writing was tiny, the words squashed against one another to make the most of the limited space, and it was difficult to read the Continental style of writing. She peered a little closer.

My dear Suzanne,

You must excuse any mistakes with my English but I am a 60 year Frenchwoman living in France. It is time to put my affairs in order as I have a serious illness. You do not know me so you may be thinking what that has to do with you. I will explain.

Why was this woman writing to her? What did she want? A feeling of dread – that something awful was about to be disclosed – took root in Suzanne's bones. She licked her lips and read on.

I do not want to wait until it is too late before sending you something very precious to your grandmother who died many years ago.

Suzanne gave a start of surprise. Her grandmother! This woman had sent something of her grandmother's? But Suzanne didn't know her grandmother. Didn't even know her name, and nor did her sisters. As far as she knew, there'd been almost no contact between her mother and her parents, so why was this Marguerite, who must be a relative of Maman's, writing to *her*?

Curiosity overtaking finishing the letter, Suzanne cut the string of the package and removed a small polished box, the colour of deep red wine. She held it to her nose and sniffed.

It smelt like an old leather book. There was a tiny brass button, which she pressed to release the lid . . . then gasped. In its own little golden velvet slit of a cavity lay the most beautiful ring she had ever seen. It was diamond-shaped, with more than a dozen glittering stones. A much larger stone lay at its centre. She gave the ring a little tug to release it, then held it in the palm of her hand. It really was the most exquisite-looking piece of jewellery. Setting it down gently on her embroidered dressing table cloth, she hurried to the window, and even though it was daylight, she pulled the blackout curtains together. Then she switched on her bedside light and held the ring under its glow. The ring sprang into life. It twinkled and dazzled – all the colours of the rainbow winking up at her.

She slipped it on the ring finger of her right hand but it was much too loose so she tried her middle finger. A perfect fit. Then realisation struck. This was not some piece of costume jewellery – some trinket as she'd first imagined. She picked up the small leather box and studied it. The lid was lined in pale gold satin, hardly discoloured with age, with a beaded gold trim that bordered the whole of the cavity. But what caught her eye was the black lettering in the lid, on the lining itself, with a crown above the words 'By Appointment'.

BY APPOINTMENT
J. CHAUMET
SR DE MOREL & CIE
LONDON PARIS
NEW BOND STREET PLACE VENDOME

154 12

It looked like a French company that had a shop in London. This ring was a very special piece indeed. In a daze she took up the letter again.

You will not need me to tell you that this is a ring of the highest quality. It was your grandmother's ring when your grandfather received his doctorate and they became engaged. As you can imagine, she loved it. She always wanted you to have it. We always talked about our Suzanne and hoped you were happy. Wear it and think of her. She was a wonderful mother to us, and if you had met her you would think her a wonderful grandmother.

Now completely baffled, Suzanne reached for the second sheet, which had been carefully cut in half. Whoever this Marguerite was, the lady was obviously mindful of wasting paper.

I was married to a very dear man but he was killed in the Great War. I do not have any children but I have a younger brother of whom I am very fond. This may come as a shock to you, and if it does I am sorry, but I feel obliged to tell you my dear brother is your father.

Suzanne froze. Was the woman mad? What on earth was she talking about? She *must* be mad. Or playing a joke. She read on.

You have never met my brother and he has never met you, but he has loved you since the day you were born and always sent you letters and cards on your birthday until the war, but now there is no more contact between our countries. But he once told me your maman has never mentioned your reaction and this is why I felt I should write to tell you the truth of your parentage. I do know your maman always sent him a photograph of you each year which he treasures. I have seen them so I feel I know you even though we will never meet.

Suzanne felt completely numb. Her brain couldn't take in any more. She rubbed her brow, willing herself to understand what this Marguerite was saying. She turned over the half sheet, barely taking in the final words.

Goodbye, my dear. I wish I could meet you, my only niece, and see you wearing the ring but it is not meant to be. I only hope one day when this terrible war is over you will be united with your loving father. It is his dearest wish.

With loving wishes that you have a full and happy life.

Marguerite

Suzanne couldn't fathom it. Maybe she'd missed something with such small writing. She read the letter again . . . slowly, this time. What did it all mean? Why hadn't Maman told her and her sisters that her own mother had died? Or with the war, did Maman even know? A shiver ran across Suzanne's shoulders. Her thoughts scrambled. She couldn't make sense of them. Her mouth tasted sour. She went to the bathroom and put her open mouth under the cold tap. When she raised her head she caught sight of herself in the mirror above the basin. Her face was slack with shock and disbelief. Dad wasn't her father! The man she and her sisters all adored wasn't her dad. *Her* father was French. But Marguerite hadn't even mentioned his name. Why? Had she left it out to protect him?

And then it was as though someone had punched her in the face. Her mother must have had a lover! If everything Marguerite had told her in the letter was true, it was the only explanation. Bile rose in her throat. Her mother – always so strict, always so proper where her daughters' morals were concerned – but apparently it didn't apply to herself. Her mother had led a life of deceit and lies.

A wave of terrifying fury swept over her making her reel. She clutched the edge of the washbasin.

Another thought struck her. With trembling legs she stumbled back to her room and picked up the outside wrapping paper of the parcel. The postmark was definitely London. So how on earth had it reached here from a closed France?

She felt inside the cardboard box one more time and her fingers closed on a small shiny card that was standing upright against the side. She drew it out and turned it over. It was a photograph of a beautiful woman, probably in her forties, almost as fair as herself, with darkened eyebrows and deep-coloured lipstick on a full, wide mouth. She gave a sudden intake of breath. It was a mouth that might have been her own. Suzanne stared again, then put her hand over the eyes of the woman. The mouth and chin, the jawline . . . She took her hand away. The eyes were different, but the nose, the shape of the woman's face, even the hairline . . . she looked more like this aunt than she did her own mother! Which meant Marguerite's brother must truly be her natural father. She shook her head. It still didn't seem possible. It was like a bad dream that she couldn't wake up from.

She hesitated a few moments, then slipped the photograph in the pages of James's school prize.

There were so many questions. And only one person who could answer them.

Gently, she set the ring into its cavity, snapped the lid shut, and tucked the box into her dressing gown pocket. She poured her mother's tea and went upstairs. Softly, she tapped on the bedroom door. There was no going back.

'*Entre, chérie.*'

Her mother was sitting on the edge of the bed, slipping her feet into a pair of mules. She looked up at Suzanne with a hopeful smile and Suzanne knew her mother thought there might be a chance she'd changed her mind and would go to the music school.

'Good morning, Maman.' She felt the word choke in her throat. 'The postman's just been.'

Her mother rose and held out her hand. 'Another bill, I suppose.'

'No, there's nothing for you, Maman. It's something that came for *me*.'

'And you wish to share it with your *maman*.' Her mother smiled more broadly this time.

'Yes. It's a letter. I'll read it to you.'

'Sit on the chair, *chérie*, and I will listen as I attend to my hair.' Her mother went over to her dressing table and picked up her hairbrush.

For a few moments Suzanne stood and watched her mother's reflection in the mirror as she brushed the lustrous dark waves with no hint of grey. Even without her make-up, when she relaxed her expression, Maman was beautiful. She hardened her heart. Her mother was treacherous.

'My dear Suzanne,' Suzanne read. 'You do not know me, but I am a Frenchwoman living in France—'

Suzanne glanced up. Maman's back was rigid, her face a pale mask in the mirror.

'Who has sent this letter?' her mother demanded in a tight voice.

'Let me finish reading it.' Suzanne drew a deep breath and continued. When she read that it was her grandmother's engagement ring, her mother flung down the hairbrush and twisted round.

'You have this ring?'

'Yes, I—'

'Show it to me.'

Suzanne reluctantly took the little box from her dressing gown pocket and handed it to her mother. Simone opened it and stared for a number of seconds, silent. Then she snapped shut the lid and put it in one of the small drawers in her dressing table. Plucking a key from a bone china pot on the dressing table top, she locked the drawer and pocketed the key.

Suzanne watched her mother's actions with disbelief.

'No, Maman,' she protested. 'The ring is mine. My grandmother wanted me to have it.'

'You will give me the letter to finish,' Simone said, turning and stretching out her hand.

There was nothing she could do with her mother in such a mood. Suzanne handed it over. Her mother silently read it, her mouth moving as she did so. Then without warning she tore the sheets in half, then quarters, and tossed the pieces into the wastepaper basket.

'So . . .' Her mother stared at Suzanne, her face contorted with fury. 'The woman has told you everything. She could not respect me enough that I tell my own daughter in my own time.'

'"Respect" seems a funny choice of words in the circumstances,' Suzanne said. 'Well, Maman, you can tear up my private letter all you like.' She forced down the roll of anger.

'But I think I deserve an explanation. I find out I have a French aunt who tells me—'

'Your *aunt*.' Her mother's lip curled on the word. 'She has no right to send this letter from an occupied country. Does she have no idea how dangerous this is?'

Suzanne took a step back. 'What do you mean – dangerous?'

'Because, my dear Suzanne, your father is a resister. He is in the French *Résistance*. And the Gestapo are looking for anyone who resists their abominable *régime*. That is the reason why Marguerite at least had the sense not to mention his name. He would never work for the Nazis. I know – knew him well,' she hastily corrected herself.

'You *knew* him well? Or do you still *know* him?' Suzanne's voice was ice.

'We are no longer in contact.' Simone sniffed and reached for her handkerchief.

Suzanne refused to soften. Maman could put it on when she wanted her own way. 'Then maybe *you* will explain as my *real* father cannot. All my life I've taken for granted that Dad is my father. I find out through a *letter* from this unknown aunt that I have no blood of his flowing in me whatsoever.' Her voice shook with anger. 'Instead, I have the blood of your *lover*!'

'Stop it at once!' Simone pounded her fist on the dressing table. 'How *dare* you speak to me like that!' She fixed her furious gaze on Suzanne.

'I dare, *Maman*—' Suzanne's tone was heavy with sarcasm '—because as you know full well, it happens to be true. But I'd like to know the full story of this *love affair* with—' She broke off, letting out a heavy sigh. 'With whatever his name is.' A dreadful thought occurred to her. 'What about Raine and Ronnie? Are they Dad's? Or have you had other lovers?'

She couldn't stop herself. It was as though a floodgate had opened within her. She didn't care how much she hurt her mother. She only knew the ache in her heart that she'd been deceived all these years would never go away.

'Of course both your sisters are Robert's,' Simone said very quietly.

'So I'm the only odd one out?'

'There is no difference. All remains the same.'

'Remains the same?' Suzanne snorted. 'No, Maman. Nothing is the same. My sisters aren't even my full-blooded sisters.'

'Do not be ridiculous. They are your sisters in every sense of the word. I am the mother of all three of you. My blood flows through your veins. Keep that in your head. And remember it is the family that matters.'

'The *family*.' Suzanne couldn't stop the fury that enveloped her. 'You have no idea about family *or* how to be a loving mother. You've lived a lie, you've made me live a lie – Raine and Ronnie too – you've been deceitful, and worst of all, you've betrayed Dad – who was still the best father in the world. I don't want another one, thank you.'

'Suzanne, you forget yourself. I refuse to discuss the matter while you are in this mood.'

'How do you expect me to be?'

'I expect you to be civil.'

'And I expect you to give me back the ring. I want it, Maman. It's mine.'

Her mother turned and gave a tight smile. 'You will have it back when you tell me you will attend the audition and enrol at the Royal Academy of Music. And you will not mention anything of this letter to your sisters until we speak to them when we are all together. Until that time, I do not want to hear another word from you until you apologise.'

'You will wait a long time for me to do that,' Suzanne said. 'I'm not the one at fault here – you can't force me to promise anything.' She jerked her head away before her mother could see the tears streaming down her cheeks. 'And I won't let you threaten me.'

She closed the door as quietly as she'd entered.

Chapter Sixteen

Suzanne mooched along the village High Street, Rusty leading the way, her mother's words ringing in her ears. She decided she was perfectly justified in speaking to her mother in the way she had. Her mother should have told her about her father long ago.

And what about Dad? Had he known about her mother's affair? If so, how had he come to terms with the fact that his wife was carrying another man's child? Had Maman come clean with him? Had Dad forbidden his wife to go to France again, knowing her lover was probably still waiting for her? Was that the reason why they never went? And what about *his* feelings for the new blonde-haired baby that wasn't his, born less than nine months after his wife returned home? Suzanne swallowed. She tried to put herself in his shoes and could only admire and love him more. He'd never once given any hint that he loved her any less for not having his flesh and blood.

Suzanne shook her head in despair. She needed time on her own to digest all this – away from Maman. She dismissed the fleeting thought that her mother was probably feeling quite shocked herself that her daughter had found her out. Well, that was *her* fault for not being honest.

What should she do about James's birthday? She'd left a

note on the table, not even bothering to sign her name or writing 'Maman' at the top as she usually did, but just a curt message saying she'd be back later, giving no set time or where she would be. Her mother had more or less forbidden her to go, only because she didn't care for Mrs Mortimer's supposed influence on her daughter. But this was merely a simple, innocent invitation to a birthday tea, although the state Suzanne was in, might she put a dampener on the occasion? It could be the last time James would see his mother for several weeks – even months.

But she so wanted to see James again. He was sensible and would know what to say. She stopped abruptly on the pavement. Whatever was she thinking of? She wouldn't dream of telling him that her dad was not her father after all, but that her mother's French lover *was*. No, that secret had to be buried. She mustn't ever let anyone know the shame of it. Oh, how could Maman do such a thing and think it would never be discovered?

She hardly registered Rusty whine as he pulled the lead, desperately trying to strain ahead. It was only when he twisted round and sent her an imploring look and gave a short bark that she slowly began to walk along the High Street again.

How could she spend the next couple of hours before going to the Mortimers'? What about the library? But she couldn't leave poor Rusty outside waiting that long. She'd have to take him home. And then Maman would pounce. No. She was out now, and she wasn't about to go home. Rusty would have to meet James and Mrs Mortimer, that's all.

Suzanne rang the bell, her heart thumping at the thought of seeing James. To her surprise the door was opened by a stocky young man with ginger hair and freckles, and narrow eyes that looked as though they missed nothing as he broke into a beaming smile. She took a step back and Rusty barked.

'Hello. You must be Suzanne. I'm Lance Boswell.' He thrust out his hand. 'Nice dog.'

'It's my sister's. Rusty, stop it!' She looked at Lance. 'I'm early, but I—'

'Oh, don't apologise,' Lance interrupted. 'I'm sure our James will be delighted. Come on in.'

'I'm not sure where to put Rusty. He's quite a good boy at home but he's not used to going in other people's houses.'

'Bring him in. They won't mind at all. They love animals.'

Disappointed she wouldn't get a chance to speak to James on his own – though not about Maman, she reminded herself – she followed him into the hall. She couldn't help noticing his limp and remembered James had told her he'd been sent home with a bad leg wound.

'James'll be down in a mo,' Lance said. 'Mrs Mortimer is in the kitchen if you want to see her. Here, let me have Rusty.'

'Thanks.' Suzanne handed him over. 'I'll go and see her. Maybe I can be of help.'

Suzanne gave a brief tap at the kitchen door and opened it. Beatrice Mortimer's face was a little flushed as she brought out a batch of teacakes from the oven. She shut the oven door and pulled upright, smiling.

'There you are, my dear. I'm so glad you could come.'

'I hope I'm not too early. It's just that I had to get away – have a walk—' Suzanne stuttered. Then to her embarrassment she suddenly broke down in sobs. She fumbled for her handkerchief.

'My dear, whatever's the matter? Here, come and sit down.' Mrs Mortimer pulled out one of the kitchen chairs and took Suzanne by the arm. 'Have you had any lunch?'

Suzanne shook her head. 'No,' she mumbled. 'I—'

'Don't say another word before you've had something to eat,' she said. 'I've just this minute made a pot of tea as Lance – James's friend – can't stay long, so just as well you're early so you can meet him.' Mrs Mortimer cut one of the teacakes open as she chatted.

Suzanne watched, mesmerised, as a curl of steam rose. Mrs Mortimer spread a thin amount of butter over the two pieces, whisked them onto a plate and put it in front of Suzanne.

'You might need to let it cool off a minute,' she said, 'while I pour the tea.'

As she handed Suzanne a cup of tea James put his head in the door.

'Hello, Suzy.' He grinned with pleasure. 'Lance told me you were here. And you've brought Ronnie's dog. He looks in a lot better shape than when I last saw him outside the air-raid shelter – poor little chap.' He paused and came into the room. 'Suzy, are you all right?'

Out of the corner of her eye she saw Mrs Mortimer surreptitiously shake her head at her son.

'She's just going to have a cup of tea first, James. You go and talk to Lance. We shan't be long.'

To Suzanne's relief he nodded after giving her another quick glance of concern before he disappeared.

'I'm sorry . . .' Suzanne began again.

'Don't worry, my dear. Just have your tea and tell me if the teacake has worked. I had to make them without yeast and not as much dried fruit as I'd have liked.'

'It's delicious,' Suzanne said, enjoying the warm, comforting taste. 'Thank you so much. I don't know what's the matter with me – breaking down like that.'

'You haven't had bad news, have you?' Mrs Mortimer said,

when Suzanne had eaten the last crumbs of the teacake and drunk a second cup of tea.

But she could only stare miserably at James's mother. She trusted her without reservation but she didn't want James to know about her mother's infidelity. She might feel it was her duty to tell her son what kind of family Suzanne came from. Suzanne hesitated. It wouldn't be right to involve Mrs Mortimer. If Maman found out her shameful secret was out in public . . . No, she couldn't say anything. No matter how shocking her mother's news, no matter how angry she was, she had to stay loyal. It was what Maman had always drummed into them.

'I expect going to talk to the woman at ENSA is part of the reason,' she said numbly.

'Ah, so you've been to see them? And what did they say?'

'They've offered me a place with the band as a singer.'

'That's wonderful.' Mrs Mortimer beamed. Then her smile faded. 'I suppose you're feeling bad at the thought of stepping into your friend's shoes – is that what's upset you?'

'I suppose it must be,' Suzanne said faintly. Yes, that had been terribly upsetting. But it wasn't the reason today.

'Don't feel in the slightest bit guilty,' Mrs Mortimer said, joining her at the table and sipping her tea. 'She wouldn't want that.'

'I know.' Suzanne swallowed hard. 'And it's James's birthday. I don't want to spoil it.'

'You could never do that.' She studied Suzanne. 'Why don't you go and freshen up. There's a cloakroom off the hall – the furthest door on the right. There's a clean towel out.'

Suzanne gave Mrs Mortimer a quick grateful smile as she got to her feet. Under the tap she rinsed her stinging eyes and dabbed them with the towel, then glanced at herself in the silver-framed mirror above the sink. Her eyes still looked red but they didn't sting so much. Thank goodness she'd put her hair up this morning as it was still in place. Her pink lipstick had faded, though, and she hadn't thought to bring it with her to touch it up.

When she returned to the kitchen she could hear James's amused laughter at something Lance must have said. He had a lovely laugh – rich and infectious. She smiled – the first time since that letter.

Mrs Mortimer gave her a nod of approval and picked up an enamel bowl of pink blancmange and a glass bowl of jelly in the shape of a rabbit. She set them on a tray with a serving spoon, then handed Suzanne a small plate of fairy cakes decorated with hundreds and thousands. 'I know this is children's party food but it's at James's request.' She chuckled. 'So if you're feeling better, shall we lay the table?'

James and Lance were in deep conversation when Mrs Mortimer called them into the dining room.

'Come on, Rusty. You never know. There might be a titbit for you if you're good,' James said as the dog followed him.

'Sit under the table, Rusty,' Suzanne commanded, 'and don't say a word. You must be seen and not heard in Mrs Mortimer's house.'

'He's lovely,' Mrs Mortimer said. 'James told me how your sister rescued him. I expect he's well and truly settled in now.'

'Mmm. With us, but not with our mother,' Suzanne said. 'She doesn't think dogs have any place in the home. But at least she's resigned now that he's here to stay, and Ronnie absolutely adores him.'

'Your young sister's a sweetie,' James said. 'She immediately took him from me when we had that air raid. She said she was going to take him home and try to find out where he came from.'

'She didn't try very hard,' Suzanne quipped, and everyone laughed.

All of a sudden she felt her shoulders dropping and her jaw relaxing. She was in convivial company – even Lance who she could tell was one of James's valued friends. When James brought up the subject of ENSA, Lance was every bit as keen to hear all the details.

'I'm not certain I'll be able to join,' Suzanne said a little hesitantly, taking a bite from her ham sandwich. *What a treat!* It was ages since she'd tasted ham. And mustard too! 'I need permission from my mother because they're going abroad sometime soon, and she's very much against it.' Oh, dear, had she said too much? But surely it was all right as long as she wasn't being specific as to when ENSA was going or where. And as she was hazy on one and had no idea on the other, it must be all right.

'I'm sure your mother will give her permission knowing how much the soldiers appreciate a pretty girl singing to them,' Lance said, giving her a wink.

Suzanne felt her cheeks glow. 'That's just the trouble as far as my mother's concerned.' She tried to lighten the remark with a smile as she stole a glance at James. He was grinning.

'Don't take any notice of Lance,' he said. 'He's a charmer, if ever there was one.'

Lance stayed an hour, then got up.

'I hate to leave you all,' he said, his smile widening as his eyes settled briefly on Suzanne. 'It was particularly good to meet you, Suzanne. I hope it won't be the last time.' He turned to Mrs Mortimer. 'Thanks, Mrs Mortimer, for inviting me. Wouldn't have missed it for anything, but the regiment is calling for me and I must respond. They really can't do without me, more's the pity.'

James sprang up and shook hands with him.

'Best of luck, Boswell,' he said. 'Just be sure you come back in one piece. That means both legs intact.'

'I probably want that even more than you,' Lance grinned. 'Oh, don't come to the door. I can see myself out.'

Mrs Mortimer stood up and began to collect the dirty dishes. When Suzanne made to help her she said, 'No, no. You and James go into the sitting room. It's his birthday and we can't leave him on his own . . . nor Rusty.'

Rusty gave a short bark, making her jump. She'd almost forgotten him. And she'd almost forgotten the afternoon tea was to celebrate James's birthday. If only she'd managed to get him something remotely like a proper birthday present. But he and his mother had been emphatic that she was not to bring anything. She thought of the bookmark tucked in her handbag. She wouldn't give it to him after all. It would be too embarrassing.

'Go and sit on the sofa, Suzy.' James shut the sitting room door and took his place next to her, Rusty sitting at his feet and looking up at him adoringly.

'He's trying to thank you for rescuing him at the air-raid shelter,' she said, giving him a half-smile.

'I'm pleased I did. It was my first introduction to the Linfoot family.'

He wouldn't say that if he knew.

'Then Lance beat me to it by telling you how pretty you look.' He gazed at her appreciatively. 'And you are . . . very pretty.' He smiled. 'Suzy, sit back and relax. You seem all on edge. Is it because of ENSA?'

'I'm worried that I've never sung professionally.' It was all she could come up with.

'I don't think you need to. I bet they thought your voice was perfect.'

'I think they're desperate.' She gave a wry smile.

'Oh, no. They wouldn't have you if they didn't think you were up to it,' he said. 'So is that it – that you haven't taken them up on their offer?'

She hesitated. Somehow she never wanted to tell James a fib, let alone a lie. He was worth more than that. She shook her head.

'No, I'm determined to join now I've spoken to them. I've already met some of the people going, and the pianist helped me a lot with the audition. He was really nice.'

'The pianist, eh?' James was looking at her. 'I hope he doesn't become *too* nice.'

'Not in that way,' she said, smiling, and feeling a tiny twinge of delight that James actually sounded worried. 'He's old enough to be my father.' The word faltered on her lips.

'See that he stays that way,' James grinned and then was immediately serious. His gaze became more intense. 'Suzy, there's something else wrong. Something you're not telling me. You know I'm your friend and you can tell me anything. It won't go further, I promise.'

'There's nothing to tell,' Suzanne said miserably.

'I don't believe it – you're holding back something that's upsetting you. You were crying when I came to the kitchen.'

'I need to get away from my mother,' she blurted. 'That's half the reason why I want to join ENSA now.'

'She's not that bad, surely?'

She turned her head away from him, but he brought her back to face him. The tears fell and angrily she brushed them away.

'What is it?'

Should she? James was looking at her with the same concern as when he'd taken her to the hospital to find out about Wendy and Rosie. She could rely on him. She swallowed hard. 'It's not a nice story.'

'It doesn't matter whether it's nice. You'll feel better when you've told me.'

Maybe he was right. She couldn't face Maman feeling like this.

'I don't know where to start.'

'Plunge straight in,' James said. 'Nothing's so bad when you share it with a friend.'

She cleared her throat. 'I had a letter from a Frenchwoman called Marguerite this morning. She'd put it in a package containing a beautiful diamond ring, which she said was my grandmother's and that my grandmother wanted me to have it. I was surprised as I never knew my mother's parents, but it turns out it was nothing to do with them. Anyway, this Marguerite has a younger brother and—' She stopped. She wasn't sure she could bring herself to say it.

'And?'

'He—' She glanced down at her hands, clenching and unclenching, and let out a shaky breath. Then a storm burst inside her and she put her head in her hands and cried while James held her, saying nothing until she'd cried herself out.

When she finally looked up, the tears still running down her cheeks, he said softly, 'This man must be important.'

'He's important to my mother,' she exploded.

He pulled back at her venom. 'What are you saying?'

'I'm saying he's my *father*!'

James's eyes widened in astonishment. 'Good heavens!'

'Is that all you can say?'

'Hang on, Suzy, don't get mad at *me*. I realise it must be a terrible shock but—'

'You don't understand. My mother had a *lover*! Probably still has, for all I know.' She gritted her teeth. 'She betrayed my dad. It's disgusting. *She's* disgusting.'

'Suzy, don't speak of her that way. You may not be aware

of the circumstances at the time. You shouldn't judge her for something that happened a very long time ago.'

Suzanne shot to her feet causing Rusty to bark. 'You have no idea what you're saying. *Your* family is normal.'

'No family is normal,' James said quietly. 'Come on, Suzy. Sit down.'

'No, I'm going home. I've still got a lot of questions to ask her.'

'I'll come with you.'

'No. Stay here. You're going away Monday so it's not fair to your mother. I'll say goodbye to her. She's always been so kind, but she wouldn't like me if she knew what I've told you – any more than you will when you think about it.'

'You're being really silly.' James stood facing her. 'And if you don't mind my saying so, I think you're being too harsh on your mother.'

'I *do* mind your saying so. You don't know my mother to make any comments on her behaviour.'

'Suzy, listen to me. This isn't anyone's fault. It happened. And it doesn't make me think any the less of you at all, if that's what's bothering you. It makes no difference whatsoever. And if it hadn't been for her . . .' he hesitated '. . . indiscretion, you wouldn't be here. Have you thought of that?'

'I've thought of everything,' she snapped, 'and it *does* make a difference – a *big* difference. Such a difference that I shan't be seeing you any more.'

She could hardly believe what she was saying but the words spewed from her mouth as though she had no control.

'You can't mean what you're saying.'

He went to put his arms around her but she shrugged him off.

'I *do* mean it. Every word.'

James's mouth hardened. 'If that's your wish, I'll see you to the front door.'

Rusty followed, his tail low. She slipped his lead on, then stepped outside, fuming that James had stuck up for Maman. Then she remembered and turned round.

'Will you apologise to your mother? Tell her I wasn't feeling well . . . or something.'

He nodded and shut the door behind her.

If it hadn't been for Rusty she might have rushed back – told him she was sorry. That she didn't mean it. But the little dog strained ahead, knowing he was going home to see his proper mistress.

Chapter Seventeen

Suzanne hung on for dear life to Rusty's lead, keeping her eyes fixed on the small energetic creature in front, her head thick with self-recrimination. She'd been perfectly horrible to James. He'd only been trying to help – she knew that. He didn't deserve the way she'd spoken to him. Sick at heart she felt she was lurching from one calamity to another. And now she had to face Maman.

'And where have you been, Suzanne?'

'I went to James's birthday party.'

'So you have defied me.' Simone's eyes flashed with anger.

'I'm old enough to make my own decisions about a friend inviting me to their birthday party, Maman. You must remember I'm no longer a child.' Her voice was ice cold.

For once, Maman didn't mention Rusty. Suzanne marched past her mother without another word and took him up to Ronnie's room where he went straight into his basket and closed his eyes. She patted his head. He knew Ronnie would be home soon.

Once in her own room, Suzanne peeled off her clothes and pulled on her old skirt and blouse. She ripped the pins from her hair, letting it fall where it may, then sloughed off her shoes and flopped onto her bed. She put her hands behind her head and lay on her back, her mind crammed with thoughts that she didn't like. She'd ruined James's birthday. Whatever must he think of her? What must his mother think of her? They'd never treated her with anything but kindness. How could she have told James she wouldn't be seeing him any more? It was the last thing she wanted. But she'd been so terrified he'd think of her as illegitimate. But he'd said he didn't think any less of her. So why hadn't she taken him at face value? Why was she hurting herself? But if he'd truly meant what he'd said, then why hadn't he insisted on accompanying her home and not simply taken her at her word?

Because you didn't give him a chance, the small voice said. *You were so wrapped up in yourself. How Maman's actions affected* you. *You refused to acknowledge that James was decent. That he'd never divulge your secret. And would never be ashamed of you. Maman's right on one thing – you acted like a bad-tempered, badly behaved child today.*

Oh, James. She bit her lip to try to stop the tears. She'd cried enough in one day and there couldn't possibly be any more tears left. But she was wrong. She turned over and sobbed her heart out into her pillow. Everything had gone wrong and she didn't know how to put things right.

'Suzy, are you coming down?' She felt Ronnie's firm tap on her shoulder and bolted upright.

'What's the time?'

'Suzy! You've been crying!' Ronnie's voice was shocked.

'I haven't had a very nice day.'

'Has this anything to do with Maman?' Ronnie asked.

'Why do you say that?'

'Because she's acting funny. She's ever so quiet, like she's deep in thought. Not like her at all.'

'She's probably got one of her heads,' Suzanne answered. She couldn't dredge up any sympathy for her mother. Her own head felt as though it were full of sawdust.

'No,' Ronnie said. 'It's not that.' She stared at Suzanne. 'Why wasn't your day very nice? Did Maman forbid you to go to James's birthday party?'

'She tried to, but I went anyway. Then I ended up being horrible to him.'

Ronnie's eyes were wide. 'Why on earth . . .?'

'I don't want to go into it.'

'So that's what's upset you. Well, you know the answer.'

'I don't seem to know any answers these days,' Suzanne said wearily.

'You know jolly well what you have to do – you have to bloody well go and see him and apologise before he goes back to his ship.'

'There's no need to swear,' Suzanne reprimanded.

'I *do* need to,' Ronnie shot back. 'James sounds too nice not to fight for. You'd better tell him you're sorry or you'll have me to deal with. Now, come on downstairs. You can help me with supper.'

'I'm not hungry.'

'No, you've had a delicious tea at Mrs Mortimer's. But *I'm* hungry and Maman will be. So don't be so selfish. That's not like you either.'

Supper was a silent affair. Simone picked her way through a small serving of the inevitable stew and Suzanne barely touched hers. Ronnie ate with her usual gusto, but after a minute of chatting and getting little response she finished her meal without speaking.

'I'll wash up,' Suzanne said, standing to clear the dishes. She glanced at her mother whose head was lowered. 'Ronnie, you get on with your homework.'

After a few minutes Simone entered the kitchen.

'I hope you have calmed down,' she said.

'I'm perfectly calm.' Suzanne banged some clean plates onto the rack. She swung round. 'But I have some questions I need to ask.' She plunged straight in. 'Were you *ever* going to tell me that Dad wasn't my real dad?'

'I do not wish to discuss this any further. It is not the right time.'

'When *will* be the right time to discuss him?' She couldn't use the word 'father'. There was only one, and that was Dad.

'I will tell you everything you want to know after the war is over,' Simone said. 'But for now, it is better you know nothing. When the war began that was the decision I made. And when it ends you will be old enough to understand.' She picked up the tea towel and wiped some knives and forks. 'Although I now have doubts you will ever understand.' She put the cutlery in the drawer.

Suzanne was silent for a few moments, consciously taking deep breaths.

'I can't force you,' she said, 'but I want my ring back. Marguerite wants me to have it.' She glared at her mother. 'And those letters she mentioned. They're *mine*, addressed to *me*.'

'I will keep everything safe until the war is over.'

'You can't keep me tied to your apron strings forever. I'm going to join ENSA and I'm asking that you sign the form to give permission for me to go abroad wherever they want me.'

'You are wilful, like Lorraine. I am deeply disappointed.'

Oh, Maman, you don't know how disappointed I am in you.

Her mother's features seemed to droop. She momentarily closed her eyes. 'Very well. I will sign if you promise me one thing also. Your father may be in great danger. He is working for the *Résistance*. For France. And you are French – the same as me. It is your country at stake. So you will always keep him and his identity a secret from your friends . . . even your sisters.'

'But Maman, I don't even know his name—'

Simone held up her hand. 'There will be no argument. Someone might recognise the name of Marguerite. Listen to me, Suzanne. I will let you join this ENSA – if you make the promise.'

Suzanne's heart beat rapidly as her mother's eyes fixed upon her.

But I've already told James my aunt's name.

She bit her lip hard to stop herself from saying the words. James was a man she could trust implicitly. He'd seen how upset she'd been and would have instinctively known she'd taken him into her confidence. But not to tell her sisters? Or at least Raine. It wasn't possible. How could she keep something so important from them? They would never gossip to anyone if she explained how crucial it was to keep it a secret. Did Maman have any idea what she was asking of her? For a dreadful moment it flicked across her mind that her mother was trying to put a wedge between her and her sisters. She fixed her eyes steadily on her mother, not knowing what to answer.

'*Alors*, Suzanne. Do you promise?'

Suzanne hesitated. Her head felt it would burst from all the possible outcomes this promise might cause. But if she didn't do what her mother insisted she would never get away. By promising, she would be able to join ENSA and focus on something worthwhile. Put some miles between her and Maman. And one day read the letters from this stranger who had sent her birthday cards every year and whom she must accept was her father. But only in blood, she fiercely reminded herself. Dad would always be her father and nothing would change that.

But promising her mother not to say a word to her sisters would endanger the one precious thing she put above everything except her music. It was the love and laughter and confidences she and her sisters had shared ever since they were children when Ronnie was only five, Suzanne eight and Raine ten, and had made a pact that they would never keep secrets from one another. And up until now they had never broken it.

That night in bed Suzanne played the same imaginary scene over and over like a stuck gramophone record that Raine and Ronnie would find out one day that she was only their half-sister. Because Maman had forced her into this terrible situation of not being allowed to confide in them. But Raine and Ronnie would sense something, wouldn't they? Suzanne pictured Raine's stricken expression, never forgiving her for keeping a secret of such magnitude that it would have an effect on all their lives.

A shiver ran across her shoulders. It still didn't seem possible that Dad was not her real father.

And then her mother's words resounded in her head:

Your father may be in great danger. He is working for the Résistance. *For France. And you are French – the same as me. It is your country at stake.*

She set her chin. Only for *his* sake would she keep her promise to her mother.

But it was after two before she finally let go and fell asleep, dreaming fitfully of James who informed her it would suit him perfectly if he never saw her again.

Chapter Eighteen

When Suzanne woke early Sunday morning, the sun already making shadows through the blackout curtains, James was the first thing on her mind. What if something happened to him at sea? She would never forgive herself to know they'd parted in anger. And if she were honest the fault lay entirely with her. Even Ronnie had immediately told her what she had to do. She had to apologise before it was too late. Before he sailed tomorrow.

Follow your heart, Dad always said. Well, Dad might not still be around but she was going to follow his advice. She sprang out of bed. She wouldn't even bother with breakfast. She had to see James straightaway. Tell him how sorry she was she'd been so hateful. When she ran over in her mind the things she'd said to him she felt thoroughly ashamed. She'd been about to toss away the one friendship that meant everything in the world to her.

Twenty minutes later she slipped out of the back door.

There were few people about this early. The milkman was finishing his rounds and she could see the village florist working in the back of her shop as she passed, but nothing was open. She kept up a fast pace and hadn't got even halfway before she spotted a dear familiar figure walking towards her, his shoulders hunched, his head bent as though deep in thought. She stopped in her tracks. Then he lifted his head and in that moment, before he was aware of her, she saw his expression of utter dejection. Guilt washed over her as she called out his name.

'James!'

He startled but didn't quicken his pace. It seemed to take an age before he reached her.

'You're out early.' He wasn't smiling.

She flushed, her insides tightening. She hadn't given a thought to the possibility of James wanting to keep things how they'd been left. How *she'd* decided they should be left. How could she have misread him so completely?

'Um, I was . . . I thought I needed some fresh air . . . I should have brought Rusty,' she added, trying to find an excuse but hearing herself sound even more pathetic.

'Yes, he would probably have appreciated it,' James said. He looked her directly. 'Were you going somewhere in particular?'

'Not really.' Oh, why couldn't she be truthful? What was the matter with her? She was turning into a coward.

'Shall I make it easier for you?' James said. He put a light hand on her shoulder. Her heart stopped. 'I think you were coming to see me. Am I right?'

'Yes,' she stammered.

'You know I sail tomorrow?'

'Yes,' she said again. She couldn't think of any more words.

'So you came to say goodbye.'

Her heart jolted. Yes, it would have to be goodbye – he was going away tomorrow. But only goodbye for now. Not forever.

She couldn't drag her eyes from him as he glanced round. More people were appearing on the streets. Housewives with their baskets on their arms, determined to be as close as possible to the front of queues already forming, dog walkers, shopkeepers rattling up shutters from their windows, and a horse pulling a cart clip-clopping by, its owner not unkindly persuading the animal onwards.

'This isn't the right place to talk,' he said. 'The café should be open by now. We'll go there.' He shot her a look. 'Have you had breakfast?'

She shook her head, wishing with all her heart that she could tell what he was thinking.

'Seems I'm always feeding you breakfast,' he said, taking her arm.

The café – even this early in the morning – was full of people, mostly men, smoking. He steered her to a table by the window adjacent to the entrance.

'At least we'll get a breath of air when people go in and out,' he said.

A young girl in a none-too-clean apron came over and he ordered a pot of tea, then looked up from the menu. 'Are the scrambled eggs powdered?' he asked her.

'No, sir,' she said. 'All our eggs are fresh . . . 'cept when we run out, o' course.' She giggled.

James gave the girl a glimmer of a smile, then caught Suzanne's eye. 'Scrambled eggs on toast for you, Suzy?'

'Yes, thank you.' She clung on to the fact that he'd used the friendly diminutive of her name.

The young waitress brought their tea almost immediately and Suzanne took grateful swallows, which almost burnt the back of her throat. She didn't care. James was across the small table from her. That was all that mattered. Unless this really was goodbye. She fought down another wave of guilt until the same girl brought their tea and plates of scrambled egg and she realised how hungry she was.

'Eat,' James said. 'It's far better to talk on a full stomach.'

Some minutes later Suzanne put her knife and fork together on the empty plate.

'Better?' James asked. He'd finished before her and was leaning back a little on the upright chair.

'Much better,' she said, refilling their cups.

'Now, what was yesterday all about?' he said. 'Nothing to do with your mother. I'm talking about your decision for us not to see each other again.'

She wished they were sitting somewhere alone. Anywhere except in the crowded, noisy café. But he was waiting for her answer.

She swallowed hard. 'I shouldn't have said what I did. I suppose I was angry and upset. It's still raw. My mother's confession was such a shock and I was so certain you wouldn't want to—'

'Stop!' He put his hand in the air, drawing a few curious glances from the nearby tables, then brought it down to cover hers. 'You're going to say you thought I wouldn't want to know you after your mother's news – weren't you?'

She bit her lip and nodded, only aware now how her skin tingled from his touch.

'I thought you knew our friendship was special,' he said, so softly she had to lean forward to hear the words. He pressed her hand. 'Didn't you?'

'I thought it was.'

Why was he speaking as though it was now in the past?

'Well, then, if it's special, how can something that happened twenty years ago to your mother possibly alter it in any way?'

She stared miserably at her plate. 'I don't know.'

'Come on,' he said, rising to his feet. 'Let's get out of here.'

It was good to be outside, away from the stuffy, smoky

atmosphere. James took her hand in his as they walked. She didn't care where he was taking her as long as he still held her hand, his fingers strong and warm as they curled round her own.

'I can't be too long,' she said, after a few minutes. 'I didn't leave a note so they'll wonder where I am.'

'I won't keep you out for long,' James said. 'But I want to know why you were coming to see me.'

'I wanted to apologise and . . .' She pressed her lips together.

'And what?' he prompted.

'And tell you I didn't mean it,' she said quickly before her stupid pride took over again. She stopped and looked up at him. His warm eyes held an expression she couldn't interpret. 'I was very rude – and that's not like me.'

'The war is changing all of us,' he said. 'We may not be alive next year, next month, tomorrow . . .'

She shuddered.

'Emotions run high when really it should be a chance for people to be honest with each other. Don't you think?' He ran a finger lightly along her jaw, making her quiver.

'Yes, I do,' she said, trying to keep her voice steady, 'and that's why I'm so upset with my mother for not being honest.'

'I daresay she had her reasons. Life isn't black and white, Suzy. There are swathes of grey areas in between that make things interesting and exciting. People fall in love – sometimes at the wrong time. They can't always think straight and things happen.' He tilted his head towards her. 'Do you know what I'm saying?'

'Yes,' she said in a small voice. 'But I can't just forgive and forget like you're supposed to.'

'Then forgive and remember,' James said. 'That's even more important but possibly more difficult. And if you can't do that, then just forgive. It's your mother we're talking about – not some stranger who doesn't deserve your love.'

Was he right? She needed to think about it.

'We'd better turn for home. You must get back before they send out a search party and I need to do my packing.'

They walked in near silence until they were only a stone's throw from the cottage.

'I don't want you to get into trouble so I'm going to leave you here,' James said. 'Then you can just slip in and no one's any the wiser.'

In a moment he'd be gone. She had to say something – do something. And then she remembered and opened her bag. She'd been too angry yesterday on his birthday when he should have had it. It wasn't wrapped but it would have to do.

'Your mother insisted I bring nothing for your birthday,' she said. 'But I wondered if you'd like this for your book when you're on the ship.' She handed him the bookmark with its purple tassel and the letters 'SL' she'd embroidered.

He stared at it for a full minute and she turned away, thoroughly embarrassed. It was completely the wrong thing to give him and he didn't know how to say it.

'Did you make it?'

'Yes,' she said. 'It's all I could think of. I know you love reading, as I do.'

'I've never had a handmade bookmark,' he said. 'It's lovely. But it's yours. It has your initials.'

'I know. I can't even pass it off as new, can I?' She gave an embarrassed laugh.

'I'll treasure it and think of you every time I get my book out.' He kissed her cheek. 'By the way, how are you getting on with *The Pickwick Papers*? My mother told me you'd borrowed it.'

Suzanne flushed. 'Do you mind?'

'Of course not. I'm delighted. I might have to test you on it, mind.' He sent her a wink.

'I've only read the first hundred pages,' she confessed, her cheeks still warm. She wouldn't tell him that most nights she'd read part of a chapter before sleep overcame her, but whenever she was about to turn her light off, she'd give the book a tender kiss. He'd think her completely soppy.

'Don't forget me, Suzy.'

'I won't.'

'And you promise to write?'

'Yes, I promise.'

He looked at her, then put both arms round her and held her to him. She could feel the steady beat of his heart. He tilted her chin. Unconsciously, she parted her lips and he lowered his head.

A door noisily opened.

'Suzanne! Where have you been? I was worried to death. Come in at once!'

James laughed. 'Don't look so cross, Suzy. That's mothers for you. She's just protecting you.' He looked towards Simone and smiled. 'Here she is, Mrs Linfoot, safe and sound. Please don't blame her – it was all my fault for taking her out for breakfast on my last day.'

He swiftly kissed Suzanne on the forehead and before she could answer he'd vanished from sight.

'Before I sign I must speak to someone who is in charge of this entertainment group,' Simone said, as she spread the mixture of butter and margarine on her toast at her usual late breakfast that morning.

Suzanne unconsciously tensed her back. She shouldn't be surprised that Maman was making a further condition. It was probably to be expected. To be fair, her mother was already worried about Raine's safety flying aeroplanes – war or no war – and now her second daughter was about to travel to some foreign place that might prove dangerous, too.

Keeping her tone calm, she said, 'That would be Miss Foster.'

'Where is her telephone number?'

'I don't have it. But the operator will put you through.'

After what seemed like an age Suzanne heard her mother say good afternoon to Miss Foster. She heard a murmuring from the other end, and her mother ask what country they would be going to.

'So you cannot tell me where my own daughter will be living?' Maman's lips clamped together in frustration as she cocked her head to wait for Miss Foster's reply.

'I see.' Her mother shook her head.

Maman didn't 'see' at all, Suzanne thought resignedly. Well, there was nothing she could do to influence what her mother would say, so rather than be on tenterhooks in the hallway she decided to go and say hello to Rusty.

Ten minutes later her curiosity got the better of her and she came back into the house.

'I have been calling you,' Simone said when she walked into the sitting room. 'I have spoken to Miss Foster. She seems a sensible woman. And she has promised you will be guarded day and night. So I will sign the form.' She gave Suzanne a sharp glance. 'That is, if you will keep *your* promise not to tell your sisters our discussion.'

'I promised, Maman, and I will keep to it,' Suzanne said.

What on earth would she say if she knew her daughter had already spilled her secret to James Mortimer?

Chapter Nineteen

Now, Suzanne stood dazedly in front of a huge map of the world in one of the offices of the Theatre Royal in Drury Lane. Where would they be sending her? A frisson rushed through her as she studied the different countries. She almost wished today was the day she'd be travelling abroad, but no one knew yet when that was likely to be.

A plain girl with spectacles and a shy smile knocked and came in.

'Miss Linfoot?'

'Yes?'

'Please come with me. They're ready to fit you for your uniform.'

Suzanne's eyes widened. It was the first she'd heard about wearing a uniform. She followed the girl along a corridor to a separate room where a balding man was doling out what looked like skirts from shelves stacked with various items of clothing to another young woman with the brightest red hair Suzanne had ever seen. The woman looked up as Suzanne walked in.

'Hello,' she said with a smile, her freckled nose crinkling. 'I'm Betty Graham. Who're you? Which troupe are you in? Are you going abroad? What do you do? I'm with George Johnson's band. I play the sax. Leaving in a fortnight, though it's all a big secret where we're off to. I do think they should tell us so we know what to pack.' She paused for breath and giggled. 'Sorry, love, I always do this. Don't let people get a word in. I'll shut up and let you speak.'

'I'm with the same band . . .' Suzanne started.

'Before you have your cosy chat, miss, would you please let me finish giving you your uniform so I can help someone else.' The balding man rolled his eyes.

'Oh, of course.' Betty shook out one of the khaki garments and frowned. 'Oh, they're shorts. I thought it was going to be a tunic and skirt.'

'You'll have a skirt for any formal occasion,' the man said. 'But you'll be going to a hot country – no doubt about that.'

'Do you know where we're headed?' Betty asked.

'No. And if I did, I wouldn't tell you. No one ever knows until they arrive. Not even us here. You've been through security regulations, I take it?'

'Not yet,' Suzanne said quickly, 'but we do know everything has to be kept secret.'

Betty pulled a face. 'Well, I just hope it won't be too hot,' she said, turning to Suzanne. 'I always go bright red with my skin.'

Suzanne gave her a sympathetic smile as the supplies man reached behind the counter. 'Now, Miss Linfoot—' he removed a stubby pencil from behind his ear and ticked something on his notepad '—I have you down for the same outfit as Miss Graham.' He reached for two short-sleeved khaki shirts, two pairs of the long shorts and one skirt, then removed a short-sleeved tunic and held it in front of her. He nodded. 'This size should do.'

He added a tie, two pairs of socks, and plonked a couple of peaked caps on the counter. 'One each,' he said, jerking his head towards Betty who stuck it on her head immediately.

'How do I look?'

'You look very smart,' Suzanne said, chuckling. 'I feel I should be saluting you.'

'Is there a mirror?' Betty asked the supplies man.

'Not in here,' he said with a slight curl to his lip. 'Maybe in one of the dressing rooms. If you're ready, then you can go next door for your shoes. Make sure they fit – not too tight as your feet will swell in the heat and you won't get a second choice.'

'I didn't even know we'd be wearing uniforms – ENSA's not the military,' Suzanne ventured.

'I'll tell you why, young lady.' He caught her eye. 'It's so you don't get arrested and shot as spies.'

'What!' Betty's eyes were wide with alarm as she stared at him from under the peaked cap with its ENSA insignia pinned above a large flat bow.

'That's Jerry for you. If you're captured and you're in officer's uniform – which these are—' he nodded to the pile of clothes '—at least you'll be treated properly. If you go off course and was in frocks, they'll assume you're up to no good . . . next thing you know, they've pulled the trigger.'

Suzanne's scalp prickled. Thank goodness Maman was not here to listen to this. She would have steered her out of the door there and then.

'Oh, surely that's an exaggeration.' Betty giggled nervously as she pulled off the cap and shook out her red curls. 'Are you really saying we're now officers? That we're allowed to go in the officers' mess?'

The supplies man nodded. 'That's right. But don't take my warning lightly. It's not an exaggeration. Ask anyone.' He acknowledged a grey-haired man who'd just walked in. 'Sorry, ladies. I need to help this gentleman.'

'Thank you,' Suzanne said over her shoulder as she and Betty left, their arms full of khaki clothing.

'I didn't think we'd be that close to the enemy,' Betty said quietly, her voice trembling a little.

'Well, we've chosen to entertain the boys who're close to them, so we must be taking some risk,' Suzanne said. She glanced at Betty. 'I suppose we could pull out now – go back home and forget it.'

'Are you going to?'

'No.' Suzanne's voice was firm.

'Nor'm I,' Betty said, but she didn't sound quite so convinced. Then she brightened. 'Still, at least we'll be together.'

After they'd chosen their shoes and boots, they were taken to see a nurse for their vaccinations.

'What do we have to have?' Suzanne asked.

'Yellow fever and typhoid,' the nurse said as she took one of Suzanne's arms and dabbed it with something cold, smelling of rubbing alcohol. She barely felt the needle go in.

'Now the other arm,' the nurse said. A few moments later she looked up and smiled. 'There. All done.'

'I really hate this,' Betty said from behind her, rolling up her sleeve, as the nurse prepared the next syringe.

'Just think what the men are going through getting shot at every day,' Suzanne said soberly. 'They'd probably give anything just to have a needle stuck in them instead.'

No sooner had she uttered the words than there was the sound of a groan and a heavy thud. Suzanne swung round. Betty was on the floor in a dead faint.

'I should take her to the café for a strong, sweet cup of tea,' the nurse said to Suzanne after she'd gently pulled Betty up into a sitting position and they'd helped her onto a chair. 'I'll get you some water, love, and you'll be right as ninepence.'

She went over to the washbasin and ran a small cup of water and handed it to Betty.

'But you've still got to give me the jab,' Betty stuttered, as she took a few sips, her orange freckles standing out like bright dots of paint.

'Don't worry, love. I did it while you were asleep. You wouldn't have felt a thing, so off you go. Turn right out of here and along the corridor. Your nose should guide you – or the rattle of the cups.'

Suzanne took Betty's arm, sensing the girl was still shaky, as they made their way to the café. A few people were sitting at tables, and one or two looked up curiously, then resumed their conversation. When Suzanne had settled Betty, she went to the counter and bought two cups of tea and a few Rich Tea biscuits.

'You must think me daft being so scared of a needle,' Betty said, as soon as Suzanne put the tray on the table and set the tea in front of her.

'I don't at all,' Suzanne said. 'I felt really sorry for you. But better that than risk getting a horrible illness.'

'I s'pose you're right,' Betty said, taking great gulps of her tea.

'Well, at least your colour's come back.'

'I feel all right now. Thanks for the tea.' Betty smiled and crunched through a biscuit, then let her gaze linger on Suzanne. 'I don't even know your name.'

'You haven't given me a chance,' Suzanne chuckled. She felt she was going to like this Betty with her outright manner. 'It's Suzanne Linfoot.'

Betty blinked. 'Oh, very posh. Mind if I call you Suzy?'

'No, I don't mind,' Suzanne laughed. 'My sisters always do, and my friend, Wendy.' She gulped. *And James.*

'Then we're friends already,' Betty said, grinning. 'What do you play?'

'The violin, but they auditioned me as a singer. I'm not at all experienced,' she added apologetically. 'What about you?'

'I play the sax,' Betty said. 'You know, Suzy, I expect this is going to be something quite different, playing to really big audiences – out in the open.' She looked at Suzanne, her grin back in place. 'All men.' She gave an exaggerated wink. 'We shouldn't have much trouble getting ourselves a boyfriend.'

'I'm not joining up to find a boyfriend,' Suzanne said, hating herself for sounding so prim.

Betty's eyes widened. 'Oh, that must mean you already have one. Do tell. I want to know every detail.'

Suzanne felt her cheeks flush. The trouble was, she wasn't used to blurting out personal things to strangers. She'd always had her sisters to talk things over with if she couldn't work it out herself. But being away, heaven knew how many thousands of miles from them, her life was bound to be so different that it would be hard for them to understand, let alone give advice. Now she had the extra burden of carrying a secret that affected the whole family, and Maman had made her swear not to breathe a word. A rush of resentment for her mother putting her in such a position forced her to look away from Betty.

'You're blushing,' Betty pounced, clapping her hands. 'You're obviously courting. Do you have a photo of him?'

'I'm not courting,' Suzanne said firmly, willing the image of James to disappear and the rush of blood to her cheeks to subside.

'But you have your eye on someone,' Betty said, her mouth drooping with disappointment, then catching Suzanne's steady eye she giggled. 'I shall only think we're real friends if you let on.'

'There's nothing to say,' Suzanne replied, feeling a little guilty that she wasn't being completely honest. She smiled. 'But I promise you'll be the first to know if anything changes.'

Chapter Twenty

The days dragged by, Suzanne still churned up about her mother's love affair that she'd only admitted when faced with the evidence in Marguerite's letter.

James was wrong about forgiveness. No matter how Suzanne tried to act normally with her mother, she felt uncomfortable, as though she was playing a part. Equally, Maman didn't open up any further conversation about the Frenchman. Maybe it was the only way to get through this, Suzanne thought. She couldn't wait to get away.

One evening Betty telephoned her and Simone took the call.

'It's a friend of yours – Betty somebody. She says she's one of the musicians.' Her mother gave her a stern look. 'Which is what *you* should have been instead of this singing nonsense.' She made the word 'singing' sound like something unimaginably coarse as she shook her head and handed the receiver to Suzanne.

'Oh, Suzy, you know on our list of things to take with us?'

'Yes – I haven't got mine all together yet, have you?'

'No, not all. But did you notice there's no mention of bunnies?'

'Bunnies?' Suzanne frowned.

'Yes, you know – sanitary towels.'

She'd never heard them called 'bunnies' before and was glad Betty couldn't see the telltale flush of her ignorance.

'Oh, yes . . . of course.' She didn't want to admit she hadn't given them a thought. But Betty was right. Where they were going – maybe even in the desert – they might not be able to buy them.

'I'm taking some with me, in case,' Betty said. 'And I suggest you do the same. We don't want to get caught out,' she laughed.

Suzanne couldn't help smiling into the receiver. 'Thanks for the tip, Betty. I'll be sure to bring some extra . . . bunnies.'

'Good. I'm glad I remembered. But heaps more interesting than bunnies – have you bought your clothes yet? You'll be needing special evening things, being a singer.'

ENSA had confirmed they would be providing a small wardrobe for the performers as well as the uniform. They'd sent clothing coupons to Suzanne with a letter requesting her to buy the necessary items for a posting in a warm country, and to include two evening gowns. This was the perfect opportunity to heal some of the tension between her and her mother, because Suzanne had to admit Maman's taste was impeccable when it came to clothes. Excitement gripped her once more.

'Suzy, are you still there?'

Suzanne brought herself up sharply. 'Yes, Betty, I'm still here . . .'

Betty chatted on a bit longer but Suzanne was already dreaming of her not one, but two glamorous gowns. Up until now, she'd never owned anything remotely resembling an evening dress.

* * *

As soon as Suzanne made her promise to her mother, Simone immediately took charge of what clothes she'd be taking.

'We'll go to Bromley,' her mother said. 'That is where we will find everything.'

But there was little variety in the shops and what there was seemed terribly expensive when Suzanne totted up the value of the coupons. And if she really was to go on the stage and sing – a shiver of fear replaced her earlier excitement – she would have to look the part, as Maman always insisted.

Her mother was in her element and although complaining at the lack of choice, her eye alighted on exactly the right cream skirt of crisp cotton, teamed with three short-sleeved blouses, two colourful patterned ones and the other white with a V-neck and pretty pearl buttons. Two cardigans completed the sets.

'We will have a coffee, and then buy the evening gowns,' her mother told her.

This proved a far more difficult purchase. Time and time again Maman spotted something beautiful and looked at the label, wincing as she put it back.

'We will go to Garlands,' she announced as she drained her coffee.

Suzanne's heart sank. Raine had worked in that dress shop for a few months while she was waiting to join the ATA, and wasn't keen on Mrs Garland, the owner. She'd been mean with Raine when it came to giving her any commission, even though she admitted she'd never had such a good salesgirl who would often model the clothes to a hesitant customer, and so clinch the sale.

'Isn't Mrs Garland even more expensive?' Suzanne said.

'Yes, but she will allow me a discount.'

'I'm sorry, Maman, but I really don't want to buy the

dresses in Garlands. She caters for the older woman with plenty of money. And besides, she's a gossip.'

Maman frowned. 'You are talking of my good friend, Suzanne.'

'I know, and I'm sorry.'

'Maybe we are both tired, *chérie*. We will have a second trip to Bromley next week. We have time.'

It was gone nine in the evening when the telephone rang. Maman sprang up to answer it, grumbling as to who could be phoning at such a late hour. In her haste she left the door open and after some moments Suzanne heard Maman say:

'But I am her mother. You may tell me.' Then a half a minute's pause. 'Very well. I will fetch her.' She called from the hallway. 'Suzanne, it is your Miss Foster. She would like to speak to you.'

Her mother sounded peeved. What could have gone wrong?

With beating heart she picked up the receiver, aware of her mother behind her.

'Suzanne?'

'Yes, Miss Foster.'

'Change of plan. The date has been moved.'

Oh, no. A delay would mean more difficulty with her mother in this mood, obviously annoyed Miss Foster hadn't confided in her.

'I'm sorry this is such short notice but we are leaving tomorrow evening. So please be here at the theatre by 3 p.m. latest.'

'Um, I haven't—'

'There isn't a problem, is there?'

'N-no.'

'Good. I will see you tomorrow. Please be prompt.'

The receiver clicked.

She hadn't had a chance to tell Miss Foster that she hadn't yet bought her two evening gowns. There wouldn't be time to go into Bromley tomorrow. She'd have enough to do to go to the chemist and the village shop to buy the rest of the items Miss Foster had included before she caught the train to London in good time.

'I am not so sure of this Miss Foster after all,' Maman said with pursed lips when Suzanne explained the reason for the call. 'You cannot stand on a stage unless you have the appropriate dress. You must tell this woman you cannot go after all.'

'There must be something that would do until I find the right one,' Suzanne said desperately. Surely her mother couldn't stop her now it was this close. 'Oh, I know. I can take the flowered one I made when Raine and I went out together that time.'

That evening seemed a long time ago. Such a lot had happened since then. She'd been a young girl. Now she'd grown up and was ready to do her bit.

'That is a summer dress,' Maman said, her lip curling. 'It is pretty but not suitable at all for the evening. You have been given the instruction to buy two gowns – and you will go with not even one.'

'I'm sure something will turn up when I'm out there – wherever I'm going,' Suzanne said firmly. 'I doubt the soldiers will bother that I'm not in full evening dress after what they go through every day.'

'Nevertheless, I will find you something.'

Suzanne was up in her room by the time her mother briefly knocked on her door and swept in with several dresses over her arm. Suzanne recognised a couple of them – they'd been glamorous in their time but Maman had had them long before Dad lost his money and they'd been forced to move to Downe. Besides, her mother's figure was different altogether. For a start, Maman was shorter with a more generous bust and hips. No, she couldn't possibly wear her mother's dresses.

Maman's face was concentrated as she separated the gowns and laid them on what used to be Raine's bed.

'Maybe this one.' She held up a heavily sequined royal blue dress with a deep neckline and long sleeves.

Suzanne's heart plummeted. Maman always looked wonderful in her clothes. She had that marvellous French deportment, but this one would look hideous on her. She desperately fished for an excuse.

'Maman, we're going to a hot country so I don't really want long sleeves. And I don't think you'd approve of such a plunging neck on me.'

Her mother narrowed her eyes, then studied the dress, then looked at Suzanne. 'Hmm. I always fill this out in a feminine way but maybe you are a little young for something so sophisticated.' She selected another one. 'Try this one.'

The dress was black in a lightweight satin, relieved by a moss-green border at the cowl neckline, which formed cap sleeves. The same colour edged the deep-cut back that ended in a small flat-tied bow. The dress was narrow and closely followed the curve of a woman's hips before it fell in swinging sections to the ankles.

'I've never seen you in this,' Suzanne said. 'It's rather lovely.'

'It was a mistake. I was not tall enough to carry it off. But Robert . . . Dad . . . chose it for a special evening and I did not want to hurt his feelings. But you are taller. I think it will look very elegant. And you are an excellent seamstress.

You will make it fit properly.' She picked up the other dresses. 'Come with me to my room and see in the mirror. It will give you the idea.'

Suzanne followed her mother into the bedroom and held it up against herself as she looked in the mirror. Strangely enough, the black didn't make her look old at all with her fair skin and blonde hair. The dress would be fairly straightforward to alter, she thought, and fashions for evening wear hadn't changed that much since the Thirties.

'Will you be happy to wear a gown of your *maman*?'

'I don't mind,' Suzanne said.

Was Maman trying to call a truce? Well, if she was, it wasn't going to work.

Suzanne hardened her heart.

'You know I still do not approve of this singing.'

'I know, Maman, but I feel happy that I'm finally doing something.'

Her mother nodded and for once said nothing more.

Back in her own room, Suzanne gathered the items she needed to pack, remembering to take her sewing kit and checking there was enough black cotton to alter Maman's dress. Then she reached under the bed for her suitcase, the one she'd used when they'd moved house a few years ago. It was really Dad's. A canvas one with leather corners and a leather strap. They'd given it to him in the last war when he was demobbed. She opened it and immediately imagined she could smell the scent of him.

What would he say if he could see her now? Would he be disappointed that she hadn't carried on with her music; refused to attend such a fine music school in London? Or would he be proud she was finally making a practical contribution towards the war effort? She didn't have to think very hard. He would be proud. He always told her to follow her heart – it would never let her down. And this was exactly what she was doing.

James's face suddenly dipped into the foreground. She hoped it wouldn't be too long before he wrote.

Suzanne dreaded saying goodbye to her mother who she knew was still against her going, but now it was time to face the inevitable.

'I'm off now, Maman,' she said as she stepped into her mother's bedroom.

Her mother looked up with tear-stained eyes. For a moment Suzanne softened. Should she say something? She hated to leave her mother like this.

'I am sorry I . . .'

Maman was apologising for not telling her about her French father? Suzanne stood stock still, ready to put her arms around her mother. Forgive her.

'. . . that I am not successful to make you see sense about this ridiculous notion of singing . . .'

Suzanne closed her eyes against any further reprimand.

'Goodbye, Maman. I'll write when I arrive.'

She gave a perfunctory kiss to her mother's proffered cheek, then closed the door behind her. Who was she trying to kid? Maman would never change.

'You're doing the right thing,' Ronnie said when Suzanne came downstairs. 'I almost wish I was going with you – I would if I could sing,' she added with a giggle.

Suzanne chuckled. 'You'd hate every minute,' she said, ruffling her sister's short curls. 'You're always ready for bed at nine o'clock, which is probably the time I'll be starting work.'

'I know,' Ronnie said, sombrely. 'It's just that you and Raine seem to be having all the fun.'

'Your turn will come,' Suzanne said. 'But in the meantime you have Rusty to look after – and Maman, of course.' She winked at Ronnie.

Ronnie pulled a face. 'I shall keep out of her way as much as I can. Thank goodness I've got the vegetables to look after.' Her eyes filled with sudden tears as the full force of her sister's departure took hold. 'You will write often, won't you?'

'Of course I will.' Suzanne hugged her. 'But Raine says she only hears from you occasionally. I could be thousands of miles away so I'll want to hear all the news and gossip, and how you both are. I know I'll get homesick so I want you to promise to write regularly. Will you do that?'

'All right,' Ronnie said. 'I promise.'

'I'd better go now or I'll miss my train.' She gave Ronnie a last hug. How she'd miss her. 'Oh, Ronnie, one thing.' She held out a letter. 'Could you please deliver this letter to Mrs Mortimer – you know, James's mother. It's just to tell her I'm going away and that as soon as I know where I am, I'll drop her a line.'

'Have you heard anything from James?' Ronnie asked curiously.

Suzanne felt her cheeks warm. 'No, not yet.'

But when she stepped out of the front door with her suitcase, Micky, the ginger-haired post boy, was leaning his bicycle against the wall, on his rounds delivering the second post.

'Three today,' he said. 'One for your mother. I think it's from that pilot sister of yours.' He looked at the second one. 'One from her for you, too. And one more for you,' he added, staring at the third envelope. 'Funny.' His forehead wrinkled. 'I don't know this writing.'

'Thank you, *post boy*,' Suzanne said firmly, reminding him of his job. She stretched her hand out to take the letters from him, her heart beating furiously, as she glanced at the envelope.

Yes, it was from James. She recognised the writing from his note in the Charles Dickens book. She smiled to herself. His writing had hardly changed. Tucking her two letters into her handbag she ran back up the path.

'Ronnie,' she called. 'There's a letter from Raine for Maman. I'll leave it on the hall table. Must rush. Bye.'

Chapter Twenty-One

There was no space anywhere on the train to London for Suzanne to even open her letters, let alone read them, squeezed in the corridor amongst the standing crowds of servicemen and women, several men in RAF uniforms with their pilots' wings and stripes displayed on their uniforms. How proud Raine must have been when she'd been given her wings. What good timing to receive her letter today. She smiled at the image of her older sister coming back from one of her deliveries and settling at a table in the crew room to write as much news as she was allowed. Well, she wouldn't be doing anything near as risky as Raine.

She shifted her suitcase a fraction towards the window to give the RAF chap next to her a little more standing room for his feet. He blew out a stream of smoke above her head and smiled at her. She tried to smother a cough as she shyly smiled back.

'Going anywhere nice?' he said, jerking his head towards the case.

'I don't know.'

He raised his eyebrows. 'Really? How's that?'

'I'm a singer with ENSA,' Suzanne said, then worried as to whether she was allowed to even say that much.

'Every Night Something Awful,' he grinned, looking down

at her with twinkling eyes, reminding her a little of James. 'Didn't you know that's its real name?'

'The real name is Entertainment National—' Suzanne began.

'Yes,' the pilot interrupted, still grinning. 'I know that's its proper name, but everyone calls it by the more descriptive one.' His gaze lingered on her face. 'Only teasing.' He paused. 'So you're a singer?'

'Yes. I'll be singing in a band.'

He looked impressed. 'Then I hope I'll be stationed somewhere nearby so I can hear you.' He hesitated. 'So you don't know exactly where you'll be going?'

'No,' she answered, immediately conscious of ENSA's security measures. 'Only that it's abroad. And even if I knew, I wouldn't tell you.'

He grinned. 'I wasn't testing you, but you're right. But just in case I see you again, I should introduce myself. Flight Lieutenant Phil Havers at your service.' He paused as he glanced around. 'I'd bow to you if there was room.'

She couldn't help smiling at his nonsense. 'Suzanne Linfoot. Pleased to meet you.'

At that moment the train came to a juddering halt with a screech of brakes, throwing her against him. He put a steadying hand on her arm. 'Careful, Miss Linfoot, you don't want to go throwing yourself at strange men.' When the blood flared to her cheeks, he said, 'Sorry, I couldn't resist that. And now I've made you blush.'

'It's not that – it's terribly hot in here,' she said, trying to cover up her embarrassment. Oh, dear. She had a lot to learn about men.

They chatted some more – or rather Phil did – until the train slowed right down with much grinding and squealing of brakes. 'Well, Miss Linfoot, it looks like we've arrived in

London, so I wish you all the best, and hope we might meet again one day.'

'I hope so,' she said politely.

But the only man with twinkling eyes she wanted to meet again was James Mortimer. She swallowed. How long would he be at sea? What if a U-boat attacked them? What if he got ill? What if . . .?

Stop it!

All kinds of things could happen but probably wouldn't. She had to hold on to that thought. At least she had a letter from him tucked into her handbag. Somehow it made her feel closer to him – gave her hope. She smiled back at Phil Havers. Anything could happen to him too.

'Good luck,' she said, extending her hand when they were on the platform.

'You, too, Miss Linfoot.' He gave it a quick squeeze and she watched as he disappeared into the crowd.

Suzanne pushed the door of the theatre open to a buzz of conversation. She could hear her heart beating in her chest. It would be the first time she'd meet the rest of the band.

She needn't have worried. Bram introduced her to the band of ten musicians, who all smiled and nodded in a friendly way. Just as she was trying to remember all their names, Betty stormed in.

'I'm sorry I'm late,' she said. 'Oh, good, Suzy, you're here. It was all such a rush with having to get packed so sudden and I haven't got half the things on the list – not even the bun—' She stopped short and giggled. 'Well, never mind that. I expect we'll all manage. Does anyone know yet where we're off to?'

'All will be revealed when we arrive,' Bram smiled. 'You'll

have to get used to everything being kept secret until the last minute.'

An hour passed. Suzanne fidgeted, wondering how long it would be before Miss Foster told them what was happening. For the moment, all she could think of were her letters she'd not had time or privacy to read.

'Betty,' she whispered, 'I need to visit the ladies.'

'Okay, but we might be asked to suddenly do a rehearsal so don't be long.'

'I won't.'

She found the ladies' cloakroom and pushed open the door at the same time as an elegant black woman was about to leave. The woman nodded, giving her a radiant smile as she held the door open. Suzanne, feeling overwhelmed, only just remembered her manners and smiled back as she thanked her.

Thankfully, there was no one else in the cloakroom. Suzanne sat on a gold-trimmed theatre seat someone had thoughtfully placed outside the cubicles and took the letters from her bag.

Please don't let anyone come in until I've read them. Raine's first.

She unfolded a sheet of paper with her sister's familiar large-looped writing.

21st May, 1943

Dear Suzy,

Thanks for your letter about joining ENSA and sorry it's taken me so long to reply. Hope you receive this before you leave. Am so proud of you for standing up to Maman and making that decision. And you're now a singer! Well, well. Saying that, you do have a gorgeous voice – don't know why we've never thought of you singing professionally before. The boys are going to be bowled over with you!

I've been flying all over the country but am terribly envious you're going abroad. Can't wait to hear where they're sending you, though I may have to wait a long time for that reply as post will be very slow and your letters are sure to be censored.

Ronnie seems happy enough at the moment and thank goodness Maman has allowed her to keep Rusty (after a fashion). Neither of them write very often – Ronnie because she hates sitting down and writing letters and Maman because she's still not pleased with me, although I think she's now resigned to the fact that I'm not leaving the ATA until the war's over – whenever that is. You're definitely the most regular letter writer, so please keep up the good work. I love hearing from you and am longing to hear about the band and your songs.

Wouldn't Dad be proud of his daughters? If only he hadn't died. Sixty was no age really.

Well, I'd better close for now and will just end with two words. Good Luck!

Raine X

Suzanne's eyes filled with tears. Dearest Dad. Yes, he would be proud. For a fleeting moment she thought of the Frenchman – a man out there somewhere who happened to be her father. A tear trickled down her cheek. The war was making everything impossible. People she loved were now far away. And one in particular whom she'd so wanted to hear from . . .

She tore open James's envelope, inwardly smiling at the image of Dad reprimanding her for not using a paper knife.

Normally, she was as meticulous as him, she thought, as her eyes drank in the first lines.

20th May, 1943

Dear Suzy, (I hope you don't mind me calling you Suzy as it rather suits you, especially if you are to be a singer!)

I've been really busy so apologies for not writing sooner. I wanted to get this off before we sail tomorrow. When we're at sea it's difficult to write letters and be able to send them, but when we stop in a safe port we can collect and send post. If that doesn't happen it's not unknown for a pilot leaving for England to be bombarded with requests to take any letters with him, so one way or the other I'm hoping my letters to you will be delivered. I can't say anything about where we'll be heading, more's the pity.

I'm longing to know how you are. If you joined ENSA you may even now be rehearsing. You might even be sent abroad. If so, I wish I knew where!

Keep safe wherever you are and whatever you do. This war will be over one day and I'd like to think we'll see each other again.

Please write when you can. Any news of home, however ordinary you might think it is, would be very welcome.

Yours,

James

She read the letter again, more slowly so she didn't miss anything. He'd be at sea by now. What if they ended up in the same place? But even if they did, it was highly unlikely they would meet. He was bound to his ship, for one thing.

And anyway no one had said or even hinted where *they* were heading. Betty had asked Miss Foster outright, but she'd said they would have to get used to not knowing until they arrived if they were serious about belonging to ENSA. All their movements had to be top secret.

'It's so that the enemy doesn't get hold of any information if they sink us,' Miss Foster explained grimly.

Suzanne's stomach fluttered. She hadn't actually given being sunk any real thought. But of course it was possible. Anything was. She just had to hope for the best, like everyone else.

Suzanne folded the letter a little uncertainly, not sure what to make of it. James sounded somehow distant in his letter when she compared it to that terrible day he'd taken her to Bromley hospital. When the news had been so shocking about poor Wendy, he'd been so understanding . . . so affectionate, although she'd hardly appreciated it at the time. She remembered how he'd kissed her forehead, and held her in his arms, doing his best to comfort her. And he had. She didn't know what she would have done without him.

Then Sunday when she'd apologised to him he'd instantly forgiven her. When they'd stood near to home and he'd taken her in his arms, she'd been sure he was going to kiss her. If it hadn't been for Maman interrupting . . .

Next time they met she would make sure it happened. She would kiss *him*.

Her cheeks flamed with the idea.

But was she reading things between the lines that weren't even there? After all, he'd only asked her to write when she could. And at the first opportunity she'd do just that. But now it was time to go back to Betty and the others.

She found Betty talking to other ENSA people at the theatre bar. One woman stood out from the crowd even though she was seated. But it wasn't only her dark skin that drew Suzanne's eye. Her face glowed with animation, and her wide-apart brown eyes shone with a brilliance as she laughed with two of the musicians, drawing attention to her mouth, boldly painted in ruby red. She was the same woman who had held the cloakroom door for her at the theatre.

'I wonder who she is,' Betty muttered with awe.

'Oh, I've met her already,' Suzanne said casually, then laughing at Betty's look of astonishment. 'But we could go and say hello.'

The unknown woman glanced up as Suzanne approached her table, Betty for once hanging back, dumbstruck. The woman's smile was wide, showing gleaming white teeth.

'Hi, honey,' she said, then smiled. 'Oh, we bumped into each other just now.' Still smiling, she glanced behind Suzanne. 'Bring your friend and come and sit with us?' She patted a vacant seat with an elegant hand. 'Tell me your names.'

'I'm Suzy Linfoot, and this is Betty Graham.'

The woman grinned and stuck her hand out. 'Pleased to meet you both. Adelaide Hall.'

Suzanne's jaw dropped. 'Not the famous jazz singer?'

Adelaide beamed. 'Well, whaddya know! You've heard of me.' She threw her arms in the air and laughed with joy.

'I've heard you sing on the wireless. I love your voice but I've never seen a picture of you so I wouldn't have been able to recognise you. I can't believe you're here in person and—' Suzanne broke off, flustered. Whatever would Miss Hall think of her, babbling on like that? She gathered herself together. 'Are you travelling with us, Miss Hall?'

'Oh, do call me Adelaide . . . everyone does. Say, is there anyone serving around here?'

Suzanne glanced round at Betty, amused to see her friend's mesmerised gaze was still fixed on the famous jazz singer.

'I must say I'm hungry,' Betty said, eventually finding her voice. 'We haven't eaten since noon and that was only a sandwich.'

'We need to hang around to hear our instructions first,' Adelaide said in a relaxed tone.

Finally, Miss Foster came in and clapped her hands. The café fell silent.

'Everyone in the band, would you please listen carefully. The coach that was to take us to the station has broken down. They will try and send us another one but if not, we will have to wait for it to be repaired.' She looked at her watch. 'We don't know how long that will take – it could be several hours.'

There was a collective groan.

'This sort of thing happens all the time,' an older man with steely grey hair and eyes to match told Suzanne and Betty. 'I'm used to it. Anyway, there's no point in complaining.'

'Have your tea, and I'll give you an update as soon as I'm told,' Miss Foster said.

Adelaide rose to her feet. 'I'm gonna see if I can't find some chow.' She disappeared.

Elizabeth Foster came back a half an hour later.

'Not good news,' she said grimly. 'They can't get hold of another coach so we're going to have to sit it out. I've asked the café to provide supper for you all, but please clear up your own trays afterwards.'

The announcement was greeted with a cheer. Soon everyone was tucking into fried eggs and baked beans and tinned tomatoes with toast, almost in silence, but there was a contented murmur when knives and forks were neatly put together afterwards.

'I needed that,' Betty said as she took her tray with the dirty dishes over to the counter. 'I feel I can tackle anything they throw at me now.'

'You might regret saying that,' a very tall blonde woman with heavily made-up eyes and lips, cut in. She plonked her tray down and stuck her hand out. 'Cat Bliss – cellist.'

What an odd name.

'How do you do,' Suzanne said politely. 'Suzanne Linfoot.' She turned to Betty. 'And this is my friend, Betty Graham.'

'What is your forté?'

What on earth did she mean?

'Do you sing? Act? Play an instrument?' Cat Bliss said impatiently.

'Betty plays the saxophone and I'm a singer.'

She felt self-conscious telling a stranger she was a singer when she'd never sung professionally but Cat Bliss nodded, appearing to take her at her word, studying them both with what looked like a practised eye. 'Nothing that some lipstick and eye make-up wouldn't improve,' she said finally, her gaze fixed on Suzanne. 'I could give you a few tips.' Before either girl could answer she'd left their table and stopped by another.

Betty shot Suzanne a look and giggled. 'Get her,' she said. 'I tell you something, Suzy. I'm not going to let her get her mitts on my face.'

'She's probably all right,' Suzanne said, wanting to give her the benefit of the doubt, 'but I wouldn't want to get on the wrong side of her.'

It was almost midnight before Elizabeth Foster announced that the coach had arrived. She stood at the theatre door ticking off their names on a clipboard as each member passed through. There were at least two dozen performers who climbed up the steps, Suzanne being one of the last, hoping Betty had found a seat.

'Here, Suzy,' Betty called from the back.

Her eyes stinging with tiredness, Suzanne trudged down the aisle and lifted her case on top of an already growing pile near Betty.

As soon as everyone had boarded, Miss Foster nodded to the driver and the coach moved off.

'I know it's late and you're all tired,' Miss Foster said, standing near her seat by the driver, 'but this is a good chance for me to run over a couple of house rules – particularly important for those of you who are new to ENSA.' She let her gaze rest on Suzanne and Betty. 'This tour is not to be taken lightly. Anything can happen. The Germans could strike at any time. You must always be on the alert. Never forget we are still at war.'

Betty shrugged. 'I'd rather face Jerry than another needle,' she whispered, giving a nervous giggle.

'I'd rather face Jerry than Miss Foster,' Suzanne whispered back, and the two of them stifled their laughter.

Miss Foster threw them a warning glance. 'Furthermore, entertaining the troops is not to be regarded as an opportunity to have a bit of fun with the boys. In fact,' she added sternly, as though to a gaggle of naughty schoolgirls, 'there will be no personal interaction *of any kind* with them. I'll be doing everything in my power to keep you all safe, so long as you never disobey orders. If you do, you will be sent home immediately.'

Suzanne and Betty looked at one another. Betty grimaced. This was serious.

'Anyone any idea where we're headed?' a man called out when they'd been on the road fifteen minutes or so.

'Nah. Could be anywhere. It's all a big secret.'

'I reckon we're going to Euston Station,' someone else said.

'Not sure about that,' the first man called out again. 'We're coming up to Piccadilly Circus.'

At Euston railway station everyone was herded onto a train of only four carriages already three-quarters full. Suzanne and Betty became separated, and Suzanne spent the next hour cooped up with a mixed group of people she didn't recognise, but at least she had a seat at a table for four in the dining car. Several men were forced to stand in the aisle. Desperate for some kind of conversation, she asked a lady at her table who looked to be in her fifties if she was a member of the band.

'No, love,' the woman said, chuckling. 'I couldn't strike a note if you paid me – except maybe the triangle.' She threw back her head and roared. 'I'm in *Present Laughter*. Noël Coward,' she added when Suzanne looked puzzled, 'though I've only got a minor part in this one. Once you're my age the starring roles suddenly disappear, but at least it will cheer the boys up. Fern Miller has the star part.'

'Oh, I do hope I get a chance to see it,' Suzanne said, delighted she would see Fern again.

'Talk of the devil – look who's here,' the woman said.

'Marjorie, darling, I hoped I'd find you amongst the gathering. Is there room for me?' Fern Miller emerged from the crowd.

'We were just talking about you,' the woman called Marjorie said. 'I was telling this young lady . . .' She glanced at Suzanne. 'Sorry, love, I don't know your name.'

'It's Suzy,' Fern said in that familiar husky voice 'She looked at Suzanne and smiled. 'I was on another coach and wondered if you were with us. I'm so pleased. It's what you needed after that horrible business.'

The woman called Marjorie was staring at Suzanne. 'You two know each other?'

'We met at the theatre,' Fern said, casually taking out a cigarette holder from a smart black patent handbag and fixing a cigarette in the end. She lit it and deeply inhaled. 'How's that little girl . . . Rosie, isn't it?'

'What a memory you have,' Suzanne said admiringly.

'It comes with being an actress, darling.' Fern gave a throaty laugh.

'I should think she's out of hospital now,' Suzanne said. She swallowed. 'I just hope she's not having nightmares.'

'One hopes there won't be any lasting damage,' Fern said. 'But for now, let's think of nicer things.'

The carriage came alive, Suzanne thought, when Fern got chattering and telling funny anecdotes about previous plays she'd been in and the things that had gone wrong. She couldn't help laughing along with several others who were egging Fern on and joining in. If the people in the band were as nice as these actors and actresses, she was going to have a little fun herself for the first time in her life.

Chapter Twenty-Two

Everyone was tired and irritable by the time the train finally stopped hours later in Sheffield. Elizabeth Foster told everyone they could alight and stretch their legs before the final lap of the train journey, and to make sure they bought a sandwich and a cup of tea, as she wasn't at all certain when they'd next get a proper meal. Suzanne was swept up in the stampede for the refreshment room, but by the time she reached the top of the queue there was no sign of any food.

'Sorry, love,' the woman behind the counter said. 'All the sandwiches are gone. If we'd had notice you were all turning up I could've ordered more bread and fillings.'

Suzanne's stomach rumbled noisily. Embarrassed, she found some coins for the tea.

'Here's some biscuits for you, love,' the woman said, putting a few in the saucer. 'Have them on me.'

Suzanne thanked her and squeezed through the crowd, trying to find a space to drink her tea. She'd just managed a couple of sips when the bell rang and everyone rushed out to get back on the train. Swallowing another mouthful and muttering under her breath, she grabbed the biscuits and ran along the platform, only just in time before the train heaved its way out of the station.

Dawn was breaking when someone shouted, 'We're

coming into Liverpool! I live here. I needn't have come all the bleedin' way to London.' There were a few murmurs of sympathy.

An hour later they were packed onto another coach.

'Looks like we have a long sea voyage in front of us,' someone else said. 'We're heading for the docks!'

Suzanne forgot her hunger as she gazed up at the enormous grey hulk of a troopship that Miss Foster had pointed out was the one they would be sailing on – the SS *Orbita*. It was teeming with soldiers and sailors and airmen leaning over the rails to watch the happenings below, and officers representing all the forces shouting instructions. Suzanne blinked in amazement. There must be thousands of people on board. She spotted some Wrens and nurses hanging over the rails, laughing and waving at the newcomers, and impulsively she waved back. A pair of nuns nearby were quietly surveying the scene, one of them turning to the other to make some remark. Whatever would Raine and Ronnie say if they could see her now? Their timid, unadventurous sister about to embark on the most adventurous journey of her life. She didn't dare contemplate what Maman would have said.

'We've been promised breakfast as soon as we're all settled,' Miss Foster announced to the group, 'but first we'll be going through customs.'

'Breakfast can't come too soon,' Betty said, linking her arm through Suzanne's. 'Did you get anything to eat when we stopped, Suzy?'

'A few biscuits and two gulps of tea,' Suzanne said, relieved at the thought of some food at last. 'What about you?'

'An egg sandwich with a black mark where the yolk met the white,' Betty complained. 'It was so dry it must have been made days ago. Not even any salt.' She looked at Suzanne with a contrite expression. 'Oh, but poor you. At least I got something. I promise I'll give you some of my rations at breakfast.'

'No need to go that far,' Suzanne chuckled. 'But I must say, I'm starving.'

The ENSA group boarded the ship, the girls to much cheering from the troops, and wolf-whistling in Fern's direction as soon as they recognised her. The actress gave a royal wave as she tottered up the gangway in her high heels with plenty of male arms outstretched to help her up the final steps. There was another huge cheer as Adelaide, in a pale blue suit, practically danced her way onto the deck, calling out to the boys, and blowing kisses in all directions.

'Give us a song, Adelaide,' one of them shouted.

'Later, later.' She grinned as she disappeared through one of the doors.

Suzanne and Betty joined the rest of the ENSA group for scrambled eggs and a surprising rasher of bacon for breakfast, and afterwards took part in the lifeboat drill. To her relief Suzanne found a quiet moment in the six-berth cabin she was to share with Betty and four other performers.

The others had gone to explore the ship, and she'd told them she'd catch up with them in a few minutes. She hadn't been quick enough to grab a lower bunk – Millie and Rhoda, two young dancers, and Lily, their principal, had bagged them – but it didn't really matter, Suzanne thought. She'd have Betty for company on the top level and whoever else joined them. But for now she wanted time to think about how to answer James's letter. She was in the middle of rereading it when the cabin door swung open.

'Oh, there you are,' Betty said, looking up at Suzanne who was hurriedly folding James's letter. 'Am I interrupting anything?' Before Suzanne could answer, Betty carried on. 'Come and have a look over the ship. It's marvellous, although you can hardly move for fellers – also marvellous!' She giggled and flopped onto Rhoda's bunk. 'Who's the letter from, if it's not too rude?'

Suzanne sighed. She'd have to get used to Betty's constant chatter and personal questions.

'Just a friend,' she said, putting the envelope back in her handbag.

'The way you looked just now when I came in, I think it's from someone who's more than a friend,' Betty grinned. 'Come on, Suzy, tell Auntie Betty. I love romantic stuff.'

'Then don't look at me,' Suzanne said, laughing. 'It's not a romantic letter though it is from a man. But a man who's a friend, not a boyfriend.'

'Oh, shame.' Betty pulled a face. 'But that's not to say it won't turn into a romance,' she said, her expression brightening.

'You're incorrigible, Betty,' Suzanne said, jumping down from her bunk. 'Come on, let's go and have a look round.'

They were out on deck just as the engines started up. Twenty minutes later the horns blared making the girls jump. Then the great ship slowly began to inch its way out to sea to become part of a convoy of several enormous white ships, one of them covered in large red crosses.

'You know, Suzy, I can't believe it's happening. I'm going to love being on this boat.'

But an hour later Betty's face began to turn a sickly shade.

'Are you all right, Betty?'

'No.' Betty held on to the deck's rail, her eyes riveted on the gentle swell of the water. 'I don't feel that well. You might have to ask the Captain to flag down that hospital ship.'

She was attempting to joke, but Suzanne could see how pale her friend's face had turned. Surely, Betty wasn't going to get seasick.

'But it's quite smooth,' Suzanne told her, surprised.

'Not to me, it isn't.' Betty's hands gripped the rail as a larger wave made the ship rock slightly.

'Take deep breaths,' Suzanne said, instinctively. 'The fresh air will help.'

'No, I – oh, Lord—' With that, Betty leaned over the rail and vomited.

Suzanne rushed to her side and waited until the retching subsided. As Betty straightened and clung to her, Suzanne found a handkerchief to wipe the girl's forehead.

'There. Are you feeling a bit better?'

'A bit.'

'Why don't I get you back to the cabin and you can have some water and lie down for a while?'

'Yes, all right.' Betty gave her a wan smile, and for once was silent as Suzanne put her arm around her and led her back to the cabin.

'Do you want me to stay with you?'

'No,' Betty said firmly, and shuddered. 'I feel awfully tired. Maybe after a nap I'll feel better.'

'I'll come back and see how you are in an hour.'

Suzanne closed the cabin door behind her and made her way up to the first flight of steps when she heard someone call her name from above. She tilted her head to see Fern Miller beckoning to her.

'Come on up,' Fern shouted above the noise. 'It's quieter here than where you're standing.'

Obediently, Suzanne climbed two more flights. Fern was right. There were only a few scattered groups of people, mostly crew, in deep conversation.

'We're on the bridge,' Fern said, smiling. 'The rest of the mob aren't allowed up here, but the Captain recognised me and told me I was welcome any time to watch the sunrise. So I'm taking him at his word.'

'But he doesn't know *me*,' Suzanne began, feeling she was trespassing.

'You're my guest,' Fern chuckled.

'Sunrise was hours ago . . .'

'Never mind that,' Fern said. 'Just look at the view.'

The SS *Orbita* was the fourth ship in the convoy, and when Suzanne looked behind her she could see the other ships slowly following the white trail of bubbles.

'By the way, I asked the Captain where we were heading. He refused to tell me, and instead asked for my autograph. But I said if he spilt the beans he'd get a signed *photograph* of me.' She gave her throaty chuckle as she studied Suzanne. 'If I tell you, Suzy, you have to promise to keep it a secret until it's announced, or I'll be in deep water.' She glanced over the rail, then threw her head back, laughing at her own joke.

She wasn't an actress for nothing, Suzanne thought, hiding a smile. And today she looked every inch the glamorous star with her pleated white dress just below the knee and a wide straw hat with a navy spotted scarf tied round it.

'All right, I won't say a word.'

Fern gave a dramatic pause. 'He became very mysterious by saying I'll know by something huge sticking out of the water and it's not an iceberg.' She laughed again. 'Well, my dear, you know what landmark he's talking about, don't you?'

Suzanne shook her head.

'We're going to be entertaining the lads in Gib!' Fern said triumphantly, adjusting her straw hat a fraction. 'That's where we're headed – well, the ENSA lot, anyway. I don't know about all the other ships – they'll probably go further in.'

'Gib?' Suzanne frowned.

'Gibraltar – Rock of . . . You must have learned about it in school.'

'Oh, of course.' Geography was one of her favourite subjects, but she'd never heard it abbreviated. From now on she would casually use this form when she was allowed to mention it.

'Suzy?'

Suzanne jumped at the sound of Fern's husky tones.

'Sorry, Fern, I was miles away,' she said.

In truth, she'd been thinking of James and wondering where they'd sent him. Then she hugged herself. She really *was* miles away.

Chapter Twenty-Three

June 1943

It had been a tedious journey. After three hours at sea the engines had stopped and they'd gone back to Liverpool with no explanation. Suzanne had tried to fill the time by altering Maman's gown, but space was so tight in the cabin and there was no quiet corner on deck so she'd given up. They'd waited a day in Liverpool's harbour before the ship steamed out again.

All sorts of rumours were flying as to where the ship was headed, but despite Fern's spilling the beans to her, Suzanne managed to keep it a secret even from Betty who every few hours roused from her sick bed asking if there'd been any announcement as to where they were going. Every night of the next eighteen days they were in complete darkness. The blackout rules applied on the ships as strictly as they did at home, Suzanne thought ruefully, but at least it became warmer with each day. There was no doubt they were sailing south. Finally, the Captain announced they were entering the Straits of Gibraltar and everyone cheered.

'Not all of you will disembark though,' the Captain added. 'You will be given your instructions by your CO in due course.'

Morocco and Spain flashed their lights on both sides of the straits, guiding the way, the town of Tangier alight with its twinkling winking lights, seemingly untouched by war, as a beacon of hope. When the harbour finally came in sight, the Captain announced that he was sorry it had taken a couple of days longer than expected but he'd had to dodge a U-boat that was stalking them.

'Thank goodness he didn't tell us as it was happening,' Betty said, joining Suzanne on deck with one of her rare appearances. 'I'd have had kittens if I'd known an enemy submarine had us in his sights.' She gave an exaggerated shudder.

There'd been great excitement when the Rock was first spotted – a speck on the horizon – but you couldn't miss that shape, one of the sailors told her. He said the Rock was made of limestone and was probably the largest in the world. Suzanne was fascinated with these details, remembering the fuzzy black and white photographs in her school geography book. By now the whole ship was cheering that they were bound for Gibraltar.

'We're some way yet from Gib,' the sailor said, squinting into the distance. 'We should be going in at dawn, I reckon.'

Suzanne was determined to be up early to see the Rock as they sailed closer.

'Whatever time is it?' Betty croaked as Suzanne was silently pulling on her clothes.

'Twenty past five,' Suzanne whispered. 'I shan't be long. I just want to see how big the Rock's got since we went to sleep.'

'I haven't slept a wink,' Betty said with a groan. 'But we must be getting closer to shore because I haven't been sick for the first time since we got on this damned boat.'

'Close your eyes and try to sleep now. I'll be back in an hour.'

Poor Betty had been bunk-bound for almost the whole journey, miserable with constant nausea and seasickness. Suzanne had felt a twinge of guilt every time she'd had to leave Betty, although her friend always said she would rather be left alone.

This early morning the sun's rays were lazily hovering at the base of the massive craggy peak that descended at a gentle angle before it met the Atlantic. Suzanne leant over the rail on the deck below the bridge, enjoying the fresh breeze in her hair and the fine spray of water on her face. The Rock seemed to get bigger by the minute. There were very few people about and she almost had the deck to herself.

Wendy should have been standing here enjoying the spectacle. Wendy practising her songs. Wendy meeting Betty and Adelaide and Fern. But it wasn't to be. Suzanne's bare arms chilled with goose pimples. How lucky she was to be alive and well. To be with such a wonderful group of people, giving up their careers to entertain the soldiers. And how fortunate she was that she had Betty as a friend.

Betty would have got on well with Wendy. Their personalities were not that dissimilar.

She swallowed the tears, salty as the sea beneath her.

I won't forget you, Wendy.

'Marvellous, isn't it?'

The strident voice jolted Suzanne out of her pensive mood. She turned to see Cat Bliss coming up behind her, waving a pair of binoculars.

'It is,' Suzanne said, abruptly, not wanting any company at this particular moment – least of all Cat's. There was something about the woman . . . She couldn't put it into words exactly, but she knew Betty felt the same.

'Looks like we'll be entertaining the troops in Gibraltar,' Cat said.

'So it appears.' Suzanne gazed straight ahead out to sea, hoping Cat would take the hint she didn't want to talk.

They stood in silence for a minute until Cat regarded her in her critical way.

'You should wear a hat, you know,' she said, 'with that fair skin of yours.'

'I wanted to feel the air on my face,' Suzanne said defensively. 'It's too early to burn and anyway I'm going in in a few minutes.'

'I'd better follow suit,' Cat said. 'All this sea-spray is playing havoc with my hair – making it all go frizzy – even wearing a hat.' She shrugged and gazed at Suzanne. 'Is your hair bleached?'

The question took Suzanne by surprise. 'No, of course not.' She automatically put her hand to her hair.

'Hmm. It's such a pale blonde, I wondered.' She took another step closer and instinctively Suzanne stepped back. 'No, you don't look English at all . . . You look almost Scandinavian . . . or German,' Cat sneered, making Suzanne flinch.

'Well, I'm neither,' Suzanne managed to say.

Without warning her eyes filled with tears. She no longer knew her background. What her real father looked like. But he'd have dark hair, being French. What was he doing this minute? Was he still on the run? Or had he been caught? If so, would they torture him? Shoot him? Or had he already been shot? She swallowed hard. Even thinking about the possibilities sounded like something from a horror film. But how would she ever know?

'Oh, dear, have I hit on a nerve?' Cat raised one eyebrow and smirked.

Suzanne shook her head and in defiance of Maman's voice asking her where her manners were, she turned her back and walked away.

Suzanne was relieved to see Betty – although her friend was still wan from her long bout of seasickness – joining in the excitement of disembarking and setting foot on dry land.

'I wasn't keen on staying in a foreign country,' Betty confided, 'but being Gibraltar's part of the Empire, it's okay, because you know where you are with the language and everything.'

'Just look at those palm trees, Betty.' Suzanne pointed, when they were on the way to their hotel. The palm trees, lazily swaying in a coastal breeze, framed the turquoise sea as the bus trundled along. 'I really know I'm abroad now. I've always wanted to see them in real life ever since I saw photographs of them the first time. Aren't they marvellous?'

'They are,' Betty agreed. She turned impulsively to Suzanne. 'Oh, Suzy, I think I'm going to love being in Gibraltar.'

The ENSA troupe had piled their luggage in a corner of the foyer of the small hotel. It was late in the afternoon and everyone had dived to the bar for drinks and were now sitting at tables chattering and laughing. Miss Foster stood up and rapped smartly on her table.

'May I have your attention, please. I need to go over a few things, but first I have some sad news to report.'

Immediately, there was a hush.

'One of the ships in our convoy was torpedoed two days ago and I'm afraid there have been over a hundred deaths.'

There was a cry of disbelief from the ballet dancers, but most people sat stunned.

'We didn't hear anything,' Betty muttered.

Suzanne felt too sick at heart to speak. Her whole being was with James. In her head she said a little prayer for his safety.

'We don't know the exact figures. But it shows we are still at war and this is no picnic for people who joined ENSA thinking it was going to be an easy option. But it should be a rewarding experience for you all and you can be proud of doing your bit to keep up the morale of our wonderful servicemen and women.'

There were loud cheers and clapping.

'Let's give our thanks to Captain Baker. He safely got us through, so please raise your glasses to him even though he won't be disembarking.'

When the toast had died down, Miss Foster continued. 'We're stopping in Gibraltar for what might turn out to be a few days, so we'll be giving some shows while we're here.'

'I thought we were *staying* in Gibraltar,' several people muttered.

'Where are we actually going, then?' one of the actors called out.

'Sorry, Jim, you know better than to ask. You all know the rules by now.'

'I think you'll have to leave me here,' Betty said in a low voice, her face ashen; Suzanne guessed it was the thought of facing another stretch at sea.

'But the good news is—' Miss Foster continued, throwing Betty a sympathetic glance '—this time we'll be travelling by aeroplane. That's why there could be a bit of a wait as the troops obviously take priority.'

Suzanne gave a sharp intake of breath. She'd never dreamed she'd be going in an aeroplane. She wasn't sure if this was good or bad news. But Raine had more than once said how she adored flying. Anticipation fizzed through her.

Excitement mixed with fear of the unknown. She gritted her teeth. She'd wanted to do something definite to help the war effort. And whatever she chose to do was potentially dangerous in some way, as Miss Foster had said just now. You had to face it. Dad would have called it growing up. She'd already embarked on a journey that even Raine had never experienced – travelling beyond England's shores.

A cheer went up at this news. Betty turned to Suzanne and smiled for the first time in days.

'There is a God, after all,' she said, and Suzanne squeezed her hand.

'We'll be staying in this hotel for however long it takes for us to board an available aeroplane,' Miss Foster continued. 'I'm afraid it's a bit shabby. You'll find the staff are mainly Spanish because they took the jobs left by the civilian population when so many of them were evacuated early in the war. You'll have to just make do.' She looked at her notes. 'Now you may wonder what to do in the meantime. But tonight you can all relax and maybe have a look round the town. Have supper out. I'll leave it to you. But absolutely *no* discussions in public where you can be overheard about where you've come from, where you guess you might be going or when you'll arrive, how long you're staying, because that's how security can easily be breached.' She paused. 'Remember, servicemen and even citizens could actually die from what seems like an innocent remark.' She let her stern gaze fall on everyone.

'Regarding tomorrow . . .' Miss Foster's expression softened as she continued '. . . ENSA has received a most flattering invitation from the Governor of Gibraltar, Sir Noel Mason-Macfarlane, to entertain some important guests arriving tomorrow evening at his residence. The trouble is, I'm obliged to pick only four of you. If I ask for volunteers I'm afraid you'll all raise your hands, so *I'm* going to make the decision. They've requested musicians and singers, rather than comedians and dancers.'

'That lets us out,' one of the dancers said, an annoyed edge to her tone. 'So what are the ones left supposed to do?'

'You will be rehearsing,' Miss Foster said firmly. 'We have to rid ourselves of the inappropriate term some of the public call us.'

'What? Every Night Something Awful?' Fern said. 'Tommy Trinder came up with that one. I think it's rather sweet.' She gave one of her husky laughs to the group's amusement.

Betty giggled and Suzanne smiled. Fern had lightened the atmosphere.

'I have the names of the people I would like to take with me to the Governor's Residence,' Miss Foster said when the laughter had died down.

Suzanne put her cup down with a shaking hand, making the saucer rattle. Her mind buzzed with a mass of contradictions. Part of her longed for her name to be called so she'd have the experience, and maybe even have a chance to meet Sir Noel with his double-barrelled name, and part of her was terrified it would be. She took in a breath and pulled back her shoulders. She was the newest member as far as she could make out, so Miss Foster would definitely not be calling her name. Besides, she, more than anyone, needed to rehearse before she went anywhere near a stage.

'Fern, I'd like you to be one of the four.'

'Really?' Fern raised a dark eyebrow. 'You know I don't sing *or* play an instrument.'

'I know, but you'll look gorgeous and they'll love having a famous actress chatting to them.'

'Then I'd like to take Adelaide.' Miss Foster looked across at the black singer who nodded happily.

'What would you like me to sing?' Adelaide said.

'Definitely the one you made really famous.' Miss Foster actually smiled. '"I Wanna Be Loved".'

Suzanne couldn't help an amused smile. Miss Foster was usually so stiff and starchy that Adelaide's song title didn't trip lightly off her lips.

'And a couple of jazz numbers,' Miss Foster continued. 'Then Bramwell, of course, seeing as he's the pianist.' She looked across at him. 'You can sing a few Noël Coward songs, Bram, or whatever else you fancy, as well as accompanying Adelaide and . . .' Miss Foster paused, 'our newest singer . . .'

Everyone stopped murmuring.

'Suzy Linfoot.' Miss Foster took off her glasses and gazed round the room. 'Suzy, where are you?'

'Stand up, Suzy,' Betty hissed.

Flushing with embarrassment, and pulse racing, Suzanne rose to her feet, aware of curious looks from some of the group she hadn't yet spoken to.

'Ah, there you are.' Miss Foster smiled. 'All right, Suzy?'

'Um, yes, of course.'

'Good. Those of you going to entertain tomorrow will meet here at six o'clock sharp. Two cars will collect us. Any questions? No? Then that's all I have to say for the moment, except to wish you a pleasant few days and as soon as we have an available aircraft I'll let you know.'

Suzanne sat down again. Betty turned to her.

'I'm so pleased for you, Suzy,' she said. 'It will be marvellous experience for you.'

'Don't you wish you were coming to play your saxophone?' she said, worried Betty's feelings might be hurt.

'Not likely,' Betty said. 'I still feel queasy from that rotten boat. I thought it was never coming to an end. I'll be all right now I'm on dry land but I don't feel like doing anything just yet – except maybe get a decent meal inside me.'

It was only when Suzanne was in the stark room she was sharing with Betty, in a bed not nearly as comfortable as the bunk on the ship, her friend softly snoring a few feet away, that she had a depressing thought: there wouldn't be enough time to alter her mother's evening dress. She could tell it would take at least three, if not four, solid evenings to unpick the seams and carefully cut away the fabric, keeping the same shape, then sew it back together by hand. She had nothing to wear for what was bound to be a prestigious venue. Everyone would be looking glamorous. . . except her.

It was too embarrassing to admit; she would make an excuse to Miss Foster that she'd thought about it and didn't feel at all ready until she'd had some rehearsals.

'You've gone awfully quiet,' Betty said as the two of them were having breakfast the next morning in the dingy dining room. 'Didn't you sleep very well? I went off like a top,' she added, as usual not waiting for an answer, 'even though the mattress is bloody uncomfortable. This hotel is a bit of a dump, isn't it? I hope we don't have to stay here long.' She stopped to draw breath and looked at Suzanne with wide eyes. 'Sorry, Suzy, I asked you a question and didn't give you a chance to answer. Are you all right?'

'Yes, I'm okay. I couldn't get off to sleep at first, that's all.'

'I didn't snore, did I?'

'Only quietly.' Suzanne paused. 'That wasn't what kept me awake.'

'So what is it?'

'I don't have the right thing to wear tonight so I can't go on.'

Betty frowned. 'Couldn't you find anything before you came?'

'It's difficult to shop with my mother. She's French and everything she buys has to be minutely inspected for quality – which you're not necessarily going to get these days – and because we were called at an earlier date to travel there was no time.'

Betty tutted. 'Oh, that's a bugger. I can't help you there. We're totally different. I'm shorter than you and probably a good size bigger.' She sucked in her breath. 'Let's think. There has to be a way.' She looked at Suzanne. 'I've got it. What about Fern? She's a bit taller than you but about the same size. She's also rich and glamorous. I'm sure she'd find something to lend you.'

Suzanne's spirits lifted for a few seconds, then plummeted. 'No, I couldn't possibly ask her.'

'She can only say no.'

'It's a cheek. It's not like asking a friend. I hardly know her. It doesn't matter. I'll speak to Miss Foster and tell her I'm not prepared.'

But Miss Foster wouldn't take no for an answer.

'I'd like you to do this, Suzy. It will be good experience for you. We'll just get you to sing the two songs you've rehearsed with Bram. You won't be so nervous in someone's drawing room with just a few people, and it will give you the confidence when you stand up and sing to hundreds.'

No, it's the very opposite, Suzanne wanted to say. *A huge crowd is more anonymous. Singing in someone's drawing room where all eyes will be on me is far more daunting.* But Miss Foster had patted her on the arm and already hurried away before Suzanne could ask if it was possible to run through her two songs with Bram again.

The following evening Suzanne took her flowered dress out of the wardrobe. The saving grace was that Gibraltar was very hot so the evening would be balmy. A summer dress might not look so odd, unlike the time when she'd worn it for that dance at the Palais in Bromley just before Christmas. It was the first evening she and Raine had ever been out together without Dad or Maman. She gave a start. Thinking of Raine, she realised with a stab of dismay that today was her sister's birthday. With so many changes going on in her life she'd lost track of the days. But it was the first time she'd ever forgotten any of her family's birthdays. She grimaced. This war was having an effect on everything.

She hoped Raine would have the chance to go home and see Ronnie and Maman for a day or two, although her sister rarely made a thing of her birthdays, and would no doubt be just as happy amongst her ferry pilot friends and working today like any other day.

This evening she'd be working as well, if you could call it working. Who would be there? It certainly wouldn't be the troops she'd signed up to entertain. But she supposed it was important to the Governor that his guests enjoyed themselves. She pictured herself standing up and opening her mouth but nothing coming out. Cold perspiration trickled down her back as she became more and more alarmed at the prospect. A bath would help her relax.

She ran the regulatory five inches, all the while wishing she could have another rehearsal. But no one had seen Bram. In the end, to try to take her mind off the evening ahead, she'd asked Betty if she'd like to have a wander around the town. Betty had immediately agreed.

Here, the shops were filled with all kinds of goods that were rationed in England. Suzanne and Betty stared open-mouthed through a shop window displaying many styles of shoes and advertising silk stockings. It even sold cosmetics. They ignored the temptation and walked on.

'Let's buy a bar of chocolate each,' Betty said, 'and eat the lot in one go.'

Suzanne laughed. 'We're so used to making it last a week, we'd be sick.'

'Not me,' Betty said. 'Come on, let's go in this one. I'll treat you.'

There didn't seem to be any sign of rationing in the grocery shop either. Suzanne was amazed to see British makes of tea and biscuits and tinned foods stacked on the shelves beside the wonderful variety of fruit and vegetables neatly arranged in slatted wooden crates. A Spaniard, his black hair well oiled, and his mouth in a sulky downturn, served them.

'They've even got cigarettes and alcohol.' Betty pointed to one of the shelves.

'I've never seen you smoke,' Suzanne said, as she unwrapped her bar of Fry's chocolate cream and surreptitiously popped a square between her lips, savouring the moments. It was heaven. She tucked the rest of the bar in her handbag.

'No, but if I did . . .'

They'd laughed and linked arms as they strolled through a bazaar, fingering the Moroccan textiles with the smell of fish in their nostrils emanating from the nearby market.

'You might find something here to wear for this evening,' Betty remarked, admiring the gorgeous brightly coloured patterns, so different from the drab colours they were reduced to in England.

But when they looked through some of the racks they found they were mostly bolts of material rather than made-up garments. And when they spotted some dresses they were all knee-length daytime dresses. Nothing remotely resembling an evening gown.

'Let's go and have some tea,' Betty suggested. 'I'm boiling hot, aren't you?'

'Good idea,' Suzanne said. 'And here's what looks like the perfect café – right in the shade.'

Sipping mint tea from a glass mug and gazing up at the castle on the hill from Grand Casemates Square was perfectly delightful, but at the back of Suzanne's mind was the terrifying thought that in only three more hours she'd be the focus of attention, not even dressed correctly, and performing to people she didn't know. It wouldn't be at all like playing her violin with the small orchestra for the people in the village hall. Why on earth hadn't she had the courage to speak up and tell Miss Foster she simply wasn't ready. But if she had, Miss Foster might have decided to send her home if she came across as that nervous. And that was something Suzanne couldn't bear the thought of. Maman would never stop telling her she shouldn't have gone in the first place, and what a stupid girl she'd been to give up her classical music. And now she'd lost her chance of a place in the school.

Maybe she should ask Cat Bliss if she would help do her make-up to give her a bit more confidence and try to get to know Cat at the same time. Suzanne certainly didn't want to get off to a bad start with anyone. Meanwhile, she would snatch the opportunity of answering James's letter.

It was more difficult than she'd imagined. She started it twice and got herself tied up in knots. In the end she kept it brief, telling him they'd reached a big rock. The officials might not black that bit out. She hoped he was well and keeping out of danger. At that point she swallowed hard.

Suzanne picked up her pen and finished the last line of her letter:

Please know I'm your friend and thinking of you.

Keep safe.

She blinked. The same last words Maman had said on the morning of her departure.

But she mustn't dwell on that.

So how should she end the letter? James had put 'Yours', but that was just a quick way of signing off to almost anyone. For a dizzying moment she wished she really was his. She sighed and dipped her pen in the ink bottle, simply writing Suzy.

Suzanne stepped out of the stained bath, reaching for a towel, which was small and thin with use. She tried to dry herself, gave up and threw it over the side of the bath. The warm air would have to finish off the job. She stepped into her underclothes, which instantly clung to her damp skin, then took the flowered dress off the hanger. She remembered making it with a bolt of material a housewife had given Maman because she'd had no spare saucepans to give when her mother was collecting aluminium for the war effort. Who would have thought that the next time she'd wear the frock would be in Gibraltar singing at the Governor's Residence.

Then she realised the enormity of what she was being asked to do and immediately her heart started to hammer. Pull yourself together, she told herself. If you could do that violin solo, surely you can sing a couple of songs without going to pieces.

It was after five o'clock by the time Suzanne gently knocked on Cat's door.

'Hello, Cat . . .' she began as she entered. Cat Bliss was varnishing her nails. She looked up.

'Oh, it's you.'

Suzanne recoiled at the cold tone.

'I was wondering . . . you said something about helping with make-up, so I wondered if you could help me with mine for tonight.'

Cat stared at her. 'I said I could give you some tips – I didn't say I'd do it.'

'Oh, I-I'm sorry – I must have misunderstood.'

'A bright pink lipstick would be the best colour for you,' Cat said. 'Give your mouth a bit of precision.' She shook her head and tutted. 'Goodness, I didn't realise how light your lashes are. They don't show up at all. You'll need several coats of mascara.'

'I don't have any,' Suzanne said, cross with herself for sounding apologetic. 'Or a bright pink lipstick. I'll just have to make do with what I've got.' She looked directly at Cat. 'I'm sorry to have disturbed you.'

'Well, I shouldn't worry about the make-up,' Cat said. 'No one will notice your pale face, I don't suppose, if you've a halfway decent voice.' She waved her bottle of nail varnish in the air. 'Now, if you'll excuse me . . .' She bent her head to varnish another nail.

Chapter Twenty-Four

There was a knock at the door.

'Just a moment,' Suzanne called as she pulled her dress over her head and put her arms through the cap sleeves. She opened the bedroom door and gave a gasp. Fern was standing there smiling from ear to ear, looking stunning in a sleek white gown that hugged her figure and draped to the floor. Her hair was dressed in a beautiful shiny dark chignon, decorated by a white artificial flower, and she was wearing silver high-heeled sandals, long white gloves, and carried a white fur stole over her arm. In her hand was a tiny sequined bag on a silver chain.

'Aren't you going to invite me in?' she asked in her husky tones.

'Oh – yes, of course.' Suzanne stood aside while Fern wafted through the door and into the room, thankful her side was neat, even though Betty's space looked as though it had been through a whirlwind. 'You took me by surprise. How lovely you look.'

'Thank you, sweetie.' Fern cast her eyes round. 'Oh, dear,' she said, 'I wouldn't call this much of a room. It's so small for one thing, and incredibly dreary . . . rather like the entire hotel,' she added. 'And by the looks of it you haven't even got it to yourself.'

'I don't mind,' Suzanne said quickly. 'It's nice having Betty's company.' She looked at Fern curiously. 'Are you staying here as well?'

'Yes, but I made them change my room. I'm on the top floor now so I have a view of the Rock. I insisted they gave it a thorough clean but the place is still a dump.' She gave Suzanne a rueful smile. 'Never mind all that. The cars will be here to fetch us in . . .' she looked at her watch '. . . exactly twenty-two minutes. I just wanted to see you on your own to give you some Dutch courage. I felt you might need it. But I can talk while I help you into your evening gown.'

Suzanne wanted to curl up. She looked down at her dress. Surely it wasn't that bad. She willed herself to raise her eyes to Fern who wore a slight frown.

'I'm already wearing it.' Suzanne tossed the words away with a short laugh as though it mattered nothing to her either way.

Fern's eyes widened and she shook her head. 'Suzy, we're going to meet some top-notch people,' she began. 'Everyone will be dressed to the nines . . . including *you*, sweetie.' She looked Suzanne up and down. 'Back in five minutes . . . stay where you are,' she added sternly.

True to her word, Fern was back within minutes, a pale-coloured creation, neither beige nor apricot, but somewhere in between, over her arm. 'Try this.'

Suzanne stood a little embarrassed in her brassiere and French knickers in front of Fern. She only had one pair of stockings to her name, but as the weather was so hot, she couldn't bear the thought of wearing them, in spite of the vision of Maman's horrified expression of her daughter appearing in such a grand venue with bare legs. Fern slipped the gown over her head and carefully placed her arms through the lace-encrusted chiffon sleeves. The V-necked bodice was flowered lace, following the line of Suzanne's bust, and narrowing into a pleated waistline caught by a gold buckle, where the gown then slithered to the floor.

Fern stood back and looked at her.

'Turn round,' she ordered.

Suzanne spun round, hardly believing she was wearing something so very beautiful.

'Is there a full-length mirror anywhere?' Fern said.

'No.' Suzanne smiled. 'Only the one on the dressing table.'

'That's no good. You need to see yourself full length.' She looked down at Suzanne's feet, clad in white wedge-heeled sandals.

'I think they'll have to do,' Fern said resignedly. 'Your feet are much smaller than mine so I can't help you there. Now, have you gloves?'

'No.'

'Well, I don't think it matters much with the elbow-length sleeves on the dress.' She paused. 'I have to say, Suzy, you look a million dollars. But why aren't you made up?'

'I was just about to put my lipstick on when you knocked at the door.'

'No, I mean a proper make-up. Why didn't you see Cat Bliss? She usually offers to do our make-up. She learnt how to do it when she worked in Selfridges in their cosmetic and perfumery department. She's a dab hand at making one look marvellous . . . not that you don't already look marvellous.' She gave her husky laugh. 'But she would have made you look professional and that helps to give one confidence.'

Immediately Suzanne heard those words, any shred of confidence she'd tried to muster ebbed away. Then she reprimanded herself. Cat Bliss had as good as slammed the door in her face, but she mustn't let that woman shake her self-belief. Her mind raced on. It would be different if she'd been asked to play her violin – even her piano. But singing was too new for her to judge herself. The cloud of self-doubt once more descended upon her.

'I did ask her,' she told Fern, 'but she said she'd only offered to give me a few tips on how to do it. It doesn't matter. I never wear any normally, except a touch of lipstick, so I don't suppose I'll miss it.'

Fern raised her eyes to the ceiling.

'Hmm. A pity.' She looked at Suzanne. 'But maybe it's just as well because I think she uses too much on her own face and might have ruined your looks.'

'I don't think she likes me much,' Suzanne confided, 'although I've never knowingly done or said anything to upset her.'

Fern gave a throaty laugh. 'She's jealous, my dear. She's used to being the cat's whiskers around here, if you'll excuse the pun. And now she's got some competition. You're very lovely in a totally natural way, and most importantly, you don't realise it.' The older woman looked at her watch. 'You'd better put your lipstick on, Suzy. That's really all you need, come to think of it. Then we need to go *pronto*.'

Suzanne nodded, speechless. She went to the sink and quickly dabbed on her precious coral lipstick, then picked up the black velvet bag Maman had bought her for her eighteenth birthday. Her dress sounded like the gentle rustle of tissue paper as she followed Fern out of the door.

Two sleek black embassy motorcars were waiting outside the hotel when she and Fern stepped out of the entrance.

'Mmm, two fabulous Rolls,' Fern murmured appreciatively.

Although the air was still very warm on Suzanne's face, the sky was overcast. She hoped it wouldn't rain as she had no umbrella. Neither had Fern, she thought, watching the actress hold her head high as she stepped over to the two motorcars. Suzanne felt her own chin tilt upwards. It was Fern's dress that made her hold herself straight. As though that alone had changed Suzanne's personality. She wanted to giggle as one of the drivers leapt out of the second car and opened the rear door for them. But then she thought of standing on her own in one of the Governor's grand salons and singing to some highbrow people. Her stomach curled into a knot. Words of the two songs she'd sung no more than a handful of times with Bramwell tumbled around her brain. She couldn't remember how either of them even began.

She gave a sideways glance at Fern, sitting only a foot away from her. Fern caught her eye and winked. Suzanne smiled back, thankful the actress was with her. She allowed her body to sink into the tweed-covered upholstery, taking a few deep breaths, doing her best to relax. After all, her songs would take hardly more than three minutes each. Nothing awful could happen in six minutes – could it?

The Governor's Residence towered over its neighbouring buildings even though it was modest in design.

'It used to be a Franciscan friars' convent, so Charles, one of the actors, told me,' Fern remarked, 'but apparently the powers that be decided it would make a suitable governor's residence.'

Minutes later the car turned into Main Street and at the southernmost end pulled up outside the convent, a solid-looking building, which would have looked rather austere with its plain-looking chapel adjoining, Suzanne thought, had it not been for the decorative colonnaded porch signalling the entrance.

She was relieved to see Bram, who'd made himself scarce all day, standing with Miss Foster, and when the driver helped Adelaide from the rear door, Suzanne gasped. The singer overshadowed them all. She was wearing a long emerald-green gown, the short sleeves made entirely of black net designed to look like feathers with another wide band of black 'feathers' adorning the edge of the dress at mid-calf. Glittering earrings dangled to the level of her pointed chin, with a matching clip in her sleek black hair. Green high-heeled sandals completed the vision.

'You look glorious, Adelaide,' Suzanne told her in an undertone.

Adelaide gave a grin of delight. 'And you look like a very glamorous English rose,' she said.

A male member of staff stood on the steps to greet them. He peered at their invitations, then ushered them inside.

The small ensemble was shown into the reception room, the size of Suzanne's old gymnasium at school. It was already buzzing with chatter from several small groups scattered around a handful of empty tables that were laid with white damask cloths. Tealights adorned the tables, their soft light falling on the gleaming cutlery and making the crystal glasses sparkle. Suzanne was amused to see a very large candelabra on top of a grand piano at the far end of the room. No one was playing, although two gentlemen were nearby, talking animatedly on some subject or other and every so often breaking into laughter. She wished she could hear what they were discussing with their heads bent towards one another.

Where were all the women? The wives of these men? So far she could only see a few beautifully dressed, very English-looking ladies, heavily jewelled, and except for their different hairstyles and the colours of their dresses, they all appeared to come from the same kind of moneyed background. For a few moments she was sure she couldn't compete with all this sophistication, until the swish of her dress reminded her that at least no one would suspect by her appearance that she wasn't in their class. *And I'm not sure I'd want to be,* she thought, as she watched them, their tinkly laughter sounding false as they kissed the air near one another's cheeks.

'May I introduce you to some of our guests, madam?' a uniformed officer at her elbow enquired, and she was swept up in a sea of introductions.

A waiter appeared with a tray of champagne just as Fern was making her way towards her. 'A glass of champagne for madam?'

Suzanne hesitated.

'Have one,' Fern ordered, lifting two beautiful crystal flutes from the tray and handing one to Suzanne. 'It'll do you good. Help you to relax.'

A full hour passed, the talk becoming more animated, with sudden roars of laughter. Suzanne found herself actually so enjoying meeting the guests that she almost forgot why she'd been invited. Most of the conversation was about the war and how long it might go on for. She listened intently, hoping she might learn something as to the whereabouts of the Royal Navy in the Mediterranean, though it didn't seem likely with all the notices she'd spotted about 'Keeping Mum'. But she couldn't shake off the feeling that James might not be that far away. She smiled to herself as she imagined his look of surprise if he could see her right this minute in her beautiful gown, ready to entertain these people who were miles away from the bone-weary troops she'd imagined she'd be singing to.

Suzanne couldn't take her eyes off Adelaide who was at the centre of a group of men. Even though Fern had told her Adelaide was in her forties, she didn't look anywhere near, with her sturdy but trim figure, the emerald dress showing it off to perfection. Suzanne took another sip of champagne as she watched Miss Foster walk over to her and say something in her ear. Adelaide nodded and excused herself. With total assurance she shimmied over to the piano, where Bram was already seated, giving a back view of the dress, draped almost to the waist, drawing attention to her polished bronze skin.

People were still continuing their conversations as Sir Noel Mason-Macfarlane stepped forward. A stern-looking man, Suzanne thought, inwardly quaking. His moustache reminded her of Mr Hitler's, and she shuddered inwardly.

The Governor walked purposefully into the centre of the room. He looked around, his sharp eyes missing nothing, then held up his hand for quiet. Instantly the hubbub died away, to be replaced by a roll of thunder. There were a few chuckles from the guests and Sir Noel gave a wry smile.

'It looks like we're in for a good old storm,' he said. 'But being British we carry on regardless. And on that note, we're charmed to have the wonderful Miss Adelaide Hall here tonight to sing for us before she travels onwards to her next stop – so please give her a warm welcome.' He waved his arm towards the piano. 'Ladies and gentlemen, Miss Adelaide Hall.'

Bram looked up at Adelaide and gave her a smile, but it wasn't his usual ready grin, Suzanne observed. Surely *he* wasn't nervous.

Adelaide took up a nonchalant stance as she leaned against the piano's curved lid. *Oh, to have that confidence,* Suzanne thought enviously. Adelaide was the height of sophistication, much like Fern. In those moments Suzanne knew she would never be able to attain such an attitude. Well, here was her chance to improve, at least. She'd watch and learn from a professional.

Adelaide threw her infectious smile around the guests,

but just as she opened her mouth to introduce her song there was a sudden roar and an almighty bang, making Suzanne jump. Her breath came fast. She put her hand on top of one of the chairs to hold her balance. Another bang. Suzanne felt the blood run from her face. It must be an air raid! She swung round. Why weren't people diving for cover? But no one seemed in the least bothered as they carried on talking. And then she heard the rain lashing furiously against the windows. Of course it wasn't an air raid. She'd almost made herself look a complete fool.

'The perfect time for me to sing "Stormy Weather",' Adelaide said with a rich chuckle, making everyone laugh.

There was a crack of lightning followed by another crash of thunder. Taking no notice, Adelaide looked towards Bram and nodded. He played an introduction. Suzanne watched as she sang the first few bars quite slowly, but very particularly, and then she completely altered the rhythm. What was so fascinating was the way Adelaide didn't stick at all to the melody. Suzanne could hear Bram playing the tune underneath Adelaide's voice, but the singer had her own style and paid little attention. Every movement Adelaide made with her hands reaching out to the audience, or clasping them to her chest, Suzanne tucked it all away in her mind.

'*. . . keeps rainin' all the ti-ime.*' Adelaide finished the song on a clear high note, deliberately facing the windows, and ending on a hoot of laughter.

There was an immediate burst of clapping. As it died down, Bram nodded for her to begin a jazzy number Suzanne wasn't familiar with. The woman had a superb range, able to sing low and sultrily, then improvising with strange spine-tingling sounds without words, until finally she was back to the story of a lover she'd let go and now wanted to love him again. Suzanne felt her foot tapping in time, watching in open-mouthed admiration as Adelaide moved her shoulders and swayed her hips to the music, all the while smiling, and ending this time on an even higher note. When she'd finished three numbers she thanked Bram and nodded and beamed at the guests. Then she bowed in different directions to catch everyone's eye, and waltzed off to more enthusiastic clapping.

'Thank you, Miss Hall . . . Adelaide,' Sir Noel said. 'I enjoyed your performance very much and I know all the guests did, too. We feel lucky to have such a famous singer in our midst, and I'm hoping you'll sing again for us later. But until then we'll have a short break and then invite our second singer of the evening.'

Immediately, Suzanne's heart raced. Oh, why had she agreed to do this? It was madness. She suddenly thought of her sister flying different aircraft in all weathers. If only she had her confidence. Raine would have laughed at Miss Foster's suggestion that she sing at the Governor's Residence and would have immediately said she'd give it a go.

I just hate making a fool of myself in front of people, Suzanne thought. *If I'm going to do something I like to be prepared. Do it well. And I'm not prepared at all. It's going to be a disaster. If only I hadn't had that champagne . . .*

'Suzy, are you feeling quite well?'

Miss Foster's voice made Suzanne startle.

Now was the time to say something. She bit down hard on her lip.

'Y-yes, I think so, but—'

'If you're worried about your songs, don't be,' Miss Foster said. 'Just look around you. Everyone's had far too much to drink already, and they won't notice the odd mistake.'

As usual she didn't bother to wait for any response.

Suzanne looked around the room, hoping to see where

Fern was. The actress was talking to the Governor and a fair-haired man, older and more casually dressed than the other men, yet somehow he had a presence. As though he was aware of her gaze he looked straight at her and even from the distance she saw he had the brightest eyes. Quickly, she looked away, not wanting him to think she was staring, and forced herself to say hello to an elderly couple who seemed delighted to chat to her.

In hardly any time at all Suzanne broke off from chatting with one of the lady guests who'd just asked which was her favourite opera, as the Governor called for silence. Her heart immediately thumped so hard she felt it would slam through her chest.

'We're ready to begin the entertainment again with our second singer this evening,' he said, looking towards Suzanne. 'So please give the young lady a warm welcome.'

There was a ripple of polite clapping.

Suzanne didn't know how she managed to walk over to the piano without tripping over the trailing skirt of Fern's gown, her legs were shaking so much. Like Adelaide, she put her hand on the piano but it was to recover her balance rather than trying to look like a professional. Bram gave her a weak smile that made her wonder whether he was concerned for her performance. Maybe he thought she wouldn't be good enough. She forced herself to smile back. After all, that was the song she was going to start off with.

He nodded and played the introduction. She glanced over to the people, hoping Fern had kept her promise to be close by, when she spotted Cat Bliss. For a moment Suzanne froze. What was she doing here? As far as she remembered, Miss Foster hadn't read her name out. She immediately averted her eyes, not wanting to be influenced by such a sour expression on Cat's face. She saw Bram looking up at her and nodding to come in. But what was the first line? She couldn't remember it. Her mind went blank. Bram played the introduction again and mouthed the words.

Thank you, dear Bram.

She opened her mouth, but to her dismay Bram stopped abruptly and began to shake. Sweat poured off his forehead and trickled down his cheeks, and he drew out a handkerchief and wiped his face.

Before she could ask him what was the matter he struggled to his feet.

'I'm awfully sorry, everyone, but I can't carry on.'

The shaking became violent. He obviously had a temperature. No wonder no one had seen him all day.

'Bram, sit down again. I'll go and fetch help.' Suzanne started towards Miss Foster, but the Governor was already speaking to one of the waiters who nodded and went straight over. He helped Bram up from the piano stool and the two men disappeared.

'Will they call a doctor, Sir Noel?' Miss Foster was asking as Suzanne stood tentatively back from the pair of them, feeling worried about Bram and at the same time strangely disappointed she wouldn't be singing after all.

'Oh, yes. No need to worry on that score,' the Governor said. 'What a pity our entertainments broke up. I was looking forward to hearing the young lady—' He broke off as he caught sight of Suzanne. 'Ah, here's the young lady herself. I'm sorry you didn't have a chance to sing to us this evening, my dear,' he said, turning to her.

'I'm only sorry Bram's not well,' Suzanne said.

A shadow fell over them.

'Perhaps I can help.'

It was the fair-haired man, his eyes the brightest blue as he glanced at the small group.

'*I* play the piano,' he said with a trace of an accent.

Was he German? He had that appearance. She didn't dare look fully at him again.

'That's marvellous news,' Miss Foster gushed, looking at him and smiling. 'It would just be a couple of modern songs.'

'I would be most honoured.' He gave a hint of a bow.

Suzanne's stomach fluttered all over again. First Bram being taken ill and now she'd be singing with a stranger accompanying her.

You're being an utter baby, she told herself. *Pull yourself together. There's a war on, for goodness' sake.*

Taking a deep breath she walked back to the piano and waited for the foreign man to take his seat. She watched as his hands wandered over the keys without actually making any sound. They were nice hands. Long sensitive fingers. True pianist's hands.

He looked up. She'd never seen anyone with eyes quite that blue.

'What you would like to sing, Miss . . .?'

'Suzy,' she said. She might as well use that name. Most of the ENSA people did and Wendy said it was more suitable for a jazz singer. She swallowed.

His back straightened and he hesitated. Then he smiled. 'So, Miss Suzy, what will it be?'

'"I'll Never Smile Again".' She looked at him. 'Do you know it?'

'*Ja*. I will play the introduction and give you the sign when you will begin.'

Ja? So he is German. But he couldn't be a Nazi or he wouldn't be walking about freely. The Governor would have clapped him in jail, surely.

'Tell me if this is the correct key.'

He played a phrase and she nodded.

And then her attention was completely focused on the music. Bram had been perfectly fine on the piano, but *this* man, older than Bram – maybe in his fifties – there was something special about his playing . . . the way he almost caressed the keys.

She looked away. If she wasn't careful she'd miss her introduction. She took in a breath, trying to block out the guests who were still chatting and clinking glasses. She imagined herself playing and singing. She found herself singing. James was in her heart and she was singing to him. Her heart soared.

'I'll never smile again . . . until I smile at you.'

She turned and smiled at the pianist.

He smiled back at her – a smile so full of warmth it enveloped her.

Suddenly there was a silence. Her eyes had been half closed. Now she opened them and took in the room. No one spoke, but all eyes were on her. She caught her breath. Had she made a complete idiot of herself? Would Miss Foster send her back? But whatever happened, she'd loved every second of singing. And this lovely man had accompanied her in exactly the same way as she would have accompanied herself.

As she turned to him, worried now with such a wall of silence, the man rose from the stool. Not only Miss Foster but she'd let him down too. Worse, she'd let herself down. Her stomach felt hollow. And then the clapping started. Someone called out *'Brava'* and the foreign pianist nodded to her and then to the scattered audience. He turned to her again and smiled. She extended her hand and he took it briefly.

'Thank you so much,' she said, her voice small now, against the noise of the clapping.

He inclined his head. 'I very much liked playing for you, Miss Suzy. You have an unusual and very beautiful voice.' He paused. 'But we are keeping your audience waiting, so what is your next song to be?'

As he finished speaking there was a crack of electricity overhead, then a roll of thunder so loud Suzanne thought the ceiling was about to hurtle down. Suddenly the room plunged into darkness, save for the few tealights that only sent out a glow. A woman swore as she fell to the floor. There was the sound of glass shattering.

Seconds later a male guest shouted, 'Was that you, darling?'

'Depends on which lady you're addressing,' came the swift reply, giving rise to hoots of laughter.

Suzanne stood where she was by the piano thinking she'd be safer than wandering around and maybe bumping into someone and causing another accident. Waiters were already lighting thick white candles, and in their soft light Suzanne could make out the figure of Miss Foster hurrying towards her and the foreign pianist.

'Thank you for stepping in, Mr . . .' She raised a questioning eyebrow but he only nodded. She turned to Suzanne. 'You sang it well, my dear. But because of poor Bram and no proper light, I think we'll call it a day. There'll be plenty of time when we get to our camp. I've told Sir Noel that we'll be going back to our hotel now, as I want to be there in case there's any news of Bram, so we'll go and say our goodbyes. Please be at the entrance in ten minutes.'

As Miss Foster hurried off, the pianist carefully pulled down the piano lid. His expression was serious as he stood and said quietly, 'I am sorry not to have played for you the next song.' He took her hand and raised it not quite to his lips, then turned and walked away.

'C'mon, honey.' It was Adelaide. 'We need to go.'

Suzanne felt a rush of relief. The other guests' chatter and laughter was beginning to grate on her. It had been a strange evening amongst strange people she had nothing in common with . . . except the German pianist. She'd felt completely comfortable with him.

She shrugged. What she needed now was to find the cloakroom. With a bit of luck she might have five minutes to calm herself. It must be the shock of thinking the crashes and bangs had been an air raid. Or perhaps it was the relief of overcoming her nerves and singing her first song in public. And an even greater relief that the audience had seemed to enjoy it.

Chapter Twenty-Five

'How did it all go last night?' Betty said the following morning at breakfast in the shabby little dining room of the hotel.

'Bram was taken ill.'

'Oh, no. What happened?'

'I thought he didn't look himself when he was playing for Adelaide – she went on first.' She quickly filled Betty in.

'How awful,' Betty said, scraping margarine onto a piece of toast. 'But how lucky someone stepped in so you were able to do your bit.'

Betty went on to talk about the other women – asking for details about what they were wearing.

'By the way, you looked gorgeous in Fern's gown, the glimpse I got of you in the dark when you came in,' she said. 'Sorry I was too tired to talk – I think I was knocked out after being so sick on the ship.'

'I'll feel better when it's safely in her wardrobe again,' Suzanne said fervently. 'I was always conscious it wasn't mine.' She took a piece of toast from the rack. 'It was so kind of her to lend it to me,' she added quickly, 'but after the initial excitement of wearing something so beautiful, I realised it wasn't quite *me*, if you know what I mean.'

'It did make you look older, if that's what you mean,' Betty said, 'but that may not be a bad thing. If you look too young and vulnerable to the airmen, they might take advantage of you.'

Suzanne flushed. 'They've already had it drilled into them that they have to treat us with respect,' she said. 'And I'm certainly not going to encourage them to do anything but that.'

James. He was the only one she would ever want to encourage. She wondered how long she'd have to wait before she heard from him again. She could picture his face still, but she wished she had a photograph of him, though they hadn't really got to that stage. The war had seen to that.

'You haven't told me about Adelaide,' Betty said. 'Did you like her voice?'

'She was smashing,' Suzanne said, her face aglow. 'It was so funny when she sang "Stormy Weather" and the thunderstorm started.' She wasn't going to tell Betty she'd thought it was an air raid. 'Then she sang a couple of jazzy numbers. I wish I could sing like that. I do wish you could have heard her, Betty. Your sax would have sounded marvellous with her singing.'

'Probably best I didn't,' Betty said, crunching her last piece of toast and jam. 'I'd have been terrified to play with someone that famous.'

'I'm longing to hear you play,' Suzanne said at the same time as Fern swept into the dining room as if she were entering the Ritz.

'Ah, there you are!' Fern made a beeline for their table.

Out of the corner of her eye Suzanne saw Cat watching with eyes like slits. Just like the animal she was named after, she thought with a ripple of unease.

'You were absolutely charming, sweetie,' Fern said, bending to kiss her cheek. 'And that voice. You had us all in tears.'

'Thank you.' Suzanne blushed. 'I'm sure your beautiful gown had something to do with it.' She looked up. 'Can I bring it to you after breakfast?'

'Do. Third floor. Room twenty-eight.'

'May I have your attention, please?' It was Miss Foster. Everyone quietened down and heads turned towards her. 'You'll all be pleased to know we have a plane at our disposal today – much sooner than we thought.'

There was a huge cheer from the tables.

'Where're we going?' one of the dancers asked.

'When we arrive I'll tell you where we are,' Miss Foster admonished, 'and not a moment before.'

'I've got a bet on – Sicily,' an older man called out. Suzanne remembered he'd told her he played the double bass, but she couldn't for the life of her remember his name.

'Bit dangerous there at the moment, Norman,' Miss Foster said, 'so you might well lose your bet.' Her eyes swept over the group, missing nothing. 'Please, everyone, pack your things and be in the foyer at ten o'clock sharp.'

'What about Bram?' someone called out.

'He's a little better this morning, so he'll be coming with us.'

Back in their room, Suzanne took Fern's gown off the hanger.

'I'll just pop this upstairs, Betty,' she said, putting it over her arm.

'Don't be long – we need to get packed—' Betty broke off, her mouth slack as she pointed to Fern's dress. 'What's that?'

Suzanne looked down. 'What do you mean?'

Betty put her hand on the skirt and gathered the folds towards Suzanne.

Suzanne stared in horror. An ugly red stain – as though someone had thrown a bottle of dark red ink over it.

'Oh, Betty, what is it?'

'It looks like red wine to me.'

'But I didn't have any red wine,' Suzanne said, her heart pumping. 'I had a few sips of champagne – that's all.'

'*You* couldn't have done it because it's at the back of the skirt. Someone must have had an accident and not had the decency to tell you and apologise.' Betty let the material drop back into place. She stared at Suzanne. 'Or somebody has it in for you and did it on purpose!'

Suzanne covered her eyes with her hands for some seconds. 'But who would have done anything so horrible? I've hardly even spoken to anyone, and the ones I've met seem so nice.' She bit down on her lip. 'No, it can't be that. Someone would have seen it happen and said something.' A thought struck her. 'Although maybe they didn't. The storm put the lights out and it was pitch-black for a few moments until the waiters lit some candles. A woman fell as it was. It could have been her and she might not have realised in the dark what had happened.' She looked at Betty. 'What on earth am I going to tell Fern?'

'The truth,' Betty said. 'That's all you can do, Suzy . . . tell her the truth.' She looked at Suzanne. 'Do you want me to come with you?'

'No,' Suzanne said. 'I have to sort this out on my own.'

Suppose Betty was right and it hadn't been an accident – if someone really had spilt the drink on purpose. There was only one person who might possibly have tried something so mean, but she wouldn't even hint at it to anyone until she had proof.

Taking the dress from Betty, she said, 'I deserve Fern's anger, but how I wish I'd kept my own dress on. It would have felt more like me anyway. I was nervous every minute I wore Fern's.' She gulped. 'Wish me luck, Betty. I'll go and confess straightaway and offer to pay for the dry cleaning as I wouldn't dare wash it.'

'Good luck, Suzy,' Suzanne heard Betty call as she left the room, the dress forlornly dangling over her arm.

Her footsteps clacked on the bare treads as she made her way up the three flights of stairs. Room 28 was marked just to her right as she reached the landing. And underneath the room number was pinned a hastily written note:

Suzy, just go in and put the dress on the bed. Thanks. Fern x

Blast! Suzanne stood there uncertain what to do. She couldn't just leave it with the stain unexplained. But she didn't want to take it back downstairs again, either. Well, the only thing would be to wait until Fern returned. Surely she'd be back in a few minutes.

But the minutes ticked by and there was no sign of Fern. And in ten minutes they were due to meet in the lobby, ready to catch their plane.

'Suzy! You need to come and finish packing!'

It was Betty, shouting up the stairs. Suzanne rushed to the door.

'I'm coming,' she called.

She'd have to take the dress back down with her.

There was still no sign of Fern when the ENSA group boarded the coach to take them to the airport.

'Miss Foster, have you seen Fern?' Suzanne asked as she was ticking off all the names.

'She won't be coming with us on our plane,' Miss Foster said. 'She's staying behind with a few other actors to try a new play out on the boys this evening. They should be joining us in a day or two.'

Fern would think she'd forgotten to give the dress back.

Betty, sitting next to Suzanne near the back of the coach, gave her a sympathetic glance. They watched as Cat Bliss made her way down the aisle, stopping by and smiling or having a word with every ENSA member – except one. Suzanne watched wide-eyed with disbelief as Cat marched straight past Adelaide as though the singer didn't exist. As she came parallel to Suzanne and Betty's seat she nodded.

'Morning.' Cat smiled, and there was a gleam in her eyes. Suzanne deliberately turned her head.

The coach was hot and stuffy by the time they arrived at the airport. Most faces were flushed but Bram still looked pale. Thankfully, it had only been a short journey, and maybe he'd be able to rest when they arrived at wherever they were staying.

As they stepped off the coach, the heat met Suzanne like a blast.

'Cor, we don't get weather like this in Blighty,' Betty said happily, turning her face upwards towards the sun.

'I'm rather glad we don't,' Suzanne said. 'I just go red and blotchy, which doesn't look very attractive.'

'It's because your skin's very fair like mine,' Betty said, 'except I'm a ginger-nut and you're a typical English rose. The complete opposite to Adelaide. But I love hers.'

'I do, too,' Suzanne said with enthusiasm. 'And it doesn't matter what colour she wears, she always looks marvellous.'

'I agree,' Betty returned. She lowered her voice, even though no one was near them. 'I've never seen a black person up close until now, have you?'

'No, I haven't, let alone spoken to one. But she's so friendly and natural. I hope we'll get to know her more and hear about America.'

'I hope so, too,' Betty said fervently. 'But you know what? Cat dislikes her.'

Suzanne held her breath. 'Why do you say that?'

'Did you notice she didn't even say good morning to Adelaide when we were on the coach? Just marched straight by. No acknowledgement whatsoever, the way she did everyone else.'

'Yes, I *did* notice. And I wonder if anyone else did,' Suzanne said.

'You said Cat was at the party last night, didn't you?' Betty frowned. 'Even though Miss Foster never called out her name.'

'Yes, that's right.'

'I wonder how she managed to wangle that invitation.' She hesitated. 'You know something, Suzy. I know I probably shouldn't say this, but I have a niggling feeling she might have had something to do with that wine stain.'

Betty slipped her arm through Suzanne's as they went through customs and onto the airfield. It was a warm feeling between friends and for the first time since she'd seen the stain, Suzanne forgot all about the dress and how Fern would react. What had given her a frisson was the sight of the aeroplanes lined up and to know she would soon be on one of them. Raine would have pointed out all the different makes, Suzanne thought. Oh, if only her sister could see her now!

The double row of canvas seats in the aircraft faced one another in not the most comfortable-looking arrangement. Then Suzanne berated herself. What did comfort matter when soldiers – often only her age – who'd be going off to fight, carried the overwhelming possibility they might not ever return.

'We'll be going sideways,' Betty said miserably. 'That's enough to make me feel sick.'

'Don't think about it,' Suzanne said, taking a seat and pulling Betty down next to her. It'll be an adventure.' She turned to her friend. 'Did I tell you my sister's a pilot in the Air Transport Auxiliary? And she absolutely adores it.'

'No, you didn't mention it,' Betty said, sounding impressed. 'Well, she's going to be very proud of you for spreading your own wings. Trouble is, you won't be allowed to tell her where you are or where you've been until this damned war is over. Same as Andy.' Her smile faded.

'Oh, is Andy a boyfriend?' Suzanne asked curiously.

'No, he's my brother – and a rear gunner. He says it's the most dangerous place to be – at the back of a plane. You're totally on your own, and ripe for getting shot at.'

'Oh, Betty.' Suzanne put her hand on her friend's arm. 'I'll say a prayer that he'll keep safe.'

'If you believe in that sort of thing,' Betty said grimly. 'I'm afraid I don't.'

'I know with the terrible things going on at the moment it makes you wonder.' Suzanne felt the knot in her stomach tighten. 'But sometimes I feel that's all we can hang on to.'

Everyone stopped their chattering as the aeroplane's engine revved up for take-off. Betty grabbed Suzanne's hand, giggling with terror. The plane seemed to make a mad dash along the runway, and just when Suzanne thought it would never leave the ground, her heart almost stopped when there was a sudden roar and they were up, feeling the tilt as it gained height over Gibraltar.

'Now we're on the last lap of our journey,' Miss Foster said from her seat at the end of the row opposite Suzanne and Betty, 'I can divulge where we're going to be based . . . it's Malta.'

There were one or two cheers but Lily, the principal dancer, sitting the other side of Suzanne, drew in a sharp breath. 'I thought it'd been bombed to smithereens.'

'That's true,' Miss Foster replied. 'The Island suffered terribly but the last raid was at the end of last year. Of course we can't be complacent—' she pushed her glasses up her nose '—but we wouldn't be going there if the situation hadn't vastly improved and it's no longer considered to be a danger zone. I particularly wanted us to go to Malta because the people were so brave. As well as losing their loved ones and their homes they almost starved to death. Some of you might know all this, but those who don't need to understand what the situation was until end of last year. Few merchant ships got through and our boys defending the Island insisted on having exactly the same food rations as the islanders. It makes you proud to be British.' Miss Foster sniffed and gave Lily a brief smile. 'And the Maltese . . . it didn't matter what the enemy threw at them, they refused to be beaten. And when King George awarded the whole Island with the George Cross in April last year – something unheard of – it couldn't have been better timed.'

Everyone went silent, digesting this information. Suzanne tried to visualise herself as one of the Maltese girls, terrified of the bombs dropping day after day, night after night, yet still refusing to give in. It was a frightening thought. She mustn't think along those lines, but she hoped Miss Foster would invite the civilians sometimes to a concert. It seemed the least they could do.

'That'll be all,' Miss Foster said and opened one of her files to jot down some notes.

'I just wish there was a window so we could see out,' Betty said. 'This dark tunnel atmosphere makes me feel claustrophobic.'

'Raine says she feels as free as the birds when she's

whooshing along, but of course she's got the best seat in the house.'

'Mmm.' Betty's eyes were closed, still hanging on to Suzanne's hand.

'Just think.' Suzanne nudged her friend after some minutes. Betty's eyes popped open. 'We must actually be flying above the clouds. I bet they look like cotton wool. I wish we could see them too, but isn't it fantastic even imagining?'

'I suppose.' Betty sounded unconvinced. 'I'll think it's even more fantastic when we've landed . . . and I haven't been sick.'

'You won't be,' Suzanne said. And even though it was extremely bumpy at times, she proved to be right.

Chapter Twenty-Six

The Dakota military aeroplane made a smooth landing at Luqa Airport. If anything, it felt even hotter than Gibraltar as Suzanne stepped off the plane and onto the paved runway. Several fighter planes were dispersed around the periphery and Suzanne glimpsed several craters on the airfield, which must have been caused by bombs. Picturing the exhausted RAF boys defending the Island, she couldn't help a shudder as she tilted her head to the blue cloudless sky.

Perspiration broke out on her forehead. She lifted her chin and blew out her cheeks, stirring a few strands of hair before they settled damply around her face again.

'I guess we'll have to get used to this heat,' a voice behind her called.

Suzanne turned to see Adelaide grinning as she caught up with her.

'Do you have weather like this where you come from?' Suzanne asked a little shyly, increasing her speed to keep pace with the energetic woman alongside her.

'I'm from Brooklyn, New York,' the American woman said, 'and that can get pretty hot in the summer, too. My tough old skin can take it . . .' she gazed at Suzanne '. . . whereas your delicate lily-white one most definitely *can't*. It's one of my few "being black" advantages.' She gave a chuckle.

'Do you still live in America?'

'No, honey, I came to London before the war started – nineteen-thirty-eight.'

'How long will you stay in England?' Suzanne asked curiously.

'Oh, I'll never go back.' Adelaide tossed her head. 'I much prefer living in England. I have some good friends there.'

It seemed strange to Suzanne that you could leave your country and live in another for the rest of your life. She'd always heard how marvellous America was. And from the little she'd heard, the war didn't seem to have altered their way of life much. Apparently, there was no rationing of food or clothes or petrol.

'Black people aren't treated the same as whites,' Adelaide went on. 'We're still slaves in many people's eyes in America . . . especially in the South. So I knew I'd never make it to the top all the while I lived there. That's the reason I went to England. It was like a breath of fresh air being treated as a human being who has a heart and soul. Not being called names or told not to come in by a certain door because that was reserved for "whites only".' She gave a rueful smile. 'The band I sing with are all black, and we've been welcomed with open arms wherever we've performed. Now there's a war on . . . well . . .' She shrugged. 'I want to do my bit. That's why I joined ENSA. And coming to Malta is as good as anything I can think of at the moment. By the sounds of it, the islanders have had a real rough time as well as the servicemen, and I reckon they need cheering up, too.' She glanced at Suzanne. 'How about you? Why did you join?'

But Suzanne was so confused by what Adelaide had said about American people not treating black people the same that she couldn't bring herself to talk about her own situation. It must have been awful for Adelaide to uproot and leave her family. But she'd obviously made the right decision. Suzanne swallowed. Until lately, she'd been sure of her roots and where she belonged. But now, there was so much uncertainty. She had *two* French parents. Even though her mother had told her, it hadn't really sunk in. She wasn't English after all, as she'd taken for granted all her life. She was totally and utterly French. Even more strange, her sisters were only half-sisters.

Tears sprang to her eyes. She needed her sisters right now. Needed to talk to them. Have Raine's reassurance that of course she belonged. That she was their sister in every way. And she needed Ronnie's down-to-earth way of speaking. '*Snap out of it, Suzy,*' she almost heard her younger sister say. '*You're being too dramatic for words. You're our family as much as we are yours.*'

But, even if she could talk to her sisters right this minute, nothing they said would alter the fact that it wasn't completely true.

'What were you and Adelaide talking about when we got off the plane?' Betty said. 'It looked like the two of you were in deep conversation.'

'She was telling me why she came to England to live just before the war started,' Suzanne said. 'Apparently, Americans aren't always very nice to black people and she knew she'd never be celebrated as a professional singer if she stayed.'

'I've heard that, too,' Betty said. 'Even in the American army, the black soldiers have to be in separate quarters and march separately and everything.' Betty pulled a face. 'I never really understood the reason and I still don't. After all, they're laying down their lives as well as anyone else.'

'I know,' Suzanne said. 'I felt terrible just hearing Adelaide say that black people are treated like slaves. Thank goodness she hasn't had that kind of reaction in England. I'd be ashamed if she did.'

'What about the way Cat Bliss treated her earlier?' Betty said with raised eyebrow.

'Maybe we're seeing things that aren't really there,' Suzanne said, hoping it was the truth.

The band had been allocated to the Hotel Victoria, a modest building, but thankfully, lighter and brighter than the one in Gibraltar, Suzanne was grateful to note. But although the room was much larger, there were *three* single beds, each separated only by a narrow bedside table.

'I just hope Cat isn't going to be the third,' Betty said.

'If she is, we'd have to make the best of it,' Suzanne said mildly.

'Oh, no, we won't,' Betty returned. 'I shall go and see Miss Foster.'

There was a soft knock on the open door. Suzanne whirled round, her fingers crossed.

'Well, I guess I'm down to share with you gals, if you don't mind. It's only for a few nights until they find me a room.'

It was Adelaide, smiling her wonderful smile.

'You don't know how pleased and relieved we are,' Suzanne said, smiling back. 'And as you're the most famous, we'll even let you choose which bed.'

'Thanks for not saying, "as you're the eldest by far",' Adelaide chuckled. Her eyes dropped to the three beds. 'I'll take the middle one . . . be Momma and stop any fighting.'

'Hello, sweetie. Have you and Betty settled in?' Fern said as she entered the officers' mess in the garrison building at lunchtime the following day.

Suzanne's stomach lurched. 'Fern, I must see you in private.'

Fern raised a pencilled eyebrow. 'All right. Why don't we take that table on the far side?'

'Do you mind if we go to the hotel?'

'Which is . . .?'

'The Victoria.' Suzanne paused. 'Are you there as well?'

'No, I'm just along the road with the Noël Coward actors – and it's a darned sight better than the one in Gib.' Fern looked at Suzanne and smiled. 'Don't look so serious. It can't be that bad.'

If only you knew, Suzanne thought, as they walked the half a mile to the hotel.

The lobby was light and filled with vases of flowers, a real contrast to the one in Gibraltar. They were greeted by a smiling receptionist who handed Suzanne her key.

Suzanne's heart was in her throat as she led the way to the first floor and the room she shared with the others.

'This is *nice*,' Fern said, then stopped. 'But you're sharing with two more.'

'Yes,' Suzanne said. 'Betty and Adelaide.'

'And is that okay?'

'We're all very different from one another,' Suzanne said, 'but they're both smashing. I know Betty quite well by now, and we're both keen to find out more about Adelaide. She pretends to be a mother to us but it doesn't come off. She's more like an older sister. It's rather exciting having a famous singer with us. But it's only for a few nights.'

Fern looked doubtful. 'They need to buck up about it because she's a huge star in England.'

'I know, but she doesn't seem to mind.'

Fern regarded Suzanne. 'The evening in the Governor's Residence went very well, I thought . . . that is, until poor old Bram was taken ill and that fair-haired chap took his place.' She gave Suzanne an encouraging smile. 'But if that's what you wanted to talk to me about – being worried how you sounded, then don't. You had me almost weeping. My dear, you have a beautiful voice. I could have listened to it all evening. But the main thing is . . .' She looked hard at Suzanne, 'did *you* enjoy singing one of my favourites?'

A lump formed in Suzanne's throat. 'Yes . . . oh, I don't know . . .'

Fern smiled. 'I might add that the dress suited you down to the ground and you looked absolutely sensational.'

'I was awfully nervous . . .' Suzanne stopped. She swallowed hard, then said, 'Fern, I must ask you – did you notice anyone come up to me . . . from behind?'

'What do you mean?'

'I have a terrible confession to make. When I was about to carefully fold your dress the next morning to return it to you, Betty noticed a horrible red stain at the back. She thinks it was red wine and that someone must have spilt it on me. *I* didn't have any wine – all I had was a small glass of champagne all evening.'

Fern's smile faded. 'Show it to me.'

Suzanne took it from its hanger in the wardrobe and spread the dress on the bed, the back of the skirt facing upwards and showing the stain.

Fern frowned as she lifted a fold of material and inspected it closely.

'Betty's right,' she said. 'It's definitely red wine, which is a sod to come out – if it ever does. And the material is so delicate I daren't use anything strong on it for fear of making it worse.'

Misery clouded Suzanne's vision. A tear escaped down her cheek.

'I'm so very sorry, Fern.' Her voice shook. 'I wouldn't have let anything like that happen for the world. I just didn't notice . . . didn't feel anyone . . .' She burst into tears.

'My dear girl,' Fern was beside her in an instant, her arm around her. 'This isn't your fault. I don't blame you one bit. It must have happened when the lights went out with the storm. Do you remember that woman who fell? It was more than likely her. She wouldn't have known . . . well, not until the lights came on again and she saw her empty glass. And even then she might not have realised she'd actually spilt it on someone's dress.' She gave Suzanne's arm a little shake. 'Don't look so distressed, sweetie. I *do* have other gowns. But you don't. That's what I'm sorry about.'

'I don't mind that,' Suzanne said, sniffing. 'I just wish I knew what happened.'

'Here, use this.' Fern thrust a handkerchief in Suzanne's hands. 'It must have been an accident and she was too cowardly to tell you.' She waited for Suzanne to blow her nose, then asked, 'Have you spoken to Miss Foster about this?'

'No, I wanted to tell you first.'

Should she say anything to Fern about her and Betty's thoughts that it might not have been an accident? Suzanne hovered, then decided there was no proof at all and it would be terrible if she pointed a finger to someone who was innocent. Even if that person was Cat.

'Come on, sweetie, wipe your eyes and forget it.'

Chapter Twenty-Seven

Suzanne was too busy rehearsing the following morning to think further about Cat Bliss. The room at the back of the Mess building had suffered bomb damage by the look of some shattered windows, but Miss Foster had decided it was perfectly fit to use.

'You can't stick at "I'll Never Smile Again", Suzy,' Bram said, seeming to have finally recovered, as he glanced up at her from the piano. 'What other songs would you like to sing?'

'"Chattanooga choo choo",' Suzanne said without hesitating.

'Hmm. You really need a couple of other singers with you on that one – and we've only got you and Adelaide with this band.' He looked up at her. 'Hey, that's an idea. Shall we ask her if she'd like to join you? I think that might go down really well with the chaps.'

'I'd love it,' Suzanne said fervently. 'And I'd be honoured if she'd agree to sing with an amateur.'

'Get this straight, Suzy – from now on, *never* refer to yourself as an amateur. You're a professional – okay?'

'Yes, sir.' She gave him a mock salute and he grinned.

'Right, now that's settled we'll get Adelaide on board. She should be along in—' he looked at his watch '—half an hour. Meantime, as you're keen to do something a bit lively, let's try you with "Don't Sit Under The Apple Tree". You know that?'

Suzanne nodded.

'Good. We'll be performing tonight with the band and I want you to be word and note perfect.' He handed her the song sheet. 'I'll play it through once, then you come in.'

'You're not quite there yet,' he said when she'd finished.

'Oh, that doesn't sound very good.'

'Singing's fine, but I want some energy. Use your hands. Give me some action. Here, let me show you.'

Bram stood away from the piano and began to sing. He had a pleasant voice, but the way he put it over was . . . well, it was terrific. Suzanne could see exactly what he was getting at. He was smiling round at a phantom audience, using his hands to express the words and feelings, and when he came to the bit about marching home, he pretended to march in time to the music, making Suzanne smile.

'That will look so much better when *you* do it,' he said, chuckling as he sat down at the keyboard again. 'Especially in that lovely dress you wore at the Governor's place the other night.'

Suzanne's smile faded.

'Just think what the words mean,' Bram carried on, 'not just for themselves but what they mean to the boys listening. Put some spark into it. Speak to them when you sing. Get right into their hearts.' He paused and ran his hand through his hair. 'Actually, the best advice I can give you is to catch the eye of just one chap and sing to him with all your heart. Then every soldier, I can guarantee, will think you're singing to him alone.'

Trying to push the reference to Fern's dress aside, she sang it again, then shook her head on the closing phrase. It was worse than the first time. It had sounded falsely gay to her ears when she didn't feel that way at all. And her arm movements felt even more forced and unnatural.

'And again,' Bram said, a disappointed expression on his face.

'I can't,' she said. 'I'm . . .'

Bram gave her a sharp look. 'What's the matter, Suzy?'

'I don't know,' she said miserably. 'I'm just not up to it.'

'Come and sit down with me.' He gestured to a couple of armchairs. 'Now,' he said, 'let's just go through a few things. First of all, you didn't feel comfortable singing the last song, which is a faster tempo, even though you seem to shy away from the ballads. I wonder why that is.'

'I'm not sure . . . maybe it's because I'm not confident my voice is good enough, and it might get lost more in a faster rhythm.'

'There's something else you're upset about.'

She shook her head.

He looked at her intently. 'You feel it should be your friend here and singing to the troops this evening, don't you?'

She bit her lip hard. 'I think . . . maybe you're right.'

'May I make a suggestion. Why don't we leave the jazzy numbers to Adelaide who is very experienced. It's where her voice belongs and where she's dynamic when she puts it across. It suits her personality. Then you and I will work on the ballads . . . which is where I believe *your* voice and *your* personality belong. But I'll let you both sing "Chattanooga choo choo",' he finished with a twinkle. 'How does that sound?'

'Did I hear my name?' It was Adelaide, smiling as she waltzed into the room.

'You did,' Bram said. 'Would you please this little gal enormously by singing with her the "Chattanooga choo choo"? She seems to have set her heart on it.'

'I'd love to,' Adelaide said, her smile spreading. 'Shall we give it a go right away?' She stood by the piano and waved for Suzanne and Bram to join her.

Adelaide made everything fun. She laughed, she threw an arm around Suzanne's shoulder if she faltered, and she made Bram start again. Then she winked at him and mouthed something and he grinned and joined in the chorus as he accompanied them:

'Get aboard, All aboard, Chattanooga choo choo,
Won't you choo choo me home.'

Adelaide gave her infectious laugh and, still at the mic, spoke the words as Bram did a few more trills: 'C'mon, y'all, the train's about to leave and I'm gonna be on it.'

'That's more like it,' Bram said, as he rolled his fingers over the keys to a dramatic end. 'I think the boys are going to love this one.'

'Actually, it sounded real good when you joined in, Bram,' Adelaide said, throwing him a beaming smile. 'So on the night do the same.' She turned to Suzanne. 'Are you okay with it now, Suzy-girl?'

'Yes, it was fun. I loved it, too, when we all sang together.'

'Right. Let's press on.' Bram flicked through the song sheets. 'Do you want to stay and listen to Suzy, Adelaide?'

'Sure – if that's all right with you, honey.'

Suzanne nodded weakly.

'Is there a special song you'd like to sing, Suzy?' Bram said. 'A favourite? Choose one that would really pierce the hearts of the chaps and remind them of home.'

Suzanne closed her eyes. She imagined being on a stage with hundreds of exhausted airmen and sailors who hadn't had any live entertainment since the worst of the bombardment was over. Poor Malta had been bombed worse than anywhere, so Miss Foster had told them, though she and

Betty hadn't had time yet to walk to Valletta to see for themselves. The islanders had remained stoical, grateful to all those airmen and sailors who hadn't been home for maybe a couple of years or more. Men who had left their sweethearts and wives and children in England, wanting this war to be over so they could go home and be part of their families again. She swallowed hard.

'Do you know "The Very Thought Of You"?' she asked.

Bram immediately played the introduction. Suzanne sang with her whole heart.

'That hit the spot perfectly,' Adelaide said, coming up to her and kissing her cheek. 'I'll leave you two to it and I'll be back in, say, an hour?'

Bram worked Suzanne hard, saying he wanted her to have a half a dozen songs that she would feel totally comfortable with. They were all slow songs – love songs – and she finally allowed herself to become immersed in the music and the words.

Maybe I'll get through the evening all right, after all.

'We're rehearsing again with Bram after lunch,' Betty said. 'He has a list of songs he's gone through with you and Adelaide, and he wants to spend a bit of time with the band to see how we sound with you both.' She paused. 'You all right?'

'A bit nervous, that's all.'

'Don't be. If we make a mistake no one's going to know. We're not playing to professionals.'

'I know, but I want to do my best.'

'Worst thing you can do is worry about it, so don't.' Betty mopped the last few drops of tomato soup with her bread. 'Bram said we'd be free at three-thirty so what about you and me having a swim? The exercise will do you good and take your mind off this evening.'

'I can't swim.'

Oh, why had she never let Raine or even Ronnie teach her? Ronnie loved nothing better than throwing herself in the water. But she'd always held back.

'It doesn't matter. You can come and watch me.'

Betty was right. It would be something to do.

'But be warned,' Betty said. 'Remember Miss Foster told us it's not a normal sandy beach like you'd get at home.'

'I can still take my shoes off and paddle on the edge,' Suzanne said, smiling.

'I don't think you'll be able to even do that,' Betty said. 'Apparently, to swim here you have to dive off a rock.'

'Oh, no.' Suzanne shuddered.

'Malta's probably not the right place to learn to swim,' Betty said seriously. 'Anyway, I'll meet you at the gate just after three-thirty. Bring a towel. That's about all you'll need.' She glanced at Suzanne. 'Oh, meant to say – there's a letter for you in the hotel pigeonhole.'

James! Suzanne's feet on wings, she raced back to the hotel and snatched the envelope from the cavity. Turning it over she saw it wasn't from James after all. It was the first letter she'd had from Maman since she'd been away.

Taking it up to her room, she slit open the envelope. They hadn't parted on the best of terms, she thought. Both of them had been careful not to mention her French father, but there was that underlying anger in her that try as she might, she couldn't shake it off.

She unfolded the sheet. Why did she suddenly have a feeling of dread? She began to read.

Suzanne, ma chérie,

I was relieved to receive your letter but it told me very little. I know you cannot say <u>where</u> you are but you can *say how you are. That is more important to me. It was truly a sad day when you left even though Véronique does her best to keep me cheerful. But I close my eyes and see my lovely daughter singing to our dear soldiers and I am certain you bring them closer to home. I do not think I have ever heard you sing. I look forward to the time.*

Every day since you were old enough I have wished to have the courage to tell you about your French father. But every time I thought today is the day, something would happen. You were growing up and studying your music and I thanked God you have something precious. I did not want to say anything that would destroy such talent by upsetting you. Music is always a great comfort to me and I know it is the same for you. And then my dearest Robert died. That should be when I made my confession. But it seemed even more important to keep the secret when we were all thinking of Dad and missing him. It would make his death even worse with such a revelation.

Do not think I am proud for what I did in the heat of a moment. But if I did not, I would not have my beautiful middle daughter. So I cannot be too angry with myself.

When you come home we will sit down together and I promise I will answer all your questions about your father. I dare not even write his name – just in case. He does not know you but he loves you. And I loved him. You will not understand this – you are too young and inexperienced – but I also loved Robert. He was my husband and the father of Lorraine. I had to make an impossible choice. I chose Robert. It was the right decision as I could not break his heart and deprive him of

Lorraine, his little daughter. It did not matter for me – my heart was already broken.

Dad loved you like his own, right from the beginning. When I told him all those years ago that I was carrying you he said he still loved me and forgave me. Dare I ask your forgiveness as well, my Suzanne?

Your loving Maman xx

Chapter Twenty-Eight

She had to concentrate. Put Maman's letter out of her mind for the time being. She'd think about it later, after the concert was over. Her hands trembling, Suzanne managed to secure the final button at the side of her flowered dress, remembering the last time she'd put it on and how Fern had insisted she needed something more glamorous.

Pressing down a stab of guilt at the thought of Fern's ruined gown, Suzanne glanced at the clock on her little bedside table. Just gone six. The performance didn't start until half-past eight but she should be in the officers' mess eating supper with the rest of the band. It was no good. If she tried, she knew she'd never be able to swallow anything.

'Are you coming to eat something before we go on?' Betty put her head round the door.

'I'm going to see Cat,' Suzanne said decisively. 'Ask if she could possibly help me with my make-up. She wouldn't last time but I want to see if she lets anything slip.'

'I'll come with you,' Betty said immediately, her eyes gleaming.

Cat called, 'Come in,' to Suzanne's knock, and when the two friends walked in she was taking out the last of her pin curls from the front of her upswept blonde hair. 'Oh, it's you,' she said to the dressing table mirror, fluffing the curls with her fingertips.

'And me,' Betty put in. 'I've told Suzy you might have a few spare minutes to make her up as she'll be in the limelight this evening. And if so, I'd love to watch and maybe pick up a few tips. The dancers you've made up today look super.'

Cat's expression remained sceptical. 'I suppose you'd better come in then, and *you* . . .' she grabbed a pile of magazines from one of the chairs, dropping them on the floor, and gesturing to Suzanne '. . . can sit here.'

Suzanne wasn't expecting this. Maybe it was because she had Betty with her and the woman didn't want to appear rude in front of a witness. Betty gave Suzanne a surreptitious wink.

'I haven't got time to do your hair,' Cat said, her mouth in a grim line. 'You should have it rolled up so you don't look like a schoolgirl.' She sighed theatrically. 'I suppose I could put some make-up on you.'

'Thank you.' There didn't seem much else to say.

Cat set to and unscrewed a jar. She smoothed some cream over Suzanne's forehead and cheeks and chin, then down her neck. At first, Suzanne felt herself tense, but after a few moments she decided to relax and enjoy it. Obviously, Cat knew what she was doing. Maybe she'd been wrong about her.

After some minutes Suzanne opened her eyes to see Cat spitting into a small oblong compact. What on earth . . .? But before she could object, Cat was coating her lashes with the paste. After a few moments Cat's long fingers patted some colour onto her cheeks. Suzanne opened her eyes again and watched Cat pick up a huge powder puff, which looked as though it could have done with a thorough wash. Next breath it was being puffed over her entire face and neck.

'Now for your lipstick . . .' Cat picked out a gold-coloured lipstick case from the half dozen on her dressing table and swivelled up a bright red, brighter than any lipstick Suzanne had ever worn, and quickly outlined, then filled in her lips. 'Okay, you're ready,' Cat said, stepping back to look at her with a critical raised eyebrow. 'All you have to do now is change into that glamorous affair you wore at the Governor's Residence the other night. That is, if you've managed to get that ugly stain out.'

What!

'You mean you know about it?'

'Of course I do. So does the whole of ENSA.'

'You saw someone do it and you didn't tell me?' Suzanne said, her voice rising. She'd got it all wrong then. It couldn't have been Cat, after all.

'Not my business.' Cat shrugged.

'Was it an accident?'

'Who knows?' Cat said. 'But from where I sat, it didn't look like it.'

'So someone did it on purpose?' Suzanne flashed as she stared at Cat. 'Who was it?'

'I wouldn't want to say,' Cat said, her eyes narrowing.

'You must. I have to know. The dress wasn't mine. That was what was so awful. I had to return it, damaged, to Miss Miller who was kind enough to lend it to me. I've never been so embarrassed.'

'I'm sure she's got plenty more,' Cat said. 'Someone that famous. So I shouldn't worry.'

'But I do,' Suzanne said. 'I'm determined to get to the bottom of it. Explain to her what happened. But I can't until you tell me who it was.'

'Well, don't look at me,' Cat said. 'I wasn't anywhere near you all evening, in case you didn't notice. The only person

I saw standing behind you with a glass of red wine in her hand was the darkie.'

'The darkie? Who are you talking about?'

'Adelaide Hall, of course.'

'Why would Adelaide do anything like that?' Betty said.

Cat glanced at Betty, then back at Suzanne. 'I expect she's jealous of you – a natural blonde with fair skin . . . and young enough to be her daughter. She's probably got a chip on her shoulder. Most of them do.'

'Who's "them"?' Betty demanded.

'Darkies, of course.'

'It's a shame you feel like this.' Suzanne shot up from the chair, retrieved her bag and looked directly at Cat.

Keep your voice level, Suzy. Don't let Cat see how angry you are.

'Besides being such a wonderful performer with a fabulous voice,' Suzanne said, 'Adelaide's a lovely person who I've never heard say anything bad about anyone.'

'Unlike some people,' Betty said, throwing Cat a glare. 'Come on, Suzy, we've stayed too long as it is.'

'What a bitch,' Betty said when they were back in their room.

'I honestly didn't know what she was talking about,' Suzanne said. 'And when she said she was referring to Adelaide, I felt ashamed of her. "Darkie". What a horrible word. This is the sort of thing Adelaide says she used to put up with in America, and that's why she came to England, but you don't expect anyone English to be so horrible.'

Betty shook her head. 'She certainly wanted you to believe it was Adelaide who spilt the wine over you. She despises her just because she's black, and she wants to get her into trouble.'

'But why would she want that?'

'Because deep down it's Cat who's the envious one. I think her aim is to get Adelaide sent back to England.' She looked at Suzy with raised eyebrow. 'And for some reason Cat's not keen on you, either – a natural blonde when she has to bleach her own hair – and the word's got round what a beautiful singing voice you have – so she's killing two birds with one stone. It's so simple. Everything she's accusing Adelaide of is exactly how *she's* feeling – she's eaten up with jealousy, and fear that she's not good enough. And deep down she knows she's not even nice enough.'

'But they say she's a talented cellist. And if she only smiled more she's a very attractive girl. So she doesn't need to be jealous of anyone.'

'Ha!' Betty said, over her shoulder as she picked out a plain black dress with a glittery silver bodice from the wardrobe they shared. 'You've been sheltered. There are some rotters out there. And she's one of them.' She paused while she removed her sundress and pulled the evening dress over her head. Then she slipped her feet into a pair of court shoes, gave a last quick glance in the mirror, and said, 'I'll leave you to it, as the band is having a last rehearsal before we go on.' She studied Suzanne. 'I'm not sure about the make-up job. It's very glam but it doesn't really look like you.'

'Well, I haven't a lot of time to remove it,' Suzanne said, going over to the dressing table mirror and peering at herself. She stepped back in surprise.

'Goodness, I've aged ten years!'

'She probably did it on purpose.'

'Actually, I don't feel comfortable at all. I'm going to wash it off.'

'Here, take this.' Betty handed her a jar of Pond's Cold Cream. 'I'm going. See you in a bit.' She turned at the door. 'I'm really looking forward to hearing you sing, Suzy.'

'Not half as much as I'm looking forward to hearing you play the sax,' Suzanne laughed.

But as soon as Betty disappeared, Suzanne's nerves threatened again. Once she'd finished she might as well walk over to the outdoor platform where they were going to perform. There was bound to be someone from ENSA, even if they were not in the band, who she could talk to. She needed to forget that in three-quarters of an hour she'd be on that stage. Sighing, she opened the jar of white cream, already marbled orange from Betty's own foundation, and stuck her finger in. She smeared a large blob of it over her face, then scrubbed off Cat's artistry with a face flannel.

Two men were setting some oil drums in a row on the airfield near the officers' mess as Suzanne wandered over to see what was going on. They placed several boards on top of the drums and one of the men jumped up and down on it, making it shift and creak.

'What's that for?' she asked.

They both looked up and grinned.

'It's the stage, miss.'

Suzanne took a horrified step backwards.

'It doesn't look safe.'

'For you, darlin', we'll make it safe,' the stocky one said, grinning so hard his face wreathed into weather-beaten lines.

'It can't be for the entire band.'

'Oh, no. It won't hold *them* up with all their instruments,' the second man said, giving her a cheeky wink. 'They'll have to play at the side of our magnificent stage and hardly be noticed. But so long as the spotlight's on *you*, love . . .'

Were they teasing her? She wasn't sure, but she smiled back.

It was a half hour before Betty appeared.

'Bram sent a message to Miss Foster saying he thought he'd better rest until this evening, so I hope he'll make it,' Betty said, taking the saxophone out of its case. 'Apparently, he feels quite low again, so he should see a doctor tomorrow if he hasn't improved.'

But as the band began to drift in, Bram was not one of them. It was quarter-past seven.

'Doesn't look like we have a pianist,' Betty said.

'Do you have the music?' Suzanne asked.

'Yes, for some of the pieces where we accompany a singer, but most of the swing band music we know by heart and if we don't, we improvise.' She looked at Suzanne with a raised eyebrow. 'Why?'

But before she could answer Betty she was startled by Miss Foster hurrying over the grass, panting a little, as she came up to the two of them.

'Suzy,' she gasped as she tried to catch her breath, 'I believe you play the piano.'

'Yes, I do.'

Miss Foster clapped her hands together.

'You'd be doing us a huge favour if you could stand in as the pianist this evening and also for Adelaide's rehearsals tomorrow. Bram's had another setback. I'm insisting he goes to the doctor tomorrow.' She gave Suzanne an imploring look. 'Do you think you could?'

'I've never played jazz before,' Suzanne said, 'but I'll have a go.'

'Well, it would certainly get us out of a spot,' Miss Foster said, her face relaxing. 'Pity there's no time for a rehearsal. But don't worry, we'll work something out tomorrow so you'll be able to sing, too. All right?' She gave a quick smile and was gone.

'Suzy, you can sing without the piano,' Betty said. 'You'll

have me and the band behind you. You'll recognise me – I'll be this one.' She contorted her face making Suzanne laugh. Then she fished out the music sheets from her saxophone case and handed them to Suzanne. 'Show 'em, Suzy.'

Sailors and airmen began to gather nearby, chattering and laughing, and pointing to the stage now occupied by the band. What a shame it wasn't a nice grassy airfield and they could sit on proper chairs instead of having to stand on rough ground. But that would probably not have even crossed their minds. Suzanne bent her head to study the music. She could instantly tell it was the kind that could easily and effectively be improvised. A frisson ran through her. Occasionally at home, if Maman wasn't around, she'd had some fun with these kinds of pieces on the piano after her violin practice and had thoroughly enjoyed herself. But this was real.

She caught Betty's eye as the band was tuning up. Betty sent her a thumbs up and Suzanne gave a shaky smile in return as she climbed onto the stage. How good it was to have down-to-earth Betty as her friend. Bob, the other cellist, took the platform in one leap.

'Bob, I hear Bram's still poorly—'

'Worse than that, Suzy. It sounds like the malaria is back with a vengeance so he's been taken to hospital. Probably be there for at least a fortnight, poor sod—' He broke off. 'Sorry, shouldn't swear in front of a lady.'

'It doesn't matter a bit. This war makes you swear,' Suzanne said. 'But I'm worried about Bram.'

'He was in Africa before this tour. That's where he picked it up. He'll recover, but it leaves us without a pianist.'

'I play the piano,' Suzanne said, 'though admittedly not in a jazz band. Miss Foster asked me if I'd step in tonight and Betty's given me the music.'

'Oh, that's a relief,' Bob said. 'Bram usually makes the introduction so why don't *you* take the mic.'

Panic caught in her throat. Bob nodded encouragingly.

She stepped forward to the microphone. This was the first time she'd ever used one. She didn't know how close or how far away she needed to be. There was still loud chatter from the audience, although several men looked towards her and one of them near the front hissed his mates to shut up.

She cleared her throat. 'Ladies and gentlemen . . .' she began, but there was no change in the noise level.

'Perhaps I should just say "Gentlemen",' she said, giving the words some extra power, but they were swallowed up in a high-pitched whistle. She gently tapped the head of the microphone, though what good that would do, she had no idea. She took a deep breath. Start again, she told herself, and this time with more force.

'GENTLEMEN!' She scanned the rows, smiling as she did so. There was a definite lowering of the noise level. 'I'm afraid our usual pianist has been taken ill so I've volunteered to take his place – temporarily, of course.' There were a few chuckles. 'So I hope you'll forgive any mistakes,' she added with a growing confidence that the microphone now appeared to be working. 'We'll start with a Glenn Miller favourite – "In The Mood".'

She sat at the piano and adjusted the seat, glancing towards Betty who raised her saxophone and put her lips to the mouthpiece. Suzanne nodded to bring in the band. She could tell immediately they were good. And when Betty stood and played a short solo piece on her saxophone, and Reg jumped up and answered it with his trumpet, Suzanne laughed out loud as she found the notes on the keyboard. Betty was superb. She suddenly realised how lucky she was to be here with such a talented group of people, all loving music. Yes, it was different from playing her music at home, and nothing could ever take away her love of classical music – that was in her head as well as her heart. But jazz – it made her long to spring to her feet and dance. To feel free. To let her body take hold of the rhythm, the beat of the drum, the vibration entering into the very soles of her feet through the rickety boards of the stage, as she worked the pedals.

'In The Mood' was over too quickly. The band played a few more numbers, most of which she didn't know but was able to improvise. After every piece of music the audience went wild, many of them jumping up and whistling and clapping.

In the break Bob asked her if she would like to sing a few songs.

'No need to try to do this from the piano,' he said. 'It takes a special skill to do both. Just stand behind the mic and sing your heart out.' He looked at her. 'Think you can?'

'I think so,' she said soberly. This was it. This was singing to many hundreds. This was why she'd joined ENSA.

'What would you like to sing?'

'"Don't Sit Under The Apple Tree . . ."'

'. . . *with anyone else but me*,' Bob finished and grinned. 'Yep. And what next?'

'"It Had To Be You".'

'That'll get them. And . . .?'

'What about "Harbour Lights"?'

'Perfect. We'll end with that one.' He paused. 'Are you ready?'

'As ready as I'll ever be.'

'Then I'll announce you,' Bob said. 'So let's give it to 'em.' He turned to the audience.

'All right, lads,' he said, his mouth close to the microphone. 'I think you'll agree this young lady can certainly play the piano—' At this there was a loud roar of approval. 'But she can sing, too. So will you put your hands together to give her a warm welcome.'

After the clapping died down, he stepped back to allow Suzanne to take his place at the microphone. Her chest clenched so hard that for a few seconds she was unable to breathe. But as soon as the band played the introduction and she smiled and began to sing, hearing her voice ringing out, her nerves faded. All she wanted to do was to show these brave young men, many her own age by the looks of them, how grateful Britain was that they were fighting Hitler. She could see the grins as they recognised the song, and when she began the chorus some instinct made her embrace them with her arms wide and nod for them to sing. They immediately joined in and were especially vocal when it came to the bit about marching home. She remembered how Bram had stood up and pretended to march, and so she did the same actions. There was raucous laughter and cheers and another round of clapping.

Suzanne looked in every direction to ensure she was acknowledging all the soldiers. It was a good song to start with, she thought. They really looked as though they'd thoroughly enjoyed it, especially when they all came in with the chorus.

The music changed to a softer, slower tone. As she sang her way through the notes, she hoped every soldier thought she was singing just to him, even though she was singing only to James.

'*. . . it had to be you.*' She spread both arms wide to tumultuous cheers and applause.

And then her favourite song of all: 'Harbour Lights.' Bob was right. It was so appropriate this close to the harbour. She imagined she could see the ships from here. Was James in one of them? A tear threatened and she blinked it away. She would sing just to him. Where was he? Would they ever meet again? When she'd finished and heard the applause it startled her out of her reverie. For a few seconds she stood there wondering where she was.

'More!' several of the boys shouted to her.

Bob beckoned her over. 'Why don't you sing a couple more?' he said.

Out of the corner of her eye, Suzanne spotted Adelaide standing to the side, looking towards her, smiling and clapping her hands.

'Could I sing "Chattanooga choo choo" with Adelaide?'

'I'll ask her.' Bob cupped his mouth and called her name, then waved for her to come over.

'I'd love to,' Adelaide said, her lovely wide smile directed at Suzanne. 'Shall I lead us in?'

'Please,' Suzanne said.

She was rewarded by heads moving in time with the beat, some of them singing or humming the tune. When they'd finished, Adelaide swept her arm out to Suzanne, and the cheering and whistling started again. It was several minutes before they allowed her to stand down and Adelaide to take over.

Suzanne blew out her cheeks when she and Betty and the rest of the band were finally back at the hotel. It had been quite a day.

'Suzy, I'd like a word.'

'Yes, Miss Foster.'

'While we're waiting for Bram to get well, would you kindly continue to play the piano? I'm sure the band will be most grateful.'

'I'd be happy to.'

When she and Betty were in their bedroom, Suzanne said, 'I haven't had a chance to tell you, but you're a superb saxophonist. I could never play that instrument in a million years.'

'Oh, there's really nothing to it,' Betty said airily. 'Only hours of practising day after day, week after week, year after year . . .' She gave Suzanne a huge wink.

They both burst into giggles and gave one another a hug of delight that the evening had gone so well – until Suzanne remembered Bram.

'It's so awful about Bram,' she said. 'I wonder if we'd be allowed to visit him.'

'As soon as we're allowed, you and I will be his first visitors.' She paused. 'Suzy? What's up?'

Suzanne was staring numbly at the letter she'd tossed onto her bedside table to think about later. The letter from Maman. The letter Maman thought would make everything all right.

'Nothing,' she said. 'Nothing at all.'

Chapter Twenty-Nine

July 1943

Suzanne quickly fell into the ENSA routine of playing the piano for Adelaide who wanted to rehearse some new numbers and accompanying herself with her own songs. She was also immersed in new jazz numbers, rehearsing the piano part with the band. But after the excitement of the two, often three shows they were now giving every day, she would suddenly be overcome with a feeling of guilt that she was enjoying herself so much when so many people were living an appalling life under occupation in mainland Europe.

Suzanne knew that post took weeks – sometimes months – to arrive, and that there'd probably be a very long delay before she heard from James, but Raine and Ronnie could have dropped her a line. Her younger sister had never liked writing letters but she'd promised Suzanne she'd write regularly and tell her about how they were coping. She pushed her mother's letter to the back of her mind. Maman was only contrite because she'd been found out, Suzanne thought bitterly. And although she worried constantly about Raine, she knew her older sister was considered an excellent pilot and wouldn't take any unnecessary risks. Every night before she turned off the lamp on her bedside table, she would study the small framed photograph of her and her sisters. Dad had taken it when they'd gone camping one summer at Hastings – the summer before they'd been forced to move house.

The only one who had really enjoyed that holiday had been Ronnie. Suzanne smiled at the image of her sister helping Dad put up the tent and setting out the sleeping bags. Ronnie hadn't minded in the least how many curious spiders or field mice or any other creature came through the tent flap to have a look at the goings-on. Maman had hated every minute of that holiday, threatening Dad that she couldn't stand it a moment longer and was going to pack up and go home, with or without the rest of the family. It should have been a week away, but three days later Dad had had to give in, much to Ronnie's fury, whose favourite time of the day was swimming in the sea regardless of the fact it had not had time to warm up. Dad would have enjoyed the break just as much as Ronnie, Suzanne knew, if Maman hadn't made his precious few days a misery by her constant complaints.

But he'd taken a photograph of his three daughters. She picked up the frame and kissed it. It was a memento that Maman had wanted no part of and had refused to be in it. She'd given the photograph to Suzanne who'd found a frame in a second-hand shop and had always kept it at home by her bed. Now, it felt like the only link to home, and she wished she had just one of Maman and Dad as a couple. Come to think of it, she didn't believe she'd ever seen one of just the two of them in any of the albums Maman kept in her wardrobe.

Did Maman have a photograph of her real father?

Suzanne screwed her eyes shut, trying to form a picture

of how he might look. Then she forced the fuzzy image away. It was too disloyal to Dad. She blinked back the tears. How hard it must have been for him to love another man's child and never let her suspect – not once – that she was any different. And equally hard for her real father to know she existed but had never set eyes on her, she thought, with her innate sense of fairness. She made a promise with herself that one day, after this awful war, she'd go to France and find him – no matter what Maman said.

'Is Bram allowed visitors yet?' Suzanne asked Miss Foster after the morning's band rehearsal.

'Well, they're moving him to another hospital today – it's in Sliema. They only finished transforming it into a hospital yesterday ready for the wounded. Why don't you wait until he's moved and see him there?'

'How far is Sliema?'

'Not far. There's a bus. It will take maybe half an hour.' Miss Foster paused. 'Why don't you go and visit tomorrow morning? We won't be having a rehearsal.'

Next morning the three women – Suzanne, Betty and Adelaide – were on their way to the officers' mess for breakfast as a change from the meagre offerings of the hotel, when they heard the roar of a plane overhead.

'Hope it's one of ours,' Betty commented, tilting up her head.

'If it wasn't, I imagine we'd have heard the siren,' Suzanne said, secretly crossing her fingers.

'It's an American plane,' Adelaide said, narrowing her eyes up at the sky as the plane got nearer. 'Looks like a Flying Fortress.'

'Gosh, how do you know that?' Suzanne said.

'Oh, years of studying,' Adelaide chuckled. 'I don't know. You just pick up these things. Specially since the Americans entered the war. It's a four-engine bomber, anyway.'

The officers' mess was buzzing with Americans in their smart uniforms, all seeming to talk at once. One or two stared at Adelaide before resuming their conversation.

'What's going on?' Betty leaned across to ask at the nearest table.

'You just wait and see, ma'am,' one of the men said, grinning.

'Aw, don't keep the little lady in suspense, Jackson,' another said. 'It's not a secret . . .'

'I think I can guess,' Adelaide said, 'but I won't say any names in case I'm wrong. Someone very important is arriving today – and obviously an American, right?'

'You may be right,' the first man said as he glanced at his watch. 'C'mon, guys, let's go.'

Half an hour later, when the three women left the mess, the scene in front of them looked as though half the American Air Force was on parade and the whole Island appeared to have turned out. They stood watching along with the rest of the ENSA troupe as an official-looking car headed towards them. At the same time the US Air Force band were setting up and tuning their brass instruments.

'Well, we now know it's definitely a prominent American,' Betty said, excitedly.

'Who do you think it is?' Suzanne was bursting with curiosity.

'Have a guess,' Adelaide said.

'I only know of two famous Americans – one's the President, and I doubt *he* would come to Malta, so it only leaves one.' Suzanne looked at Adelaide. 'Would it be General Eisenhower?'

'I'm pretty sure it is.' Adelaide twinkled at both women. 'I'm taking bets if you disagree.'

A uniformed driver stepped out and opened both passenger seat doors and a uniformed smiling woman stepped out. Then the General himself emerged in full regalia, to the enthusiastic welcome of the Maltese people, many of them workmen in their dungarees and caps who had broken off work to join in. Their cheering and clapping brought a lump to Suzanne's throat. What those people had been through was unimaginable.

The noise of people's chatter quietened as the band began to play the first notes of 'The Star Spangled Banner'. The Americans saluted as they stood looking towards their flag, proudly fluttering in the light breeze, and the workmen stood to attention and removed their caps as a mark of respect until the end of the anthem.

'So there's our Ike looking very handsome, and *she* . . .' Adelaide nodded towards the woman who had accompanied the General, her dark curly hair not much tamed by her forage cap '. . . is your famous Kay Summersby, personal chauffeuse and secretary to Ike.' She rolled her eyes, then grinned. 'And much more if the rumours are true.'

'Oh, how delightful,' Betty said, laughing. 'We need a bit of spice on the Island.'

'And they're the very ones who are sure to provide it,' Adelaide said, as she and Suzanne joined in the laughter.

After the excitement of the arrival of the American general and his glamorous British secretary, Suzanne and Betty caught a bus to Sliema. Even though she was worried about Bram, Suzanne couldn't help enjoying the ride – Betty exclaiming every so often about each new scene that unfolded. The bus took them through Valletta, which they'd not yet explored, and Suzanne was enchanted by the narrow winding cobbled streets, the architecture of so many of the houses with their decorative enclosed balconies filled with window boxes of brightly coloured flowers, and children playing in the streets. But then the bus would turn a corner and the charming scene would turn into what looked like the end of the world as they came upon an entire street of rubble. Where would everyone have gone when they no longer had a home? A church had lost its spire and roof and much of its interior. Now it was simply a shell. What events it would have seen in all the years – the centuries: weddings, christenings, funerals . . . and now it was beyond repair.

The bus suddenly tooted its horn, swerving to avoid a horse and cart piled up with a mishmash of household goods looking like rubbish, the driver's expression grim with determination. Suzanne clutched Betty's arm as she started to topple into the aisle.

'We have to be like the islanders and not get downhearted,' Betty said, as she pulled Suzanne back. 'If we let it get to us, Jerry's won. We have a job to do as much as anyone else. And this afternoon, don't forget, we're putting on a show for the Maltese people. It was wonderful to see how they all turned out this morning for General Eisenhower.'

'I'm looking forward to it,' Suzanne said. 'If only Bram would get better and come back.'

'Meanwhile, you're doing a great job,' Betty said. 'And that's what we have to tell him so he doesn't feel he's letting down the band.' She suddenly rapped on the bus window. 'Oh, just look at that, Suzy. Doesn't it make you proud to be British!'

Suzanne leaned over Betty's arm and broke into a huge grin. 'A red telephone box! How wonderful – standing defiant in its own little spot under the tree with those sweet little houses to keep it company.'

Betty laughed. 'You should write a song for the boys about coming across a defiant red telephone box in Malta bringing Blighty closer to home.'

A strong smell of disinfectant mixed with unmentionable odours made Suzanne screw up her nose as they walked into the new Sliema Triage Centre. Suzanne asked at reception where Bramwell Taylor was and they were directed upstairs to a ward with a double row of what looked like camp beds. Nurses were moving swiftly in all directions carrying bedpans, trays, mops and other unrecognisable equipment. There was a low murmuring from the wards, and some groans. A Sister, sitting at the head of a long table in between the beds, looked up from her paperwork, her eyes sharp.

'Good morning. You've come to see . . .?'

'Bramwell Taylor.'

'And you are—'

'Friends. Close friends,' Suzanne quickly added. 'We're all in ENSA, entertaining the troops.' Oh, why hadn't she thought to wear her uniform.

'I know we're not real family but we all feel as though we are,' Betty chimed in.

The Sister hesitated. She picked up her watch chain. 'Ten minutes.' She waved her arm. 'He's in the third bed on the right-hand side.'

'Thank you,' Suzanne said, taking Betty's arm before the woman could change her mind.

The figure lying there had a blanket up to his chin. His face was pale and his eyes were closed.

'Bram,' Suzanne said softly.

Immediately, his eyes opened and he smiled at the two girls.

'Hello, ladies. It's kind of you to come.'

'It's not kind – we wanted to.' Betty pulled up a chair.

'How are you feeling?' Suzanne asked.

'I think I'm on the mend,' he said, though to Suzanne he didn't look at all as if he was. 'But I keep worrying about the band.'

'Well, don't,' Betty told him. 'Suzy's doing a marvellous job. Did you know she's a pianist as well as a singer? She's filling in for you until you get back.'

'That's wonderful,' Bram said, his eyes suddenly brighter as he turned his head on the pillow to look at her. 'I've missed you all. Tell me everything.'

'We all miss you, too – terribly. Do you know how long you'll be here?'

'They say another few days,' Bram said with a grimace. 'I know I look awful but I really am feeling better. It's this damned malaria. I caught it on an earlier tour in Africa and it gets me every so often, but this was a particularly bad dose.' He looked at them both. 'There seems to be a lot of action going on lately. I've heard scores of planes coming over – presumably all ours, but I don't suppose you girls know anything about it?'

'As if they'd discuss any plans with us,' Betty laughed. 'Although a famous person came to the Island this morning, didn't he, Suzy?'

'Who's that then?' Bram asked.

'None other than General Eisenhower,' Suzanne grinned. 'And I think you're right about something going on, Bram. Last night we had probably triple the usual number at the concert.'

'There you are.' Bram's tone was triumphant. 'Sounds to

me like something's up.' He tutted. 'Oh, I do hate missing everything.'

'Then you need to get well quickly and get out of here,' Betty said in her usual blunt manner.

After several minutes Suzanne was on the verge of telling Betty they ought to be heading back to camp when the same Sister came striding over, her alert eyes missing nothing as she eyed Betty, then Suzanne, with what looked like renewed interest.

'Do either of you sing?' she said.

'Suzanne does,' Bram said. 'She has a lovely voice.' He gave Sister his most charming smile. 'Sister Young, this is Suzanne who sings, and Betty who plays the saxophone.'

Sister Young nodded in acknowledgement, then hesitated, wrinkling her brow as if having a tussle with herself.

'Would you like to come next time and sing to the patients?' she said, looking at Suzanne.

The question took Suzanne completely by surprise. 'Um, yes, I'd be happy to . . . if you think they'd like it.'

'I think they'd enjoy it very much.'

'What do you think they'd like to hear?'

'If you can come up with a few Vera Lynn songs, the boys will be more than happy – but please come in your uniform, then the boys will feel you're one of them.'

'Yes, of course.' Suzanne turned to her friend. 'May I bring Betty?'

'For moral support, unless you'd like me to play the sax,' Betty said with a grin.

Sister Young nodded. 'Moral support will do nicely.' Her mouth twitched at the corners. She looked at Bram, then turned back to the girls.

'Mr Taylor needs to rest now,' she said, firmly.

'We'll see you in a few days, Bram.' Suzanne caught hold

of his hand and gently pressed it. 'Now you have to do as Sister says, and rest.'

To Suzanne's delight Miss Foster handed her a letter when she arrived back at camp. She recognised the handwriting. It was Mrs Mortimer's beautiful script.

My dear Suzanne,

Suzanne's heart jumped when she read the first line from James's mother.

James told me he was going to write to you, so I hope you don't mind his mother dropping you a line as well! I hope by now you've heard from him. Don't worry if there are long lapses. It's very hard for him to send letters when he's at sea, but he always does his best to stay in touch. There's no need for me to tell you how much he likes and admires you. We both do.

Your mother is adjusting to her present situation. I sometimes see her in the village and the other day I invited her to tea. We actually had a pleasant hour, but she obviously frets about all you girls and wishes you and Lorraine weren't so far away. But you mustn't worry about her. She's much stronger than she realises.

I hope it's going well with the concerts. You and the ENSA troupe will be giving our boys such a lift. I would love to hear you sing, Suzanne. Your speaking voice is so melodious I can just imagine how you sound when you're singing.

I've volunteered to keep a diary for Mass Observation and am still busy with anything the Red Cross asks of me. Friends tell me this all keeps me out of mischief!

Well, my dear, I think that's all the news. Don't worry about answering this – I know how busy you must be. If you are happy to write to James, then he is more important and I know he'll be looking forward to hearing from you that you're safe and well.

With much affection,

Beatrice Mortimer

What a nice person Mrs Mortimer was. How lucky James was to have a mother like her. Suzanne knew she was being disloyal to Maman, but she couldn't seem to shake off her anger towards her. Maman and her betrayal. Forcing her daughter to live a lie without even knowing it. Suzanne's mouth tightened. The only person Maman thought of was herself, no matter how she always pretended her daughters came first. It was all a lie . . . all—

Stop it! You're becoming just as bad . . . You're going to have to answer that letter sooner or later. And you're going to have to come to terms with it. You have a French father. And nothing will alter it.

All of a sudden she wondered what kind of a person he was. She knew he was working for the Resistance, but she didn't know anything of his personality, or his hobbies – nothing personal about him at all. Yet she was his very flesh and blood. Did he like music? Somehow that answer seemed important.

She rubbed the back of her neck that suddenly felt sore. Maybe the mystery was best left alone. She might uncover more than she'd bargained for if she started asking too many questions.

* * *

When Suzanne stepped onto the stage that evening in Maman's elegant black gown she'd finally found time to alter, she gasped. The audience had exploded. ENSA had already entertained the Maltese in the afternoon, the islanders having turned out in droves with their children, some of them showing terrible signs of war with missing limbs. Suzanne swallowed hard when she saw children trying to cope with only one leg or arm, or with their arms stretched out in front of them, stumbling along blindly, and the parents' drawn faces as they carried small chairs to set on the hard-baked ground for the little ones. Fern, always a wealth of information, had told her the Island had been close to starvation – even the water had been rationed.

'Until we turned the tide at the end of last year,' Fern added gleefully when Suzanne gasped. 'That was when the merchant ships, with the RAF flying overhead to protect them, apparently arrived almost intact in the Grand Harbour. Can you imagine the welcome those ships must have got from the islanders – and our lot, of course – knowing there was food and fuel on board? And no one bombing them as they were unloading?'

Such a terrible situation only a few months ago seemed impossible to take in. How glad Suzanne had been this afternoon, with the band, bringing these stoical people some joy. And how they'd responded! Their hands must have been raw with clapping after every song, but the cheers were extra loud for the jazz band and Adelaide.

It was humbling to watch the servicemen still pouring in, the ones nearest to the platform staring up at her and whistling. She realised what a responsibility all the ENSA troupe shared. Thousands of men squeezed together for as near a view of the 'stage' as possible. For a few moments she heard her heart echoing in her ears, the muscles in her legs turning to water. It was overwhelming. Then she got a hold on herself. She was the same person singing as she was this afternoon and yesterday when the audiences were far more modest. Nothing in essence had changed. There were simply more men to sing to, to bring England a little closer.

She drew in a deep breath. The band was used to her now, instinctively finding her rhythm.

She caught the eye of a naval rating who gave her a wink. A month ago she would have been embarrassed. Now, she smiled at him and nodded and he gave her the thumbs up. He reminded her of a younger version of James. Dark-haired, strong features, a winning smile . . . She swallowed. She would sing her songs just to him, pretending he was James.

Dear God, please keep James safe.

The band went through the usual routine, then Adelaide sang a couple of new numbers: 'Do Nothing 'Til You Hear From Me' and 'I Can't Give You Anything But Love, Baby', jazzing it up and lifting the hem of her skirt, doing a tap dance while the band played before she came in on the second verse. The troops went wild; they whistled and cheered and clapped to her smiling bows. Adelaide, grinning from ear to ear, her teeth gleaming in the dusk, waved her over and Suzanne joined her in their now-famous version of 'The Chattanooga choo choo', to the delight of several American Air Force squadrons. One or two called out invitations to go back to America with them when the war was over, although Suzanne noticed several Americans throwing Adelaide cold, disapproving looks.

'Some of them can't stand the sight of a white woman singing with a black woman,' Adelaide said under her breath to Suzanne as they bowed to more cheers.

'I hoped you hadn't noticed,' Suzanne said, embarrassed.

'Trouble is, honey, when you have black skin you notice

everything, and you soon realise you have to grow that black skin thick as a rhino.' She patted Suzanne's arm. 'Your turn, Suzy.' Adelaide stepped down from the stage, then looked up. 'By the way, honey, that dress looks terrific on you.'

The naval rating was still looking at her intently. Really, he didn't look a bit like James after all, Suzanne realised . . . but she could still imagine. She put her hand on the microphone and closed her eyes, letting the soft warm breeze cool her skin, imagining she was watching the harbour lights.

She pictured James waving to her as his ship sailed away one evening. Her heart beating a little too fast she sang the story . . .

'. . . *but you were on the ship*

And I was on the shore . . .'

She imagined herself waving back, tears falling down her face as the ship faded into the distance, imploring the harbour lights not to steal James's love from her.

The men waved their arms and stamped, whistling and cheering. One officer shouted '*Bravo*'. Several called for an encore.

James, come home to me . . . Briefly, she closed her eyes, oblivious to the audience. He was out there somewhere. She could feel it in her bones.

Chapter Thirty

'Anyone want to come with me to the beach?' Adelaide said one cloudless Mediterranean morning when they'd finished rehearsing.

'I'll come if you want some company,' Suzanne said. 'Having a walk might do me good as my stomach's playing up.'

'Is it the curse?' Adelaide asked.

Suzanne flushed. 'Yes. But I'd love to come and watch, and maybe catch up on some reading.' She was still only a quarter of the way through *The Pickwick Papers.*

'Betty?' Adelaide enquired.

To Suzanne's surprise Betty's cheeks went pink.

'Oh, um, I—' She broke off and gave a self-conscious laugh. 'Actually, I'm going into Valletta in a few minutes with Reg.'

'Reg on trumpet?'

'That's the one.' Betty laughed again. 'He just wanted to get away from camp for a couple of hours so I said I'd go with him. I need a few bits, if I can find them in the shops, which is doubtful.'

'Sounds like a date to me,' Adelaide said, chuckling. 'The trumpet sweet-talking the sax.' She winked at Suzanne, then said to Betty, 'Give him my love.'

'And mine,' Suzanne joined in.

'Go now, the pair of you,' Betty ordered, waving her arms at them, 'before the temperature gets too hot outside.'

'I think it's already too hot in here,' Suzanne quipped. 'In fact, it's reached sizzling point.' The three of them collapsed into giggles.

'Okay, Suzy,' Adelaide said, 'are you ready?'

'Just let me get my towel and stuff and I'll be with you in a few moments.'

Suzanne brushed away the thought of how lovely it would be to just walk along the beach with James. All right, it wouldn't be a beautiful tropical beach – she'd discovered they were all rocky in Malta – but nevertheless . . . She sighed. She hadn't heard from him since that first letter and was beginning to feel on edge. Every day she prayed he was safe. That was the main thing. Whether she heard from him or not.

'Look at all those ships,' Adelaide said, as she and Suzanne walked as close as they were allowed by the fenced-off Grand Harbour, with notices every so often that this was a danger zone. 'I've never seen so many in one place. There must be thousands.' She sniffed and wrinkled her nose. 'Smell that oil, Suzy. It's overpowering. And when I went for a walk yesterday it looked as if they're building a new airfield not far from ours in Luqa.'

Adelaide was right. The Island was becoming crowded, not only with all kinds of aircraft flying into the airports, but ships of all sizes were fighting for space in the Grand Harbour as well as the usual cargo ships. Every day extra troops were arriving – not just British but American and Canadian as well, easily spotted by their smarter uniforms.

'And going by last night's concert, I'd say it's gonna be

something big.' Adelaide's brown eyes widened as she regarded Suzanne. 'You know what I think, Suzy? I think they're preparing for some sort of attack.'

A ripple of . . . what was it? . . . fear? . . . excitement? – ran along Suzanne's spine. 'Well, if there is, we won't know about it until afterwards,' she said. 'It'll be top secret.'

'Oh, wouldn't I like to know where those ships are heading.' Adelaide shielded her face with her hand.

'Not just the ships,' Suzanne said, tilting her head to the sky where three planes circled overhead to land, the fourth breaking away on its own. Would it be going to the small island of Gozo where they'd been told there was another airfield mainly used by the Americans?

She strained her eyes to take in the scene. Sailors were hurrying in all directions with loaded trolleys, hands on board waiting to haul them up, officers shouting orders, while screaming seagulls zoomed overhead, for all the world as though they were taking part in the action. It was certainly an impressive sight.

Why did she have such a strong feeling that James was somehow involved? That he would be on one of those ships. She shook herself. It was purely her imagination running wild. Why should he be exactly where she was at this moment? *But he has to be somewhere,* a small voice told her. *He could be here as easily as anywhere else.* And he'd said he hoped she was being sent to the Med. The more she thought about it, the more possible it seemed.

After walking for twenty minutes or so they found a tiny bay and cautiously made their way down some hand-hewn steps to the rocky beach. A few people were scattered around. Suzanne spread her towel on one of the hard rocks and gazed towards the inlet, admiring the way the sun caught the tips of the waves, making them sparkle like sequins.

Adelaide quickly unbuttoned her dress, pulling it over her head, her bright yellow swimming costume ready underneath.

'I'm going to have a nap first,' she said. 'For some reason I couldn't get to sleep last night. Probably missing you and Betty now Elizabeth's found me a single room.' She chuckled. 'Seriously, can you wake me after half an hour or so? I don't want to sleep the afternoon away without a swim – that is, if I even get to sleep on this truly rock-hard mattress.' She threw her towel on one of the flatter rocks.

'I won't be able to stay out in the sun that long,' Suzanne said, adjusting her hat. She could feel perspiration already beading on her forehead. 'I'll turn into a lobster.'

'Try to find some shade then,' Adelaide said, as she stretched out on her rock and closed her eyes.

What a lovely woman the jazz singer was, Suzanne thought. How lucky she and Betty were to have met her and become friends. She tried to make herself as comfortable as possible, choosing a rock close by that was shaped almost like a seat with somewhere to lean her back. She picked up her book but something made her glance round. A figure caught her eye. It was Cat. She was alone on a rock some distance away, sitting with her arms folded around her bent knees, seemingly staring out to sea. Suzanne was thankful she wasn't looking in her direction. She had no desire at all to speak to her and see that lip curl when she spotted Adelaide. She quickly buried her head in her book, thankful Adelaide was already asleep.

It wasn't easy to read. The wind had got up and was whipping the pages of her book. When she looked down to the bay she noticed the waves, which had been so calm a few minutes ago, were rolling. Should she wake Adelaide? Tell her perhaps she should go for her swim now in case it became even more blustery? But Adelaide hadn't slept well the night before and this was her chance to rest.

She stared at Adelaide, lying on her back, already snoozing, her arms protectively held against her chest, her book face down by her side, her black lashes feathering her cheekbones, the smooth, polished skin. Really, Suzanne thought with admiration, you couldn't tell she was over forty. She wondered for the hundredth time why Cat was so rude about her. It wasn't as though Cat was unattractive. She had her own style and she'd noticed some of the servicemen turn their heads to stare after her. Maybe she'd had her heart broken by someone. But that still wouldn't be an excuse to be so cruel.

Out of the corner of her eye, Suzanne kept a watch on Cat – who at this minute was smoothing something on her creamy-white body. Suzanne thought again about Cat's insinuation. There was no question in Suzanne's mind – Adelaide had nothing to do with the wine stain. Well, she'd never mention anything to her about what Cat had said – especially calling her that awful word.

In spite of the wind, and tired out from the recent journeys she'd undertaken, Suzanne felt her eyelids droop. She tried to fight it and open her eyes wider but when it happened for the second time she told herself ten minutes wouldn't hurt in the sun and allowed herself to drift off.

The next thing she heard was a scream. Suzanne's eyes shot open. What on earth . . . A hand was frantically waving in the sea! A woman's head bobbing up and down. Another scream. Someone was in trouble! She looked across to where Cat had been sitting and there was no sign of her. Adelaide was lightly snoring.

'Adelaide! Wake up!' She shook the woman's shoulder.

'Wasser matter?'

'Someone's in trouble in the sea! And I can't swim!'

'Dear God.' Without hesitating, Adelaide sprang up. 'I'll get her,' she shouted as she scrambled over the rocks, then dived straight off one of them. Suzanne stood rooted, furious with herself for not being able to help, holding her stomach to ward off the sudden sharp pain of her monthlies. Her heart pumped wildly at the thought of jumping off such a steep drop. But she couldn't just stand there. Sweat poured from her body as she forced herself to clamber to the edge of the rocks and look down. She watched as Adelaide swam rapidly towards the lone figure. If only she could help Adelaide . . . Suzanne shuddered at the thought of the sea closing over her head.

Stop thinking of yourself, she told herself angrily. *There's someone in real trouble out there.*

She strained her ears to listen.

'HELP! SOMEONE PLEASE HELP!'

It sounded like Cat, but she couldn't be sure. Whoever it was, Adelaide would save her; of that, Suzanne was certain.

Minutes later Adelaide half dragged the girl back to where Suzanne was trying to keep her balance. She was a taller figure than Adelaide, but Adelaide was strong. It *was* Cat. She was ghost-pale, her eyes closed, her lips with an unnatural bluish tinge. Suzanne managed to reach down her other side so Cat was between them. The girl felt limp and heavy as Suzanne did her best to hold on to her, thankful when she and Adelaide got her back to the rocks where they'd put their belongings.

By now Cat was making terrible choking noises. Suzanne was relieved. It meant she was alive. Adelaide set the girl onto her bottom on the hard ground, then with one arm firmly round her waist to keep her in position, she used her other hand to push Cat's head down on her chest and rapped her smartly on her back. Then again. And again. Suzanne noticed Adelaide take in a huge breath and thump her hard. Cat suddenly gave a gurgle that sent shivers down Suzanne's back. A gush of sea water spewed from Cat's mouth, forming a puddle on the stones.

'Wh-what . . .?'

'It's all right, Catherine,' Adelaide said soothingly. 'You're safe now.'

Cat's eyes flew open. She looked at Adelaide, then shook her head as though to clear it, then turned her head and vomited. Moments later she began to shiver, her teeth chattering, even though the sun was still hot. Seeming to give up, Cat fell back against the rock.

'We need to take her back to the hotel and call the doctor,' Adelaide said in a warning undertone to Suzanne.

'How will we do that?'

'Stay with her. I'll see if I can find a café or something and ask if they'll let me use their telephone. I'll try to be as quick as I can. She should be all right now she's been sick, but keep talking to her. Try to make her talk back.' Adelaide put her towel over the shaking body, then quickly threw her dress over her costume and vanished.

Suzanne held Cat's limp hand.

'Cat? Can you hear me? It's Suzy.'

There was no response. A minute ticked by.

'Cat, *talk* to me.' Suzanne squeezed her hand.

Was she still alive? A feeling of dread enveloped Suzanne as she bent low over the figure, and to her enormous relief she saw the steady rise and fall of Cat's chest under the towel.

It seemed like hours went by. Oh, where *was* Adelaide? Surely she would have managed to get help by now. Cat stirred and opened dull, expressionless eyes.

'Cat,' Suzanne said, keeping her voice calm. 'Don't worry. I'm here. Adelaide's gone to fetch help.'

Cat blinked several times but said nothing.

'It's me . . . Suzy. Can you speak?'

Cat blinked again. She opened her mouth. 'Wh-what happened?'

'You were swimming out of your depth.'

Cat slowly shook her head. 'No. No. Cramp.' She tried to struggle up but Suzanne restrained her.

'Just sit quietly for a while, Cat. You've had a shock. Adelaide's gone to fetch help so we can get you back to the hotel.'

'Adelaide? What . . .?' Cat shook her head as though trying to clear it.

'She saved you from drowning.'

Cat's eyes were like the stones on the beach as they rested on Suzanne. She cleared her throat and spat. 'I had cramp.' She paused between each word and thrust her jaw up. 'Do you understand? It was just bad luck.' She stared at the towel. 'Is this yours?'

'No, it's Adelaide's. You were shivering. She—'

Before Suzanne could finish her sentence, Cat had thrown it to one side as though it were on fire.

'I need to make something clear. I don't want that woman's dirty black hands anywhere near me.'

Suzanne looked at her with her mouth open. She could hardly believe what she was hearing. Adelaide had just saved Cat's life. A shadow fell over them.

'That's fine by me.' It was Adelaide's rich voice.

Cat turned her head away.

Curling inside with embarrassment, Suzanne put her hand on Adelaide's arm, and glanced up at her. Adelaide looked impassive but Cat's cruel remark must have badly upset her.

'They're sending a car to come for her,' Adelaide said. 'I think I'll be going. Will you stay with her to wait for the car?'

'I suppose I'll have to.' She looked at Adelaide. 'But after that outburst . . . oh, Adelaide, I wish you hadn't heard what she said.'

Adelaide shrugged. 'I'll see you back at the hotel, Suzy.'

'No, wait a moment . . .' How could Cat let Adelaide go without a word of thanks? She took the girl by the shoulders.

'What are you doing?' Cat's eyes were eerily like the animal she'd named herself after.

'Maybe you didn't realise, Cat, but you were drowning. You were screaming for help. I can't swim, but Adelaide rushed in after you and saved you . . . She saved your *life*!' Suzanne could hear her voice rising in anger, but she didn't care. She wasn't going to have Adelaide hurt by this unfeeling person.

'It's all right, Suzy,' Adelaide said in a cool voice as she directed her gaze towards Cat. 'I'm sure someone would eventually have come to her rescue. Someone with lily-white hands. Mind you, waiting for the perfect rescuer – well, it might have been too late.' She nodded towards Cat. 'The car should be here any minute,' she said, and moved away.

'I'm disgusted at your behaviour.' Suzanne looked Cat full in the face, then ran to catch up with Adelaide. She slipped her hand through the black woman's arm, and Adelaide turned to smile.

'Thank you, darlin', but it really doesn't matter.'

'Well, it does to me,' Suzanne said.

She wondered if Adelaide would feel any different if she told her that Cat had insinuated that it was the 'darkie' who had been standing behind her with a glass of wine in her hand and deliberately spilt it over Fern's gown. Well, she would never let Adelaide know what Cat had said.

Adelaide chuckled. 'Stop looking so serious, Suzy,' she said. 'I've had worse things than someone not being gracious enough to thank me for doing them a good turn.'

'But you weren't just doing a good turn, Adelaide,' Suzanne said. 'You saved her *life*. And she didn't even bother to thank you. I find it quite unbelievable.'

'I don't. She can't bear the idea that it was a black woman who saved her. But that's her problem – not mine.'

Adelaide looked away, but not before Suzanne saw the hurt in her eyes.

Chapter Thirty-One

Miss Foster was all smiles at suppertime as she came into the restaurant where she'd arranged for the ENSA troupe to meet. She held a canvas bag.

'I'm pleased to say that I have post for some of you.'

There was a loud cheer.

'But before I hand it out, I want to make an announcement. You may have all noticed that things are hotting up here. The harbour and airfields are packed with ships and aircraft. And you were all aware of the huge audiences recently. We can't have a repeat of last night when hundreds couldn't hear or see what was going on. So from tomorrow we'll be doing three music performances a day. One at four o'clock, one at six-thirty, and the last one at nine. We'll put the dancers on at two, and the actors at half past – so the smaller audience can get closer to the stage.'

Suzanne made a mental note to see Fern in the Noël Coward play.

There were groans from a few people. Miss Foster ignored it.

'Any questions?'

'No, Miss Foster.'

'Good. Then it's settled. And I can give out your post.'

'So long as someone has written to me, it can be a letter from the devil himself,' Betty said loudly.

'Hope you can read German then,' Bob called out, and everyone laughed.

Suzanne steeled herself to be disappointed. She would *not* let on that she was worried or upset in the least if there was nothing for her. But to her surprise and joy Miss Foster handed her three envelopes.

She quickly scanned them. Maman's script, Ronnie's hurried hand, and one she recognised instantly – from James! Oh, life was wonderful!

'You look happy, Suzy.' Betty came over to her five minutes later, her own face beaming. 'I know I am. Andy's written – finally – and he's safe. At least he was when he wrote this six weeks ago,' she added, her smile fading.

'Oh, Betty, I'm so happy for you.'

'I worry about him all the time, but I don't like talking about it in case I tempt fate.'

'I'm sure he'll keep safe,' Suzanne said. But how did anyone know that? They were simply words you said to someone in the hope that they'd prove to be true.

'Who did you hear from?' Betty asked.

'My mother and one from my young sister who hates writing letters, so I'm honoured.'

'And the other . . .?' Betty jerked her head towards the third envelope that Suzanne held tightly. 'Or would you rather not say?' She sent Suzanne an exaggerated wink.

Warmth spread fast to Suzanne's cheeks. 'Oh, it's just from James.' She tried to sound nonchalant as she glanced at Betty who raised an eyebrow. 'Don't raise that eyebrow, Betty. He's just a friend, as I've told you before.'

'Not by the look of your red face,' Betty smirked. 'What say we find somewhere and read our letters in peace? We could even read bits out to one another – though I don't expect you to read the juicy bits.' She giggled.

'Sorry to disappoint you,' Suzanne said, her cheeks still hot, 'but there won't be any juicy bits. So shall we forget it and go and have supper?'

She liked Betty very much – was getting really fond of her – but she wasn't prepared to share her letters, even with her friend. She wanted to be on her own when she read her precious letters . . . especially the one from— No, she mustn't think like that. Her family came first. But still she hugged herself to think he'd written. She'd save his until last.

There was a definite buzz in the restaurant, most of the ENSA group having received a letter or two from home. The only person who was sitting on her own, slumped in a corner, was Cat.

'She looks unhappy,' Suzanne said.

'I'm not surprised, the way she carries on,' Betty said. 'Sorry, Suzy, but I can't feel any sympathy for her now you told me what happened at the beach today when Adelaide saved her from drowning.'

'I'm not fond of her,' Suzanne admitted. She gave Betty a rueful smile. 'But I can't bear to see anyone look so unhappy. She probably hasn't heard from home.'

'Then go and speak to her,' Betty said, and rolled her eyes.

'I don't like to. She might want to be on her own after today. I'm sure she's still in shock.'

'You're going to drive me mad. Just go and see her, if you really must.'

Suzanne made her way between the tables. She was starting to recognise the actors and actresses in the Noël Coward play. Fern was chatting to a handsome man but looked up and smiled as Suzanne went past.

'Everything all right?' Fern asked.

'Yes. I'm just going to speak to someone.'

Fern lifted a brow, then nodded and continued chatting to the group of actors. Suzanne stepped over to Cat's table. The girl was holding her head in her hands.

'Cat?'

Cat looked up, her eyes tear-filled. 'What do you want?'

'I wanted to know if you've recovered from this afternoon. You were looking very poorly.'

'I'm perfectly all right,' Cat said tersely.

Suzanne sat down. 'Tell me to go if you want,' she said, 'but I know something else is the matter. Please—'

'Leave me alone,' Cat snapped. 'I tell you I'm perfectly all right. I don't need you playing Mummy.' She blew her nose. 'I expect it's a cold coming.'

She rose up and abruptly left the table, leaving a sandwich and a cup of tea, which Suzanne could see was hardly touched.

'I'm off to bed,' Betty said as soon as the evening show had finished.

The audience had been much smaller at the two evening shows – probably no more than a hundred, and Miss Foster had already announced she was cutting out the afternoon one tomorrow. Suzanne was determined to find out what the situation was in the Grand Harbour. She had a bet with herself that all those ships had sailed quietly away this afternoon. Where were they headed? Could James possibly be on one of them? But if that was the case, he would have come to one of the concerts. Well, wherever he was, at least she'd heard from him. She only hoped Betty would be asleep before she herself went up to bed and could finally read her letters.

Suzanne quickly undressed and brushed her teeth to the

sound of Betty's heavy breathing. She hopped into bed and switched on her bedside light. Eagerly, she slit open her sister's envelope.

Dear Suzy,

I hope you're enjoying wherever you are. I'm so envious, although if you're somewhere hot, and by the list of stuff that woman told you to pack, and the uniform shorts, I might change my mind. Working in hot sun would be awful.

Guess what? I've got a Saturday job in the vet's. Don't worry – I won't be performing operations! Not for a few weeks, anyway! But I'll be feeding the animals, talking to them when they're scared – that sort of thing. And cleaning up after operations! I'm excited. And the vet is allowing me to bring Rusty!

Maman is the same. She likes to put on an act but I can see through it. I don't take any notice and then she's all right again. Sometimes I feel sorry for her. I caught her looking at a sparkling ring the other day in her bedroom and she started to cry.

Suzanne gasped. Ronnie must mean her beautiful diamond ring! She'd only had it for a few minutes before Maman had practically snatched it from her. So why was her mother crying over it? Surely she didn't feel guilty that she hadn't let her daughter have what was rightfully hers. Or did it bring back buried memories?

She sighed and carried on reading.

Not sure why but when she turned and saw me she stuck it back in its box and shoved it in a drawer – hoping I hadn't seen it I suppose. I didn't like to ask about it. I expect Dad gave it to her and it brought back happy memories.

But Dad hadn't given it to her. It was never Maman's.

That's all. You know I hate writing letters but I like receiving them, so please write back immediately!!!

Ronnie XXX (extra big kisses!)

P.S. I keep thinking of you singing your heart out to our boys. Bet they're all in love with you!

P.P.S. Wish I could see you in action!

Suzanne chuckled. Her younger sister was irrepressible. But she sounded happy, particularly with her Saturday job. If there wasn't a war she would encourage Ronnie to study to be a veterinary nurse. But if the war went on much longer, the odds were strong that she'd end up as a Land Girl. Which may not be so bad, Suzanne mused. At least Ronnie would be out in the fresh air with the farm animals. Yes, she'd do all right, whatever she went into, if it was practical, and not in some office where she'd feel trapped.

Now for Maman's. Guiltily, she opened the envelope. She still hadn't found the words to answer that first one. Taking in a deep breath she read:

Suzanne, chérie,

I am trying hard to imagine your life wherever you are but it is difficult. I still wish you would go to the excellent music school and then I would know exactly where you are and not worry. But I have to remember I am not the only mother who worries about her children.

Life goes on the same. We hear air raids in London

from time to time, but we are thankful they keep away from Downe.

I met Mrs Mortimer in the newsagent's the other day. She invited me for tea and it was pleasant although we do not always see things the same.

She asked about you and sent her regards. She said she would like to write to you but I told her it was unnecessary. You already have a mother – you do not need another one. I politely asked about her son. She has not heard but says it takes weeks and sometimes months when he is at sea. I am sure he is a big worry for her.

That is all my news. I had a letter from Lorraine. She is well and so is Véronique. And I must try to keep brave but I miss your dear dad so much.

Your loving Maman xx

We *all* miss him, she thought, irritably. But how typical of her mother not to give Mrs Mortimer the address to write to. Suzanne was glad Mrs Mortimer hadn't taken any notice. Her mother was clearly terrified her daughter would become too close to James's mother. How ridiculous that was. But Raine would say it was typical. Maman had to have full control over the family. It was a miracle that Raine had managed to pull away from her and follow her dream to be a pilot.

And *she* had her own dream to follow, which again didn't meet with her mother's approval. Thank goodness Ronnie was her own person and could stand up to her.

But it was strange that the tone of this letter was so different from that first one. Maman hadn't even reprimanded her for not having received a letter. A thought struck her and she glanced at the date, then quietly opened the small drawer of the bedside table so as not to disturb Betty. She took out her mother's letter where she'd shoved it in disgust and checked the date. As she'd suspected – it had been sent a week later. She'd received the two letters out of date order. So that's why no reprimand. Her mother would still be waiting for her forgiveness. Not allowing herself another moment to dwell on her mother's outpourings she slit open James's letter and automatically looked at the date. It was written only days after the last letter and had taken all this time to follow her out here. Her blood stirred within her as she read:

My dear Suzy,

I wonder if you ever received my letter. The post takes so long these days especially with everyone on the move, and I'm sure by now that you are somewhere abroad. I understand the need for censorship, but it is frustrating that I could be near and never know it! I'm really hoping you have already written to me and that I might receive something from you very soon!

Did they find you a spot as a violinist or even pianist? Any of those would suit you, I'm sure. Suzy, I keep thinking of you. Wouldn't it be wonderful to spend some proper time together? There's so much I want to say that I can't in a letter. But I want to know you more. See your lovely face. Watch you smile. It lights up your face.

I think I'd better end this now before I get too carried away!!!

With fondest thoughts,

James

Suzanne let her eyes linger over the last paragraph. What did James want to say that he couldn't say in a letter? Her face warmed at the thought of him getting 'carried away'. After all, he hadn't even kissed her properly.

But she loved his letter. It was as though he was there, talking to her, telling her she was in his thoughts. It gave her a warm glow that she mattered to him. She wanted to let him know he mattered to her, too. But he hadn't received her letter and when he finally did, he'd see she'd kept it friendly but quite formal. It was only because she'd tried to match his previous tone. Nothing would have been more embarrassing than if she'd made something of their short acquaintance that didn't exist, and therefore he hadn't reciprocated. But here was his letter in front of her. She could read it over and over and it would keep him close. He would tell her again and again that he wanted to get to know her better. That he thought her lovely.

She shook herself.

If I'm not careful, I'm in danger of getting big-headed.

She allowed herself a wry smile. And then she gave a deep sigh. Everything was so different these days. None of the usual rules applied. They were in the middle of a war and things moved fast. If there was a chance of happiness people had to grab it.

She'd write back straightaway, and with luck James might receive it not too long after that first letter.

Chapter Thirty-Two

'Do you fancy coming with me again to see Bram this afternoon?' Suzanne asked Betty after rehearsal a couple of days later.

'I won't today, Suzy.' Betty put her saxophone in her case and wiped her forehead on a handkerchief. 'I'm so hot. I can't bear the idea of sitting in a bus in this heat so I'm going off for a swim. But you go. Sister's probably already told the patients you're going to sing to them so you don't want to disappoint them.'

'I'll feel funny singing without any music,' Suzanne said.

'Well, don't. You're lucky with that voice. It's good enough not to need any accompaniment.' She paused. 'Give Bram my love and tell him I hope he's out very soon. We need him.'

'I will. He'll also be keen to know the latest goings-on at the harbour and the airfields. I want to tell him how all the ships disappeared yesterday, and this morning when I went for an early walk I noticed nearly all the planes had gone as well.'

'If they're not preparing for an invasion I'll be a monkey's uncle,' Betty said. 'I just wish we knew where. But at least it might be the start of the Allies booting out the Germans in the Med.'

* * *

On the bus to Sliema again, this time in her ENSA uniform, Betty's words gave Suzanne a glimmer of hope that one day they'd all be leading a normal kind of life. Everyone in the forces would be sent safely home to their families and she would enlist in the Royal Academy of Music – if they'd have her, that is. In her heart she dreamed her friendship with James might develop into something special, but even then, she would still want to continue her music studies. She daren't think further.

When Suzanne walked into Bram's ward she had a shock. Many more beds had been jammed in, leaving barely a foot in between. A strong smell of male bodies and Dettol permeated the ward. Some patients were moaning in their sleep, their white faces screwed up in pain. Two other men whose beds were adjacent to one another were playing cards. A few were sitting up in bed reading.

Why were there so many more injured soldiers than a few days ago? Some kind of battle must have taken place. And where was Bram? He wasn't in the same bed she'd left him. Feeling more than a little self-conscious when she realised she was the only visitor, she walked through the centre of the room, glancing on both sides, but there was no sign of him. Her heart beating with fear that he'd had a relapse, she stopped a passing nurse.

'Could you please tell me where Bramwell Taylor is,' she said.

The nurse looked her up and down, and nodded, seeming to think her uniform entitled her to visit one of the patients.

'He's been moved to another ward – next door.'

'Is he all right?' Suzanne asked anxiously.

'So far as I know,' the nurse said. 'Do excuse me . . .' She hurried off.

Suzanne stepped into the adjacent ward and saw Bram

immediately. He was sitting on the side of his bed, his back to her, chatting to another patient.

Not wanting to disturb him, she made to sit on the chair squashed next to Bram's empty bed, but at the sound of her step Bram twisted round, his chubby face alight when he saw who it was.

'How lovely to see you.' He turned back to the man in the next bed. 'Sorry, old chap. A good friend has just turned up.'

Bram climbed back into his bed.

'You've come to sing to us, I hope.' He smiled encouragingly as he made himself comfortable propped up by the pillows.

A nurse, plump and smiling, came hurrying up.

'Would you be Miss Linfoot?'

'That's right,' Suzanne smiled back.

'Sister Young told me you're going to do a few songs for us, so any time you're ready . . . they've already got some requests.'

Suzanne gulped. She looked along the lines of beds. These boys were all battered from some kind of attack, yet some of them were sitting up in bed, thumbs up, giving her their welcome. It was very humbling. *Right,* she thought, *here I go*.

'Hello, everyone,' she started. 'Sister Young tells me you'd like me to sing a few songs. Has anyone got anything special they'd like to hear?'

'You sing whatever you want, love,' one of them said. He put his book down and winked at her.

Suzanne remembered Sister Young had mentioned Vera Lynn.

At first her voice was a little tremulous, knowing how important it was for the men to hear something that would remind them of home. And then she sang the chorus.

'There'll be bluebirds over the white cliffs of Dover,
Tomorrow, just you wait and see . . .'

Several of the men joined in, making the back of her eyes prick with tears, but giving her the confidence to really sing out. After she'd finished there was an enthusiastic round of clapping.

'What about "Harbour Lights"?' another man called out. He was older than the rest, his face lined with strain. 'Do you know that one?'

'It happens to be one of my favourites,' she said.

She put her heart into the song, finishing to an even louder clapping, then sang 'I'll Never Smile Again' and 'Imagination'. She noticed the older man clapped by banging one hand on the bedside table. The other sleeve of his pyjamas was empty. Suzanne swallowed.

'More! More!' they called.

'I need a few sips of water,' she said, smiling at them.

'Nurse, bring the lady a glass of water.' He was hardly more than a boy, with a cheeky grin, as he stopped one of the passing nurses. 'Then she'll have enough spit to sing us another.'

There were a few chuckles and an orderly brought her a glass of water. She took a few sips.

'"We'll Meet Again"', the man with one arm called out.

She nodded to him. 'All right. But it's the last one. I've also come to visit a patient.'

'Lucky bugger, excuse my French,' another man called out.

'And I'm only going to sing it if you join in the chorus – those of you who can,' she added.

'Off you go then, love.'

She glanced across at Bram who was beaming. When she'd finished he gave her the thumbs up.

'Delightful, Suzy,' he said. 'And by the sound of the cheering and clapping, they all thought the same.'

'I hope they enjoyed it as much as I did,' she said.

Sister Young bustled up, beaming.

'You've really cheered these boys up,' she said. 'In fact, there's someone in the ward next door who's asked if you would stop by his bed. I left the door open so the patients could hear you there as well, but most of them are quite poorly and need plenty of rest so I didn't invite you in.'

'Come back and see me before you go,' Bram said.

'I will.'

Sister Young's voice quietened when she and Suzanne stepped into the adjacent ward. It was a very different atmosphere, made so by most of the patients being fast asleep.

'He's in the last bed but one by the window on the left,' the Sister said. 'Don't keep him too long.' She hurried away.

Suzanne walked through the two rows of beds and tiptoed towards the man who'd requested her to stop by. He was lying down, perfectly still, his head bandaged, with one of his arms attached to a drip. His other hand was outside the sheet. His eyes were closed, but she could see dark bruising beneath them. He'd obviously fallen asleep and she shouldn't disturb him. But something made her step closer. That hand was familiar. She caught her breath.

Her legs were shaking so much she nearly lost her balance as she stood looking down at the man's face, a vivid shade of red.

'James,' she said softly, 'it's me, Suzy.'

His eyelids fluttered open but his eyes didn't seem to be focusing. Dear God, had his sight been affected by his head injury? Would he go blind? Was he already? A feeling of nausea threatened to suffocate her.

'James, it's me, Suzy,' she repeated.

'I know,' he rasped. 'I heard someone say your name. I thought I was dreaming. That was you next door singing just now, wasn't it? Tell me I'm not dreaming.' His voice faltered in disbelief.

'You're not dreaming.' She bit back the words, 'dearest James'. Oh, thank heavens he was speaking – sounding almost normal. 'ENSA asked me if I'd fill in for one of the singers.'

He gave a slight nod. 'Your singing . . . magical. Had a feeling you weren't far away.' His voice faded.

'I felt the same,' she said, truthfully. 'I know you probably don't want to tell me what happened at this moment, but have they said anything about your injuries?'

He put his hand to his head, feeling the bandage. 'I don't remember. I can't remember anything. I don't remember – just the water. They said I was—' His eyes stared.

He tried to struggle up, but Suzanne gently pressed him down on the pillow again.

She took his hand.

'Am I home? I can't remember.' He was beginning to sound agitated.

'Shhh, now, don't upset yourself,' Suzanne said, feeling his hand tremble in hers. 'It will come back to you in time. You're in Malta, in a hospital not far from me.'

He didn't seem to know anything about his injury or what caused it. She mustn't pursue it when he was obviously in a state.

'It's the shock – it probably blocks out the horrible things that led up to it. Try not to worry.'

He smiled . . . a shadow of his dear smile. She paused, wondering if she should mention her deepest fear for him. No, she mustn't because if he couldn't see . . .

His eyelids flickered as he turned his neck slowly towards her. 'I'm so glad you're here, Suzy. You look as beautiful as ever.'

She drew in a deep breath of relief. She wouldn't go on any longer or she'd frighten him. *Just talk to him naturally,* she told herself. He'd get better. He'd look like James again.

'I'm going to be sick.'

A nurse who was tending a man in the next bed looked up. Immediately, she came over and brought James into a half-sitting position while Suzy held the bowl under his chin. He turned his head and retched several times but only a thin slime came up. The nurse picked up his glass from the bedside table and he took a sip of water, then jerked his head away. She guided him down on the pillow again and wiped away the sweat on his forehead.

'Are you Lieutenant James Mortimer's wife?' she asked Suzanne.

Sure that her face was as red as poor James's, and realising she was still holding his hand, Suzanne gently laid it back on the bed.

'No, but—'

'You must be his fiancée then,' the nurse said.

'Oh, um, I'm—'

'Because he must be kept quiet for a few days, so visits are limited,' she said. 'But of course we'd make an exception for a wife or a fiancée.' She sent Suzanne a wink.

Suzanne thought quickly. 'We haven't set a date yet.'

'These things are difficult to arrange with a war on,' the nurse said, smiling. 'But thank you for giving your time to sing to us. It brought England nearer to the patients.' With a nod she turned to give her attention to another patient who had just come into the ward on a trolley.

'What did that woman say?' James said, his voice heartbreakingly weak.

Hoping he hadn't realised what the nurse had said about her being his wife or fiancée, Suzanne said, 'She's one of the nurses looking after you. She said you need to be quiet for a few days to recover.'

'You will come back?'

'Yes, soon, but not until you've had time to rest.'

She thought she saw a flicker of disappointment as his face seemed to drop . . . his lips momentarily parted.

'James, I don't want to tire you but—'

'I'm sorry, I keep falling asleep. Got a bit of a headache. Don't worry.' He looked at her and this time she thought his eyes looked a little more clear. 'I like hearing your voice. I've never heard you sing before. It was wonderful. I wish you could have sung in this ward as well. But when you go I won't believe you were here.'

'Yes, you will because Sister Young will tell you,' Suzanne said, a little shakily, 'and I'll come and see you as soon as I'm able. By then you'll feel a bit better. It will take time, but you'll get well – I know you will.'

'Come soon, my love.'

She leaned over and dropped a brief kiss on his nearest cheek. He gave a half-smile and seconds later his breathing was rhythmic. He was asleep.

Quietly, she rose and went back to say goodbye to Bram who was reading. He put his book down.

'Bram, you're not going to believe this, but the man asking to see me is James Mortimer. His mother lives in our village. He's in the Navy. He was very kind to me when I needed help—' She broke off, churned up again at the thought of Wendy.

Bram looked directly at her. 'You look quite flushed, Suzy. It seems there's more to it than you just knowing him, and he was kind to you.'

'I like him very much,' she said, 'but there's nothing romantic.' She gave a short laugh. 'You're as bad as Betty, reading things in that aren't there.'

She wasn't prepared to discuss James with Bram. Rumours too easily flew amongst the ENSA members.

'I wonder.' Bram grinned as he kept his eyes on her.

'Do you know when you're coming out?' Suzanne asked, desperate to change the subject.

'Tomorrow,' Bram said. 'I'm feeling much better. So you won't need to come to the hospital again as I'll be back at the camp . . . unless, of course, you have a reason to visit a certain other,' he added with a mischievous twinkle.

She couldn't help smiling. 'Don't make something out of nothing, Bramwell Taylor,' she admonished. 'Just come back soon. I'm getting fed up with trying to hold the fort.'

On the way out Sister Young waylaid her.

'Did you have a word with Lieutenant James Mortimer? He seemed quite agitated to meet you.'

'Yes, I did. And the strangest thing – I know him.'

'Ah.' Sister Young smiled. 'It's a small world. I'm sure he was delighted to see a friend.'

'I think he was.' Suzanne hesitated. 'Sister Young, what happened to him? He doesn't seem to remember anything to do with his injury.'

'That's normal,' she said briskly. 'His ship was torpedoed. He was in the water for two hours or more. Lucky he didn't drown. But he's suffering from hypothermia.' She glanced at Suzanne. 'But don't worry too much. He's young and strong.'

'Thank you.'

She couldn't say any more to the kind Sister or she would have choked.

On the bus travelling back to camp, she was relieved she didn't have Betty chattering away, asking questions. She needed to be quiet. To take it all in. James seemed to be confused about what had happened but he'd get better. He had to. If she didn't believe it, she'd be no help to him at all. And she wanted to help him more than anything in the world. She might just as well admit it. She was head over heels in love with him.

But oh, James, your lovely eyes – sometimes grey, sometimes blue. How they used to sparkle when you laughed. Now, it's as though you're only a shadow of yourself.

Finally, the tears rolled down her cheeks and she fished for a handkerchief. Two elderly ladies sitting opposite were watching her curiously.

'Are you all right, dear?' one of them said.

'Yes, thank you. I expect it's a cold coming.'

She managed a wan smile but she couldn't help noticing how they gave one another sceptical glances. She had to stop herself from bursting into sobs. James would recover. She had to believe it. He was in the safest place. And he'd called her his love.

Chapter Thirty-Three

Suzanne couldn't stop thinking about James. It didn't seem possible that a strong, fit young man whom she'd last seen in England could be lying in a hospital bed in Malta with a head wound and obviously in a state of shock. She wondered if anyone had let his mother know. Even if they had, it would no doubt be very brief and would probably have her worry even more. She'd write to her today in between the first and second concert.

But it wasn't easy. She didn't have enough medical knowledge to give any kind of assurance as to his recovery. But she must tell her something. Mrs Mortimer would want to have a truthful account, knowing she'd actually seen how he was with her own eyes. She reached for her pen and sheet of notepaper.

Dear Mrs Mortimer,

Thank you so much for your letter. It was very kind of you to write and let me know news of home.

You'll be amazed to learn that I've seen James! Unfortunately he's in hospital although not far from our camp. I was visiting our pianist who has malaria, and James was in the next ward! Can you believe it!

You may already have heard from the Navy that there was an accident . . .

Suzanne bit her lip, her pen poised. She was sure Mrs Mortimer would read between the lines and know her son's ship had been attacked, but she daren't say it in case someone censored it. She carried on.

. . . and he banged his head.

I don't know exactly what happened before he was taken to hospital. The nurse told me he needed to rest, but he could see me clearly and was speaking to me. I shall go and see him as often as I can between rehearsals and concerts. Please try not to worry. By the time this letter reaches you he may very well be out and recuperating.

I will write again as soon as I have more news of him.

Yours sincerely,

Suzanne

The 'Yours sincerely' didn't look very friendly but she didn't know how else to end it. Sighing, she folded the sheet of paper and put it in an envelope, dreading Mrs Mortimer opening it to read such news if she didn't already know.

Feeling thoroughly exhausted after two concerts, with another one in three-quarters of an hour's time, she lay on her bed and closed her eyes. In an instant she was fast asleep and didn't wake until Betty shook her thirty-five minutes later.

Bram came back to camp the following day, and the day after that, to Suzanne's relief, he was back at the piano for rehearsals.

'We've missed you terribly,' Suzanne said. 'Are you sure you're feeling up to it this soon?'

'Best rest I've had in ages,' Bram said. 'I'm fit as a flea now. I only wish I could say the same for that young man of yours—' He gave her a wink. 'Oh, now I've made you blush.'

'There's no air in here,' Suzanne said, embarrassed he was still insisting there was more to her relationship. 'Did you see him then?'

'Yes, I stopped by and had a chat. Told him I was the pianist who accompanied you at the concerts.'

'How was he?' She tensed, waiting for his answer.

'A bit confused. I imagine he has concussion.'

He must recover. Underneath it all he's strong. Sister Young said so and she had to believe her.

Bram played a couple of scales, then turned on his stool. 'How would you feel if he's left with a severe memory loss – in other words, he doesn't make a full recovery?'

She startled at the shock of his words. Not because it would make any difference at all about her feelings for him, but for James himself. He'd have to learn a different way of living. And that might well mean he wouldn't be able to stay in the Navy that she knew he loved.

She blinked away the tears.

'He's strong,' she said at last. 'I think with time and patience he'll get better.'

'It's not going to be an easy journey for him,' Bram remarked.

'I know. But I'm going to try not to think about it. I'm going to pray he'll make a full recovery. I can't think much beyond that.'

'And *I* think you're falling in love with him,' Bram said. 'And if you are, and he's a broken man, it won't be an easy journey for you either.'

'I can't think about that either,' Suzanne said, feeling sick. 'We've just got to hope for the very best.' She made herself smile. 'Bram, can we run through a new song Adelaide suggested I sing? I've brought the music with me – "Bewitched, Bothered and Bewildered". She said it would suit me, and I love the words.'

'More or less sums you up at the moment, young lady,' Bram said, lighting a cigarette. He left it dangling from the corner of his mouth as he played the introduction.

'Who's been coaching you?' he said when Suzanne had sung the last notes.

'Why are you asking?'

'You're sounding bloody marvellous. In the ward – your singing was different again from ten days ago. You just now put your heart and soul into that "Bewitched" song . . . which I don't doubt this chap, Mortimer, has something to do with.'

Suzanne tried to shrug off his remark by saying, 'I'll tell Adelaide. She's been terrific. She's the one who's shown me how to perform. It's given me so much more confidence.'

'Well, you couldn't have had a better teacher. She's a fine lady. Pity she had such a time of it in her own country and was forced to leave. It must have been very hard for her. But she's been a trouper right from the beginning of the war when ENSA was first formed. Did you know she even used to go into the London Underground at night and entertain the people who slept there until morning?'

'She's never mentioned it,' Suzanne said. 'She's so modest. And a good friend. Betty loves her, too. We all do . . . well, all except one.'

'That little madam, Cat-with-her-claws-out.'

'I don't know why she's so horrible. Adelaide saved her from drowning the other day. Cat didn't even thank her. I was disgusted and told her so, but I knew it wouldn't make any difference.'

'Adelaide has black skin. Cat can't deal with it.' Bram shrugged. 'It's her loss.' He paused, then said, 'By the way, what happened at the Governor's place when they carted me off? It must have been disappointing for you not to have sung after all – or were you relieved?' He sent her a knowing grin.

'Oh, one of the guests played the piano and offered to accompany me.'

Bram's eyebrows rose. 'Oh, really? Was he any good?'

'He was good,' she said carefully, 'but he wasn't you.'

Bram smiled, and Suzanne let out a breath of relief. She wouldn't hurt him for the world.

Suzanne managed to see James twice more during the next week, but she found him morose and silent. Conversation between them was stilted. Instinctively, she said little, just held his hand, hoping it would give him some crumb of comfort just knowing she was there. But leaving him was difficult. There were no words from him asking when she'd be coming back.

'It's to be expected,' one of the nurses told her when she had a word with her. 'It rarely happens that a patient makes steady progress. They often have a setback. Try not to worry.' She'd given Suzanne a sympathetic smile and hurried away to attend to the next patient.

On the third visit, Suzanne was pleased to see James was sitting up in bed, though still attached to the drip. His face was closer to its normal colour, but when she asked how he felt, he said he didn't want to talk about it. After another uncomfortable fifteen minutes, he made it plain he was tired.

'You shouldn't drag all this way to see me,' he said, when she told him she would leave him to rest.

'You're making it sound like a chore,' she said, her heart sinking at the tone of his voice. He almost sounded as though he was resigned to the fact that he wasn't going to get better. 'Don't you think I might actually *want* to see you?'

'I can't imagine why, when I'm in this state,' he said.

She felt a twinge of anger. 'James, listen—'

He turned his head away from her and she swallowed the lump in her throat.

'I don't want you to talk in such a way. Whatever you think, you *are* going to get well.'

'You're not a doctor, Suzy,' he mumbled.

'Stop that! Look at me!'

He turned to face her.

'Don't be cross with me.' He sounded like a little boy talking to his mother.

Immediately, she felt ashamed. How could she possibly know how he was feeling? As though he read her thoughts, he said: 'I just can't recall anything about what happened to the ship. How I got here. All I remember is water closing over my head, men screaming . . .' He began to shake uncontrollably.

It frightened her to see him like it. She jumped up. 'I'll get a nurse.'

'No, no, don't. I'll be all right. It goes.' He flopped back onto the pillow.

She held his hand again to reassure him she was there.

'I won't have you giving up. What would your mother say if she knew you were talking like this? She wouldn't think it sounded at all like her son.'

She saw his mouth droop at the corners.

'It's easy for you—' he began.

'Maybe. But I won't have you feeling sorry for yourself. You're a wonderful, brave, strong person who would do anything for anyone, and that person is still there. You just have to give yourself time. But you also have to believe you're going to be well – as I believe.'

'Why do you believe it, Suzy? You know there's a good chance my memory won't come back. The Navy will boot me out and I won't even be able to hold down some menial job. And then I'm no good to you or anyone.'

'It's only your recent memory.'

'No, Suzy. I couldn't even remember where I lived when one of the nurses asked me.' He was silent for a few moments. 'I got there in the end though, thank goodness. But I'm not the same man . . .'

Suzanne felt her chest tighten. How was she going to convince him he had everything to live for?

'What would it take for you to believe in yourself the way I do?'

He gave an almost imperceptible shake of his head.

She drew a deep breath and the words were out before she even considered whether this was a wise moment.

'If I told you I loved you, would that make a difference?'

His eyes flew wide. He gripped her hand with a strength that surprised her.

She put a hand up to her burning cheeks. What on earth had made her tell him something so serious? He'd never hinted about falling in love with her. He'd think her terribly forward. She'd been a fool to say such a thing. And wasn't the man supposed to say it first. Oh, if she could bite back the words, she would. But what was he saying? She'd missed it. Something about . . .

'Do you mean that? You're not just saying it because you feel sorry for me? Because if you *do* love me, it means you must know how I feel about *you*.' His hand was warm against her skin. 'I fell head-over-heels in love with you that first moment I met you when you tripped over in the blackout.'

'You did?'

He was smiling. 'I did. I knew you were the girl for me. But now . . .' He trailed off.

'You've remembered all that,' she said, her heart lifting with joy. 'There's not a lot wrong with your memory if you can tell me all those details. But when your ship was torpedoed your brain is blocking out the memory because it's so painful.'

'My ship was torpedoed?' He sounded surprised.

'Didn't they tell you?'

Maybe they'd kept it from him on purpose, so as not to upset him. She shouldn't have mentioned it.

'They might have done. I can't remember,' he said.

'It doesn't matter. Everything's going to get better from now on because we love each other. But even if we didn't, I want you to get better for *your* sake.' She paused. '*Now* do you understand?'

'You win, Suzy.' And this time he grinned. 'I'd better get myself right if I'm going to be courting the most beautiful girl in the world.'

They sat for a minute in silence, Suzanne happier than she'd been in her life with her hand wrapped within the strength of his. How glad she was that she'd had the courage to tell him she loved him because it seemed to have worked a miracle.

'I know you have to go, Suzy,' James said finally. 'But you'll come back soon, won't you?'

'You know I will.'

'Will you do something?'

'Anything.'

'Good.' He smiled. 'We never kissed, did we?'

'You were put off by my mother,' she said, chuckling.

'She's not here now so we don't need her permission.'

Her pulse racing, she bent over and touched his lips with hers. But as she straightened, he raised his arm and pulled her back down.

'Shall we try it again?'

'It might be easier if you sit up properly,' Suzanne said, smiling at him.

With her help he pulled himself into a sitting position. This time he took charge and his kiss was everything she'd ever dreamed of. Warm, tender, inviting . . .

'When will you come back?' he said as Suzanne bent to kiss him goodbye for the last time. He took her face in both hands to kiss her firmly on the lips again.

She didn't want him to stop. If only they were somewhere where no curious eyes could see them.

'I'll come Tuesday.'

'I love you, Suzy. Don't you dare forget it.'

'Is that an order?' She nuzzled her face in the crook of his neck. 'You'll be out of hospital soon, darling. I promise,' she told him, her voice sounding somewhat muffled.

He gave a short laugh. 'Amazing that you haven't the slightest medical knowledge, yet you're so certain.'

'You've already improved by telling me when you first fell in love with me. If you could see yourself, you'd see you look quite different. You just have to be patient.'

'I'm not very good at that.'

'I know. But you have to learn.' She kissed him again. 'I must go. We have a concert in an hour and I don't know the exact time of the bus.'

'Go then. But you'll keep your promise?'

'I'll keep my promise.'

She was glad he couldn't see her eyes fill with tears. But at least she'd had a glimpse of the James she knew. She hoped her love for him would help him get well. She couldn't give him anything more.

Suzanne could barely take in the beautiful scenic journey as the bus wound its way back from the hospital to Luqa. Her heart was light, the imprint of his kiss still tingling her lips. James loved her. That was all she needed to know.

Back in her room, she tidied her hair, hoping the boys wouldn't mind that she hadn't had time to change out of her uniform when she sang to them at the concert in exactly twenty minutes' time. She ran downstairs to find a letter waiting for her from Ronnie. This was nice. She'd only heard from her a few days ago.

Dear Suzy,

Don't be alarmed but we had some horrible news yesterday. Raine was flying with a group of other pilots when they got shot at.

No! Not Raine. Not her darling sister. Her eyes darted to the next sentence.

Don't worry – Raine wasn't harmed. I don't know all the details but she said in her letter it was our side that was firing! Isn't that tragic? I think it's worse than the enemy as it needn't have happened. Anyway, Raine was all right thank goodness but her friend Audrey died. Raine is really upset about it but she's carrying on as normal. She says these things happen in war and you have to expect it. Maman is beside herself but Raine's due some leave next month, so she'll be coming home soon for as long as a week, she said. I can't wait!

Suzanne tried to still her heartbeat, which was hammering in her chest. It could've been Raine who'd been shot down. *It could so easily have been Raine.*

Chapter Thirty-Four

Ronnie's letter played on Suzanne's mind. She couldn't get the image of the pilots flying in formation – something Raine had once mentioned she wasn't that keen on – and Audrey shot down. Poor Audrey. Raine had often mentioned her and what a character she was. Depending on the position of the planes, Raine might have actually seen it happen. Maman must be tortured with the thought that all her fears about Raine working as a pilot were well founded.

Suzanne was feeling more than tired. It had been a long day. The ENSA troupe had all gone off in a lorry to one of the other airfields, Hal Far, bombed only two months ago, so Bob had told her, and given two concerts. They'd then returned to Luqa to give an evening performance. Hurtling along on terrible potholed roads, squashed tight amongst the musicians, with Cat pulling faces and groaning, Suzanne had wanted to shake her. If that wasn't enough, the evening audience seemed unusually critical.

'Don't you know any Vera Lynn songs?' one soldier called out when she'd sung several that she didn't think Vera Lynn had made. She'd wanted a change and she'd hoped the men would enjoy them. Several of his mates shouted some names of songs she'd never even heard of. They even interrupted Adelaide, which had never happened before. Maybe some of them had been in Malta too long and were just plain exhausted.

By the end of the session her head was throbbing. She did get the occasional headache but this one felt different. Probably best to have an early night. Tomorrow was Tuesday and she wanted to look her best for James.

But in the morning when she awoke the headache had taken hold and had settled into her left eye. Suzanne had never felt such pain, but even more disconcerting was her vision. Zigzagging lights danced up and down, flashing and pricking at her. Nothing would come clear, no matter how hard she tried to focus. It was terrifying.

She tried to picture James but she couldn't. Hopefully, this pain would be gone by this afternoon and she could— She blinked, trying to clear her head. Everything went fuzzy. She must be well. She'd made a promise. He'd worry if she didn't turn up.

But she couldn't even lift her head from the pillow let alone rehearse this morning. She couldn't have sung or played her violin if her life depended on it. Sour fumes rose up her gullet.

'Betty,' she called weakly. 'Are you awake?'

There was only the sound of Betty snoring.

'Betty, I—'

The bile came up in the back of her throat and she leapt out of bed and just made it to the sink. She clung on to the edge of the sink as her head swam, then when the room stopped swaying she ran the tap to wash the mess away. Sweat from her forehead ran into her eyes and down her cheeks.

'Suzy, what on earth—' She felt Betty's arm around her. 'Come on, love, let's get you back to bed.'

'I feel terrible,' Suzanne said, holding her head as Betty helped her to settle under the sheet.

'Where's the pain?'

Suzanne put her hand up to her left eye. 'My eye feels as though it's going to drop out of my head, it's so sore and aching. And this side of my head's throbbing. I've never had anything like this.'

'I'll get you a bowl in case you need to be sick again.'

Betty stood the tin bowl they both used when washing their hair by the side of the bed.

'You need to rest. It sounds exactly like what my mother has. She calls them bilious attacks. The only thing that relieves it is a rag soaked in vinegar. I'm going to the kitchen to ask for some. Before I go I'll get you a glass of water and two aspirin and they can be working.'

Suzanne could hardly take in what Betty was saying. As soon as her friend disappeared she reached for the bowl, but the very action of bending over caused her to bring up a stream of bitter liquid. She grimaced as she hauled herself back under the sheet, her mouth sour. She took a sip of water, then lay still. Only without moving a muscle could she somehow bear it.

What was the matter with her? Was it something really serious? Betty said her mother had sick headaches every month at the time of the curse. But she wasn't due for another fortnight.

'Oh, dear, you've been sick again,' Betty said as she came into the room, which immediately filled with the sour stench of vinegar. She took the bowl away and rinsed it in the sink, then came back and patted a vinegar-soaked rag over Suzanne's forehead. Immediately, Suzanne gagged and pushed the rag away.

'Sorry, Betty,' she mumbled. 'That smell . . .'

'I'll leave you to rest,' Betty said, taking the rag and rinsing it out in the sink. 'Give the tablets a chance to work.'

'Can you pull the curtains, Betty? I can't stand the light.'

Betty swished the curtains to. 'Mum was exactly the same,' she said, turning to look at Suzanne. 'I'll check on you in an hour. Try and get some sleep, if you can. It's the only thing that works for Mum.'

'I've got to be better by this afternoon,' Suzanne groaned. 'I promised James I'd see him.'

Betty shook her head. 'You won't be going anywhere today, girl. Forget everything. Just rest. You won't be performing tonight either, so I'll let Miss Foster know.' She left the room, shutting the door quietly behind her.

At first the pain and steady throbbing on the left side of Suzanne's head stopped her from falling asleep but in the end, exhausted, she gave in.

She awoke, her mouth so dry she couldn't swallow. She ran her tongue over her lips and fumbled for her watch, but her eyes were still playing up and she couldn't read the hands. Where was Betty?

She roused herself up in bed, then forgetting the bowl she rushed to the sink thinking she needed to be sick, but nothing came up. Oh, how her head hurt. The pain behind her eye was worse. Even her eyelashes ached where they were joined to the lids, but thankfully the flashing lights seemed to have disappeared. How long had she slept?

Back in bed she gulped some water, then realised she needed the toilet. She put her feet on the floor and stood, but immediately her head swam. She sat down again.

Take it slowly, she told herself. *You'll be all right.* She heard the bedroom door open.

'Are you feeling any better?' It was Betty. 'I've been checking on you every hour but you've been fast asleep, which is good.'

'I still feel a bit dizzy.'

'Do you want the lav?'

Suzanne nodded. Her head swam.

'Are you going to be sick again?' Betty asked as she helped Suzanne along the hallway.

'No, I don't think so.'

'That's good.'

'What's the time?'

'Ten past four.'

Oh, no. James would wonder where she was. It was too late to see him now. Visiting hours were over at half past.

Betty opened the WC. 'I'll wait outside for you.'

Suzanne splashed her face in the sink, grimacing at the white reflection in the mirror. She still felt rotten but thought perhaps she might not die after all. Her mouth felt stale and dry; she ran her tongue around the inside to moisten it, longing for a cup of tea.

Back in her room Suzanne quickly dressed, cleaned her teeth and brushed her hair. It did wonders for her mood but she couldn't believe how weak she felt. She sat down on the edge of the bed. Betty watched her with a concerned look.

'You'll feel heaps better tomorrow to see James,' she said, reading Suzanne's mind. 'But for now, just take things slowly.'

Suzanne rose and put her arms round her friend. 'Betty, thank you for looking after me and—'

A sudden wail, curdling her blood, interrupted her. Betty rushed to the window and pulled open the curtains.

'Oh, my God! It must be an air raid!'

Ashen-faced, she turned to Suzanne as the siren sounded again.

'Bloody hell, Suzy, we're going to be bombed! The bloody Germans are back!' She grabbed Suzanne by the arm. 'We've got to go NOW! Don't stop for anything!'

People were rushing from their rooms, bumping into others along the hallway, as they jostled for the stairs, cursing the Germans. Adelaide came rushing down from the first floor with no sign of her usual smile.

'Thank God you're both here.'

As she spoke, there was the sound of an explosion so loud it was as though the sky was being split in two. Some of the musicians ran by on the stairs, calling them to follow. Suzanne caught hold of Lenny, the young drummer.

'Where's Cat?'

'Not seen her.'

'What's her room number?'

'Don't know, but it's second floor.' The top of his head disappeared as he rushed down the stairs.

'I'll have to go and find her,' Suzanne said, her legs trembling with fright.

'No, don't,' Betty said. 'You're not well and this building could collapse at any moment. We've got to get out now.'

'You go. I won't be long.'

Without waiting for any reply, Suzanne ran the few feet of the corridor and pulled herself up the next two flights of stairs. Her head had started to throb again, her fear taking an icy hold. She fought down a new wave of nausea.

She pounded on the nearest door and opened it. 'Cat,' she called. There was no answer. 'Cat! CAT!'

She tried two more doors. Nothing. It had to be the last one. Panting with fright she shoved open the last door and saw Cat's cello without its case standing in the corner of the bedroom.

'Cat!' she screamed. 'Where are you?'

There was a noise behind her. She spun round to see Adelaide, eyes wide with alarm.

'Come on, Suzy. We gotta get out.'

Adelaide took hold of her but before they reached the door there was an almighty crash. Then an explosion blasted through Suzanne's eardrums. Everywhere went black.

The end of the world, was Suzanne's last thought.

A voice she vaguely recognised came to her from a distance.

Adelaide's dear, reassuring face came into her vision. Was she dreaming? She felt a hand on her shoulder giving a gentle shake. She screamed out.

'What is it, Suzy?' Adelaide's voice was urgent. 'Are you hurt?'

She wasn't dreaming after all. The ache on the side of her head was real. So was the tearing pain in her shoulder. She blinked and opened her eyes. Cat's cello. Flung by the blast, it was lying on its side a few feet away.

'Cat . . .?' She didn't know if she'd made a sound.

'She was first one in the basement,' Adelaide said bluntly. 'But we're leaving . . . NOW!'

'My shoulder . . .'

'I'll help you up. There could be another bomb go off at any minute.'

The building felt ominously quiet.

'Where is everyone?' She found herself whispering as Adelaide helped her towards the door.

'In the basement. That's where *we're* going.'

'Cat's cello. She'll want it.'

'Forget the goddamned cello.'

'Adelaide . . .'

The black woman blew out her cheeks and dropped the arm supporting Suzanne. She turned back to the room and heaved up the instrument.

'I can't help you now I've got this thing,' Adelaide said. 'Nothing more – we're going. You go first.'

But when Suzanne opened the door the smoke made her reel backwards.

Immediately the two of them began to cough. Suzanne looked wildly round the room, desperately trying to recall her first aid lessons. Cat had tossed some scarves onto the bed.

Put something over your nose and mouth in case of smoke. Stay low.

She rushed to grab a couple and gave one to Adelaide, stifling a scream of pain as she tried to tie the scarf in position behind her head.

Adelaide let the cello go to the floor.

'Give the scarf to me.' Swiftly she tied it around Suzanne's face and darted to the door again. She opened it.

The smoke was worse. They could smell burning.

'Open the window!' Adelaide ordered, banging the door closed. 'We need air.'

We're going to suffocate. Or be burnt alive. James, oh, James. I love you.

Somehow Suzanne got the rusty catch to work and flung open the window, her shoulder protesting at the sudden action. There was shouting below. She stuck her head out and sucked in a deep breath of cloying air.

'HELP! Someone please help! We're trapped!'

'How many of you?' a man's voice called.

'TWO!'

'Hang on. We're coming for you.'

She saw a man wearing a helmet feed a tall ladder against the wall. Her chest tightened.

Wendy. The fire brigade had been too late for Wendy.

The inside of her mouth dried. She couldn't move. Or speak.

Adelaide practically pushed Suzanne away from the window to see out, then ducked back inside.

'Good,' she said, relief in her voice. 'The fire brigade's here. Not before time.' Adelaide brought the scarf over her nose and mouth again.

No sooner had Adelaide spoken when a man's face appeared at the window.

'Anyone hurt, miss?' he said to Adelaide.

'My friend. She's wrenched her shoulder.'

'Okay. We'll see to her. Send her down first. I'll keep a few rungs behind her so she feels secure. Then you.'

Suzanne paled. 'I can't do it,' she said, shaking violently.

'Yes, you bloody well can,' Adelaide said. 'Fix your eyes on my rear end as you go down.'

'Adelaide, I—'

'GO!' Adelaide roared, her expression fierce. 'Unless you want us both to die.'

Her breath exploding as she tried to breathe in, then out, Suzanne pushed the window fully open with her good arm. It was a long way down. She could see a small crowd but they looked like figures in a doll's house.

'BACKWARDS!' Adelaide screamed.

Suzanne turned herself round. The end of the ladder was parallel with the windowsill. Gingerly she put her leg out and felt a rung, then brought out the other leg. She felt the weight of the fireman a few rungs below her.

'Grab hold of both edges of the ladder,' Adelaide shouted. 'Feel each rung. Don't rush, whatever you do . . . and don't look down, for God's sake.'

'Take your time,' shouted up one of the firemen. 'We'll help you.'

Her forehead was clammy, her head throbbing. She wanted to be back in her bedroom with the curtains pulled. Her eyes felt as if they would drop out of their sockets with pain. She still hadn't moved. She looked up at Adelaide who stuck her thumb up. She had to do this for Adelaide who'd been so kind to her.

Taking a jagged breath, she let her right leg feel for the next rung down.

One rung at a time, Suzy. Slowly, one by one.

She was halfway down when a siren suddenly went off again, startling her. Her foot slipped, leaving her leg dangling in mid-air. She bit back a scream as she tried to regain her balance, another wave of pain shooting through her shoulder. The fireman had already reached the ground and Adelaide was making swift progress in front of her eyes. She could feel the ladder wobble with every step Adelaide took.

If she didn't soon move, Adelaide would be on top of her. They'd both fall and break their necks.

Courage, Suzy. You're nearly there.

'Keep going, love,' shouted the fireman from below.

She brought her dangling leg back onto the rung. How many more rungs? One, two, another breath, another rung, three, four, five, six, seven, eight . . . She must be close to the ground now. She felt a pair of arms around her waist.

'You're safe now, love,' the fireman said. He paused and studied her. 'Go and sit down over there.' He pointed to a wooden bench by one of the flower beds. 'You're in a bit of shock. I'll go and see to your friend.'

But Adelaide was making her way towards them as though she was perfectly used to coming down ladders from bedroom windows.

'Do we need to go to the basement?' Adelaide asked him.

'No. That was the All Clear. One of the other firemen has gone down to tell them they can come out. They were worried there was a danger of more bombs . . . but it's been a half an hour now.' He looked up. 'And the sky's as innocent as a baby. Nasty when it happened, though. There was a whole formation above us.' He sighed. 'More ruined buildings to clear up. More people homeless, just when we thought we had Jerry on the run since Christmas.'

'I wonder if you could do us a big favour?' Adelaide said.

'What's that?'

'One of the musicians left her cello in the dash downstairs. It's valuable and we don't have another. Could you possibly—?'

'If it's really important, miss. In that same room, is it?' He jerked his head to the open window.

'Yes.'

He was up the ladder and back down in a trice, triumphantly bearing the cello.

'Now which one of you's goin' to make your friend very happy?'

'You give it to her, Adelaide,' Suzanne said, her voice still shaky. 'It's your idea. Cat's lucky you thought of it.' She gazed at her friend. 'What made you go up to Cat's room?'

'Well, I rushed down to the basement with the others, then saw Betty in a panic. She told me you'd gone to find Cat who wasn't anywhere in sight. Then someone told me they'd seen her. By then *you* were missing.' Adelaide ran her tongue over her lips. 'That woman has caused more trouble than anyone I know.'

'I'm so sorry I put you in danger,' Suzanne said. 'I don't know what to say to thank you for coming back for me.'

Adelaide smiled. 'It seems to be my forte lately – rescuing people.' She looked over towards the main entrance of the hotel. 'They're coming out now.' She turned to Suzanne. 'Shall we take this damned cello over to our dear friend?'

Chapter Thirty-Five

'Anyone who's staying at the Victoria Hotel, come and see me and I'll let you know where you'll be staying tonight,' Miss Foster said in the officers' mess where most of the troupe had gathered for teas and Camp coffee after the fright of the air raid. 'Anyone not here, would you let them know the same?' She pushed her glasses up her nose and glanced down at her notes. 'I'd like to say how proud I am of all of you for staying calm this morning.' She looked towards Adelaide. 'Adelaide, I hear you came to Suzy's rescue, so thank you for showing such bravery.'

Everyone clapped and Adelaide gave a modest smile. Suzanne noticed she was the only one who was her usual groomed self. Everyone else looked decidedly bedraggled and Suzanne didn't want to think what Maman would have said if she'd caught sight of her at this moment.

'I don't want to cancel both shows,' Miss Foster continued, 'so we'll do the earlier one at half-past five, then call it a day.' She paused. 'Suzy, you're excused as I believe you've not been very well lately, and Betty told me you'd hurt your shoulder. I want you to get it looked at.'

Suzanne was relieved to be excused. The headache was beginning to recede but she felt weak – unable hardly to think straight. All she knew was that James would be worried she might have been injured – or worse. He was sure to have heard the air raid.

She'd go and see him tomorrow without fail.

Until then, she'd have an early night. Miss Foster told them the hotel hadn't been too badly damaged and that as soon as it was considered safe, they could go back for their personal belongings. However, they would no longer be staying there as repairs would be taking place as soon as possible.

'I have another announcement to make,' Miss Foster said. 'And this affects every one of you. The air raid this morning was quite out of the blue.'

'Quite out of the blue sky,' one musician piped up. There was subdued laughter, though with a brittle edge.

'We all thought the terrible attacks on Malta were over,' Miss Foster went on, ignoring the weak joke. 'That's why I felt ENSA should make its presence known. This poor unfortunate Island has had very little – maybe *no* entertainment for several years, and Basil Dean – you may remember he was the chap who formed ENSA – anyway, he felt it was important they'd not been forgotten. This may be a one-off raid, but I can't take the risk that the Malta attacks have started up again, so I'm afraid we'll all be leaving as soon as alternate transport arrangements can be made.' She stopped speaking and swept her eyes round the room.

'We have the chance to be evacuated to another country with less known risk, which is what I will be doing. I would like to know how many of you will be joining me. If so, please let me have your names. Alternatively, anyone who decides he or she would like to go back to Britain, please inform me so I can find places for you on the journey home.'

'Where are we off to?' It was Lenny, the boy drummer.

'Sorry, Lenny, I'm afraid you won't be going onwards. In fact, you'll be escorted home.'

'I don't need no escort,' Lenny said sulkily. 'Why can't I go if everyone else does?'

'You know the reason,' Miss Foster said sternly. 'Unless you'd like me to tell everyone what age you *really* are.' She paused, her head cocked on one side. 'I thought so. Well, then, there will be no need for further argument.'

'What about the rest of us?' one of the actors said.

'As usual, you'll know more details when we get there,' Miss Foster said crisply. 'It's not to be discussed with anyone or written in letters. You know the rules – and I'm deadly serious about keeping them.' Her alert gaze swept over the troupe. 'Now, any questions?'

'If we go home, will we be able to entertain the boys there?'

'Yes, very definitely,' Miss Foster smiled. 'Some of them are posted in extremely remote places and they've always welcomed us.' She paused. 'Anything else?' She cocked her ear. 'In that case, have a think about it. I need to know numbers by tomorrow morning, ten o'clock. That will be all.'

Suzanne was grateful to be on her own in the small cluttered front room of the hotel. She sat on one of the armchairs and flicked through an old copy of *The Lady* magazine which her mother sometimes read, but she couldn't concentrate. Raine's near accident had shaken her badly. But her sister was carrying on. Suzanne was sure Betty and probably most of the band would go with Miss Foster, and she wanted to be with them.

'What do you think you'll do, Betty?' Suzanne said as they sat at the kitchen table in their temporary accommodation when Betty had returned from the early performance of the concert. The B&B in the heart of Luqa village was a simple affair, run solely by the Maltese landlady, Sinjura Galea.

'You can call me Mrs Galea,' she said, smilingly. 'It is more easy.'

Her husband and young son had been killed in a bombing raid at the height of the siege. How the house had survived, heaven only knew, by the look of so many nearby streets being nothing but rubble. But Mrs Galea was kind and motherly and had made the two girls tea and a plate of cheese on toast.

'I'd like to stay with the troupe wherever Miss Foster has in mind to take us,' Betty said. 'I feel I came out here to do a job and would like to give it longer than just these last few weeks.'

'Nothing to do with lovely Reg, I don't suppose,' Suzanne teased.

'Oh, no, nothing at all.' Betty grinned, then gave Suzanne's arm a playful push. 'Course it is, you daft thing. I'm not going to let him slip through my fingers.'

'Is it really serious?'

'He says it is.'

'And do you feel the same?'

'I think so.' She drew a hand through her red curls. 'Yes, I do. But it's early days. I'm not going to be rushed.' Putting her empty cup on the saucer, she said, 'Mmm, that just hit the spot.' She studied Suzanne. 'So what about *you*? Have you made a decision about staying or going home?'

'Can we talk about it in the morning?'

'Course we can,' Betty said immediately. 'It's been quite a day.' She glanced at Suzanne with a look of concern. 'How's the headache?'

'I think the bomb put paid to that.' Suzanne swallowed the last of her tea. 'And your nursing, of course,' she grinned.

Betty chuckled. 'What about the shoulder?'

Suzanne grimaced and rubbed the hollow between her neck and left shoulder. 'It's not too bad. I think it's just a wrench.'

'Then it's two more aspirin for you, Miss Suzy, and an early night.' Betty went to the sink and began to clean her teeth. She finished and put her toothbrush back in the mug and glanced towards her bed. 'You know what – that bed looks most enticing. I think I'll turn in early myself.'

Half an hour later Suzanne lay in the unfamiliar room, her fingers softly linked across her chest. Adelaide had already told Betty she would stay with the troupe and continue the overseas tour. Idly, Suzanne wondered what Cat would do. In her mind she replayed the scene when Cat had emerged from the hotel basement and spotted Adelaide with her cello.

'What are you doing with my cello?' Cat had said accusingly, stretching out her arms to take it.

Adelaide held back. 'The reason I've got it is because Suzanne asked me to save it for you when the two of us were trapped in your room.'

Cat's eyes widened as she stared at Suzanne. 'What were you doing in my room? You had no business there.'

'Apparently, Suzanne thought she did,' Adelaide rushed in before Suzanne could reply. 'No one had seen you when the bomb went off. Suzanne ran upstairs to find you. Someone told me you'd been first down the basement, so then we had *her* missing. I went after her and we were nearly suffocated with the smoke. One of the firemen had to rescue us down a ladder from the second floor. Did you know that?' Adelaide said fiercely.

'No, I—'

'It was impossible to bring myself *and* the cello down the

ladder at the same time so I left it behind. When I got down I asked the very nice fireman if he would go back up and fetch it. I said it belonged to one of our friends. So he rescued it, though why you didn't take your precious instrument with you when you ran out of the room, God knows.' She gave Cat a steady look. 'You may take it from me if you can bear the thought that my dirty black hands have touched it.'

Cat's face flushed bright red. She bowed her head. 'I was too terrified to even think when that alarm went off,' she mumbled, 'but I've been so upset about my cello.' She looked up and stared ahead. 'It means everything in the world to me. My arm might as well have been ripped off. You couldn't possibly understand—'

'Maybe not,' Adelaide cut in. 'I'm just a two-bit singer. But Suzanne understood. Here, take it.' She held out the instrument.

'I owe you an apology, Adelaide,' Cat muttered as she took the cello, keeping her head low, averting her eyes. 'I was very rude and you didn't deserve it.'

She ran her fingers lovingly over its curves, reminding Suzanne how she would do the same thing with her violin. Then to Suzanne's amazement, Cat said, 'I've never thanked you for saving me.' This time she looked fully at Adelaide. 'You were right. I *was* out of my depth and petrified. Thank God you're such a strong swimmer.'

'I would have done it for anyone,' Adelaide said, her eyes never leaving Cat's face. 'Because none of us ever knows when we might need help one day from someone – and in that situation, who cares what colour their skin is. Remember that, in future.'

'I will.' Cat chewed her lower lip. She glanced at Suzanne. 'By the way, it honestly wasn't me who damaged Fern's dress, whatever you thought. One of the wives who was near you was waving her arm about – holding the glass – and was far too tight to realise she wasn't in control. Then the lights went out. Do you remember a woman tripped and called out? I reckon it was her.' Her eyes appealed to Suzanne as if to say, *I should never have implied Adelaide had anything to do with it when she was nowhere near you. It was a mean trick.*

It didn't matter now, Suzanne thought. Adelaide needn't be any the wiser about Cat's accusation.

Now as Suzanne lay in bed she thought about the remarkable change in Cat. Something had happened in the girl's life, she was sure, that had made her bitter, but perhaps now she could start to lose that suspicious attitude and begin to trust people. She idly wondered if Cat had made a decision as to where she was going with ENSA.

An hour later she was still staring at the ceiling. Something niggled in her mind. Cat and Maman and Adelaide were mixed up in it. Her head felt woolly. She still hadn't answered Maman's letter. Oh, she'd written an answer to the one she'd last received about the concerts and the people she was performing with, but so far she'd ignored that other one . . .

Cat – where do you fit in?

And then everything flashed through her mind, giving her the answer. Cat had judged Adelaide when she didn't even know what sort of person the singer was, all because she had a different skin colour. Suzanne put her hands to her face. She'd done exactly the same. She had judged her mother. How could she possibly know what the circumstances were between Maman and the Frenchman – her father? Even more importantly, how could she know how her mother had felt at the time – or how Maman felt now?

Even Cat had had the humility to say she was sorry for treating Adelaide so badly and Adelaide had immediately forgiven her. Her mother had said she was sorry for not telling her about a mistake she made once when she was young, hoping Suzanne would understand and forgive her . . . as her husband, Robert, had done.

Suzanne leapt out of bed and once more retrieved the letter from the drawer. This time she read it more slowly. And when she came to the part where her mother wrote that her heart was already broken, she sat on the edge of her bed, her hands cupping her face, trying to put herself into the head and heart of her mother. The tears welled. She'd tried so hard, so many times since that letter, to hold them back, but now they fell silently down her cheeks. She cried for her mother who'd had to make such a terrible choice, she cried for Dad who had loved her like his own, and would always be her father no matter what, but most of all she cried for a Frenchman who was her own flesh and blood – but whom she would never meet. Yet without him she wouldn't exist.

She dried her eyes. It was time to make her peace with Maman.

Chapter Thirty-Six

The inviting smell of toast wafted from the kitchen of their new digs to where Suzanne was drifting. Yawning, she looked over to Betty's bed. As usual her friend was curled up in a heap with one leg dangling out, and Suzanne's heart warmed at the endearing sight. Dear Betty. How kind she'd been, the way she'd looked after her.

What was the time? Suzanne reached for her watch. Ten minutes to eight! She'd been ages trying to get off to sleep last night and now it was late. Hurriedly she pulled the borrowed nightdress over her head and neatly folded it, laying it on top of her pillow. She went to the sink and had a quick wash, then put yesterday's clothes on. She couldn't wait to go back to the hotel to collect her belongings.

'Morning, Suzy. Did you sleep?' Betty sat up in bed rubbing her eyes.

'Not that well.'

'Was it because you still haven't decided what to do?'

'I'm going home,' Suzanne said.

Betty's face fell. 'Oh, Suzy. It won't be the same without you.' She threw back the sheet. 'What's changed your mind?'

'Something Ronnie said in one of her letters. Raine nearly had a fatal accident – one of her friends was shot down and killed by our own side. That's what was so awful. They could have shot Raine as their next target. Luckily, someone on the ground must have realised they were our planes.' She shivered at the horror of poor Audrey. 'I think Ronnie's having quite a job keeping Maman calm.'

'Oh, dear, that's awful,' Betty said. 'But what about James? He'll be upset you're leaving.'

'I'll be leaving him behind whatever I do.'

If he made a full recovery – and she prayed to God he would – they'd put him onto another warship, no doubt about that. She'd see him this afternoon and tell him about Miss Foster's announcement. He'd probably heard the noise of the bombs and was worrying about her. Well, she'd soon be putting his mind at rest.

'Are you ready for breakfast?'

'You go down – I'll follow,' Betty said. 'I'm not quite ready.'

Mrs Galea put a fried egg on toast and a pot of tea in front of Suzanne when she sat with two of the musicians at breakfast. It seemed the entire troupe had decided to press on to the next location. But she'd made the right decision, she was certain.

Miss Foster was in the officers' mess registering the ENSA group when Suzanne and Betty joined the queue at ten o'clock. There was a lot of chatter and people were betting on where they were being sent. Suzanne heard Cairo being mentioned several times. She wished she'd paid more attention in geography at school to see where it lay in relation to Malta.

'Suzy – what have you decided?'

'I've decided to go home,' she said. Miss Foster raised her eyebrows. 'Oh, nothing to do with ENSA,' Suzanne hurriedly added. 'I've loved every minute. But there's something at home I have to put right.'

Miss Foster nodded and put a cross against her name.

'So I'll be pleased to accompany Lenny,' Suzanne said.

After everyone had spoken to Miss Foster, she rapped on the table for their attention.

'I'm pleased to announce that you've all decided to continue on with us,' she said. 'Well, all except Suzy. She's volunteered to take Lenny home.'

Suzanne was gratified to hear several people say they'd be sorry not to have her along.

'Thank you, Suzy.' Miss Foster looked at her and smiled. 'Don't forget that when you're home, be sure to go to Drury Lane and they'll soon set you up with another troupe so you can continue your singing – or maybe even get the chance to play your violin.'

Suzanne nodded.

It won't be the same though. I won't have Betty and Adelaide and Fern.

But in place of the cold stone that had lately lodged in her chest was a warm feeling of anticipation that she'd soon be seeing Ronnie, and maybe it wouldn't be too long before Raine had some leave. But it was Maman she desperately needed to talk to.

'The good news,' Miss Foster continued, 'is that some of you may go to the Victoria hotel for a maximum of ten minutes between now and eleven to collect your things—' Miss Foster broke off for the cheers and whistles to subside. 'The workmen are coming in to carry out "first aid" repairs. The fire brigade is going to be very strict on this ten-minute slot, but I'm afraid those who were at the back of the building, which was the worst hit, will have to wait until I'm told it's safe.' There were a few groans from this announcement. 'They're not allowing anyone in those rooms until certain repairs have been done. They hope to start immediately, but as you're aware, people's homes have been destroyed from yesterday's raid, and some are more urgent than at the hotel. We have to just bear with it.'

'When is it likely we'll be off to the next place?' Bram asked.

'Could be as long as a fortnight, but for safety's sake, the sooner the better. We hope by then you'll all have your belongings.'

Suzanne was glad to be on her own for a while as the bus groaned and swayed through the bombed-out streets of Valletta towards Sliema. She needed to sort out her feelings. She was going home now and had a responsibility to Lenny so there was no possibility of changing her mind. James would be disappointed she'd no longer be able to visit him. She took comfort in the thought that it might well be a week or more before there was an available flight to take her back to Gibraltar. Who knew what might happen with everything changing from day to day?

She entered James's ward, barely able to contain her happiness at the thought of seeing him in a few moments.

'I'm afraid Lieutenant James Mortimer is no longer with us,' a nurse Suzanne recognised told her.

Her heart gave a sickening squeeze.

No! It couldn't be. Oh, James.

She stared at the nurse, desperately trying to take it in.

'Oh, nothing wrong, miss,' the nurse said quickly, seeing her face. 'He's been sent back to England. He went very early this morning on one of those flying boats.'

Suzanne staggered back, grabbing the door handle. *Nothing wrong.* That's what the nurse had said. He hadn't died. Without warning she burst into tears.

'I'm sorry, nurse.' She sniffed as she felt in her bag for a handkerchief.

'It's a natural reaction.' The nurse smiled sympathetically.

'Did the doctor mention anything about his recovery?'

'That's why he's been sent home,' the nurse told her. 'We couldn't do anything more for him. The cut on his head is healing nicely, but he just needs time and rest to recover from hypothermia. He was in a very poor state when he was rescued but he's strong. I'm sure he'll improve over the next few weeks.' She glanced at the watch on her chain. 'I'm sorry I can't tell you more. You should speak to the doctor but he's not on duty until this evening.'

She'd be performing to the troops this evening.

'Do you know which hospital he's gone to?'

'We wouldn't have that information. The Red Cross would be the best people to contact.' The nurse hurried away.

He wouldn't have been able to write her a note, even if he'd had the time, Suzanne thought sadly. He'd be so upset to think she wouldn't know where he'd been sent to, and that he was leaving her behind. Which is exactly what would have happened if it hadn't been for Maman and Ronnie, as she would have stayed with the ENSA troupe wherever they were going. Her part in the war effort might have to be shelved for a few weeks, that's all.

Her heart did a little jump. It must be fate. James was ahead of her, going back to England. And she'd soon be following. Better still, his own mother did volunteer work for the Red Cross.

Chapter Thirty-Seven

Unlike the previous journey out several weeks ago, the ship bound for England was packed with injured servicemen, mostly sailors. Never had Suzanne seen so many men with missing arms and legs. It was a disconcerting sight but somehow the atmosphere remained jolly. They were all making the best of it, joking with one another, playing deck games and substituting the missing limb with anything they could get hold of. Suzanne wondered how they'd be when they were back with their families and no longer had their mates in the same position as themselves. Jobs would be hard to find, for one thing, and they would be without all the camaraderie and support from their friends they'd been used to.

So far, everything had gone well, Suzanne mused, as she and Lenny made their way to the dining room, which was already full. They'd managed to bag two places on an available flight only three days after the air raid, and it was as though a ship had been waiting for them when they'd landed in Gibraltar, as they'd sailed the very next day.

It had been strange to be in Gibraltar again. She couldn't help her thoughts turning to that evening in the Governor's Residence when she'd first sung in public. How nervous she'd been. How she'd only sung one song because of Bram and then the storm. What a long time ago it seemed. So much had happened in the meantime. Best of all she'd told James she loved him, and to her joy he'd told her he felt the same. And now she was on her way. Every mile would bring her closer to him.

Lenny had been the only difficult part of the journey so far. He couldn't forgive Miss Foster for treating him like a child and sending him home. He'd argued that there wasn't another drummer, but Miss Foster had said in a tone that invited no backchat that they'd have to manage without.

'Miss Foster never let on, but I'm not sure you're even sixteen,' Suzanne had told him. 'But you'll get your chance. It's not likely the war is going to end just yet. We might find a band we can both join.'

Lenny had merely compressed his lips.

Apparently, he was only a couple of years younger than herself but he seemed like a schoolboy. It was difficult to keep an eye on him because he'd been allocated a bunk with the men, and Suzanne was in a cabin with five nurses. They were friendly girls, most of them having done a stint close to the front line in North Africa, one of them having lost two fingers on her right hand. They were going home to rest for a week or two and would then be sent somewhere else in the world where they were needed. They were most intrigued that Suzanne was a musician and singer.

'They're having entertainment on the ship for our first night,' one of them called Virginia told her excitedly. 'Why don't you let them know and they'll put your name down. Then we'll all come and hear you and throw tomatoes at you.' She chuckled. 'Seriously, we'd love to hear you sing, wouldn't we, girls?'

Suzanne tried to protest but Virginia said she'd go with her to talk to the chap who ran the entertainments and introduce her. The next thing Suzanne knew was that her name had been put down to sing a few songs.

'We don't have a crooner,' Mr Mason, the compère told her. 'It will be a real novelty to have a professional. Do you have your own music?'

'No. But I know quite a few songs by heart.'

'Trouble is, there's no time to rehearse. Do you think you'll be all right to come straight here at half-past seven? We'll just have you on for half an hour.'

'I'd like that,' Suzanne said, surprised she really would. It would be something to pass the time away. Who knew how long it would take for the ship to reach Portsmouth?

Suzanne and Betty had been lucky their room in the Malta hotel hadn't faced the rear. The two girls had been allowed to go back and collect all their belongings. That afternoon on the ship she washed her hair in the tiny cabin sink. Now for the dress. There was precious little space to hang anything but thankfully Maman's black dress didn't crease. She'd lay it out on the bed with her underclothes. Clicking open the locks she then raised the lid of her suitcase.

She frowned. There was something wrapped in tissue paper on the top of her case. She hadn't put it there. She didn't even possess any tissue paper. It made a rustling noise as she opened it. And there was Fern's beautiful gown!

Fern must have given it to Betty who'd slipped it in. Almost reverently, Suzanne picked it up and held it against her body, then turned it over to inspect the back. Where was that stain? She shook her head in wonder. There was no hint of any stain. Carefully she removed a note pinned to the bottom of the skirt.

My dear Suzy,

We didn't have a chance to say goodbye properly. I was sad when you volunteered to go home with Lenny and thought you might like a small keepsake from me.

The gown! It couldn't go to a nicer home. By the way, I got the stain out with salt. An old trick my mother taught me. It usually works!

Please wear it and think of me sometimes. As our dear Vera Lynn sings, I'm sure we'll meet again some sunny day!

With love and best wishes for a happy future.

Fern x

She blinked back the tears. How kind of Fern. She'd not only got the stain out but had passed on her lovely dress. How Suzanne wished there'd been time to get to know her better. Well, if she was going to be the only crooner, as Mr Mason called her, she might as well dress for the part, as Maman always insisted. This time she would do Fern's dress proud.

It wasn't easy getting dressed in the cramped space of the cabin with five other girls fluttering round, admiring the gown, thrilled when Suzanne told them it was a present from the famous actress, not to mention the swaying of the ship. But eventually she was ready, much to the excitement of the nurses.

'You look a dream,' Brenda, the auburn-haired nurse with the merry eyes, said. 'You'll knock 'em dead, Suzy.'

As half-past seven drew nearer Suzanne wondered if it had been wise to let herself be persuaded to stand up on a stage with an unknown band that she'd never rehearsed with, and amongst strangers. Then she noticed the nurses had managed to secure a table quite near the front of the stage and were smiling and beckoning her over.

'Are you feeling nervous?' Kath said when Suzanne took her seat.

'No more than usual,' Suzanne replied. 'Fern Miller said it's the adrenalin flying. She maintains it's a good thing.'

Babs ordered a jug of lemonade and the simple act of

sipping a refreshing drink with such lovely girls calmed Suzanne. She didn't have to worry too much about Lenny. He'd bluntly stated he was going to sit with some of the lads and pointed out the table to the right of the stage. He'd have more fun with them than sitting with a load of women, he'd said, though he did wish her good luck, which she'd thought was rather sweet.

The small jazz band was surprisingly good and she was soon immersed in the music, her foot tapping to the rhythm. It almost took her by surprise when Mr Mason stepped up to the microphone.

She drew in a deep breath. She knew the songs she wanted to sing. She'd sung professionally now. There was no need for nerves. But still her heart raced as Mr Mason cleared his throat.

'Thank you, ladies and gentlemen. I'd like you to give the band a round of applause. They've never played together before and are military men like the rest of the troops here, but they kindly volunteered to entertain you this evening.' He paused, waiting for the clapping to die down. 'And now I'd like to introduce Miss Suzy Linfoot, our singer for the evening. Or should I say "crooner". She's picked some beautiful songs for you, many of which I'm sure you'll know. So give her a big hand.'

Suzanne rose, the nurses clapping loudly as she left their table, swaying slightly when a sudden wave tilted the ship. She kept her head high as she walked towards the stage, the feel of Fern's gown swishing her calves. How different she felt from that first time in the Governor's Residence when she'd had no idea how to put a song across.

Quickly, she stepped up to the microphone.

'As we haven't had time to rehearse – in fact we've never set eyes on one another until this minute—' Suzanne paused for the chuckles '—I shall have to ask our pianist each time if he knows the song. So please bear with me.' She bent her head towards the grey-haired gentleman at the piano and asked in an undertone, 'Do you know "The Nearness Of You" and "When You Wish Upon A Star"?'

He nodded and smiled. 'I know pretty well all of them.'

Suzanne cleared her throat, then put her hand round the microphone stand. Hardly realising what she was going to announce, she said:

'I'd like to dedicate the songs this evening to my friend, Wendy. She was supposed to have been one of ENSA's singers – I was coming with her to entertain the troops . . . but—' She stopped and squeezed her eyes tight. 'But she died in a terrible accident.'

There was a soft murmuring, then gentle clapping from several tables. Suzanne gave them a nod of acknowledgement, then cleared her throat again.

She finished her half hour of songs with 'Harbour Lights', her heart beating hard as she thought of James, praying the doctors in England could help him. She blinked back the tears. *Please, James, get better. I love you.*

The applause was thunderous. She felt humbled that these wounded men appeared to have embraced her songs, many of them joining in the chorus of two or three.

'You were marvellous, Suzy,' Babs enthused. 'We loved it. Your voice . . . it's made for those songs. That slight husky tone with a catch . . . mmm . . . sexy.'

Suzanne laughed, a little embarrassed. 'Thank you, but it wasn't supposed to be sexy. I just feel part of the words when I sing.'

'And you can tell,' Mary said. 'You had us nearly in tears with some of them.'

* * *

The Captain's voice came over the megaphone. 'Ladies and gentlemen, this is your Captain speaking.' There was a pause. 'I have an announcement to make.' The ship fell silent. The Captain continued. 'We have heard the most welcome news that Mussolini was arrested yesterday, the 25th of July!'

There were shouts and cheers. One of the sailors called out, 'About bloody time. Now perhaps the Eyeties will be forced to come over to our side.'

'Let us hope so,' the Captain said. 'But we take nothing for granted. And I would like to remind you we're on the usual alert. So if anyone sees anything suspicious, or anyone acting suspiciously, please report it to a crew member . . . or me. That will be all.'

Chapter Thirty-Eight

August 1943

No one was there to meet her at Bromley station – well, they had no idea she was on her way home, she thought. She'd left Lenny her address and telephone number, and a promise to do her best for him if he applied to join ENSA again. He said nothing was going to stop him.

There was one taxi in the rank when she stepped out of the railway station to an ominous sky that looked ready to shed buckets at any moment. Without a second thought she grabbed it. She could wait ages for the bus and her legs were tired from all the sitting, and now her shoulder ached with carrying her suitcase. Too late, she realised she'd been using the one she'd wrenched in Malta.

The driver was chatty but for once she was glad she was not allowed to say much more than answer in monosyllables to his questions as to where she'd been and what she'd been doing. He dropped her outside the house and opened the cab door, setting down her suitcase outside the gate.

'Thank you, miss.' He pocketed the fare and a shilling tip, nodded and was away.

Suzanne's heart raced as she rang the bell, her only thought as to what Maman would say when she saw her daughter standing on the step.

The door was flung open and Ronnie's disbelieving face cracked into a beam of delight, Rusty behind her, barking and wagging his tail at the same time. He pushed past his mistress and jumped up at Suzanne and thrust his wet nose in her hand.

'Hello, Rusty,' she said, patting his head. 'Have you been a good boy? You certainly look better than when I left.'

'Suzy! Oh, I can't believe it! Here, let me take that.' She whisked Suzanne's suitcase inside. 'Be quiet, Rusty.' She put her finger to her lips and spoke in a whisper. 'Shhh. I want this to be a surprise – for both of you.'

Suzanne gave a wry smile as she followed her sister into the hall. Maman certainly *would* be surprised. Ronnie opened the sitting room door.

'Someone here to see you,' Ronnie said.

'Suzy!' Raine leapt up from her chair and threw her arms round Suzanne. 'How marvellous. I certainly didn't expect to see *you* this time.'

'Nor me you,' Suzanne said, beaming. Raine couldn't know how pleased and relieved she was to see her older sister. 'How long are you home for?'

'I've actually got five whole days – unheard of, but I was due some leave. I only arrived an hour ago – thought it was time to see Maman – and Ronnie, too,' she added, with a wink at her youngest sister.

'Is Maman here?'

'No. She's got her knitting group so she doesn't even know Raine's here, let alone you,' Ronnie said. 'And you know she and Mrs Mortimer have coffee together occasionally, don't you?' She threw Suzanne a wicked grin. 'James's mother, in case you've forgotten.'

'No, I haven't forgotten, little monkey,' Suzanne said, ruffling her sister's dark curls. 'Have they become friends?'

'Two less likely people, I should say,' Ronnie giggled. 'But somehow they're okay. They seem to find each other fascinating in their own way. It's quite amusing.'

'Oh, it's so good to see you both. I've missed you,' Suzanne said, laughing, happy to have these moments with her sisters before Maman came home.

'Where did you go when you left?' Ronnie asked.

'When Maman's here I'll tell you as much as I can.'

'How long are you home?' Ronnie pressed.

'However long I want.'

'You're not going back then?'

'Not abroad, anyway.'

'Why's that?' Ronnie persisted.

'Steady, Ronnie,' Raine said. 'Suzy won't be allowed to talk about some of the things you're asking.' She looked at Suzanne. 'Why don't you go upstairs to our old room and unpack. We can talk when we've all had a cup of tea. Ronnie, be an angel and go and make a pot.'

Suzanne's thoughts teemed as she put away her clothes in the wardrobe. What to tell her sisters, and what not to mention. If only she could confide in them. Tell them about her real father. About Marguerite's letter. But she'd promised her mother not to. Her sisters would be shocked enough to learn Dad wasn't actually her own dad, but they were going to be almost as shocked that she was breaking their rule of always telling each other everything, and never keeping secrets. But she owed it to Maman to speak to her first.

She ran down the stairs, hoping Ronnie would have made the tea. At that moment the front door opened and their mother's footsteps sounded in the hall.

'Véronique!'

'In the front room, Maman,' Ronnie answered.

'Véronique, did you—?' Simone halted in the doorway. Then her face broke into a beam of pleasure as her gaze alighted first on Suzanne and then on Raine. 'My girls are back,' she said as she rushed to take Suzanne into her arms and kiss her soundly.

'I'm here, too, Maman,' Raine said, a little peevishly as she rose from her chair.

'Of course, *chérie*.' Maman turned to her and kissed her, though with not quite the same exuberance, Suzanne noticed.

Were her sisters right? Was she really her mother's favourite? If so, was it because her mother had always loved the Frenchman? Suzanne gave an inward sigh. If it was true, she didn't want to be.

'It is wonderful to have you all with me,' Maman was saying. 'I have been so worried – especially about *you*, Lorraine,' she said pointedly as she removed her jacket and hat and put them neatly together on a side table.

'Would you like tea, Maman?' Ronnie said. 'I only made it two minutes ago.'

'No, thank you, Véronique. Mrs Mortimer – or Beatrice, as she insists I call her – gave me a cup of very good coffee. She tells me her son is in hospital.' She glanced at Suzanne and smiled. 'You see, *chérie*, I know more about him than you do.'

Suzanne gave a small smile to her mother. She'd go and see Mrs Mortimer at the first opportunity.

'His ship went down, I understand. I did not take in all she was saying. It was too horrible.' She kept her eyes fixed on Suzanne. 'I am sure he is a nice boy – well brought up – but he will need a lot of care. You must make sure you do not lead him to think seriously about you. It would not be kind for him.'

It's too late for that, Maman.

'Oh, poor James,' Ronnie said. 'Is he badly injured?'

'I hope not,' Suzanne said, a lump suddenly forming in her throat. 'But he's being treated for shock . . . and he has some horrible symptoms from being in the sea for so long. He doesn't remember any of it. But I have to believe he'll make a full recovery.'

'I'm sure he will, Suzy,' Raine said. 'At least he's in the best place.'

Words that were meant to comfort but made her even more worried.

'You appear to know much about this, Suzanne,' Maman said with a frown. 'Did Beatrice – Mrs Mortimer – write to you?'

Maman seemed more upset that Mrs Mortimer might have written to her than making any encouraging remark about James.

'She wrote once or twice, but I saw James when I was out in the Mediterranean,' Suzanne said, her lips trembling as she sought to find the words to explain to Maman how serious this was. 'His ship was torpedoed and they had to bring him back to Malta. I was visiting one of the musicians who was ill, and James was in the ward next door.'

She wasn't sure if she should be saying all this, but she knew her mother would have pressed it out of her at some point. As it was, Maman's eyes were wide.

'You have been all that way to Malta and you did not tell me this?' she accused.

'We weren't allowed to. No one knew at the time where we were going. We weren't even told until we actually arrived. ENSA is subject to the same security rules and regulations as the Air Force, and I had to sign a document. What I've said just now mustn't go any further.'

'*Alors!*' Her mother raised her eyes to the ceiling. 'You are home now, and you will not go off again. I should not have allowed it.'

'I'm so glad I went,' Suzanne said. 'If you'd seen the faces of the airmen and sailors when they came to our concerts, you'd understand how important it is for them to see people from England. They loved our shows.'

'Why did you leave, then?' Ronnie said.

'There was a spot of bother,' Suzanne said, giving her a warning signal not to say more. Ronnie gave an almost imperceptible nod back.

'What does this mean – a spot of bother?' Simone demanded.

'Nothing much, Maman. Just a bit of extra action. We all packed up and left, and most of the others went to another country.'

'That is what I mean,' Simone said, her voice rising. 'You are not safe in these places. You will stay in England and I will go with you to the music school. That is the best place for you. Then when the war is over you will have a proper career.'

'Maman, I wouldn't have missed going for anything,' Suzanne said. 'I learnt an awful lot. The whole experience has made me grow up. And I want to continue singing to the troops as long as the war lasts.'

Simone was silent.

'But I'm quite tired after the journey so I think we should discuss everything later.'

It was late that night when Maman had gone to bed early that the three sisters gathered in Suzanne's bedroom.

'Maman always comes in just at the wrong time,' Ronnie said, flopping onto Suzanne's bed. Raine sat on the edge of her old bed.

'You haven't told us properly about James,' Raine said. 'But every time he's mentioned you go pink. Is there something serious going on between you two?'

Suzanne took a deep breath and looked first at Raine and then at Ronnie. With shining eyes, she simply said: 'We love each other.'

She felt a little shy saying the words but immediately both sisters jumped up to give her a hug.

'We can't wait to meet him,' Raine said, beaming. 'If he's half as lovely as Alec I definitely approve.'

'If he's tall, dark and handsome he'll get my thumbs up,' Ronnie said, giggling.

'He's all three,' Suzanne laughed. 'But best of all he's a wonderful person. That time when I came out of the village hall after the concert – the one you didn't get to, Ronnie – and bumped into him in the blackout, he was standing in for Mr Draper, the ARP warden, who wasn't well. James was in the audience but had to rush out when the siren went off to do his duty.'

Ronnie furrowed her brow, and then she burst into laughter.

'Then *I* met him and spoke to him before *you*, Suzy,' she said. 'I met him at the shelter. I remember telling you at the time that it wasn't the usual warden. That this one was younger and much better looking . . . and so kind, the way he'd rescued Rusty.'

'Seems I'm the only one who's not met him,' Raine said, chuckling. 'I can't wait.'

Her two dear sisters. Suzanne wouldn't change anything about them for anything in the world.

Chapter Thirty-Nine

It was Raine's last day, Suzanne thought, sad on her own account, but she couldn't be sad for her sister. In spite of poor Audrey's death, she could tell Raine couldn't wait to get back to her station by the way she fidgeted as though she was bored, and was sometimes snappy, particularly with Maman. Unusually, her mother had refrained from rising to Raine's irritability.

The three sisters had had breakfast and Maman was upstairs taking her bath when Raine announced that she needed some air.

'Let's take Rusty for a nice long walk to Keston Common. We might be able to let him off his lead. He'd love that.'

'You and Ronnie go,' Suzanne said. 'I want to make some telephone calls. I still haven't been able to speak to Mrs Mortimer.' She chewed her lip. 'I'm hoping she's visiting whatever hospital James has been taken to. And then I want to phone Drury Lane and find out if there's a band that needs a singer – or I could even be a violinist, for that matter!' she added with a grin.

'You still want to entertain the troops, don't you?' Raine said.

'Yes.' Suzanne chewed her lip. 'But not before I know that James is going to recover. And I want to stay and help Ronnie with Maman for at least a few weeks.' She glanced at Raine. 'I think she worries about us more than she cares to admit. It's just a pity she always sounds so controlling when she puts her fears into words.'

Raine pulled a face. 'Maybe,' was all she said, but the tone wasn't convincing.

All seemed quiet upstairs when Suzanne's two sisters and an excited Rusty left the house. She wouldn't disturb her mother who she knew would be some time. It was a perfect opportunity to make her phone calls. She went out into the hall and at that moment the doorbell rang.

It'll be the postman, Suzanne thought, as she hurried to open the door. *He's late this morning.*

But it wasn't Micky or any other postman who stood there. The man raised his hat to her.

'Miss Linfoot,' he said. It wasn't a question but rather a statement of relief.

She blinked. It was impossible.

'Wh-what—?' She was lost for words. What on earth was he doing here? Had he come to find her for some reason?

'Do you not recognise me?'

'Yes, of course I do,' she stammered. 'You stepped in for the pianist when he was taken ill at the Governor's Residence in Gibraltar.' He nodded and smiled. 'You accompanied me the first time I'd ever sung in public.' She remembered how he'd put her at ease with his confidence in her.

'Then I am not a stranger,' he said, looking at her intently with those bright blue eyes. He smiled, that same gentle smile. 'May I come in?'

Automatically, she glanced behind her, hoping that her mother would come down the stairs and take charge, yet paradoxically she was relieved Maman was nowhere in sight.

Suzanne didn't know what to say. Her mother wouldn't

be at all pleased if she let some foreigner into the house. But she couldn't leave him on the doorstep either.

'I'm so sorry – I'm forgetting my manners.' She stepped aside to let him in. 'We'll go in the front room.' When she'd got him settled into Dad's armchair, she said, 'Can I get you some tea?'

'Just a glass of water . . . please.'

She found a glass and poured him some water, her mind racing. What was he doing in England? He was German so how was he allowed to have such freedom in England? Or Gibraltar, come to think of it. And why was he here – in Downe? It didn't make any sense at all.

When she came back into the room, he was standing in front of the fireplace, his back to her, staring at the landscape. He turned.

'Um, did you wish to speak to me about something?' Suzanne said as she handed him the water.

'Eventually,' he said. 'But first I have come to speak to your mother . . . and your father – if they are here.'

'My father died two years ago,' she said, trying to keep her voice matter-of-fact.

He blinked. 'Oh, I am sorry to hear that. It must have been a sad loss.'

'Yes, it was.'

'And your mother?'

'She's upstairs. I think I'd better call her.'

'Please do not go for a minute,' he said, and the urgency in his tone stopped her. 'I need to speak to you.'

'But I don't even know your name. The Governor never introduced you.'

He pointed to the picture. 'There is my name – Pierre Brunelle – who painted that landscape.'

She gasped. 'Goodness, you're the artist. My mother's

always loved that painting but she never told us she *knew* you. She'll be thrilled to see you.' She looked at him again and frowned. 'But that's not a German name.'

He smiled again. 'No,' he agreed. 'It is French.'

Every inch of her skin prickled. She opened her mouth but no words came out. She didn't know how to begin. What to say . . .

He stood quietly waiting, his eyes creased, his expression tight. She was only aware of the clock ticking on the mantelpiece, shifting her perspective of time and place.

If she was wrong she'd feel an utter fool. But he would never be the first to tell her. Her mother would have sworn him to secrecy. And she knew she wasn't wrong. Suzanne's eyes filled with tears as she stared at this fair-haired man, searching his face, studying every detail. He smiled at her, and his eyes cleared as though he was sure now what she would say.

'You're my father.' And when she uttered the words it was as though it was the most natural expression in the world.

He held out his arms. She moved straight into them, and he folded her close to his heart.

'How I've longed to tell you, my dearest, darling daughter. My sweet Suzanne. I've always called you my golden angel. In my heart that's who you were. But all I had were photographs.' He drew back and looked at her with a sad smile. 'You cannot know that I have waited all my life for this moment.'

He kissed her forehead, then gently moved her away from him, still holding her arms, and gazed at her.

'You have your *maman*'s beautiful eyes, the colour of violets in the rain,' he said, 'but all else is like your *Tante* Marguerite – my sister.'

Suzanne remembered the photograph her aunt had

included with the diamond ring. She recalled how she'd thought at the time she looked more like Maman's sister than Maman herself. Suzanne steadied her breath. Pierre looked the image of his sister Marguerite, and Suzanne took after them both. It must have been why she'd somehow felt so comfortable with him as he'd accompanied her on the piano in Gibraltar. She shook her head. She'd found her true father. Or rather, he'd found her. It was hard to take in. But it was the most wonderful news. She stopped her train of thought abruptly, every nerve ending tense. How would Maman take this news? Or her sisters. They would have to know the truth now.

'I knew who you were when I saw you at the Governor's headquarters,' Pierre said after some moments. 'If you could see how I trembled that night when I played the piano and you sang. All I could think of was this lovely girl with such a beautiful voice was my daughter.'

'But you couldn't have known. You only knew me as "Miss Suzy".'

He put his hand in the inside of his jacket and drew out a well-thumbed photograph. Without a word he handed it to her. Staring back at her was a pretty young girl in a party dress. Although the dress looked grey in the photograph, she remembered it was the most beautiful shade of lilac. Maman had said it emphasised the colour of her eyes. The photograph was taken before they'd moved to Downe. She swallowed, remembering her birthday party. They'd all felt so grown up. She'd been fourteen.

'This was the last photograph your *maman* sent to me,' Pierre said. 'She always sends me a photograph every year on your birthday.' His eyes never left her face. 'You have not changed much in the last four years. I will . . . *would*,' he corrected himself, 'recognise you anywhere.'

Suzanne swallowed hard. This was her father – her blood father – standing before her.

'The war came and we could no longer correspond. It would be too dangerous. Your mother knew and understood I must fight to the end for my country, but it was hard for us. I knew she would never leave Robert – your *papa*.'

Suzanne glimpsed tears in his eyes.

'But I did not know he had died.' He cleared his throat. 'I hoped after nearly twenty years he might allow me to thank him for being such a good father to you. I know you loved him the way he loved you. I think by now your *maman* would tell you about me. But I do not think she did.' He looked at her. 'Am I right?'

She nodded. 'I knew nothing until recently when I received a letter from Marguerite who I'd never heard of,' she said. 'Maman *had* tell me then.'

'It must be a great shock.' The blue eyes were anxious.

'I was upset that Maman hadn't told me the truth much sooner. I felt I'd been living a lie.'

He shook his head as though unable to take it in either.

'You must try to forgive her,' he said. 'We fell in love many years before she married Robert, your *papa*. Her parents made us separate. They didn't give her the letters I wrote. Then she came to Paris with your sister, Lorraine, who was only just walking. That was the time we bump into one another again and we know . . . knew we had not stopped loving each other.' He paused, his eyes on hers. 'Can you try to understand?'

'I'll try.'

'I only hope you will allow me to be part of your life when it is safe to do so,' he said in a quiet voice.

'I will,' Suzanne said softly, unconsciously matching his tone as she pressed the photograph back in his hand. 'I promise.' She put her heart into the smile she gave him. 'I think I'll take my mother a cup of tea. She might need it when I tell her who's downstairs.'

Suzanne knocked on her mother's bedroom door.

'*Entre!*'

Simone was in her dressing gown, sitting at her dressing table, brushing her hair. She turned as Suzanne stepped through the doorway.

'*Merci*, Suzanne,' she said as Suzanne set the cup and saucer on a mat on the dressing table. 'Did you sleep well, *chérie*?'

'As soon as my head touched the pillow,' Suzanne said, not remembering anything about the night now she was facing Maman. She hesitated.

Come on, Suzy, you've got to say it. Say it now!

'Why are you staring at me, Suzanne?' her mother demanded.

'Sorry, Maman. I didn't mean to. But I have something serious to tell you.'

Her mother was suddenly alert, her posture straight, her neck long. 'What is it, Suzanne? You have not got yourself into trouble? Please do not tell me that. I could not bear it.' Her mother's eyes bored into her.

Suzanne's jaw fell open. What was her mother talking about? Then she noticed Maman's eyes drop to her stomach. Suzanne's cheeks flamed. How could she think such a thing?

'I'm not sure what you're implying, Maman, but if you're referring to James, the answer is no. I haven't got myself into that kind of trouble.'

Her mother raised her brows at her daughter's tone.

'There is no need to be rude, Suzanne. I was merely making the enquiry.'

'You should know me better than to ask that,' Suzanne flared.

Dear God, this was already going badly. She shouldn't have risen to Maman's insinuation. It was the sort of thing that used to get Raine into trouble.

'So what is it you have to tell me?' Simone demanded.

'There's a gentleman downstairs and he would like to see you.'

She waited with beating heart. Her mother had already turned away and begun to finish putting up her hair.

'And who is the gentleman at such an early hour of the morning?' she spoke into the mirror.

'It's Pierre Brunelle.' There – she'd said it.

Suzanne could see in the mirror that all the colour had drained from her mother's face. Her eyes looked huge. Her back was rigid, the comb frozen in the air above her head. Slowly she stood up and faced Suzanne, her eyes now ablaze.

'What are you saying, child?'

Suzanne took in a deep breath to steady her heartbeat. 'I met him in Gibraltar at the Governor's Residence. The same man who painted the landscape over the mantelpiece. I know who he is.'

'You are making up things you do not understand,' Simone said, frowning. 'Go downstairs and get rid of this man. I do not want any strange man in my house. I want him gone by the time I come down.' She glared at Suzanne. 'Have I made myself clear?'

A coldness like iced water swept through Suzanne's body. She swallowed hard but the lump in her throat remained. Her mother was impatiently tapping her foot.

'Well?' Simone snapped.

'Yes, Maman. You have made yourself perfectly clear.'

Simone nodded. '*Bon*. I will be down in some minutes.

And then we will telephone the music school. That is the important thing to do today. If you have your audition very soon you will be able to attend in September.'

It was no use arguing. Suzanne walked slowly downstairs. She had to admit it wasn't in the best of circumstances that her mother should meet Pierre without having been prepared for it, but what else could she have done? Well, she wasn't going to send her father away, whatever Maman said.

As soon as she entered the front room Pierre caught her eye.

'What did she say?'

'I told her but she didn't believe me.'

Pierre flinched. Suzanne put her hand out to him, but he looked at her with such a plaintive expression, then dropped into the armchair, his head in his hands.

Chapter Forty

As soon as Suzanne had left the room, Simone dropped down heavily on her bed. Her legs were trembling with weakness.

Was it possible?

Suzanne wasn't in the habit of making up stories or exaggerating. Was someone playing a game with her? But Suzanne had distinctly said the name Pierre Brunelle. But how could he possibly be here? When she'd last heard from him a few weeks after France had capitulated less than a year after the war started, he'd already been working in the Ministry of Information in Paris for more than two years. She'd been amazed that parts of the letter hadn't been blacked out, and even more amazed to see that someone – presumably the censor – had scribbled in the margin: 'I agree!' in large letters.

Last night I went to the cinema, he'd written, *where they showed a meeting between Hitler and Mussolini. The audience booed and stamped their feet and called out rude names, so they stopped the newsreel and we were ordered to be silent, but as soon as it restarted everyone began coughing and sneezing very noisily right the way through to the end.*

She remembered smiling at the image of the rebellious crowd, knowing Pierre would have joined in. He would never willingly work for the Nazis but she had a strong feeling he had used his fluent German to France and England's benefit. Reading between the lines she knew she wouldn't hear from him again until the war was over. And it was entirely possible that she might never hear. She swallowed hard as she recalled the ending of his letter – her precious letter she'd had to destroy – partly for his sake in case it got into the wrong hands, and partly not to hurt Robert.

I love you. I always have. I always will. I will never marry unless it is to you. And I know that can never be.

But I want you to know, my darling, if I die, your name will be the last word on my lips – your image the last one in my head – your voice the last one I hear.

She'd always assumed if anyone reported him on suspicion of being disloyal to Pétain, and if he was tipped off, he would escape. But this would immediately put him on the Gestapo's list and they wouldn't rest until they'd found him. If this ever happened, Simone could only hope Pierre would somehow reach the safety of Spain. She'd not dared think that he might possibly find his way to England.

Now in her bedroom, she could see him as clearly as though he were there next to her. She squeezed her eyes shut. *Oh, Pierre.* He still lived in her heart, and there was never a day that she didn't think of him, praying he was safe, even if she never set eyes on him again. She took a deep breath, then another, trying to quieten her thumping heart.

After a minute she realised the house had gone quiet. Véronique's mangy dog – although she had to admit he wasn't mangy any longer and she'd secretly begun to like the creature – had been barking his head off but had now stopped. She frowned. Where was everyone?

Well, she'd been disturbed enough already. Her tea had

gone cold on the dressing table. She took a sip and grimaced. Ugh! How the English could drink so much tea was beyond her. But the girls always brought her one out of some kind of British tradition. She glanced at the watch Robert had given her on their tenth wedding anniversary. She still missed him. He'd been her rock. She hadn't realised how much she'd depended upon him until he'd died. She'd begged her daughters to stay near her but Lorraine and Suzanne had rebelled, just as *she* had rebelled against her own parents by marrying Robert, a kind and affectionate man, but much older, and whose father was Jewish. That had been the final straw for her parents when Robert had unintentionally let it slip. They'd presented her with an ultimatum. Either she drop the idea of marrying him, or else they would drop her from their lives.

There'd been no doubt in her mind that she was going to marry Robert whatever her parents threatened. He was so different from her own father who was even more unemotional than her mother. Over the years, when she'd matured and had had time to think about it, she realised she'd longed for a father who adored her – Robert had come along and fitted the bill perfectly. Her thoughts drifted again.

She'd decided to take Lorraine, still a toddler, to Paris, to show her parents their first grandchild, hoping the precocious little girl who charmed everyone in sight would do the same for them. Robert had wanted to go with her. It had probably been her worst decision that she'd persuaded him against the idea.

'They have to face it, Simone, that I'm your husband, the father of our child, and their grandchild. It's a ridiculous situation. I'm coming with you and that is my last word.'

Simone looked at her husband with astonishment. He'd never opposed her so strongly. Always so kind and thoughtful, so adoring, it was as though she saw another side of him that she didn't know how to handle. He was standing by the fireplace in their rented flat, his arm along the mantelpiece, flushed with annoyance, and she wasn't sure whether it was on account of her or her parents.

'Robert, be reasonable. It is best I go on my own this first time. They can get to know Lorraine and she will heal the rift. Then the next time we can go together as a family and they will make us all welcome.'

'I am not going to be dictated to on the whim of your parents and their prejudice towards my Jewish background. I'm not even a practising Jew. I was perfectly happy to bring up Lorraine and any other children we might have as Church of England. I told them at the time. So I don't see why they're taking this attitude. But as they're making this stand, I hope as my wife you will be loyal to me.'

She knew he was justified in making such an argument, but some obstinate spark within her made her snap back: 'You cannot refuse to let me visit my own parents, Robert. And you said only the other day you had a heavy workload at the firm.'

He opened his mouth but she stopped him.

'No, Robert. You must let me go. I will be home in two weeks. And that's *my* final word.'

She'd stormed out.

Although she'd stayed with her parents for the duration, the relationship had been distant. They'd even seemed to hold themselves back from getting too close to their granddaughter, and treated Simone with cordial disdain. She couldn't wait to go home. Even Paris wasn't the same as she'd remembered but maybe it was because it was colder than she'd expected for autumn and a dreary rain greeted her on many mornings when she pulled back the curtains of her old bedroom her parents had completely redecorated. She could have left after she'd seen the situation in the first few days, but she couldn't bear the idea of having failed.

But if she'd gone home to England sooner she would never have bumped into Pierre Brunelle again. Her first love. The man who'd once held her heart – and if she admitted it, always would.

He'd walked into her life for the second time and changed it forever.

Pierre Brunelle could not have been more different from Robert. For one thing, at only three years older than herself, he could never be called a father figure. He was always full of energy and ambition and talent. And those eyes – bluer than a summer sky . . . She'd been dazzled by him. They'd fallen madly in love. That had been the beginning of the trouble between her and her parents. Pierre had asked her father for her hand in marriage.

'Are you mad?' her father had almost spat. 'She's only seventeen. She doesn't know her own mind.'

'I *do* know my own mind.' Simone had stamped her foot. 'I shan't feel any different ever.'

Pierre had begged her father to allow them to at least continue to see one another, but he'd remained adamant.

'Come back when Simone is twenty-one. When you've made something of yourself. A penniless artist is not what I have in mind as a husband for my daughter.'

She'd never heard from Pierre again and assumed he'd met someone else. She'd given up thinking Pierre might come back for her. It was then that she'd met Robert when he'd come to Paris to study French.

And that had been that.

But she'd never forgotten Pierre Brunelle.

At twenty-three years old, Simone was on the last day of her visit before she was to return to England, enjoying a few precious hours of freedom because her mother had actually agreed to look after Lorraine for the afternoon. She'd strolled round the familiar cobbled streets and cafés until she spotted a small art gallery she'd not noticed before. On impulse, she decided to go in.

At first glance it appeared she was the only visitor. No one was at the shabby wooden bar that acted as a reception desk, so she wandered around, nothing really catching her eye. She followed a sign with an arrow pointing upstairs to the gallery's latest exhibition. She wouldn't stay long and afterwards she'd go and sit in one of the cafés with a coffee, and maybe even a glass of warming red wine – something else her parents frowned on.

And that's when she saw him. She would have recognised that profile anywhere. He was hatless, the thick fair hair swept back from an enviable wave, the slightly crooked nose, the strong jawline . . . He was wandering around, hands in the pockets of his raincoat, staring critically for a minute or two in front of a painting before he moved on to the next.

She froze. What should she do? Tap him on the shoulder? Say 'hello' as if it were the most natural thing in the world? Savour the look of amazement in his eyes? Ask him . . . ask him what? If he was happy with his new girlfriend? Or his wife, maybe? She set her chin. No, she mustn't do any of those things. He had stopped writing to her with no word of explanation. She must slip quietly down the stairs, lucky to have escaped more heartache.

Her heart thumping so loud he must surely hear it, she turned away.

'Simone! Is it really you?'

She swung round, not able to speak. He stepped over to her.

'I can't believe it,' he said. 'What are you doing in Paris?'

'Seeing my parents.'

He frowned. 'Oh, of course. And are they well?'

She shrugged. 'They are the same.'

He nodded. 'Did you know this was my exhibition?'

'No,' she said, 'the notice just mentioned a local artist.'

'Hmm. I'm obviously not quite famous enough yet to have my name in lights.' He smiled. That wonderful smile that made her heart leap.

He gestured to the wall of paintings. 'Tell me what you think of them, Simone.'

He followed her quietly without speaking. There were only a couple of dozen paintings. She remembered how he'd once sketched her likeness. She'd asked if she could have it, but he'd said no, he wanted it to remember her. She realised now, looking at the paintings, how talented he was.

'You're not saying anything,' he said after some minutes.

'They're good. No, more than good.'

She found herself in front of a landscape painting that captivated her.

'It's a view near my home town,' he said. 'One of the covered bridges that are famous in Alsace. I wanted to take you there – do you remember?' His voice cracked.

Tears stung the backs of her eyes. She forced herself to keep calm. She wasn't that seventeen-year-old any longer – she was a married woman, a mother. 'I like this one very much,' she said. 'Are the paintings for sale?'

'No.'

She felt a stab of disappointment. She told herself it would remind her of France. Sometimes she longed for her country so much it made her throat ache. But she knew she wasn't being completely honest. She wanted to take a little bit of Pierre home with her . . .

'But if you will come to dinner with me this evening, I will send you the painting as a present.'

She couldn't resist him. She'd telephoned her parents to tell them she'd met a friend and they were going out to dinner and she'd be late back. Her heart beat fast as she waited for her mother to say she would not be willing to look after Lorraine for that long, but to her surprise her mother agreed.

At dinner they didn't stop talking. It was as though the years dropped away. She couldn't bring her gaze away from his face, the face she still loved. Pierre in turn never took his eyes off her. Once he brought his hand up and softly stroked her jawline across the table in front of all the diners. It seemed the most natural gesture in the world.

'You're so beautiful, Simone,' he said, shaking his head, his voice full of wonder.

'Why didn't you at least write to me?' she finally dared to ask, bracing herself for his answer.

His eyes widened. 'But I did,' he said. 'I wrote to you for months after your father forbade us to see one another again. I couldn't understand why you never replied.'

A wave of fury with her parents threatened to choke her.

'I never received them,' she whispered. 'Not one of them.'

And then when she told him she was married to an Englishman and they had a small daughter, and lived in Kent, his eyes were full of regret.

He had a good job now, he told her, working for the Ministry in Paris. He also had an apartment nearby and offered her a drink before he took her back to her parents.

As they ascended in the wrought-iron lift to his apartment he bent his head and kissed her. She remembered the taste of his lips, at first gentle, exploring, probing. Then it was as though there was an explosion and his kiss became hard, demanding, possessing. When they finally drew inches apart as the lift reached his floor, Simone thought her lungs would burst, her breathing was so harsh and rapid.

She studied the shape of his hand as he inserted the key. Artist's fingers. Long and sensitive.

'We never made love,' he said, when she was once again in his arms, 'but now I think it is time.'

She only knew one thing. She wanted this man – body, heart and soul.

On the train home the next day, the weight of Lorraine on her lap, the little head pressing against her breasts, sore now with wild lovemaking, she relived those precious moments of their last hour together this morning when she'd agreed to meet him for the last time. How he'd begged her not to go.

'I must,' she said. 'I need the stability Robert gives me now I have Lorraine.' She sat the squirming little girl on the floor of his sitting room and gave her her doll. 'I couldn't hurt him and deprive him of his child. I would never forgive myself.'

'But you can hurt *me*!'

'You'll meet someone else,' she said.

'I haven't so far,' he said. 'You're all I ever wanted, and it hasn't changed.' His eyes were challenging. 'You said last night you loved me.'

'I do love you,' she said softly. 'And I always will. But I must go home.'

He'd insisted on taking her and Lorraine to the railway station.

There'd been one last kiss. She'd wanted it to last forever. His kiss was tender, then fierce, his arms hard around her as though he would never let her go.

And then Lorraine began to grizzle in her pushchair and the magic was gone. Until that moment Simone had never really understood the meaning of grief.

How happy Robert had been when she'd arrived home. How guilty, how wretched she'd felt when he'd taken her in his arms and told her how much he'd missed her and how his voice shook when he told her he loved her, then swept up his little daughter, making her chuckle.

Six weeks later the thing she'd both dreaded and desired had happened. She knew she was going to have a baby. And there was no possibility it was Robert's. How would she be able to tell him? But maybe she wouldn't need to say anything. Maybe her instinct was wrong.

Another fortnight and she knew her instinct had been right. She had to tell Robert the truth – whatever it cost her.

She would never forget the hurt in his eyes.

'Who is he?'

She swallowed hard. 'I fell in love with him when I was only seventeen. My parents would not allow me to continue seeing him. I've had no contact with him since then. I did not go to Paris to search for him, Robert. You must believe me.' She gave him an imploring look. 'I bumped into him. He invited me to dinner for old times' sake.'

Robert's mouth hardened. 'Are you sure the baby isn't mine?'

'Yes,' she said. 'I'm sure.'

'Do you still love this man?'

She had to be honest. 'Yes,' she said, 'but I am married to you and we have Lorraine.'

'I don't want you to stay with me out of duty.'

'I love you, too, Robert.' She hesitated. She had to say it. 'And if you want a divorce I will understand – and never blame you.'

'I don't want a divorce,' he said. 'I still love you.'

'You forgive me?'

Robert hesitated, but only for a split second. 'Yes,' he said, 'I still want to live with you.'

'But the baby . . .?'

'I'm prepared to take the baby as my own. To be the father – just as I am Lorraine's.'

Her eyes were wide. 'It is a serious thing to do, Robert.' She bit her lip. 'You need time to think about it.'

'I don't need to think. I would never go back on my word.' His eyes searched hers. 'You can trust me, can't you?'

She nodded. 'With my life.' Her voice was low.

'But I think the child should know one day when it's older that I'm not the true father. It's only fair. But I'll leave that conversation to you, when you consider it's the right time.'

Simone blinked back the tears. How did she deserve this man? Yes, she would tell the child one day. It was her duty, no matter how difficult it would be.

'I will do that. But there is one important thing I must ask. It is Pierre's child. He's a good man and I owe it to him to send him a photograph sometimes. Would you allow me to do that? I do not wish to do it in secret.'

'Once a year, on the child's birthday,' he said. 'That's all.' His eyes filled. 'I couldn't bear any more than that.'

She'd promised. Once a year. That was all.

Now, back in Downe, nearly twenty years later, she swallowed hard. She'd stuck to her promise rigidly. And then the war, which had put paid to any further correspondence between them.

How she'd reprimanded herself for breaking her vow to Robert and Pierre that she would tell Suzanne about him. She'd planned to do so after Robert died, but every time she'd got to the point of speaking, she'd panicked. Her daughters would think so badly of her. What a terrible example to them. She cringed now as she recalled her veiled accusation to Suzanne about having James's baby. She should have known better. Suzanne was a wonderful daughter, a girl to be proud of. And so were her other two girls – Robert's girls. She brushed away the threatening tears with the sleeve of her dressing gown.

Simone checked herself in the mirror. Her eyes looked anxious. She was certain now that her daughter had been telling the truth. But how could the man asking for her be her dearest love? *Impossible.*

She listened. There were no sounds or movement downstairs. She'd told Suzanne to get rid of him. If it really was him, how hurt he must have been, all over again, especially what he must have gone through to arrive from occupied France. Maybe escaping after he'd been locked in a cell ready for questioning – and torture. She shuddered.

I know who he is. Suzanne's words tumbled over in Simone's head. She had ordered her daughter to send her own father away. What must Suzanne think of her?

Simone's heart pounded so hard in her chest that for a moment she wondered if she might be having a heart attack. Perhaps it wasn't too late. If she hurried she might catch him up. He couldn't have got far in just these few minutes. Yes, that's what she'd do.

There was no time to dress. Thank goodness it was summer. Her satin dressing gown was concealing enough that she could run down the street – so long as she didn't bump into that Mrs Bates. Was she going to lose him again – and for good?

Without another thought she flew down the stairs but just as she reached the final three steps one of the heels of her mules caught in the brass stair rod. With a scream she hurtled face down into a heap at the bottom.

'Simone! Oh, *chérie*, are you hurt?'

She was dreaming that Pierre was speaking to her. If she could only open her eyes so she could call for help. But she had to concentrate. Pierre was saying something in her dream.

Familiar arms from so long ago, thin now, but still strong, wrapped around her. She could smell the very scent of him as though it were yesterday. In a daze, wavering between the past and what might be reality, she felt herself being picked up and carried into the sitting room, then laid on the sofa.

'Simone, my love, please talk to me.'

A gentle hand stroked the hair away from her face. Her eyelids flickered open.

There he was. The love of her life. His smile – just for her – that always made her feel she was the only woman in his world. Eyes that were still as blue as a summer sky. She drank in the dear sight of him. She'd recognise him anywhere even though twenty years had passed and his fair hair was sprinkled with grey. She put her hand up to stroke the contours of his face, sharper than she remembered, and his eyes held hers. She used her fingertip to follow the deep, bitter lines around his mouth. What had he gone through these last months to have lost so much weight? She shuddered, then tried to clear her head from the mirage before her. But he didn't vanish.

'Pierre . . . is it really you?' Her voice was small and seemed to come from a long way away.

'Yes, it's me, my darling. I've been dreaming of this day for twenty years. But I thought it would be a little more romantic than this.' He smiled teasingly. 'Tell me you're not hurt.'

'I-I don't think so.' Her head reeled. She fought against it. She tried to sit up, but he wouldn't let her. 'It was just the shock. I thought you'd gone. I didn't believe Suzanne—' She stared up at him. 'She said she knows who you are.'

'She guessed.'

'How—?'

'Hush, *chérie*. It doesn't matter. Nothing matters now. We're together again, and that's all I've ever wanted.' He looked at her. 'It is a strange moment but I do not want to forget to say something important.' His eyes glistened. 'My darling, I want to thank you with all my heart for our beautiful daughter. If only I could be there to help bring her up, but it was not to be. Your husband . . . Robert—'

Pierre's eyes were moist with unshed tears. She held one of his hands tightly between both hers.

'What about Robert?' she whispered. 'Did Suzanne tell you he died?'

'Yes,' he said giving her hand a little squeeze, 'but I wish so much I could thank him for being her loving *papa* all those years.'

Simone swallowed. She didn't deserve this man. But she resolved from now on things were going to change.

'Please, darling Pierre, it's been so long. Will you kiss me?'

Chapter Forty-One

Suzanne half ran, half walked the two miles to catch up with her sisters. If only she'd mastered riding a bicycle. Ronnie cycled to the common often with Rusty in the front basket. She couldn't help smiling at the image. Then Pierre's sad face came into focus. She still couldn't believe what her mother had ordered her to do – to send her own father away. There'd been no possibility of hurting him like that, so she'd told him she was going to meet her sisters to give him and her mother a chance for some privacy. He'd been touchingly grateful and pressed her hand. She tried to picture Maman's expression when she eventually came downstairs expecting her daughters to be there and Pierre gone. How could she have been so cold-hearted as to turn him away without at least some kind of explanation?

Thank goodness Raine had mentioned she and Ronnie were going to take Rusty to Keston Common. She was desperate to speak to them. She didn't care if her mother said she was being disloyal. Maman didn't deserve her loyalty. But her sisters did. They'd always kept to their childhood pact. And so had *she*, up until now.

Completely out of breath, her heart racing from exertion, Suzanne stopped and scanned the common. Which end would they be? The place was teeming with families, the children on their summer holidays. It was going to be almost impossible to find them. Then she remembered Ronnie saying how Rusty loved splashing in the lake. She'd try that end.

She saw Rusty before her sisters. He'd just come out of the water, shaking himself, showering droplets over some nearby children who screamed in delight. She couldn't see Raine or Ronnie but Rusty would lead her to them.

'Rusty!'

He pricked up his ears and immediately bounded over, barking and trying to jump up at her.

'No, you're all wet,' she said, grabbing his collar. 'Where's your mistress?'

A pair of arms flung themselves around her waist.

'Right here.' It was Ronnie, giggling from behind.

She swung round. 'Where's Raine?'

'Just over there, chatting to that couple. I think she knows them. I'll go and get her.'

'What's up, Suzy?' Raine said as she strolled over.

'I think we'd better sit down on that bench,' Suzanne said, pointing to the nearest one that a family was just vacating.

She sat in the middle of the bench with her sisters on either side, Rusty at Ronnie's feet, gazing up at his mistress.

Suzanne swallowed. 'I have something serious to tell you both. I don't quite know how to begin – but you know that painting over the mantelpiece in the front room?' Her sisters nodded. 'Well, the artist who did that painting – Pierre Brunelle – Maman knows him personally.'

Raine stroked her jaw. 'I think I know what you're going to say, because whenever we've asked her about it – where it was painted and where did she buy it – she goes all secretive.'

Suzanne gave a start. Could Raine possibly have guessed?

'I've always thought the artist might be an old flame,' Raine went on. She stared at Suzanne. 'Am I right?'

'Yes, you're right.'

'How exciting,' Ronnie chimed in. 'Maman had a lover before she met Dad.'

'That's partly true.' Suzanne fiddled with the strap on her bag.

'There's something more, isn't there?' Raine's voice was sharp.

'Yes.' She turned to Raine. 'There's no easy way to say this, so be prepared for a shock, but Pierre Brunelle happens to be my father!'

There was a stunned silence.

'That explains a lot,' Raine finally said.

'Have you gone completely barmy?' Ronnie made Suzanne face her.

'It's true,' Suzanne said, immediately feeling a weight lift from her shoulders that her sisters now knew the truth.

'But *Dad*'s your father,' Ronnie burst out. 'He's our dad. All three of us. You can't possibly have a different one.'

'Shhhh, Ronnie. Let Suzy finish,' Raine said sharply.

Suzanne patted Ronnie's hand. 'Pierre Brunelle has a sister called Marguerite,' she went on, 'so she's my aunt. She explained everything in a letter she wrote to me. He's a Frenchman and is working for the Resistance.'

'Where's this letter?' Raine demanded. Her eyes narrowed as she fixed them on Suzanne. 'I'd like to see it for myself.'

'I'll explain later.'

'But Dad—' Ronnie started.

'Dad will always be Dad to me, and I loved him the same as you – I still do. But Pierre is my own flesh and blood.' Suzanne looked at Raine, wanting her above all to understand. 'It wasn't just a fling. He was Maman's first love when she was only seventeen and her parents forbade her to have any more to do with him. Years later she met Dad and married him.'

'Did Dad know he wasn't your real father?' Ronnie said.

'Yes. She didn't lie to him about that.'

'My God, poor Dad,' Raine said. 'The wife he adored betraying him, then presenting him with a baby who wasn't his.'

'She and Pierre accidentally met again in Paris when she took you to meet her parents,' Suzanne said, worried at Raine's tone. 'You weren't much more than a year old. They knew they'd never stopped loving each other. That's when Maman fell for me.'

Her two sisters were silent.

'I think that's why Maman is on edge so much of the time,' Suzanne went on, understanding so much more since she'd fallen in love with James, and wanting to put her mother in a better light. 'You know how she always makes everything into a major disaster? She must think that everyone she loves always leaves her in the end. And maybe she wonders if it had been worth her loyalty to Dad when it had meant losing her life's love.' She looked at both of them. 'It must have been a terrible time for her,' she finished.

She looked at both of them. What were they thinking?

'Start at the beginning,' Ronnie demanded. 'We want to hear everything. Tell us about the letter from this Marguerite.'

Suzanne swallowed. She began with the package that had contained the diamond ring and the letter.

'That must be the ring I caught her looking at a few weeks ago,' Ronnie interrupted. 'Do you remember I told you about it in my letter, Suzy?'

'Yes, I do.'

'She wasn't at all pleased to see me at that moment,' Ronnie said, 'but what I want to know is, why did she have it in her possession when it was yours?'

Suzanne swallowed. She hated being disloyal to her mother in front of her sisters. But she had to tell them the truth.

'She said I could have it back when I went to the music school.' Suzanne kept her voice soft. 'She tore the letter into pieces, but I'd read it through so many times I remembered most of it. She detests Marguerite. I don't know why.'

'You *are* a dark horse,' Raine said after a few moments' silence. She looked steadily at Suzanne, her face a mask. 'You do realise, of course, what this means, don't you?'

'I'm not sure . . .'

Raine looked so serious that Suzanne felt her heart thud.

'We—' Raine cleared her throat '—Ronnie and I – are only your *half* sisters.'

Ronnie's head shot up. Her eyes were wide. 'Gosh, I hadn't thought of that.'

Suzanne swallowed hard. Raine was her usual blunt self, but it sounded so final. 'Does it matter?' she said. 'Does it really make a difference to the three of us? I'm the same person as I was before.'

But it wasn't quite true. She wasn't exactly the same. Without warning, tears streamed down her face. Immediately Raine threw her arms around her.

'Suzy, I'm sorry. I didn't mean it in a bad way. Of *course* you're still the same person. And we love you the same. It's just been such a bolt out of the blue, that's all. We'll soon get used to having a pure French sister.' She squeezed Suzanne's shoulder and smiled, her eyes now sparkling in their old way. Suzanne smiled weakly back. 'But it would have been easier for us all if we'd been let into the secret much earlier,' Raine added. 'We'd be used to it by now.'

'Maman made me promise. I felt awful not being allowed to tell you.'

'But you've now broken your promise to her,' Ronnie said.

'I know. But you don't know how relieved I am to tell you both. I hated going against the pact we made when we were children.'

'Glad it still holds,' Raine chuckled, then became serious again. She studied Suzanne as though for the first time. 'I suppose you don't resemble Ronnie and me that much,' she said after some moments, 'except for the eyes. Our violet-coloured eyes are the Linfoot sisters' trademark,' she added with a wink. Then she sighed deeply. 'Families. You never know, do you, what's going on?' Before Suzanne could answer, Raine said, 'Well, all I hope is that this chap Pierre stands up to the test of being your father.' She paused. 'I've just realised something. How do you know all this? The unknown aunt couldn't possibly have put so much detail in one letter.'

'He turned up a few minutes after you and Ronnie left the house.'

'What today?' Raine's jaw dropped. 'And you let him in?'

'Yes, I—'

'What if he's some kind of imposter?' Raine narrowed her eyes suspiciously.

'He isn't an imposter,' Suzanne said. 'I recognised him. You see, I met him in Gibraltar at the Governor's Residence. It was my first singing engagement. Bram, our pianist, was taken ill, and he – Pierre – stepped in and accompanied me. I was so nervous but he put me completely at ease. And he played so beautifully.'

'You mean you actually met your real father out in Gibraltar and you didn't have any idea?' Ronnie said, her voice rising with disbelief.

'How could I? But he knew *me*.' Suzanne recalled Pierre's warm smile that had enveloped her when she'd been so nervous.

'How did he know it was definitely you?' Raine's tone was incredulous.

'Because Maman sent him a photograph of me every year.'

'It's a damnable lot to take in,' Raine said. 'It feels more fiction than real.'

It was Suzanne's turn to be silent. She couldn't blame her older sister for feeling that way. It was still like a dream to *her*.

'Do you think Maman's still carrying a torch for him?' Ronnie said.

Suzanne shook her head. 'The way she behaved just now makes you wonder – but we'll soon find out.'

'What did Maman say when you told her he was at the door?' Raine asked.

'She was upstairs,' Suzanne said, desperately hoping Maman hadn't been unkind to him. 'I said who he was, and she immediately told me to get rid of him. But of course I didn't tell him anything of the kind.'

'That sounds like Maman,' Ronnie murmured.

'It was the shock, I expect,' Raine said briskly, rising to her feet. 'I think it's about time we went home and met this man – providing Maman hasn't sent him away with a flea in his ear.'

Raine didn't sound as though she was bothered one way or the other, Suzanne thought. She glanced at her older sister. She had to convince her what a lovely man Pierre was, and how she was sure they'd all feel the same after they'd met him. But where Raine was concerned, people always had to prove themselves, though she sometimes misjudged people and regretted it.

'I don't think she'll send him away once she sees him,' Suzanne said.

'Don't I wish I was a fly on the wall.' Ronnie kicked a stone along the pavement for Rusty to chase.

'Well, whatever we think of this Frenchman – and I hope it's all good – he gave us *you*,' Raine said, smiling to Suzanne's relief. 'That was his gift. And we wouldn't be without you, Suzy, for anything in the world.'

Chapter Forty-Two

'We're right near Mrs Mortimer's house,' Suzanne said, 'so do you mind if I call in quickly and ask her about James? I can't get her on the phone.'

'Don't be long,' Raine said. 'We'll wait outside.'

Suzanne's chest tightened as she walked up the concrete drive and rang the bell. She waited but there was no sound of any movement. She used the heavy knocker, which came crashing down, making her jump. If that didn't bring James's mother to the door, nothing would.

After a minute she had to concede that Mrs Mortimer wasn't at home. Suzanne could only hope she was visiting James in the hospital, wherever that was. She longed to let him know she was back in England. He'd be worrying about her, thinking she was still in Malta amongst the air raids. If only she had his address so she could write to him.

Not knowing how James was or where he'd been sent made her feel helpless, as though she'd lost her connection with him. She was certain he loved her but this separation made her uneasy. She'd try to telephone Mrs Mortimer again this evening. For now, she could only hope against hope that Maman was being kind to Pierre. She gave a long sigh as she joined her sisters. She'd know in exactly ten minutes.

* * *

As soon as Suzanne stepped through the front door she could tell that the atmosphere in the cottage had changed. A man's laugh interjected something Maman was saying. She hugged herself. Pierre. How she prayed her sisters would take to him. But whatever they thought, they couldn't deny he was family, and instinctively she felt that even Dad would have approved.

She opened the door to the front room. Pierre was sitting on the sofa with Maman's hand firmly in his own. He immediately stood up as Suzanne and her sisters entered.

'I want you girls to meet someone special,' her mother said, looking flustered, but staying seated. 'Pierre, these are my other two daughters, Lorraine and Véronique. Lorraine is a pilot in the Air Transport Auxiliary, and Véronique is still at school but she works for a veterinarian on Saturdays.'

Suzanne had to stop herself from letting her mouth drop open. Maman actually sounded proud of them. She hugged herself. In such a short time Pierre had already worked a miracle.

'I am very happy to meet you,' Pierre said, shaking hands with them. He turned to Suzanne and put his arm around her shoulders. 'And to meet my daughter again.' He looked at her. 'Have you told your sisters when we first met?'

Suzanne smiled. 'Yes. I've told them everything.'

'It must have been a shock,' he said, glancing at Raine and Ronnie.

'We're still trying to take it all in,' Raine said.

But her sister was smiling, Suzanne noticed. It was all going to be all right – of that, she was absolutely certain.

'Where have you all been?' Maman asked.

'We took Rusty to the park,' Ronnie said.

'Then I called to see Mrs Mortimer but she wasn't home,' Suzanne added.

'She is probably at the Red Cross,' Simone said. 'She does that nearly every day now. She has asked if I will help pack food parcels for the soldiers and I said I will.' She paused, her tone softening. 'I know you want to ask her about James, Suzanne. I am sure he is all right or we would have heard. But telephone her this evening so she can reassure you.'

'I thought that's what I'd do,' Suzanne said, relieved her mother understood her anxiety. She wouldn't tell her she'd tried to phone the last few evenings. This was Pierre's time and she wanted her sisters to get to know him.

'Try not to worry,' Simone said unexpectedly. 'Things have a way of working out.'

'Even if it's not for twenty years.' Pierre chuckled, turning to Simone, and taking his place next to her again.

'I hope I don't have to wait that long for news,' Suzanne said lightly.

She couldn't help smiling at the pair. They looked so right together. To be truthful it was strange to see Maman so relaxed, but perhaps her mother had accepted all that had gone before and had finally glimpsed a chance of happiness. Suzanne noticed how every so often her mother would give Pierre a quick glance as though to make sure he was really there and not some figment of her imagination. And every time Pierre would catch her doing this he would turn to her, smiling and pressing her hand.

'We will all have supper together this evening,' Simone said. 'But Pierre and I will go for a walk after lunch as we have much to talk about and it would not be interesting for you girls.'

'That's where you're wrong, Maman,' Ronnie teased. 'We want to hear *everything*.'

'*Alors*, that is not possible,' Maman said, a shade of her old character coming through, much to Suzanne's amusement.

'And we will hope the three of you will make supper. I have a special bottle of French wine I put away for a special occasion. That occasion will be this evening.'

The kitchen was too small for the three girls to work in at the same time, so Raine, the least domestic of the three, opted to lay the table and generally tidy up the front room and dining room.

'I've been thinking,' Raine said as she came into the kitchen to make tea.

Suzanne's heart did a dive. 'About Pierre?'

'Yes.' Raine looked directly at Suzanne. 'Maman looks so different, so alive. And now we know the full story – well, most of it,' she corrected herself with a grin, 'I've realised she deserves to be happy again. I even think Dad would approve.'

'And do *you* approve, Raine?' Suzanne asked, her heart racing.

'Well, of course I did meet him first,' Raine grinned. 'All right, I may have only been a year old and therefore not quite mature enough to make a calculated judgement . . .' She laughed. 'Yes, Suzy, from what I've seen of him in such a short time, I like him. In fact, I like him very much.'

'I do, too,' Ronnie put in. 'I think he's perfectly adorable.' She giggled. 'But we'd better get cracking on supper or he's going to be very disappointed.'

'What have we got in the garden we could eat tonight?' Suzanne said.

Ronnie furrowed her brow. 'There's a cauliflower.'

'Perfect. We can make cauliflower cheese.'

Ronnie pulled a face. 'There's only a small lump of cheese I was saving to grate on our baked potatoes tomorrow.'

'We need it now,' Suzanne said firmly, going to the larder.

She removed a small packet of cornflour, then spotted a plate with something wrapped in greaseproof paper. She put the plate on the kitchen table to find four rashers of bacon – a week's ration for two family members.

'I'll cut these up into pieces and fry them. They'll give it some flavour. Then I'll make a white sauce. Is there any stale bread?'

'What for?'

'Breadcrumbs. They'll go on the top with some parsley and a little of the cheese to make it nice and cheesy and crunchy.'

'How do you know all this?' Ronnie asked curiously.

'We had something similar on the ship coming home,' Suzanne chuckled. 'But we didn't have a glass of Maman's fine wine to go with it.'

'Lorraine, will you fetch the bottle of wine from the larder?' Simone said as they sat down at the supper table. 'It's on the slate shelf – at the very back.'

Raine was back in a few moments, a dusty bottle of white wine in her hand and a teacloth over her arm. She gave it a cursory wipe, then handed the bottle to Pierre.

'Would you like to do the honours?' she said to Pierre who Simone had insisted sit at the head of the table.

'With pleasure.'

Deftly he uncorked the bottle and began to pour.

'Véronique is too young for wine.'

'Maman—' Ronnie started.

'This is a special occasion,' Pierre said firmly. 'She must have the same.' He poured the golden liquid equally between the five glasses.

'I would like to say something for a toast,' he said, still standing, his eyes resting on Suzanne and then Simone.

Everyone raised their glasses. 'Simone, you will never know how much this means to me—'

He stopped, his voice cracking. Suzanne saw the tears in his eyes and could only guess how he must be feeling after nearly twenty years. She swallowed hard.

'To be with you, *chérie*,' he continued after a few seconds, 'and to be with our daughter, Suzanne—' He stopped again and looked at Raine and Ronnie. 'And meet her beautiful sisters, Lorraine and Véronique.' He paused and glanced at Raine. 'Of course I have met Lorraine already but she was very small at the time.' He gave her a quick smile and then gazed around the table. 'I want to thank you all for making me so welcome.' He raised his glass.

Suzanne briefly closed her eyes as the first sip of Maman's special wine slipped down her throat. She knew she would never forget this evening as long as she lived.

Pierre's eyes as usual were on Simone. 'I am so happy you have given them all beautiful French names.'

Ronnie burst out giggling, and Simone frowned.

'Véronique is laughing because they refuse to use them.'

Pierre chuckled. 'It does not change what is on their birth certificates,' he said, and to Suzanne's relief her mother's frown relaxed.

Ronnie jumped up. 'I'd better bring supper in before it ruins.'

'I'll help you,' Raine said.

The two girls reappeared with the dish of cauliflower cheese and three baked potatoes, all halved. Raine put two halves on Pierre's plate and a half each for the others.

'I also have something to say,' Simone said unexpectedly when everyone had scraped the last from their plates. 'Thank you, girls, for making a delicious supper.' She let her gaze linger on Suzanne. 'I have something to return to you, *chérie*.'

She leaned across the table and put a tiny maroon leather box in front of Suzanne. 'I have kept it safe for you, but now it is the right time for you to have it.'

Grandmother's engagement ring!

Feeling everyone's eyes on her, Suzanne undid the catch. Under the candlelight the ring winked and sparkled up at her.

'Oh, that's the ring—' Ronnie's voice was high with excitement, but Suzanne threw her a warning look.

Raine got up from her seat to peer at it over Suzanne's shoulder. 'Oh, it's gorgeous. Put it on, Suzy.'

'Let me look.' Ronnie jumped up.

Slowly, carefully, Suzanne drew it out of its safety slit and held it up a moment, then slipped it on her middle finger, just as she had in her bedroom that time. How different the situation was now.

'Show me,' Simone demanded. Suzanne stretched out her hand and her mother gently took it and peered at the ring. She nodded. 'It suits your hand, *chérie*.'

'May I see?' Pierre asked gently.

Shyly, Suzanne held her hand towards him.

'It is very beautiful,' Pierre said softly. 'Just like its new owner.' He smiled at her. 'You know it was the ring of my mother?'

'Yes,' Suzanne said. 'I know. And I promise to treasure it all my life and remember her even though I'll never meet her.'

'I will tell you about her and you will feel you know her the same as me.' Pierre's blue eyes lit up his thin face.

'Jelly and custard, anyone?' Ronnie asked, breaking the spell as she sprang up.

They all laughed. Suzanne beamed happily at everyone around the table, enjoying the wine. Maman looked more animated than she'd ever seen her and Pierre seemed content to simply watch their mother, his joy at being with her again plain for everyone to see.

The only thing gnawing at Suzanne, which she tried hard not to let spoil the evening and her mother's joy, was that she still didn't know about James. But while Raine and Ronnie were clearing the dishes and Simone and Pierre had repaired to the front room, Suzanne grabbed her opportunity and slipped into the hall. The number rang on and on. Her shoulders slumped with disappointment and worry, she was about to replace the receiver when she heard Mrs Mortimer say, 'Bromley 2391.'

'Oh, Mrs Mortimer, it's Suzanne. I'm so glad you've answered. I've been trying to reach you for days.'

'Hello, my love. Where are you?'

'I'm home.' Suzanne hesitated, not quite sure what to say. 'How are you?'

'I'm well, thank you, my dear. But it's James you're asking about, I think.'

'Is he making progress?'

The line went so quiet Suzanne thought it had gone dead. Her mouth went dry. She tried to swallow but couldn't.

'He's being well looked after.'

That could mean anything. Mrs Mortimer hadn't answered her question.

Suzanne swallowed. 'Would I be able to see him?'

There was a short pause. Then Mrs Mortimer said, 'I'm sure you would. Why don't you come for lunch tomorrow and I'll give you the details, as much as I know.'

'That's very kind of you but I just wanted—'

'Good.' There was another crackle. Suzanne was sure Mrs Mortimer had said something. Then she heard her say, 'Come at noon, my dear. I look forward to it.'

Suzanne heard the receiver click. Worriedly, she replaced hers. Mrs Mortimer was holding something back. She'd sounded guarded, as though she didn't want to say too much. Was it that she didn't want to say that James wasn't getting better? And she didn't want to upset Suzanne over the telephone? Was that why she'd invited her to lunch? To break it to her gently in person? Suzanne stood fixed. She needed to see him and tell him she loved him, no matter what. And hear him say that nothing had changed – that he still loved her. Whatever was wrong with him she was sure her love would help him to heal.

Slowly she walked into the front room and sat down.

'Is something wrong, *chérie*?' Maman asked immediately.

Suzanne felt every pair of eyes on her. All she wanted was to be left alone.

'No. Just tired, that's all. It's been a long journey.'

'Yes, it has.' Pierre smiled tenderly at her. He looked at Simone. 'And I should know.'

Simone sent him a loving smile.

'Did you find out how James was?' Raine said.

Suzanne shook her head, her eyes stinging with unshed tears. Without thinking she jumped up.

'I'm sorry, everyone. I think I'll have an early night. Would you mind?'

Pierre stood. He gently took hold of both her arms. Kissing her on both cheeks, he said, 'Get some sleep, my darling daughter. Everything will look better in the morning.'

In bed, Suzanne played the short conversation with Mrs Mortimer over and over again until in the end she thought she would go mad. James wasn't well. He'd had a turn for the worse. Mrs Mortimer didn't know how to tell her. The poor lady was too filled with grief and was hiding it.

Suzanne turned over for what seemed like the hundredth

time. And then floating upwards she heard music. Piano music. Chopin. She sat up in bed. She must be imagining things. She padded barefoot to the landing and put her head over the banister. The music was coming from the front room. But no one in the family played the piano except herself.

Ah! That wasn't quite true any more. She allowed herself a small smile. Her father was playing. She closed her eyes, the back of her neck to the top of her head tingling, her heart full. Reluctantly, she crept back into bed and pulled the sheet up to her chin, listening to Chopin's heavenly sonata. Within minutes she was asleep.

Chapter Forty-Three

Suzanne opened her eyes. Even though she'd pulled the blackout curtains the sun had found a crack to send its beam in. It was set to be a beautiful day. She yawned and stretched her arms above her head. She'd had the best sleep for a long time and hadn't even heard Raine come to bed. But then the worry about James washed over her. Swallowing hard she threw off the covers. Noon couldn't come quick enough.

Swiftly she pulled on her dressing gown and went downstairs to the clattering of teacups. Good. Ronnie was making the tea. But to her surprise it was Maman. She was listening to the wireless.

Simone put her finger to her lips. 'Shhhh!'

'This is the BBC Home Service. Here is the news read by Alvar Lidell on Wednesday, 18th of August. Sicily has finally been liberated from its oppressors by our Allied forces. The invasion which began on the 10th of July has opened the way to further advance into Italy . . .'

The newsreader went on in more detail but Suzanne didn't hear the rest.

'That's what we saw in Malta,' she said, her voice rising. 'You couldn't see a gap between hundreds – probably thousands – of ships lined up in the Grand Harbour. The same with the aeroplanes on the airfields.' She gazed at her mother.

'That's where James was off to – Sicily. It matches the date exactly. And the day after what I now realise was the invasion he was in hospital . . . not even remembering his ship was torpedoed,' she finished shakily. 'Oh, Maman, when I saw him in hospital he didn't look the same man. But he'll get better – I *know* he will.'

Her mother gave her a penetrating look. 'You love James, don't you, *chérie*?'

'Yes,' she said without hesitation.

'And does he love you?'

'He says he does.'

'Then that's all that matters.'

Suzanne glanced at her mother in surprise. 'But only the other day you said—'

'Forget what I said then,' Maman interrupted. 'There is a war. No one knows how long it will go on. How many more people will be lost to us. We must all take our happiness when we can.' She gave Suzanne an unexpected kiss. 'When will you go to the hospital to see him?'

'Soon, I hope,' Suzanne said. 'Mrs Mortimer didn't tell me much over the telephone last night, but she's invited me to lunch today and says she'll tell me what she knows. But I'm so worried—'

'Suzanne, you are a strong girl. A good girl. You will work things out with James, no matter what. But for now—' she handed a cup of tea to Suzanne '—would you take this to your father?'

Suzanne stared at her mother. Maman was so changed. Her eyes and skin glowed. It was as though her mother had been hiding her real self from them all these years, and Suzanne wasn't sure how to respond. Had they become lovers again? Suzanne felt her cheeks warm. Then she saw something completely foreign in Maman's eye – a mischievous twinkle.

'And before you or your sisters think anything different – I made him a bed on the sofa!'

Mrs Mortimer opened the front door almost before Suzanne's hand was on the doorbell.

'How lovely to see you again, my dear.' She kissed Suzanne's cheek. 'Do come in.'

She took Suzanne through to the back of the house and into the kitchen where the open French windows led into the garden with its sweeping lawns and flower borders.

'I was just going to pick some raspberries. They're beautifully ripe but if I leave them another day the birds will have them, which would be a pity as I've made some mock cream this morning for the first time. And before you ask how that's possible, it's butter, sugar, milk and vanilla extract. I can't wait to try it.' She smiled at Suzanne. 'Would you like to pick them and then I can get the potatoes on?'

'I'd love to,' Suzanne said. It would give her something to do until Mrs Mortimer was ready to tell her about James. All the time she didn't say how James was, Suzanne could pretend everything was all right.

Mrs Mortimer handed her a glass bowl and pointed. 'The raspberry canes are over in the fruit cages on the other side of the greenhouse.'

The sun warmed Suzanne's bare shoulders as she made her way towards the greenhouse, her flowered dress swishing over her knees. At the last minute this morning she'd decided it would be right for what promised to be a hot day. Wearing something pretty always helped in every situation, Maman had said. Raine had already left for White Waltham this morning, which only enhanced Suzanne's feeling of gloom about her sister's safety, although Raine had pooh-poohed her anxiety.

'No need to worry about *me*,' Raine had said when Suzanne and Ronnie had walked with her to the bus stop, Ronnie trying to control Rusty who was straining and whining on his lead. 'And just for the record,' Raine had added, 'I think Pierre is a dear.'

'Do you really?' Suzanne said.

'I wouldn't say it if I didn't mean it,' Raine said. 'You should know that.'

'I think he's super-duper,' Ronnie said.

'You've been watching too many American films with that language,' Raine laughed, ruffling Ronnie's hair. She turned to Suzanne. 'And try not to worry about James until you know the latest.'

Her sister's encouraging words sounded in her ears as Suzanne walked past the Victorian greenhouse towards the fruit cages. She could see the raspberry canes sticking up. And in the distance was the tall figure of a gardener, his back to her, bent over a hoe. Mrs Mortimer was jolly lucky to be able to keep one these days, she thought idly. He was probably too old to be in the forces. His straw hat was pulled low over his head, presumably to protect himself against the sun beating down on this hot August day. Idly, she wished she'd worn hers.

She'd go and say hello to him so he didn't think she was some interloper. But when she was only twenty yards or so away from him she stopped abruptly, sucking in her breath. He'd half turned and straightened, tipping his hat back as if pausing for a few moments before resuming.

She startled. It wasn't the stance of an old man at all. There was something about him. Something familiar. Her heart went still. Then she found herself sprinting over the grass.

'James! Oh, James!'

He whipped round.

And then he tore off his hat and flung down his hoe, his dear face – the face she adored – wreathed in smiles.

'Suzy!'

She hurled the raspberry bowl on the grass.

He half ran towards her, his arms outstretched, and she flew into them. He wrapped her tightly against his chest, so close she could feel his heart beating – a strong thudding rhythm against her own.

'Oh, my darling, I can't believe you're here.' Suzanne stroked his face, then gently ran her finger over the scar just below the hairline, still red and lumpy and raw-looking. 'Your mother didn't tell me—'

'She didn't know until yesterday,' he said. 'The hospital rang her to say they were sending me to a convalescent home. She said it might as well be here as anywhere else and they agreed, especially when she told them she worked for the Red Cross. She didn't say she did office work and had no medical knowledge whatsoever.' He chuckled. 'They turned me out more or less there and then, saying I could cadge a lift with one of the doctors who lives in Bromley. So I came here in style.' He kissed the top of her head. 'But we're wasting time talking,' he said. 'I have to do something I've wanted to do for such a long time.'

The touch of his lips on her mouth was gentle at first, and then desire swept through her and she kissed him back with such passion he pretended to reel backwards.

'My goodness, Suzy, where did you learn to kiss like that? Mind you, I'm not complaining.'

Warmth rushed to her cheeks. He laughed and kissed her again.

Taking hold of her hands he pressed them. 'Mother never gave any hint that you were coming today.'

'I rang her yesterday to find out how you were, but she

said she'd tell me what she knew if I'd have lunch with her today. When I arrived just now she asked if I'd go and pick some raspberries. She knew full well where I'd find you.'

He laughed and pulled her back into his arms, kissing her eyelids, the tip of her nose, along her jaw, until he was kissing her lips once more.

Mrs Mortimer's voice called from the kitchen door and they sprang apart, breathless and beaming at one another.

'Suzanne, have you picked those raspberries?'

Suzanne looked at James and giggled. 'It's your fault.' She retrieved the empty bowl she'd thrown down in the excitement.

He grinned. 'We'd better get to them then,' he said, 'or we'll never hear the last.'

Acknowledgements

When I tell people I write my novels in a special cabin in the garden they often remark how romantic it sounds. I'm not sure about romantic, but it is a great space away from the house that only my white rescued cat, Dougal, is always welcome at any time. In fact, I can hear him scratching at the door for me to let him in as I write this! He curls up on top of the back of the sofa and sleeps while I tap away on the computer in the office section of the cabin. And when it's dinnertime he'll walk across my cabin worktop and meow loudly for me to pack up. If I don't immediately pander to his demands he'll march across the keyboard causing havoc.

For me, it's a dream come true, so maybe it's romantic, after all.

I've very much enjoyed the research for this latest novel because I've always fancied myself as a singer entertaining the boys in the war, had I been born twenty-five years earlier! However, my heroine is a very different girl from me at that age. So many young girls like Suzanne were sheltered in those days and yet they were unthinkingly brave, putting their lives and careers at risk, and I'm not at all sure I could have risen to the challenge. With regard to ENSA, there were sometimes comments from the public that to join was a copout. Their reasoning? The entertainers had too easy and too enjoyable a time. But from the many memoirs I've read, this is not at all the case. They were often performing under very difficult circumstances such as poor food, dysentery amongst other illnesses, horrendous journeys bumping over long distances in army trucks, sometimes little or no sanitation, rarely any privacy, exhaustion, sometimes danger from being too close to the enemy . . . The list goes on. But they were determined to do their bit for the war effort and all lived to tell the tale with the exception of one attractive girl, Vivien Hole (stage name Vivienne Fayre), who died in active service at only nineteen.

I could never have completed the novel in such good shape without the input of so many people and I'm grateful to every single one. First, as always, is my lovely agent, Helen Holden Brown of HHB Agency. She always keeps me calm if things go a bit haywire, and I value her advice. Then there's my publishers at Avon, HarperCollins, with my talented editor, Katie Loughnane, at the helm, wonderfully assisted by editor, Molly Walker-Sharp. They both have such a flair for understanding my characters and their problems. Thank you, Katie, and to your whole amazing team who work hard to bring my scribbles into such stunning-looking books and get them in front of the readers.

I'm so lucky to be part of two small writing groups: the Diamonds and the Vestas, all published authors. I make up the fourth member in both cases. The Diamonds, being Sue Mackender, Terri Fleming and Joanne Walsh, meet once a month for a whole day, which works brilliantly. We usually read out our latest chapter and the other three will critique it in some detail as well as brainstorming, particularly with plot holes. The Vestas, being Gail Aldwin, Carol McGrath and Suzanne Goldring, meet just two or three times a year, usually at one of their second homes in Greece or Port Isaac.

There we'll have up to a week to discuss our work – a real luxury away from all the problems at home. We always come away with a healthy word count under our belts, feeling a resurgence of energy to press on to the end.

And then there's Alison Morton, thriller novelist with the successful and long-running 'Roma Nova' series. She and I are each other's critique writing partner, our red pens in hand, poised to spot any weakness. Although we write in completely different genres it works like magic. Thanks, also, Alison, for your suggestion that I send Suzanne to Malta – it proved the perfect location for my story.

I must mention Derek Wilkins' 'Troopship Diary' 13/12/43–24/01/44 where 'The People's War' published extracts from his journey from Liverpool to Gibraltar/Durban on the SS *Orbita* during those tumultuous war years. It gave me a real insider's impression of what it was like to be on one of those ships undertaking such a hazardous voyage.

Another mention must go to Trevor Moorcroft, brother of best-selling novelist Sue Moorcroft who so kindly put me in touch with him. What the two of them don't know about Malta isn't worth knowing! Trevor is particularly knowledgeable on its history and put me right on hospitals and airfields on the Island in the war. Many thanks, Trevor.

And last but never least is Edward Stanton. He wouldn't normally read the kind of novels I write, but since he's my husband he's forced to – and twice over! Luckily for me, he has a marvellous eye and ear for anachronisms, and can advise me on all sorts of details involving military aeroplanes, antique motorcars and bikes, ships and submarines, the military forces, prominent characters of the era, etc. Annoyingly, he's unnervingly accurate.

Author's note

I have tried to be faithful to historical facts so far as I've been able to confirm, but would like to make the following comments:

ENSA was definitely in Malta but I was never able to find out the exact dates so I took the liberty of 'my' troupe going out in June 1943 when it should have been safe to do so.

However, even though the Siege of Malta was supposedly over in December 1942, I discovered in my reading material that there was one more attack on the day I describe in the novel – 20th July, 1943, and which was totally unforeseen. Frightening though it must have been, especially for the islanders who had already suffered so terribly for so long, it was a gift for me as an author as it solved a major problem towards the end of my story.

General Eisenhower *did* fly into Malta on the day I describe but there was no mention that his personal chauffeuse, Kay Summersby was with him. That said, she often accompanied him on his various flights as his personal secretary. For the purpose of adding a little spice to Ike's visit, I decided to bring her in.

In her time Adelaide Hall was as famous a singer and entertainer as Josephine Baker, though I haven't met anyone yet who's heard of her. I have kept as accurately as possible to any historical facts I've included about her, such as packing up and coming to England in 1938 because of the way she was treated as a black woman in the States, and yes, she really did go down into the Underground and sing to the hundreds of people huddled together in makeshift beds for the night as protection against the bombing.

However, there is no record of Adelaide going to Malta to entertain the troops, but she was a long-standing member of ENSA and travelled widely in Great Britain and Europe to sing to the troops during the war years and was immensely popular. I'm sure that given half a chance, she would have gone to Malta like a shot. And who knows – perhaps she did!

I've thoroughly enjoyed listening to her on my CD. She had an unusual voice, perfect for jazz and scat singing, and in the snippets I've read about her she comes across as a thoroughly nice person. I hope she would be pleased to see the way I've portrayed her. On saying that, she was no push-over in real life, and nor is she in *A Sister's Song*.

Read on for an exclusive extract from the next Molly Green novel . . .

A Sister's War

Chapter One

Downe, near Bromley, Kent
October 1943

The lights dimmed in the cinema until the auditorium went dark. All Ronnie could see was the swirl of cigarette smoke and the silhouette of the heads and women's hats in the rows in front. The chattering audience stopped as one accord. She felt her friend, Lois, give her a nudge.

'Not long now 'til the film.' Lois was breathless with excitement.

'It's Pathé News first,' Ronnie whispered.

'That's the bit I hate. It's always more bad news. I just came to see the film.' Lois pulled a small bag of boiled sweets from her handbag and handed one to Ronnie. 'Joan Crawford is my favourite. She always plays good parts – makes mincemeat of the men.' She giggled.

'Shhhh!' A man with a large head, and boxer's shoulders, who was sitting in front of them half turned, waving his hand towards her. 'Some of us would like to hear the news.'

Ronnie recoiled. 'It hasn't actually started yet,' she said, feeling a rise of annoyance.

'This is Pathé News,' came the newsreader's voice everyone recognised. 'Today, the 13th October, Italy has declared war on Nazi Germany, just one month after Italy surrendered to the Allies.' He paused, as though he knew there would be a positive response from the cinema-going public.

The audience sent up a roar of approval and several people clapped their hands, Ronnie and Lois amongst them.

'Best news we've heard for ages,' Lois said, turning to Ronnie, the light from the cinema screen making her eyes dance with excitement.

The newsreader continued a few moments longer and then switched to another subject.

'Women and girls are taking over more and more of the men's jobs. Here are some of the girls in the Land Army doing a marvellous job keeping food on our tables . . . just look at this young lady actually driving a *tractor*!' The newsreader's voice rose in disbelief. 'These girls are certainly wearing the trousers.'

There were a few male chuckles. One man in the audience called out, 'Not in my house, they're not.' More laughter.

Ronnie watched intently as three Land Girls dressed in jodhpurs, their jumpers tucked into their waists and belted, were being filmed working on a farm. Ronnie immediately slumped. The trouble was, she'd already applied three weeks ago to join the Land Army – actually, three weeks and two days to be precise – convinced they would grab her when she read the messages of several recent posters she'd seen pinned up in the library and the village hall hoping to persuade girls to join. One colourful poster had really caught her eye. It showed a smiling Land Girl with dark curly hair, a little longer but not unlike her own, her hand resting on a horse's neck, and an amiable pipe-smoking farmer looking on. The message along the top of the poster read: '*We could do with thousands more like you . . .*' and underneath the picture was a yellow banner with black writing: *Join the Women's Land Army.*

She'd dashed home, breathless with excitement that her chance had come, and filled out the application form without telling her mother her intentions. What would have been the point? Ronnie had mentioned it a couple of times to her sisters and although Raine and Suzy had cautioned her about the hard, monotonous work, which didn't worry Ronnie one jot, Maman had shot her idea down in flames. Being a Frenchwoman, Simone couldn't bear the idea of one of her daughters with dirty, broken fingernails and wearing men's clothes, digging the land for victory, or otherwise.

Every morning when she'd heard the postman rattle the letterbox, Ronnie had flown downstairs, followed by an exuberant Rusty barking his head off. This morning she'd been certain that today would be the day she'd hear. But there was nothing . . . until the second post at noon.

'*Chérie*, you have a letter in the front room on the mantelpiece,' Maman had said, leaning over the banister when Ronnie had come in from tending the vegetable plot. 'It came a few minutes ago. I will be down in one minute so do not open it until I am there with you. We will read it together.'

Ronnie's heart gave a flip. It must be about the Land Army. And Maman was trying to take control as usual. Ronnie set her jaw. She was almost seventeen – perfectly old enough to open her own letters. She'd wanted to be indoors before the noon post came for this very reason but Rusty had begged her to take him for a walk, the way he'd looked at her with his warm, brown, beseeching eyes.

Please don't come downstairs before I've read it on my own, Maman.

'Come on, Rusty. I'll allow you to read it with me.'

Rusty followed her into the front room, his claws making a clicking sound on the hall lino.

Ronnie grabbed the long envelope partly tucked behind

one of a pair of silver candlesticks, a remnant of the old life they'd had before Dad had lost a lot of money and had gone into debt.

Probably one of the reasons why he'd died so suddenly at only sixty, she thought grimly. He'd always tried to keep up with Maman's demands and standards. Her heart squeezed at the thought of her dearest Dad and the stress it must have given him when he realised what he'd brought upon the family.

All this was racing through her head as Ronnie ripped open the envelope and pulled out the single sheet. She glanced at the heading. She was right. It was from the Ministry of Agriculture and Fisheries and the Land Army came under their umbrella. Heart beating in her ears she read:

Dear Miss Linfoot,

We thank you for your application form to join the Land Army but regret—

Ronnie broke off reading. Regret? Surely . . . Biting her lip and willing herself to go on, she continued:

. . . but regret we must on this occasion turn down your application. Our minimum age is seventeen and a half, and you are not yet seventeen. This is because the work is often heavy, having been carried out by the men before war was declared. However, we are encouraged by your enthusiasm and hope that in a year's time you will apply again, whereupon we would expect you to be successful.

Thank you for your interest.

Yours sincerely,

Ministry of Agriculture and Fisheries

Ronnie was disgusted to see that the person who'd written the letter hadn't even had the courtesy to sign it.

'You are reading your letter without me,' Maman said, sweeping into the room in her usual style of a thirties' actress. 'Did you not hear me?' For once, she didn't ask Ronnie to remove 'that dog'.

Ronnie shoved the letter back into the envelope, her eyes stinging with anger. The war would be over by the time she reapplied.

'Yes, I heard you – but Maman, it's addressed to *me*. I should be allowed to open my own post.'

'Who is it from?'

'No one important.'

'Let me look.' Simone stretched her hand out.

Ronnie was on the brink of refusing to give it to her. But what difference did it make? She hadn't been offered an interview and she'd already told her mother she wasn't going back to school. She wasn't brainy like Raine, or musically gifted like Suzy, and didn't see the need for two more years of mathematics and history and French and all the other subjects she wasn't good at. But she excelled in biology and natural history. She knew she had a way with animals and was at her happiest when she was outdoors. The Land Army would have given her all those things. And now her hopes were in pieces.

Sulkily, she handed over the envelope.

Simone pursed her lips as she read the letter. Then she looked up. Ronnie noticed a gleam in her mother's eyes.

'*Chérie,* I do not like that you go behind my back to write to these people. We have already discussed this. Winter will come soon and I will not have my daughter digging up turnips. What would people say? They will think we are in poverty. What would your father say if he was here? He would be angry that I allow such a thing. So I am very happy they will not take you. This will be the end of the conversation, even when you are of the right age. You will find a worthwhile job or I will send you back to school.'

Simone had torn the letter into pieces and thrown them on the unlit fire.

Still bristling with Maman's unfair dismissal of the Land Army, Ronnie was brought back to Pathé News with the newsreader's latest clip.

'Yes, women and girls are working in the munitions factories . . . here they are, cheerfully changing into boiler suits and rubber shoes, wearing gloves and masks as protection against poison and dangerous fumes from the explosive material . . . here's one of the girls filling the exploder and finishing the shells. If it wasn't for the fair sex performing what was once considered men's work, there wouldn't be enough ammunition to send to our boys in the field. We couldn't carry on the fight. That's how important this work is.'

I'd hate it. Ronnie pulled a face in the darkness. Having to repeat the same movements hour after hour, day after day, cooped up in a room with constant clanging and clattering above the chatter of the girls. It was a wonder they weren't all deafened with the row. Besides, it was obviously dangerous to be amongst all those poisonous fumes, mask or no mask. But I do admire them, she thought. They're getting on with it – and doing their bit for the war effort. And that's what I need to get cracking with.

'. . . and women and girls are even working on the canals, some of them as young as seventeen, taking critical supplies from London to Birmingham and back again on the Grand Union Canal. They work together in threes, from all walks of life. Here is one group in charge of a seventy-foot canal boat, with a second boat being towed behind which will carry the cargo. It's a hard, dirty, backbreaking job but these girls look fit and healthy working outside all day . . .'

Ronnie sat bolt upright, staring hard at the screen. She couldn't hear what they were saying but they were tying two boats together, working as a team. One of them, a pretty girl with a cap perched on her blonde curls, looked up and smiled and waved at the camera. The good thing was that they didn't appear to be wearing any kind of uniform, Ronnie noticed, although they all wore trousers. How sensible.

She was barely aware of the other news. And when the film, *Above Suspicion* – a wartime drama that hadn't really appealed, but Lois had gone on and on about it until she'd finally agreed to go with her – eventually came on, Ronnie scarcely paid any attention. Watching a far-fetched story about a honeymooning couple in Europe being asked to spy on the Nazis for the British intelligence, and Joan Crawford, the bride, looking ever more glamorous in every subsequent scene, didn't ring true. It all looked so artificial against the horrors she'd seen so many times on Pathé News of the brave boys, many whose lives were being snuffed out before they'd even properly begun to live, or so horribly injured and disfigured they'd never lead a normal life again. Co-star, heartthrob Fred MacMurray, didn't accelerate Ronnie's heartbeat one scrap. No, what was making her heart thump so hard she felt it might burst through her chest, was the thought of doing something worthwhile – something she thought she'd be good at. She was as certain as Lois sitting in the seat next to her that working on the canals, which she knew nothing about – had never even been on a boat – was the very part she felt she was destined to play.

But how would she talk Maman round to giving her permission?

Reading List for A Sister's Song

Greasepaint & Cordite: How ENSA Entertained The Troops During World War 11 by Andy Merriman
Entertaining The Troops 1939 - 1945 by Kiri Bloom Walden
East With ENSA: Entertaining The Troops In The Second World War by Catherine Wells (A memoir)
We'll Meet Again: A Personal And Social Memory Of World War Two by Vera Lynn (Part memoir)
A Dancer In Wartime by Gillian Lynne (A memoir)
Drury Lane to Dimapur: Wartime Adventures of an Actress by Doreen Hawkins, wife of Jack Hawkins (A memoir)
Malta: The Thorn In Rommel's Side by Laddie Lucas (A memoir)
Fortress Malta: An Island Under Siege 1940 - 1943 by James Holland
Churchill And Malta's War 1939 - 1943 by Douglas Austin
Malta Convoys by David A Thomas

Acknowledgements of Extracts from the Songs Mentioned:

"Chattanooga Choo Choo" p. 54, 121, 263	Songwriter: Mack Gordon, pub. 1941
"Don't Sit Under The Apple Tree" p. 91, 277	Songwriters: Lew Brown/Charles Tobias, pub. 1942
"I'll Never Smile Again" p. 124, 240	Songwriter: Ruth Lowe, pub. 1940
"Stormy Weather" p. 235	Songwriters: Ted Koehler/Harold Arlen, pub.1933
"It Had To Be You" p. 278	Songwriter: Gus Kahn, pub. 1924
"Harbour Lights" p. 294	Songwriter: Frances Langford, pub. 1937
"The White Cliffs Of Dover" p. 317	Songwriter: Nat Burton, pub. 1941

Now you've finished Suzanne's story, why not go back to the beginning to read about her sister, Raine?

Available in ebook and paperback now.

If you love the Victory Sisters series, why not curl up with another heart-warming story from Molly Green?

Available in ebook and paperback now.

War rages on, but the women and children of Liverpool's Dr Barnardo's Home cannot give up hope. . .

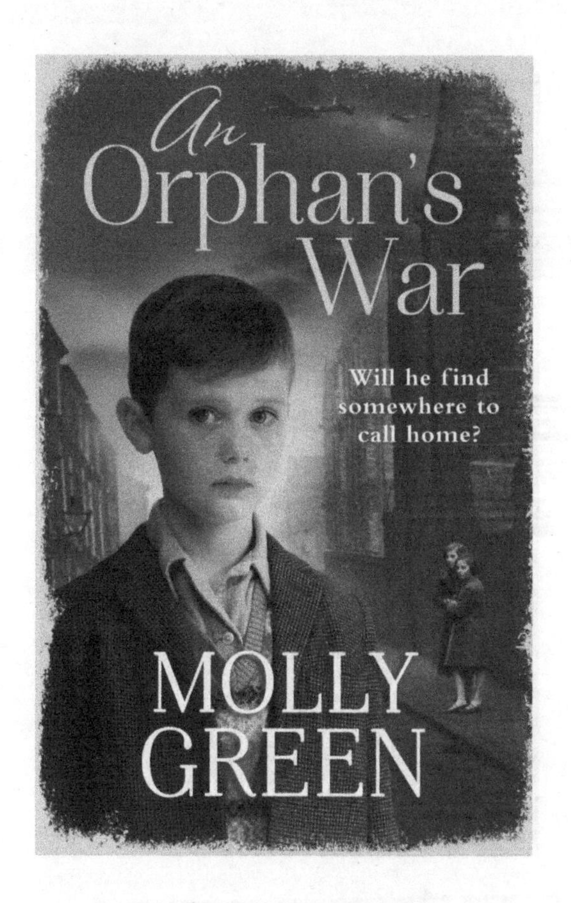

Available in ebook and paperback now.

Even when all seems lost at Dr Barnardo's orphanage, there is always a glimmer of hope to be found. . .

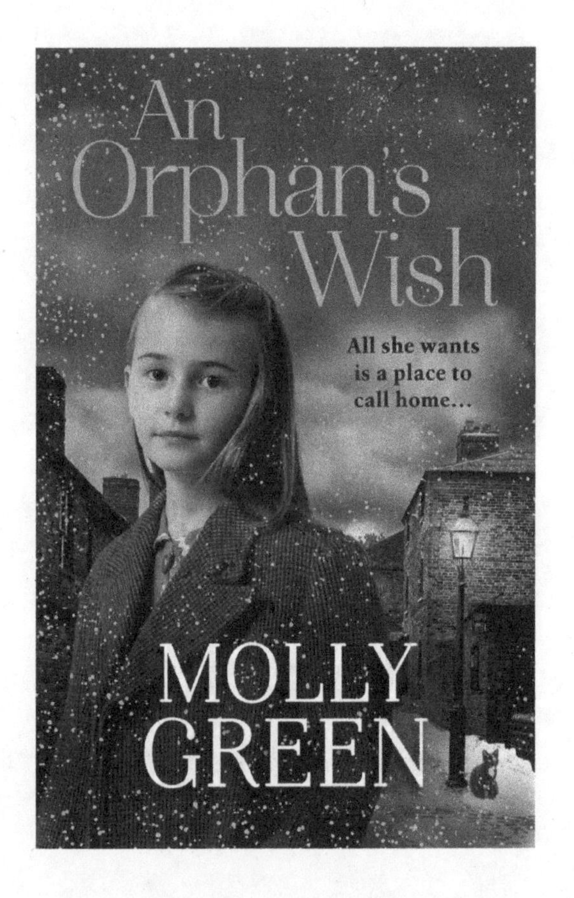

Available in ebook and paperback now.